Addiction & Pestilence

Book I

Slaying Dragons: A Journey Through Hell

E.M. Kelly

Addiction & Pestilence
Second Edition
Published by: Great Blue Hill Publishing
All rights reserved.
ISBN-9781730704338

Copyright © owned by E.M. Kelly
First edition published 2016

Cover design: Aero Gallerie

Addiction & Pestilence is a work of fiction. Names, characters
and places are products of the author's imagination.

A very special thank you
to someone I am privileged
to not only call my editor,
but also my friend.

Rich Heebner

For my wife, Natalie
For all that you do
For always being there
For our family
For all the bullshit you have endured
I love you

Slaying Dragons:

One who overcomes addiction to drugs or alcohol; defeating evil or the Devil.

And I saw when the lamb opened one of the seals,
and I heard, as it were the noise of thunder,
one of the four beasts saying, Come and see.

- Revelation 6:1

And I saw, and behold a white horse:
and he that sat on him had a bow;
and a crown was given unto him:
and he went forth conquering, and to conquer.

-Revelation 6:2

Chapter 1

Tuesday, October 27th
11:27 A.M.

The little black mass appeared out of nowhere. It floated and danced like a butterfly, yet it stayed in the same place.

Karen carried out the heavy basket of laundry and placed it under the clothesline, looked back at the house and yelled, "Jimmy, bring Momma out the bag of clothespins." Jimmy got up off the kitchen floor, picked up his red toy car, grabbed the bag of clothespins and made his way out the back door.

"Here, Momma," Jimmy said as he dropped the bag of clothespins at her feet and took off running after the bright yellow and purple butterfly that just passed through his legs. "Vroommmm!" he said as he flew his car behind the bright butterfly that danced its way from shrub to shrub.

Jimmy followed the butterfly around to the front of the house but had to stop as it flew across the street. He could go to the sidewalk, but the street was forbidden by his mother. "Aw," he pouted as he pushed his red hair out of his eyes and stood watching the bright butterfly land in the grass in front of his friend Tommy's house.

He turned to head back to his mother when he noticed a second butterfly, black as midnight, near the middle of the front yard. Jimmy ran straight up to it and stopped. He bent over, putting his hands on his knees, and leaned in to get a closer look at the pitch-black butterfly. Narrowing his eyes, Jimmy quickly realized it wasn't a butterfly and that it must be some sort of strange bug he hadn't seen before.

The floating black mass mesmerized him. He searched it with his eyes, trying to find its legs, when he noticed something start to extend out of the little mass. It looked like a string of some sort was growing from it. Jimmy brought up his right hand and slowly moved his index finger towards the newly formed black string, which was now starting to spin.

Jimmy's eyes widened as the hovering black thingy began to pulse as his finger reached closer to it, and its growing appendage now spun faster like a small tornado. "Cool!" the boy exclaimed, his index finger now only an inch away from it. Suddenly, little sparks that looked like static electricity began swirling inside the black mass.

"Momma! Come look at this!" Jimmy shouted with amazement as his finger came so close to touching the black hovering formation. He was about to pull his finger away when one of the little sparks jumped from the black mass.

"What?" Karen shouted as she turned her head towards the front yard. Suddenly, a bright flash of light filled everything and a loud horn sounded, shaking the Earth under her feet. The phenomenon was so intense that Karen dropped to her knees. Once she was able to stand again, she hurried to the front yard.

The little black mass was now a dark, shadowy figure that moved across the yard and hid in the shade of the large oak tree next door as Karen came sprinting around the corner.

"Jimmy!" Karen screamed at the sight of her son's smoldering clothes, laying in a pile on the lawn.

Chapter 2

Wednesday, October 28th
9:30 A.M.

Eight miles to the west, Brian Phillips sat confined in his room. Outside, the morning sun broke through the clouds as a dark, shadowy figure made its way across the landscape, up the drive and into the east wing entrance of Concord Labs.

It had begun.

Harry Stoneham, a federal security guard, sat reading the paper in front of the security monitors for Concord Labs, known to the local community as the Lumpton Treatment Center. He started his shift the same way every day, eating his breakfast and reading up on the news before making his rounds. He was engrossed in the headline story about a young boy from Brooksdale, the next town over, who had gone missing from his front yard, when something on the security monitor caught his eye. It appeared as if someone had entered through the secured door of the east wing, but the security system had not detected a breach, nor had the motion sensor activated. *It must have been my imagination*, the security guard thought, returning his focus on the paper.

Harry picked up his jelly donut and cursed as white powder fell onto his black tie. He picked up a napkin and attempted to clean himself when once more something grabbed his attention on the monitor, now at the far end of the east wing corridor. Again, it seemed as if someone walked past the security camera.

He reached out and pushed the left button below the monitor. To his astonishment, something dark zoomed backwards as the recording rewound. He gently tapped the button to the right which caused the film to move forward again, then watched the dark apparition move across the screen. Leaning in close and rewinding the film again, certain his eyes were playing tricks on him, Harry studied the feed and confirmed what he saw. Goosebumps formed on his arms. He could not see anyone in the hallway, but it clearly looked like a shadow of a human form. He rewound the recording a third time and thought he could see something else. Moving the film at the slowest speed, he watched intently as tiny specks floated through the air in front of the camera.

I need another cup of coffee, he thought and dismissed the dark, shadowy figure as dust particles too close to the camera lens, merely giving the illusion of a human form. After all, what else could it be?

The dark, ominous specter moved silently down the hall and passed through the airtight security door. It slithered like a snake along the walls and ceilings, staying in the shadows as much as it could and making its way past the nurses' station, towards the contamination suit closet. Once inside, it worked its way around each suit until it found the one it was searching for and stopped. Slowly, the center of the shadow started to spin and swirl. The insides churned like a hurricane and, with each revolution, started to spin faster and faster. Within seconds there was a defined eye in the middle of the swirling, and tiny sparks began to appear inside the form. It reeled even more rapidly, building energy. The previously dark center of the shadowy form now glowed brightly from the thousands of tiny sparks. Slowly the eye of the spinning storm started to protrude from the center, and a small vortex stretched out, reaching towards the contamination suit. Suddenly a tiny energy bolt shot from the black mass and struck the elbow of the contamination suit, creating a tiny tear.

Nurse Robin stood at the med cart filling the daily medications for her morning rounds when the phone rang at the east wing nurses' station. "Robin, your son's school is on the phone," Barbara, the nurse at the desk said, turning in her seat.

"What did he do now?" Robin muttered to herself as she took the phone from her coworker.

"Hello?" Robin answered.

"Hi, Mrs. Dupree. This is Nurse Swanson over at Blake Middle School."

"Is everything alright?" Robin asked.

"Well, Sean got sick in class, and it feels like he's running a fever."

"Alright, I'll be there as soon as I can. Thank you."

With a sigh, Robin hung up the phone, informing Barbara she would need to leave after finishing her rounds.

"I can tell you I don't miss those days," Barbara empathized. "My two girls were always sick."

Robin finished filling the daily medications and then went to the orange fridge labeled "Test Subjects," grabbed some fruit and pudding and put them on a tray. She then walked over to the closet behind the nurses' station, opened the door, and took out her contamination suit. After giving it a quick once over, she donned the suit, picked up the tray of food and then started her rounds.

Before starting at Concord Labs, Robin had spent seven years working for the Centers for Disease Control and Prevention (CDC) as a Registered Nurse and part of the CDC's Global Rapid Response Team, where she traveled the world, working with patients with infectious diseases. She was the bedside face of the CDC and responded to all sorts of outbreaks from malaria to Ebola.

The job was exciting, but also consuming. Her marriage eventually failed and she had grown tired of always being away from her son, so she decided to resign from the CDC. On her last day, however, men in military uniforms approached Robin, asking if she would be interested in a full-time position that required no travel. They explained she would continue her work with highly contagious patients and receive a sizable pay increase. Delighted to continue working in her field, she quickly accepted the job. A week later, she reported to Concord Labs, which was hidden inside the Lumpton Treatment Center.

Concord Labs worked with the world's most deadly germs and viruses—influenza virus, Ebola virus, the hantavirus—and the microorganisms that cause the Bubonic plague, pneumonia, meningitis, and cellulitic infections.

After decades of war, the American people were tired of sending their young off to fight and die. The military needed a new way to fight the ever growing number of terrorists around the world.

Two years ago, Concord Labs obtained a government contract to design a super "battlefield bug." The military wanted a virus that it could drop on an intended target and kill the enemy, but would also die off quickly in order to limit its ability to spread. Concord Labs promised that this was something it could achieve.

With the backing of the military, Concord Labs built a drug treatment center known publicly as the Lumpton Treatment Center. Within months, its doors opened and it actually treated patients. But, the facility had a secluded wing on the east side where scientists experimented on those who met certain criteria: drug addicts who had no family or loved ones to interfere with the research.

Located just a little over an hour north of New York City, Concord Labs had no issues acquiring such test subjects.

After months of failures and setbacks, Concord Labs finally had the breakthrough it was looking for. Scientists successfully extracted and combined the DNA of several viruses, bacteria, and other microorganisms. When they injected the battlefield bug into lab rats, it attacked and killed the host rat within forty-eight hours. The infected rats seemed to suffer and die from an severe cold, showing no signs or symptoms of the plague or other viruses used to develop the virus. The mortality rate was one hundred percent of the infected host rats and less than ten percent of the non-injected rats. Concord Labs had found a way to kill an intended target and to make it look like just an everyday cold, with minimal collateral damage.

Now in the testing stage of the project, the lab needed human subjects to complete its three-phase experiment. This was where the pseudo-treatment center came into play.

The goal of the first phase was to test the super bug on humans. Each test subject was infected and showed signs of a simple cold. Scientists monitored for any mutations to the virus, while the subject became sick and died two days after being infected.

With the first phase complete, Concord Labs quickly moved into the second phase of testing. It infected twenty-five selectees and placed each one in a room with a non-infected test subject. The second phase yielded the same exact results as the first phase: every infected test subject died and approximately ten percent of the non-infected test subjects became infected and died as well.

Concord Labs was very satisfied with the test results as the human study produced the same results as the study on the rats; however, there was one anomaly. One of the infected test subjects never showed signs of infection while his non-injected roommate always became infected second-hand. The non-injected test subject would soon die from respiratory complications, drowning in a yellowish-green froth originating in his lungs, and black sores covered the exterior of his body. This was exactly what both Concord Labs and the military were trying to avoid. To have terrorists die from a cold was one thing, but to have them die from something that looked like the plague was another. As a result, the lab separated Brian, the test subject, in order to determine why he did not die, and why the virus in his body unexpectedly mutated, before it moved onto Phase Three of the tests.

10:00 A.M.

Brian Phillips sat on the bed in his new room in the east wing watching the news. It had been several weeks since he arrived at the Lumpton Treatment Center. Today's top news story was about a small boy who went missing from his front yard, followed by stories of robberies, rapes, and murders. *The world seems to be going mad*, he thought as each story seemed to worsen.

Suddenly there was a loud hissing sound outside his room, followed by a knock on the door.

"Come in," Brian called.

"Time to check your vital signs," Nurse Robin said through the voice box of her contamination suit as she entered and placed the tray of food on the table at the end of his bed.

Brian simply nodded as he stared at her in the suit.

"How are you today?" she asked.

"Better than some of those folks out in the real world," he replied, pointing to the TV.

"Oh yeah, nothing but bad news lately," she commented as she grabbed the small machine mounted on a stand—known as a "nurse on a stick" by the staff who used it to check patients' blood pressure and temperature—and dragged it over to the bed.

"Open wide," she said as she removed the thermometer from the machine and stuck it under his tongue. She then opened the blood pressure cuff, strapped it onto his arm and pressed the little red button on the machine, causing the cuff to fill up and become tight. After a minute the cuff deflated and the machine displayed his blood pressure: 120/75. Robin noted the result from the machine and removed the cuff. She was grabbing his wrist, feeling for his pulse through her rubber gloves, when the machine beeped indicating the temperature reading was complete. She glanced over at the machine, while her fingers found the beat in his wrist. *Ninety-eight point six degrees—a normal temperature*, she thought as she counted off a solid eighty beats per minute.

Robin was perplexed. She had personally infected Brian not once, but twice, yet his vital signs were still normal and he showed no sign of the sickness.

"Hey, I have a few questions," Brian said.

"Shoot," she said through her contamination voice box.

"First, what the hell is a treatment center doing with contamination suits, not to mention a hissing airlock? And what happened to Howard?"

"Howard was pretty sick when he came in, and nobody knows what he was exposed to prior to being admitted here, so we're just erring on the side of caution by using the suits and airlock. Right after the 9/11 attacks and all the anthrax scares, the state and federal government approached facilities outside New York City to see if they would be interested in becoming a decontamination center, in case the city was ever attacked again. I guess the government offered huge tax breaks, so the Lumpton Treatment Center agreed. The higher-ups thought this would be a good time for a practice run with the equipment."

"Oh, well that makes sense, but what about Howard?" he asked. "It's been two days since they took him to the hospital and moved me over here."

"No word yet, but I'm sure we'll get the all clear from the hospital soon," she lied as she remembered wheeling Howard's body down to the incinerator that was hidden in the basement a few floors below. "I wouldn't worry. If it was something serious, we would have heard. Between you and me, I can't wait to get the all clear. I hate wearing these suits."

"Well I hope he'll be alright."

"I'm sure he will, but we're going to continue to check your vital signs every four hours and check your blood once a day. Remember, you're here to get treatment for your addiction, so why don't you worry about getting yourself clean, and let us take care of the rest."

Brian nodded in agreement.

"I brought you some more fresh fruit and pudding," she said as she opened the kit used for drawing blood. "Studies show that those are the most popular foods for people going through rehab."

Nurse Robin removed the thick elastic band along with the long needle and tube used to collect blood and placed the materials on a tray next to him. She then rolled up his sleeve, exposing his drug of choice by the track marks covering his arm. Upon tying the elastic strip across his upper arm, she tapped the inner crook of his elbow, found his vein and inserted the needle.

He zoned out at the sight of the needle as it reminded him of the events that brought him here in the first place. Two weeks ago he was picked up by an ambulance in New York City after someone called 911, stating a man lay unconscious with a needle sticking out of his arm behind The Lounge.

The recession had hit America hard, forcing many people into a downward spiral. He wasn't the only one who turned to drugs to cope with life's problems. New York, like most over populated cities, had a drug problem. Heroin, crystal meth, cocaine — whatever anyone wanted, they could get easily and cheaply.

Brian was a lifelong resident of the city. He grew up, went to school, and even married his wife Patricia there. Last year when the recession peaked, both Brian and Patricia lost their jobs and soon their bills were piling up. Eventually they lost their brownstone and were forced to take a studio in Brownsville.

Shortly after moving in, Patricia started socializing with an old high school friend that lived in the building, who had resorted to drug dealing in response to the hard economic times. He gave them a free sample of heroin to deal with the gloom that had become their lives. Before long, they were both hooked. After months of using, Brian was arrested for trying to sell stolen electronics to a local pawn shop.

While in jail, another inmate turned him onto God, and shortly thereafter, he vowed to kick his addiction. When released from jail, he finally landed a job at a local convenience store where he agreed to work the overnight shift, because it paid an extra sixty-five cents per hour.

One night the store was held up at gunpoint. The police engaged the would-be robber, and after a short exchange of gunfire, the robber fell. Brian, who had been crouching behind the counter, rose to see the man dead on the floor. The police called the store manager, who hurried to the location, as the store had to be closed for the investigation. After the police finished questioning him, the manager told Brian to take the rest of the night off.

He arrived home shortly after one in the morning that night, walked in and found Patricia lying on the couch. She was an ash grey color and her body was cold to the touch. He rushed to the phone and called 911, but it was too late. She had died on the couch in a stain of her own urine and feces, surrounded by drug paraphernalia.

After burying Patricia, Brian couldn't cope with the loss of his wife and soon found himself at The Lounge regularly, drinking away the pain. It wasn't long before he was buying heroin from a dealer in the back of the bar. One afternoon, he awoke in the emergency room to find a woman standing at the end of his bed, offering him help. He had reached rock bottom and had nowhere else to go, so he accepted her offer.

Two days later, the hospital transferred him to the Lumpton Treatment Center where the woman who admitted him asked about his next of kin. She flashed a wide grin when he answered, "None." The woman knew that no family meant no one would come looking for him, which meant no one to stop the human experiments.

Robin removed the elastic strip with a loud *SNAP*, releasing Brian from his zoned-out state.

"Where did you go?" she asked.

"I was just thinking of how I got here," he answered.

"It's normal. Reflection is good."

"Yeah, I guess."

"Can I get you anything?" she asked as she packed up the kit and blood work.

"How about a deck of cards?" he replied.

"I'll see if I can find one as soon as I get this blood to the lab and finish my rounds."

"OK, see you later," he said as she noted his vital signs in his chart and then left.

A few minutes later he heard the airlock hiss again, followed by another knock on the door. "Come in," he said.

Nurse Robin re-entered holding a small tray. "Sorry for the intrusion, but I forgot to give you your meds," she announced, and then injected him with a small syringe.

"Hey, are you alright?" he asked as he winched from the injection.

"Yeah, I'm just in a hurry. My son's school just called. They're sending him home sick, so I have to leave to go pick him up."

"Well, I hope the little guy feels better."

"Thank you," she replied as she jotted down the medication and dosage in his chart. "Oh yeah, I also found these for you," she said holding up a deck of cards.

"Oh, perfect—something to help fight the boredom," he joked as he took the box from her, opened it, removed the cards and started to shuffle them.

"Thank you," he added as Nurse Robin made her way towards the door, opened it and left. The door hissed as it locked behind her.

Brian sat playing cards when an overwhelming feeling that someone or something was watching him caused a chill to run down his spine. He glanced over at the exam room window that looked out at the nurse's station and thought he saw a dark, shadowy figure standing on the other side of the glass. He rubbed his eyes and looked again, but nothing was there. Suddenly he felt something was wrong— terribly wrong. The medicine started to take effect and he became lethargic; unable to hold his eyes open, he laid down and fell asleep.

Nurse Robin finished her rounds, removed her contamination suit and brought the blood samples she had collected to the lab for her friend Joe Benson, the lab's blood analyst.

Her duties completed, she left work and headed over to her son's school to take him home for the day.

11:33 P.M.

Robin sat on her sofa feeling a slight headache coming on, and her throat felt like she had swallowed razor blades. *Probably caught whatever Sean picked up at school,* she thought. *It is cold season and he gets sick every year at this time.*

Exhausted, she could feel herself falling asleep on the sofa. The cold was kicking in and it felt like it was going to be a doozy. She picked up the phone and called into work. Her voice sounded very congested as she told the night-shift supervisor she would be taking the next day off, hung up the phone and then climbed into bed.

Chapter 3

Wednesday, October 28th
15 miles south of Boston
10:47 P.M.

"You're a fucking alcoholic!" Annabelle screamed. She was holding onto the kitchen chair, her arms visibly shaking with fury. "I can't believe you had the nerve to say that to me!"

Drew couldn't remember what he had just said, but considering the tempest spewing from Annabelle, he figured it must've been a whopper of a comment. He had never seen his wife this angry before, ever. She never swore, yet she had just used the "F" word. Her words hung there, stunning him. Her face was slowly becoming red as rage washed over it. It was like watching something in slow motion, or as if time itself had slowed down. He watched as she slowly reached up, grabbed the back of the chair, leaned forward and screamed at him. Her words came out slowly and clearly, "You're a fucking alcoholic!"

She usually just called him a jerk when he drank too much, which over the months had become more frequent, until he started drinking every night, passing out on the sofa in the living room or in the kitchen chair with his head on the table.

He tried to apologize with the same old drunken slurs that she had heard more than enough times as of late.

"No! Not this time! You can't take back what you said. Every time this happens, you promise it's the last time, but you do it again the next night! I'm tired of your drinking, and I'm tired of the way you treat me when you do. I want you gone! I'd have you leave right now, if you weren't too drunk to drive, but tomorrow you're out! I can't have you acting like this every night. You're so full of anger when you drink, and the baby can't see you like this. Everyone comments on how much of an asshole you've become. What happened to you? You were a good man who had morals and believed in yourself. But you're not the man I married anymore! I'm done with you!" It all came out at once and it was the most she had said to him in weeks. Her cheeks flushed with anger.

"Do you want a divorce?" he asked.

"I think I do!" she replied before she turned and stormed down the hall, slamming the bedroom door behind her.

Drew made his way to the living room and laid down on the couch, dwelling on what his wife had just said to him. He couldn't for the life of him remember what he had said to her. Did it have something to do with her constant complaining and bitching and never doing anything about it? It must have been about her weight or something for her to have gotten so pissed.

He laid in shock, wondering what he should do. One marriage had already ended, but for different reasons, and now it looked like the second was about to end as well. *What am I going to do about my daughter?* he thought to himself. *Will Annabelle let me see her? I didn't even have that much to drink. What will I do with my clothes? I guess I'll have to live out of my car.*

He continued to ponder on what would happen and if Annabelle would tell his daughter that her daddy was a bad man once he'd gone. He stared up at the ceiling when he heard his baby girl cry out from down the hall, "Boobie, where are you?" She was looking for her little blanket that they called her woobie.

"Boobie, where are you?"

They always laughed when she asked for her woobie, because she was unable to pronounce the W sound. She must have found it, because she quickly started to settle down. He had visions of her holding her woobie close as she normally did in her crib.

He wondered once he'd gone if she would call out, "Daddy, where are you?" like she did for her woobie. The thought of not being there for her when she cried out for him broke his heart. He wanted to go talk to his wife but he knew that would only make it worse.

Drew looked at his watch—he had to be to work in five hours, but sleep wouldn't come. He found himself staring at the ceiling when his phone buzzed, and knew by the sound of the tone that it was an alert for breaking news from his local news station's app. He pulled out his phone and checked the alert message:

Amber Alert issued by
Brooksdale, New York, Police.
Details in app.

Drew swiped his finger across the front of the phone, opening the app, which brought up several headline stories. The first story was a report about a young boy named Jimmy from Brooksdale, New York, who had disappeared while playing in the front yard as his mother hung out laundry in the backyard. The Brooksdale Police had issued a regional alert for the missing boy.

The next headline story read, "Two Dead After Overnight Car Accident," followed by, "Debate Scheduled for Tuesday Night," "Eighty People Sick After Eating at Local Restaurant," "Orlando Theme Park to Open New Ride," "Rare Freeze Ruins Crops in Mid-West," "New Hybrid Car to Get 150 Miles Per Gallon." *Nothing good here, —just same old same old*, he thought, putting the phone down as he felt himself growing tired.

"Boobie, where are you?" Drew heard again just as he finally started drifting off to sleep.

Thursday, October 29th
4:37 A.M.

Several hours later, Drew woke up to his phone ringing. *Who the hell is calling me at this time of the morning?* he thought as he grabbed his phone. His head was pounding from the alcohol and lack of sleep as he glimpsed the screen to see the Caller ID display his mother's cell phone. Without the slightest hesitation, he slid his thumb across the phone to answer the call and put the phone up to his ear.

"Hello?"

"Hi, Drew. It's Rebecca," the voice announced on the other end of the phone.

"Hi, Rebecca. Is my mom okay?"

Rebecca paused before replying. "Listen, you need to come down here quick."

His heart stopped in his chest. "What happened?"

"The doctors think your mom had a heart attack and... they are asking for family to come."

"What?"

"I wish I had better news for you, dear. But they don't think she has much longer to live. She went a long time without oxygen." Rebecca's voice was shaky with concern.

Drew's mind started racing back to memories of his mother. The way she raised him to be a good boy and always do the right thing. How she tried relentlessly to provide everything for him and his sister. Usually she never had enough, but he always knew she tried... harder than his father did, that's for sure. He drifted further back to his sister. He was the last person to see her before their father had driven her to run away some thirty years ago.

"Drew are you there?"

"Yes. I'm on my way. I'll call you once I land in Florida."

He hung up and then looked up flights from Logan to Orlando, eventually finding one that departed at 6:30 A.M.

With effort, Drew forced himself off the couch, made his way down the hall to his bedroom and opened the door, using his phone as a flashlight to enter their bedroom since the light was on the nightstand next to the bed. He scanned the room, but Annabelle wasn't there. He then proceeded to his daughter's room and checked the crib. Empty.

Dammit, Drew! You and your drinking. Annabelle must have left after you passed out last night, he chastised himself as he held a hand to his pounding head, trying to quell his hangover. *I really must have drank more than I thought last night.*

With a sense of urgency creeping into his consciousness, Drew stumbled his way into the kitchen and grabbed a glass of water and several aspirin. He pulled out his phone and tried calling Annabelle, but her phone went straight to voicemail.

"Hi, Annabelle. I'm sorry about last night. Can you please call me? My mom had a heart attack and the doctors don't think she has long to live. I'm heading to the airport now to catch a flight to Florida. Please call me. I'm sorry."

He hung up the phone and texted Annabelle the same message. Heading back into the bedroom and turning on the light, Drew went to the closet to pull out the suitcase but found himself staring at the bare floor. It took him a moment to realize Annabelle had taken the suitcase. He walked into his daughter's room and checked her closet for his old gym bag, but that too was gone.

Ding. He reached into his pocket, pulled out his phone and saw a text message from Annabelle:

I want a divorce. I'm sorry about your mom and I'll pray for her, but I can't keep living this way. We'll talk when you get back.

"Can this day get any fucking worse?" he shouted as he grabbed his sweatshirt and stormed out the front door with his keys and a bottle of water.

Man, I really screwed up last night to make her go sleep at her mother's, he thought as he drove. *What the hell did I drink last night? I remember stopping of at the packie yesterday, because it was a rough day at work. Oh yeah, I grabbed an eighteen-pack of beer and a few nips from the checkout counter,* which he stuck into the front pocket of his sweatshirt. He started drinking as soon as he walked in the door yesterday, like each and every day before. In fact, Drew had been drinking so much lately that his insides were starting to hurt. B*ut what the hell; what's another drink?* he would say to himself.

His mind quickly shifted to his mother, imagining her lying in a hospital bed with all sorts of tubes and wires coming out of her. It reminded him of when he had to go and identify his father's body after he died of a heart attack some seventeen years ago. An image burned into his memory just like all of the other deceased people he had tried to save while working in Boston as an EMT after he got out of the Marines.

The drive to the airport seemed to fly by as he remembered his past life. Drew Murphy did not look back on his childhood with fond memories. He thought back to when he was younger and his mother allowed his father back in the house, one of the umpteen times. He always wondered why she let him back, knowing that he would only cheat on her and verbally abuse her again. Drew himself could take all of the abuse, from getting walloped with a belt to chopping firewood until midnight. He could even take the countless times he was suffocated by that man's hands. He could not stand by, though, and watch his mother cry.

Now a man, he understood why she let him back in. She needed the money to feed her kids. No matter how he spun it in his head, he knew this had to be her reason. When their dad wasn't home, days went by when they had no food to eat. When his mother did get food, she would go without so her kids wouldn't go hungry.

His hands subconsciously tightened on the steering wheel as he looked over at the harbor where his father's friend used to keep his boat — the boat that his father used to bring him out to the middle of nowhere, with no land in sight, and throw him overboard. The old man would then move the boat hundreds of feet away and stop. That man who was supposed to love and protect him would laugh as he yelled to Drew, "Swim before the sharks get you!" Once he was within reach of the boat, his father would move it again and again, until he became exhausted and would start to go under. That asshole didn't even give him a life jacket.

His memory of the boat brought back more thoughts of his childhood. He remembered the times his father would try and smother him as he slept in his bed. The pungent smell of his fingers and those long fingernails that used to clamp over his nose and mouth, suffocating him. He would struggle and fight to get free, but he was too small to overpower the man's six-foot four, three hundred pound frame. Drew struggled until he ran out of air and was about to collapse.

He felt more like a child slave than a son. His father would have him chop firewood and stack it for hours, sometimes until midnight. His mother would scream at him that Drew had to be up in the morning for school. He also remembered being hung up by his feet for what seemed an eternity until all of the blood rushed to his head and he started to turn purple. He thought about the welts on his back and bottom from the belt his father used as a whip on him, that hurt so bad he couldn't sit down. Drew lived in constant fear of that man—the man who was supposed to love him like no other. He loathed that man and on many occasions wanted to kill him, but he wasn't strong enough.

When his father finally died, a great weight lifted off his shoulders. He knelt before the casket, his hatred released. That man—that asshole—created a fire within Drew that burned with intensity. He took everything that man had dished out, even when it left him bruised and bleeding, and he never let his father think he had gotten the best of him. Somehow, some way, he kept that fire buried, down inside himself to be the best at everything he did. Drew had become very competitive and put everything on the line, every time. After all, what did he have to lose? He pushed his emotions down and hid them. For years, he built up a wall until it became impenetrable, except for when he drank. Only then, did that façade come crumbling down.

He hated his childhood because of his father and vowed to never be like him. But, here he was on the verge of becoming just that, and he couldn't stand it. Just like his mother left his father, Drew's wife left *him*. She didn't leave him for the man he was, but because of the man he became when he drank. His friends, who grew up with him and knew what he went through, forgave him for his actions when under the influence of booze. They knew the next day the wall would be back up, and they loved him because he was a loyal friend.

Annabelle didn't know much of his past, except for what he told her, which wasn't much. His friends filled her in on the gist and she had compassion for him, but his drinking had become too much as of late. Annabelle would no longer allow their daughter to be exposed to all of that repressed anger and rage that came out whenever he drank.

Drew pulled into Logan Airport and slipped on his sweatshirt, knowing that the cold wind would be blowing through the garage like a wind tunnel. As he slipped it over his head, the little airplane bottles, called "nips" in Boston, fell out of the front pocket. Reaching down, he picked them up off the floorboard and put them next to his phone in the console. He stared at the phone for a moment and then picked it up to try Annabelle again. The phone rang once but then went straight to voicemail. Unsurprised, he put the phone in his pocket and reached for the phone charger from the console. One of the small bottles sat on the charger cord. Unable to restrain himself, he picked it up, put the neck into his mouth and twisted off the cap, dumping the whole bottle into his mouth, and repeating the process with another.

Once satisfied, Drew grabbed the phone charger and made his way inside the airport, where he would soon board his plane for Orlando. And where, hopefully, the alcohol would soon kick in and alleviate his hangover.

Chapter 4

Thursday, October 29th
4:41 A.M.

Annabelle sat on the edge of her old bed at her mother's house and cried. She had packed up and left with her daughter in the middle of the night while Drew was passed out on the couch. This wasn't what she had signed up for. She wanted to be respected, not treated like a dog. Drew was a good man, but when he drank he became filled with such anger—an anger she couldn't let her little girl see again. He was never physically abusive (she knew he would never actually lay a hand on her or their little girl), but verbally... he beat her down hard, and she just couldn't deal with it anymore.

Susan, Annabelle's mother, heard her daughter come into the house during the middle of the night. Heard her put Stephanie down in the crib. Heard her sobs from the other room. *Better to talk about it in the morning*, Susan thought, knowing it was Drew's drinking that drove her here.

Annabelle had just started to finally fall asleep when her phone vibrated on the nightstand. She knew it was Drew calling to give another one of his half-assed apologies. The one where he would tell her he wouldn't drink anymore, only to pick up a drink the next night. She didn't want to deal with him right now, especially since she had a tough decision to make. To let him stay, under the condition that he attend Alcoholics Anonymous and get help, or to leave him. But she was certain he would just tell her he didn't have a problem, wouldn't go and would continue drinking. They've had that conversation more than once before. So that left her only one option. The phone vibrated again, indicating there was a new voicemail.

Annabelle loved him and knew he had been through a lot with an abusive father, joining the Marines after high school and then becoming an EMT in Boston. She was aware of the horrendous things he faced daily on the streets of Boston, things that sometimes kept him up at night. She also understood that was part of the problem—he used alcohol to help him cope with the stress of the job. At the same time, she knew he loved his job, nevertheless, even though it didn't pay much, and that he excelled at it, but it was costing them their marriage.

Her phone sounded off a short, double vibrate, letting her know a text message had been received. Without a doubt it was Drew trying to apologize and asking her to come home. A part of her wanted to text him back and tell him how she really felt, but she decided it was best to wait until she was well-rested and less emotional before replying.

But a minute later her phone vibrated again. Frustrated, she rolled over, grabbed the phone off the nightstand and read the text.

Her first thought upon reading the text was to hope his mother would be okay. She was a nice woman and Annabelle really liked her. She then thought, *How are we going to pay for the flight? And, if his mother does die, his drinking will only get worse,* which brought her back to why she was at her *own* mother's house in the first place. She had wanted to wait, but given the circumstances of Drew's unexpected emergency, she opened the message and began to type, *I want a divorce. I'm sorry about your mom and I'll pray for her, but I can't keep living this way. We'll talk when you get back.* Then, with slight hesitation, she hit send. She felt horrible, but it needed to be done.

Setting the phone back on the nightstand, Annabelle rolled back over and began to cry.

Annabelle woke a few hours later with bloodshot eyes, the lack of sleep combined with crying all night clearly written all over her face. Mascara lines ran down her cheeks like rivers cutting across the land and smeared onto the pillowcase.

She couldn't believe her life had come to this. She just wanted a happy marriage like the ones she saw on TV. But it seemed to her that Drew had too much bottled up deep inside himself. He didn't talk much about what had happened to him as a child, but whatever demons he had made sure to hide from the rest of the world, alcohol brought them to the surface.

Annabelle could understand him having a drink or two to wash away the stress of the day. For Drew, however, once he had one, he couldn't stop, and the more he drank, the more belligerent he became. He didn't have much of a filter when it came to speaking in general, but with a few drinks in him, he had diarrhea of the mouth. He would say anything to anyone, and what he said was usually hurtful.

She lay there wondering about her future and what it would hold. At some point she drifted off again and slept the whole day away.

Chapter 5

Thursday, October 29th
5:25 A.M.

Brian sat in his bed dealing cards to himself to kill time. His grumbling stomach forbade him from sleep, but he knew Nurse Robin would be in shortly with his breakfast. He tried watching the news, but it was just constant coverage of the little boy who had gone missing. Brian figured some pedophile had snatched up the boy, and he didn't want to be watching should the police discover the body, so he had decided to play solitaire instead.

Finally, a knock on his door. It was loud, but also music to his appetite and therefore welcomed. "Come in!" he yelled.

The outside airlock hissed followed by the door swinging open. A tall, black male nurse entered the room wearing a contamination suit and carrying a tray of food.

"Where's Nurse Robin?" Brian asked.

"She called out today," the man answered, his voice distorted by the suit's voice box.

"Is she alright?"

"I think she just took a personal day." The nurse placed the tray of food down on top of the cards. He then went through the same routine Robin did every morning—checking Brian's vital signs, drawing some blood and giving him an injection.

Brian's blood work from yesterday had come back negative again for the strain of the super bug, despite Robin's having attempted to infect him. So, the nurse injected him with the disease again. Once he finished, he handed Brian his daily medications, comprised of blood pressure medicine and a sedative, which made the test subjects fall asleep and allowed the virus to work faster. It was easier for the staff to perform tests if the subjects were unconscious.

"Will she be in tomorrow?" Brian asked.

"I don't see why not," the man replied as he wrote down Brian's vital signs and walked out.

Brian liked Nurse Robin, being his first caregiver when he was admitted for treatment. She was always nice to him and seemed to generally care for him, unlike some of the other staff members.

5:30 A.M.

Down the hall, Joe, stood over the blood machine with a killer headache and a sore throat that felt like he swallowed shards of glass. He had just received a call ordering him to retest the blood of all the living test subjects. When the soft alarm chimed to alert him the test was complete, he turned toward at the big grey machine, reached down and pushed the flashing red button, causing the door to open and the tray of test tubes to pop out. He carried the rack of tubes over to the fridge, opened it and placed it on the top shelf. The sample would stay there for a few days, in case additional testing was needed, before being moved to a large freezer. Just as he closed the fridge door, the printer on the shelf next to the machine came to life and began spitting out the blood test results. Joe grabbed the two pages and brought them over to his desk.

The first page contained the blood results for the female test subjects.

FEMALE TEST SUBJECTS

Rachel Ahern . . . . Positive
Lisa Bennington . . . . .Positive
Mary Childs . . . . .Positive
Janelle Forbes . . . . Positive
Bridget Goodson . . . . Positive
Nancy Harbors . . . . .Positive
Susan Reynolds . . . . Positive
Elizabeth Smith . . . . .Positive

He quickly looked over the results and noted that everything appeared to be accurate. All infected subjects came back positive for the sickness.

Joe then quickly scanned down the second page, which contained the blood results for the male test subjects, and his mouth dropped open. It was the first time he had witnessed a print out with the word "Unknown" in the results column. *What the hell does "Unknown" mean?* he thought.

MALE TEST SUBJECTS

Steven Astew . . . . Positive
Peter Baker . . . . Positive
Michael Daniels . . . . Positive
Stewart Fredrickson . . . . .Positive
Brian Phillips . . . . Unknown
Craig Stevens . . . . .Positive
Eric Wadsworth . . . . Positive
Mark Umbria . . . . Positive

His eyes darted over to the column containing the test subjects' names. "Oh, shit — Brian Phillips!" he gasped. He immediately picked up the phone and called his supervisor.

Someone picked up the phone. "Hello?" said the voice on the other end, but it sounded different. It sounded congested.

"Something has gone wrong—terribly wrong," Joe said into the phone receiver as he put his hand to his chest, starting to feel a growing tightness deep within. *No, please Lord—don't let me have it,* he thought.

"I'll be right down," the voice on the other end of the phone said.

Joe hung up, reached into his desk, pulled out the last two days' worth of printouts and started to pour over them. He needed to find out what went wrong, and he needed to find out fast.

He scoured the last couple of days' reports, searching for a clue, when the answer jumped out at him. In the upper right hand corner of the results were the initials "R.D." He remembered hearing that Robin had called in sick last night for her shift today. Panic set in, he used the mouse and clicked on the computerized Rolodex and found Robin's phone number. Squinting at the screen, he picked up the phone and dialed Robin's number.

Pick up! Come on! Pick up! he said to himself, but the phone just rang and rang.

5:36 A.M.

Robin lay on her bed at home breathing in her last breaths when the phone started ringing on her nightstand. Her body was covered with painful black sores and it was shutting down. Just as the phone stopped ringing, Nurse Robin drowned in a thick yellowish-green froth that had formed in her lungs and now seeped from her mouth.

Joe hung up the phone and left the lab heading towards the east wing nurses' station, his breathing was labored and becoming worse with each step. As he exited the lab into the hallway, the ear-piercing contamination alarm started sounding and the red strobe lights activated, indicating there was a breach. The automated emergency system immediately sent the facility into lockdown mode.

6:02 A.M.

Brian Phillips awoke to alarms sounding, security lights flashing and people screaming. Jumping out of bed and rushing to the exam window, where on the other side of the glass, it looked like a mad house as doctors and nurses ran around like crazy. He gasped as he watched one of the doctors lie on the floor with a yellowish-green froth spewing from his mouth. The same thing happened the other day when his roommate Howard became sick.

He searched the faces of all those on the other side of the exam window and saw their frightened expressions. A doctor ran up to one of the nurses and yelled, "It wasn't supposed to mutate!" as she assisted a second doctor lying on the floor, spewing froth from his mouth. Behind the nurses' station, two women yelled hysterically at each other, while others sat on the floor and wept. Scientists searched frantically through piles of paperwork as the virus spread with impeccable speed. It was like nothing they had seen before in all of the tests that they had performed. They had no time to run new tests. No time to react. Their bodies were shutting down and black painful sores were starting to form all over their bodies. Brian watched in horror as each person on the other side of the window eventually fell to the floor, coughed up froth and died.

He remained still, paralyzed with fright, staring out the window. His mind raced with the fear of catching whatever was killing everyone on the other side of the glass or worse, slowly dying of starvation. He thought he was going crazy for sure—he kept seeing a dark shadow of some sorts dance and float from one dead body to another. *My mind must be playing tricks on me*, he thought to himself, frozen in place. His eyes the only thing moving other than the rise and fall of his chest with each breath he took.

Brian tried to see if there was someone moving on the other side, perhaps someone casting the shadow. His eyes darted from body to body. He watched as a large urine stain appeared on the front of one doctor's pants whose bladder let go after he died. Soon the stain turned into a puddle of urine on the floor that slowly started to trail off towards one of the nurses who had dropped dead a few feet away from the doctor's feet. The trail zigged and zagged as it moved, and he could only guess where it would end. Eventually, the thin stream of urine turned and headed for the dead nurse. A part of him wanted to see it run right into the face of the blond-haired nurse who had been mean to him, but another side of him was disgusted by the thought of it.

Suddenly a hand pressed up against the window, startling Brian and causing him to jump. A man appeared in front of the window, and he read the man's name on his lab coat: Joe Benson. The man's face and hands were covered with black sores and he was clearly having trouble breathing as he bent over and rested a hand on his knee.

He watched as Joe Benson slowly made his way around the nurses' station, towards the closet door. Just as Joe reached the door, he suddenly had an uncontrollable coughing fit and fell to one knee. Brian witnessed Joe's chest heave up and down, just like the chests of the other nurses and doctors out there had. Joe was able to reach out and take hold of the closet doorknob. He held himself up for a second and appeared to regain his stamina as he managed to open the door.

Joe used his left shoulder, held himself up against the doorjamb and used his right hand to tug on the contamination suits.

It's too late for those suits to help you, Brian thought despondently as he continued to observe the man with sympathy.

Joe started turning each helmet to inspect them. After a second he slid the suit to the left. Brian realized that Joe was reading the names on the helmets. He slid two more suits to the left before he stopped, read the name and pulled the suit from its hanger. It fell to the floor, and Joe turned his back to the doorjamb and slid down until his butt hit the ground.

He could see Joe was sweating profusely and that his breathing had become very labored. He sat there for a minute before he leaned forward, grabbed the suit and pulled it close.

The man ran his fingers over the thick plastic suit as if he was searching for something. When Joe flipped it over, he could see the small, black, charred mark on the back of the elbow.

He leaned his head back against the wall and brought his hand up to his mouth as he started coughing again. He pulled his hand away, looked at it and let it fall to his side. Brian noticed sputum covered Joe's palm.

Brian put his open palm against the window and banged on the glass, trying to get the Joe's attention.

Joe looked up as Brian's movement caught his eye. Brian pressed his face to the window and mouthed, "What happened?"

Anger washed over Joe Benson's face as he grabbed the suit and threw it. Brian watched it land in front of his window.

The nametag that read "Nurse Robin Dupree" jumped out at him. Brian looked back up to see that Joe Benson had his arm outstretched, pointing at him through the window. Goosebumps covered his arms as he watched Joe's arm fall to his side and his head hang low.

The man slumped over and a thick mucus spilled from the mouth of the lifeless body, just like everyone else on the other side of the window. Brian jumped as Joe's eyes reopened, giving the appearance that they were staring up at him.

Still unable to move, he glimpsed the shadowy thing near the back of the nurses' station as a chill ran down his spine. He reached up, grabbed the cord for the blinds and yanked on it, causing the exam window blinds to come crashing down as he jumped into bed and curled up into a ball under the covers.

How am I going to get out of here? he thought as the air under his shelter of blankets became warm. All of a sudden Brian was having trouble breathing— claustrophobia was taking hold of him. He whipped the covers off and dropped to his knees as he bowed his head. "Dear God, please get me out of this alive and I'll do whatever you ask of me," he said out loud as he prayed.

Suddenly there was a thunderous sound that shook the building, like a thousand trumpets playing all at once.

When the noise had quelled, a familiar hissing sound followed. Someone or something had opened the door from the outside.

He turned, grabbed a towel from the small linen cart in his room and held it up to his face, hoping it would prevent him from catching whatever killed everyone else. He hesitated for a minute, contemplating whether to stay or go. *If I go out there, I can catch whatever killed everyone else. But, the door is already open and whatever was out there is in here now.*

It didn't take Brian long to make up his mind. He had survived when his roommate Howard had become sick. Besides, if he stayed here in the room he would probably die from hunger. He grabbed a larger towel, covered his face and tied it in the back. Working up enough nerve to leave, he walked nervously to the door, took a deep breath and held it, then pulled the door open to exit the room.

He made his way past the nurses' station and down the hallway, skirting his way around the bodies as he went. Each carcass was covered with black spots and had a thick yellowish-green crust on the face. Some had died right in their chairs while others were stacked upon each other near the exits at the far end of the hall. This particular section of the building was designed to be air tight, and at the first signs of exposure it would go into lockdown mode. Brian walked past the security office when something lingering in the shadows moved and caught his attention. The hair on the back of his neck stood on end as goosebumps formed on his arms when he looked through the security office window and saw the ominous dark presence swaying in front of the computer terminal. He was still holding his breath and his lungs were burning. His heart pounded so hard in his chest that he could actually feel each palpitation. He wanted out of the building in the worst way.

Time seemed to move in slow motion as his head turned away from the security office window, searching to find the closest exit. Every muscle in his body was working as hard as it could as he darted down the hall, away from the dark shadowy thing and towards the mound of bodies in front of the exit. As he approached the door, his heart skipped a beat when he noticed the red light above the door indicating that it was locked.

Suddenly there was another thunderous sound and the building shook again. This time it seemed like ten thousand trumpets were blaring, and Brian had to cover his ears. The pile of bodies in front of the door shook, a few of them falling off the pile and sprawling out across the floor. When the sound finally ceased, he noticed the red light above the door had turned green as the door swung open with a loud hiss.

He glanced over his shoulder to see who had opened it, but the only thing he saw was the ominous shadowy figure now in the hallway next to the security office. Like a startled animal at bay, Brian bolted for the open door. He wasn't sure if that thing had released him or not, but he wasn't going to stick around to find out.

Time seemed to resume its normal speed once he passed through the airtight door that led into another part of the building. He ran down a long corridor that came to the main lobby, where he found two more dead bodies. They were workers who must have been able to get out just before the security protocol initiated, which could only mean one thing: the super bug was now free. Brian ran out the front door of the lobby and into an open parking lot. The air felt cool as it rushed down his throat.

Just beyond the front steps, a woman laid dead with her purse sitting next to her stiff, lifeless body. He picked up the purse and searched through it until he found a set of keys, luckily with an alarm fob.

Hurrying down the stairs into the parking lot, Brian held the keys above his head while repeatedly pushing the alarm button. He followed the noise until halfway down the lot on the right side, when he saw the flashing head and tail lights of a silver SUV. Within moments he commandeered the vehicle and was off for the nearest police or fire station to let the authorities know what was going on at the Lumpton Treatment Center.

6:19 A.M.

Brian raced down Waltham Street, boldly exceeding the posted 35 mph speed limit, driving blindly until he realized he had crossed over into the town of Brooksdale. Luck, for once, appeared to be on his side as he came upon the Brooksdale Police Station by chance. He parked the SUV in one of the open spots and rushed up the stairs leading to the police station entrance, passing two shady looking men coming out.

"Look at this freak," he heard one of the men say as he passed them on the walkway. The man was wearing a hat with an embroidered weed leaf, and he laughed at Brian who hurried on his way.

Weed-hat guy shouted "Freak!" at him again from behind. Brian paid little mind, but was momentarily perplexed by the unprovoked mockery, until he realized it might have had something to do with the fact that he was barefoot and only had on his hospital pants.

He entered the police station and walked up to the thick glass window, frantically ringing the bell. A few seconds later a broad-shouldered police officer approached the window. Brian could tell that the cop was questioning his attire.

"Can I help you?" asked the police officer.

"Yes sir. I just came from the Lumpton Treatment Center and there's been some sort of accident."

"What sort of accident?" The police officer held a look of suspicion on his face.

"Some chemical or something was released and there are a lot of dead people up there!" he exclaimed.

The officer rested his hands on his utility belt and assumed Brian had escaped from the psychiatric ward at the Brooksdale Hospital nearby. He had seen folks like this before but never had one walk into the station.

"What hospital did you say?" the police officer asked with a hint of doubt.

Brian's face turned red. "Not hospital," he snapped with a forceful tone. "Lumpton Treatment Center," Impatiently, he placed his wrist against the window. "See? Lumpton Treatment Center."

The police officer leaned in close and confirmed the words on the wrist band.

Although he was content that this stranger was truthful regarding where he came from, the cop now suspected he was most likely high on something. "Okay, I'm going to buzz you in," he said with a disarming smile, thinking it best to get this junkie off the street.

After Brian walked through the door, the officer led him to a desk and had him take a seat.

"So tell me again what happened up at the treatment center?"

Brian left no details out as he told him about the shooting at the convenience store, the death of his wife, his admittance into the center after the drug overdose, and then repeated the story of how everyone there had mysteriously died. The only element he chose to omit, for fear of being taken for a wacko, was the inexplicable dark phantom he had witnessed.

"Did they all overdose?" asked the cop.

"No, I don't think so," Brian replied, shaking his head. "More like a virus or something, but it worked quickly and spread like fire. I've never seen anything like that before. Like something straight out of a fucking sci-fi movie!"

The police officer was not sure what to do. He figured this guy was a nut-job, but protocol mandated he at least have someone check it out, just in case. Besides, the last thing he wanted was for there to have been a homicide and he did nothing, especially if this lunatic in front of him was the killer.

The officer told Brian to sit tight, then stepped into a nearby office. Biting his nails nervously, Brian could see the cop through the office door's glass window, speaking into the phone. Within a few short minutes he hung up and came back out. "They're going to send someone over there to look around," he said as he walked over to the police radio and tuned it to the Lumpton Police Station's frequency.

Seconds passed and the radio came alive: "Dispatch to car thirty-seven and forty-five."

"Thirty-seven answering."

"Forty-five answering."

"Both units respond to the Lumpton Treatment Center for a possible homicide."

"Thirty-seven's responding."

"Forty-five's responding as well." The sirens were audible through the radio.

"Homicide?" Brian repeated, with evident irritation.

The officer, sitting close to him to prevent an escape simply shrugged. "Just considering all possibilities."

Short seconds became lengthy minutes. Brian stared at the clock. *What is taking so long?*

After what seemed like an eternity, the silence broke: "Thirty-seven's off at the Lumpton Treatment Center. I have someone up by the front door at the top of the stairs."

The police officer sitting next to Brian slowly reached up and put his left hand on his cuffs, waiting to hear what was going on. He wanted to be prepared to arrest this psycho for homicide if need be.

The radio came to life again: "Forty-five's out with thirty-seven. I have someone in a running car over here. I'm going to investigate."

Suddenly screaming came over the radio: "Forty-five, don't go near that body!" screamed thirty-seven.

The officer across from Brian slowly reached for his cuffs.

"Oh my God! What's all over her face?" Forty-five responded.

Another moment passed.

"Dave, we have more people lying in the lobby," Thirty-seven shouted into his radio, now using his partner's name.

"Meet me at my cruiser, Tim" Forty-five demanded.

The officer across from Brian now stood up, waiting to make the arrest.

Another minute passed by, feeling like an hour to Brian and the police officer with him.

"Forty-five to dispatch," crackled the radio.

Instantly the dispatcher answered, "Go ahead, Forty-five."

"We've got a big problem and we're going to need the fire department and HAZMAT team up here right away. We have about a dozen people who appear to have died from the plague or something."

"Received, Forty-five. You're requesting the fire department and HAZMAT team," dispatch answered.

The officer standing up across from Brian put his cuffs away, now knowing that the man across from him was not a crackpot.

Brian sat in the Brooksdale Police Station for several minutes listening to the events as they unfolded over the radio. The Lumpton Fire Department had arrived on scene and was waiting for the HAZMAT team to arrive before entering the treatment center to search for any survivors.

After several minutes, the phone rang. The officer rushed to answer, not bothering to close the door behind him this time. His voice, as he spoke, now sounded a bit congested to Brian.

The officer listened for a moment before speaking. "Can you send someone here? I'm the only one here at the station right now since all the other officers are out searching for that missing boy."

Brian looked around, noticing that there were no other officers in the building, and then looked back at the officer who was nodding his head as he listened to the phone.

"Okay, see you in a few minutes," he said as he hung up and returned to where Brian sat waiting. "That was the Lumpton Police Station. They're sending someone to talk to you about what happened."

7:02 A.M.

Several miles from the Brooksdale Police Station, a black sports car crashed into a telephone pole after leaving the local diner. The driver died on impact and the passenger was ejected, a hat with an embroidered weed leaf stuck on his head by a shard of glass.

Two women in a passing car stopped to help, both horrified to find the driver dead and the passenger sprawled out in the street with a mixture of blood and yellowish-green substance coming out of his nose and mouth.

A few other drivers stopped—one called 911 as they stood watching the man die.

7:06 A.M.

The phone rang again, startling Brian. The officer picked up the phone, listened for a minute and said, "I'll be right there," before hanging up.

Brian turned in his seat as the officer stood up and said, "I'm going to have you follow me."

Brian stood up, and then the officer led him over to one of the cells. Before he could react, the officer placed his hand on Brian's back, pushed him into the cell and closed the door behind him. Brian turned, grabbed the metal bars and yelled, "What the hell!"

"There's been an accident up the street I need to go to and I can't leave you unattended. Don't worry, I'll be back in a few minutes. Besides, the Lumpton police should be here soon." The officer grabbed his hat off the rack and started for the door. He made his way out to his cruiser, got in and headed up the street to the car accident. As he drove he rubbed his throat. It felt like he had swallowed razor blades.

The officer approached the scene and found about ten people standing around a motionless body. He exited his cruiser, approached the body and instantly recognized the man lying on the ground as the man who had just been bailed out of jail. He leaned over the body and noticed it was covered with black spots and that a mucus had spilled out of the mouth. His mind quickly flashed to what he had just heard on the radio about finding dead people with spots on their necks and foam coming out of their mouths.

"Everyone, get back to your cars!" he yelled through a congested voice as he slowly backed away, heading for his cruiser. He needed help and right away. He got into his cruiser, picked up the radio and suddenly started to cough uncontrollably. He put his hand over his mouth and felt a wet, warm substance in his hand. The officer reached up, turned on the overhead light and opened his eyes wide with terror as he looked into his hand covered with a thick mucus. A tightness shot across his chest and he started coughing again. The officer was unable to catch his breath as fluid built up in his lungs. He drowned sitting in the cruiser with the radio mic in his lap.

7:31 A.M.

Almost thirty minutes had passed since the officer had left Brian sitting alone in the police station, when he felt something watching him. He looked up and in the back corner of the police station loomed the ominous, dark shadowy mass he had seen earlier.

Brian's heart was racing. Fear gripped him. He backed up until his back pressed hard against the far wall of the cell. The apparition hovered and moved across the floor like a mist coming towards him. As it approached the holding cell, he noticed the air was becoming colder.

Something started to protrude from the dark phantom as it drew closer to the cell. It appeared as if an arm was extending and growing long black fingers that rose up and pointed at the lock of the cell.

Suddenly a bright flash filled the police station, followed by a deep, beastly voice growling, "Come and see." Its words gave Brian an unusual feeling—they changed something within him, altering him. They were a signal to Brian Phillips' body and to the dark presence within that it had begun.

Brian felt weightless and disoriented, like he was having an out-of-body experience. It was as if he no longer had control of his actions.

One of the menacing figure's long, black fingers touched the lock of the cell. Brian could hear the tumblers turn, followed by a loud *CLINK* as the cell door unlocked and swung open. The ominous presence floated backwards and then raised its arm again, pointing at the front entrance.

His body began moving on its own as it walked out of the cell and through the front entrance of the police station. Unable to stop himself, he climbed into the silver SUV he had taken from the dead woman at the treatment center. Brian was conscious, but his body felt like it was on autopilot, like it was pre-programmed and his mind was just along for the ride. Though he desperately fought to regain control over his motor skills, there was nothing he could do but watch as some unknown but wicked entity used him like a puppet. He was utterly helpless.

The beginning of the end was at hand, and Brian Phillips had been chosen to be the first of the Four Horsemen.

He sat upon a white horse and he brought pestilence.

Chapter 6

Thursday, October 29th
8:12 A.M.

Within minutes, Brian Phillips arrived at the Lumpton Train Station. He had never been there before, yet the entity controlling his body seemed to know exactly where it was going. He was trapped within, unable to resist what was happening. Pulling up onto the curb in front of the entrance to the station, he put the vehicle in park and exited the SUV. His bare feet touched the cold asphalt, but Brian didn't feel it. In fact, he felt nothing. He tried with all his might to stop his legs from moving. He tried screaming, spitting, jumping up and down, he even tried standing still—nothing worked. All he could do was simply see and hear, comprised of nothing more than conscious thought: a mere spectator of whatever was going to happen.

When Brian's body entered the station, he could see the dark, ominous figure near the turnstile that allowed entrance to the train platform below. As he approached the turnstile, a black arm-like tentacle extended out from the dark shadowy figure and reached out, touching the card reader slot. Instantly, he heard the click of the gate unlocking as his body passed through the entrance. His body continued toward the escalator and rode it down to the platform below. It stepped off of the escalator and walked out to where other passengers were waiting on the train. He approached two men in business suits, engaged in conversation. He could feel his body inhaling a large breath just like he did whenever the doctors checked his lungs.

His head suddenly leaned in close to the men standing on the platform and released his breath, blowing it straight into their faces. Both men instantly turned their heads, and one of them lifted his suitcase up in an effort to block Brian from breathing on him.

"What's your problem?" the businessman yelled as he made a disgusted face and backed away, covering his mouth and nose with his left hand, not realizing he just breathed in his own death. The other man, noticing Brian's odd attire, assumed he had mental issues, and briskly walked away.

Brian continued over to other waiting passengers and stood next to them, taking in deep breaths of life and exhaling death.

The commuter train heading to New York City arrived and he climbed aboard, taking a seat near a large group of passengers. Brian leaned his head back taking in deep breaths and exhaling, blowing them up towards the ceiling. The train car served as a living incubator in which everyone inside became infected. The train continued on towards the city, stopping several more times. At each stop more and more people got on, and at and each stop more and more people became infected.

Soon he exited the train, now in the heart of the New York City subway system. He made his way to one of the other train platforms, snaking through the hordes of rush hour commuters who were waiting for their trains to arrive. Within minutes one pulled up to the crowded platform, and he boarded the front of the packed car. Instead of finding a seat, he started walking down the aisle towards the back door of the train car, where he forced it open and passed from one train car to the next. In each car he walked through, he exhaled microscopic droplets of death that hung in the air for unsuspecting passengers to inhale.

Finally, he moved into the last train car where he passed a courier with a bike. The car was full of passengers, but he found an empty seat in the middle between a construction worker wearing ripped jeans and holding his yellow construction helmet in his lap, and a couple in matching workout suits, getting ready to power walk the downtown mall. In front of them sat a young woman heading to the airport for her return flight to college. In front of Brian sat a group of medical students on their way to the hospital to begin their first day of rounds. And in front of the medical students sat a group of ladies who had traveled to New York to sightsee and were now heading to catch a bus back to Boston.

Brian continued breathing in and out, spreading his invisible death. Whoever he came in contact with became infected—no one was immune. He had just made all of the passengers carriers of the disease. Within minutes they would start showing signs of the sickness. They would go about their normal routine, the sickness would inevitably follow, condemning others to their death.

The bike courier would soon make his way through a busy crowd to his first delivery stop: a high-rise office building with hundreds of white-collar employees.

The construction worker would stop at his favorite breakfast spot to order his usual sausage, egg, and cheese on an English muffin, hash browns, and a coffee, and sit in the lobby of the establishment to enjoy his meal with dozens of other patrons.

The group of medical students would return to the hospital to meet with the rest of their class before making their scheduled rounds, meeting with doctors, nurses, and many patients, most of which were to be discharged that day.

The couple in matching workout suits would begin their powerwalk through the mall, working up a sweat and breathing heavily.

The group of ladies would hurry to catch their bus for Boston, huffing and puffing to catch their exhausted breath. On the way, the bus driver would pull into a rest stop along the Massachusetts I-90 Turnpike so that the passengers could relieve themselves or purchase quick meals from the chain of fast-food restaurants, along with hundreds of other motorists.

The young college student would board her plane with many other passengers, and they would soon land in Atlanta, where many would disperse and scatter to catch their connecting flights to multiple other destinations.

The sickness would rapidly spread throughout New York City, Boston, and many other major cities. Soon it would be spreading worldwide. It was multiplying faster than the dark ominous presence could have ever hoped, *and soon the streets will start to fill with the dead*, it thought.

Chapter 7

Cassandra—Cass to her friends—sat with her head down, her long dirty-blond hair spilling everywhere. She didn't want to be in class today, but policy at the Savannah Institute of Graphic Art and Design mandated that attendance was fifty percent of the grade, so she had little choice. She'd rather be back at the cabin, lying in Greg's arms, nursing her hangover. She and Greg along with two other couples, had been on a three-day binge and now it was back to class.

A few weeks prior, they had decided to take a stroll through the woods to find a place to make love. Greg had always wanted to have sex out in the woods and *act like animals*, as he put it. They had followed a trail until it led down to a lake. From there, they had ambled along the water's edge, looking for a field or opening whereupon they could live out Greg's fantasy, when they had come across an old abandoned cabin on a small beach.

"Let's go take a look," Cass said as she grabbed Greg by the hand and led him towards the cabin.

The structure was a worn shade of brown that blended in with the surrounding foliage. The bottom step of the back entrance had rotted away and laid twisted at the base. The roof was covered in a thick coat of pine needles and the front porch had a pile of leaves up against the front door.

Cass had stepped up onto the porch and tried the front door, which was surprisingly unlocked. She had immediately thought of some horror movie she had seen as a child and secretly hoped there were no dead bodies inside. They had both cautiously entered, where they found everything was covered with white sheets. There was a thick, musty smell that hung in the air, and the floorboards creaked with their every step. In the main room sat a large sectional and two recliners off to each side. Further to the right was a small walk-in kitchen and a bathroom behind it. They had also discovered two bedrooms off the back of the cabin. The first bedroom had a queen size bed while the other had a king that almost took up the entire space.

The excitement of breaking in had turned her on, and the thought of finally making love to Greg in a bed instead of in the back seat of his car seemed very appealing. It also seemed a lot more alluring to her than having her bare ass possibly poked by branches, or worse, getting covered in poison ivy from lying on the ground doing what animals do in the wild. And with that thought, she had grabbed him and threw him on the bed, and they did what people do in beds.

After they had returned from the woods, they told their friends about their little special place they had discovered. Since then, the six of them had been spending weekends out there together.

Professor Franks stood at the front of the class discussing the project that was due on Monday. To Cass's surprise, he announced that the deadline would be postponed a week, because he had to leave town for a speaking engagement. Cass looked over at Greg and smiled with delight, the unexpected news somehow curing her of her hangover.

After class, she met Greg out in the hallway where she jumped up into his arms and planted a big kiss on his lips.

"That's awesome!" she exclaimed as she held him close. "Now that we have more time to complete the project, we can make use of the free weekend and go back to our little spot."

Greg just smiled and shook his head up and down with excitement.

Cass shifted her body to the left and slipped under Greg's arm. Out of the corner of her eye, Cass spotted their friends Jessica and Jim coming out of the classroom door behind them, followed by Shawn and Renell, who were holding hands. She took a step back just as Jim snuck up behind Greg, and gave him a big bear hug surprising him.

"That's awesome!" Jim cheered. "We just got out of that project. Beers are on me, my friend."

"Back to our little spot for a few more days?" Jessica asked.

"That's what Cass was just saying," Greg replied.

Jessica smirked at Cass and said, "Great minds think alike!"

Jim gave Greg a high-five. "Jess and I are going to hit the liquor store. Any requests?"

Before anyone else could answer, Renell stepped forward. "Shawn and I will go with you. We can stop at the grocery store along the way and grab some essentials."

"Sounds great," Cass chimed in. "I'll go get my new phone dock so we can listen to some music.

"Booze, food and music—who could ask for anything more?" Greg laughed.

"So we'll all pack for the weekend and then meet out at the cabin later?" Cass asked.

"Yup," answered Shawn and everyone else shook their heads yes in excitement.

They all agreed and, after a few more minutes of casual chatter, went their separate ways to prepare for their mini vacation.

Back in her dorm, Cass retrieved her ear buds from her nightstand and put them in her ears. She plugged the other end into her smart phone and opened her music app of choice to play her favorite song. While the music played, she started dancing around her room while quickly packing some clothes and other overnight necessities in a gym bag—she was looking forward to her unexpected weekend off. *It's been a great start to the semester with Greg and our friends*, she thought as she finished getting ready.

They had all met in Professor Franks' class, where they quickly bonded and had been inseparable since. Cassandra fell in love with Greg right away. He wasn't very athletic, or even muscular, but he was sharp. He had that uncanny ability to flip anything around on anyone to get what he wanted. Growing up, he had learned that if he complained about something enough, he could get his way. Of course, it also helped that his father was filthy rich.

She started for the door, but decided she should use the bathroom before the long walk out through the woods to the cabin.

12:13 P.M.

Danielle was glad to be back in Georgia and looked forward to seeing her friends at college. Her flight back from New York, where she attended her cousin's wedding, had landed less than an hour ago. She was glad her cousin had finally met a nice guy, especially after all of the dirt-bags she had dated. *I hope I'll get to meet the man of my dreams*, she thought as the taxi pulled up to the front of the women's dorm and the driver got out to assist her with her bag. She tipped the driver and started for the front door, when she noticed Greg, her roommate's boyfriend, sitting under a tree.

"Hey, Dannie!" Greg shouted as he waved.

She waved back with a smile and entered the dorm. As she made her way down the hallway, she saw Cass exiting their room and heading the opposite direction towards the bathroom with a gym bag strapped around one shoulder.

"Hey, Cass!" Danielle shouted, but Cass continued on her way without turning or responding. "Greg is outside!"

Danielle then noticed Cass had her ear buds in as she turned the corner. *I'll tell her when she comes back — and I'll tell her all about the wedding too*, she thought.

She entered the tiny dorm room, put her bag down and sat on the edge of her bed when she suddenly started sneezing uncontrollably. She put her hand up to her throat — it felt like she had swallowed shards of glass. Ignoring the pain at first, she started unpacking her clothes. After several minutes, Danielle realized Cass had not returned and figured she must have gone out to meet Greg.

I need to get a drink, she thought as she rubbed her throat, which felt like it was quickly getting worse. *I must be getting sick, because I have the chills now too.* She put on a sweatshirt and decided to head to the cafeteria, hoping that some hot, chicken noodle soup would help.

Danielle entered the cafeteria and was surprised at how busy it was. She figured it would have been empty at this time of day, but then checked her watch and realized it was still lunch time.

She entered the line for the soup when her friend Barb rushed to her side and asked, "How was the wedding?"

"It was wonderful! My cousin looked so beautiful," she said followed by a sneeze that launched green and yellow snot all over the crook of her elbow as she brought her arm up to her face.

"Are you okay, Dannie? You don't look so good."

"I'm fine. I must have picked something up while I was in New York."

Chapter 8

Thursday, October 29th
9:32 A.M.

Earlier that same day, Drew's flight landed fifteen minutes ahead of schedule. The drink he had on the plane combined with "the hair of the dog" he had earlier, were finally kicking in and curing his hangover. He stopped at the little store inside the terminal and purchased a pack of gum and a sleeve of mints, hoping to mask the smell of alcohol on his breath as he made his way to the car rental service desk. He breathed a sigh of relief as he walked away from the car rental counter, having successfully secured a rental without suspicion. Of course it helped the young kid who waited on him had on a wrinkled shirt, unwashed hair, and he reeked of weed mixed with BO... evidently too stoned to notice, or care about the smell of booze coming from Drew.

Once situated in the rental car, he pulled out his phone to check for any missed calls or messages during the flight, but it showed neither. Breathing a despondent sigh, he looked up the address for the hospital, plugged it into the car's GPS and set out on his way.

Upon arriving at his destination, Drew entered through the revolving door of the lobby and up to the older woman sitting at the front desk. He exchanged pleasantries with her and provided his mother's name. The woman typed in the provided information, squinted at the screen and gave him the room number before directing him toward the elevator.

Drew made his way down the long corridor, wondering what he was going to find once he got to Room 627, where his mother had been admitted. He never really paid much attention to it since he was always in and out of hospitals as an EMT back in Boston, but the scent of the place suddenly gave him a sense of familiarity. Maybe it was the smell of hope or despair — maybe both combined — or just the chemicals used to clean the halls, but nonetheless hospitals had a unique smell. Today it reminded him of his childhood and especially of his father's passing. Certain odors provide the mind with little identifiers that restore once-forgotten memories, no matter how well-hidden or suppressed. He wasn't looking forward to going through that again, especially since he hated his father and all of the horrible things that he had done to him. But, he had nothing but love and respect for his mother, and he wanted to be here for her.

He stepped inside the elevator and pushed the number six. As the elevator ascended, Drew felt butterflies in his stomach. The anticipation of seeing his mother on her death bed started to make him feel queasy. *Please let her have turned around and be sitting up when I walk into her room.*

The elevator finally stopped, and he stepped off and turned right. Passing the nurses' station where a young nurse sat with her head down, writing in a chart, he found his mother's room a little farther up on the left. As he approached the room, he could hear voices coming through the doorway. Drew took a deep breath and was about to enter his mother's hospital room when suddenly a big red cart came rolling through the doorway. A nurse was pushing the cart, followed by two doctors and another nurse. He knew what the red cart was as he'd seen it hundreds of times — it was a code cart used for when a patient went into cardiac arrest.

Drew backed up, allowing the hospital staff to exit the room, and then finally stepped inside. He saw Rebecca standing near his mom while another nurse was busying herself, picking up all kinds of open wrappers and little EKG pads, some of which were stuck to the floor.

Rebecca looked up and saw him standing there. Her eyes darted to her best friend laying in the bed and back to Drew. His heart sank. He knew by the look on Rebecca's face that he was too late. His mother lay there motionless. Tears started to well up in his eyes.

The nurse could feel a presence in the room and turned around. She was surprised to see the stocky man with huge shoulders and menacingly large, tattooed arms standing there with tears streaming down his face.

Rebecca, cutting the silence, spoke to the remaining nurse, "This is her son who just flew down from Massachusetts."

The nurse quietly walked over to the trash barrel, dropped all of the collected garbage in and then removed her gloves. "I'm very sorry for your loss," she said as she also discarded the gloves and left the room.

Rebecca made her way around the bed and gave him a big hug and kiss on the cheek. He leaned down hugging her small skin-and-bone frame.

"She passed peacefully and without pain," Rebecca said gently.

He nodded silently while looking at his mother.

Rebecca spoke again, "I'll give you a moment alone with her." She placed a supportive hand on his shoulder before stepping out of the room.

Drew moved awkwardly over to the side of the bed. He reached out and took his mother's frail hand into his. It was small and weak in comparison. He remembered how strong and beautiful her hands were when he was younger and they would wash dishes together. She would come home tired from work, yet still found time to go out to play catch with her son when he had asked her to. He remembered how she could not only throw a perfect spiral, but could teach him how to throw one too. She wouldn't have her son out there tossing the ball to himself.

He recalled all of the times she was there for him—never letting him down. Tears continued running down Drew's face. *You were always there for me, but when you needed me the most, I wasn't there for you.* He looked down at her aged face. She was still beautiful, but soft lines had now taken over, and her once-brown hair was now completely gray. The intubation tube still hung out of her mouth, something he was accustomed to seeing in his line of work, but it looked out of place. It wasn't the last memory he wanted of his mother but it would have to do.

He wiped his nose on the sleeve of his arm and used his thumb to wipe away the tears from his eyes. A single tear fell from his hands and landed on her face, just below her right eye. Drying his hands on his pants, he reached up and wiped it from her cheek.

I can't believe you're gone. It seems like yesterday we were talking about girls and what I wanted to do after high school. Drew reflected back to one particular summer, a hot, Saturday morning when he was a teenager in high school. He remembered his mom pulling into the parking lot of the Purity Supreme, their local super market. His mother had turned off the old Chevy truck engine and turned towards him in her seat, putting her hand on his leg. "I love how you chase your dreams," she had said. "You can do whatever you put your mind to. Life isn't easy and you'll be tested, but never give up. Even when you're down, never give up. God knows I've wanted to give up, but I never did. I'm so proud of you. I love you, son!"

He found himself wiping away more tears as they blurred his vision.

"I love you too, Mom," he said aloud.

"Drew, these men are here to take your mom away," Rebecca said from behind him.

Drew found himself on his knees next to his mother's bed, his head on her shoulder and her hand still in his.

He wiped the tears away one last time, stood up and walked out into the hallway. Rebecca followed him and again gave him a sympathetic embrace.

"With our age, your mom already had everything planned out for when this day inevitably came," Rebecca explained. "The funeral home already knows of her wishes. All we have to do is inform them of her passing."

Drew nodded his head, but was looking down at the floor. *Did she know this day was coming? Was she feeling sick and didn't say anything? I wish Annabelle and I had made that trip down last year to see her, but we just couldn't get the time off from work.*

"I suppose we should go over to the funeral home and let them know so they can come pick her up," Drew said.

"It's not far from here."

"Where did you park? I'll walk you to your car and then I'll grab my rental and follow you over to the funeral home."

He was relieved his mom had made all of her own funeral arrangements. She had left instructions that she opted for cremation and wanted two services. The first of which was to be held at her church down here in Florida, and afterwards her ashes were to be sent back up North with Drew. Once he returned home, she requested that another service be held at her old church up in Massachusetts, so that all of her oldest friends could say their goodbyes. She also instructed that all of her possessions be donated to the church, except for her pictures—she wanted him to have those. She lived with Rebecca, who was her best friend, but the house was

Rebecca's. He was glad his mom didn't own the home, because of the nightmare he went through trying to sell his father's house after he passed away.

"Will you be staying until the service?" Rebecca asked while holding an old shoebox.

"Probably not. I have to get back to work. The funeral home said it will be several days before she can be cremated, so I'll fly back once the service is scheduled and I can pick up her ashes."

"You're welcome to stay here, if you'd like," Rebecca said.

"Thank you, but I already rented a hotel and I'll be flying back once all of the arrangements are made." *Plus, tonight will be a heavy drinking night*, he thought.

"Well the offer is there," she said and handed the shoebox to him.

"Are these Mom's pictures?"

"Yes, they are. As I said earlier, being our age, your mom and I knew we should plan everything out. She told me where to find the box of photos."

He opened it and saw a picture of him with his mom when he was just a little boy. She had her arm wrapped around his shoulders with that big smile of hers that she always wore. He had once heard it was easier to smile than frown—and even though life had been tough on her. A verbally abusive and cheating husband, plus trying to feed hungry kids, didn't make for a great ride.

Drew could feel the anger growing inside him at the thought of all the hell his father put them through, and quickly covered the box. "I'll look at these later," he said.

Rebecca could tell he was getting emotional and figured he didn't want to cry in front of her again.

"Well I should probably get going and try and book my flight home," he said standing up.

Rebecca stood and gave him another hug. He pulled her in close and said, "Thank you for being such a great friend to my mom."

"It was my pleasure. She was a wonderful woman."

"Yes she was."

4:59 P.M.

Once in the car, he checked his phone. No calls or texts from Annabelle. As he drove, he dialed Annabelle, hoping she would answer. The phone rang once and went straight to voicemail. Further up the road, he noticed a large sign for a liquor store and pulled in. He sat in the parking lot and tried calling Annabelle a second time. Again the phone rang once and went to voicemail, indicating she was ignoring his calls. He slammed the palm of his hand against the steering wheel.

"Fuck it!" he said as he got out of the car and walked into the liquor store.

Chapter 9

Thursday, October 29th
5:08 P.M.

Brian was screaming and kicking on the inside, but nothing he did stopped his body from moving. He couldn't even control his own breathing. He tried holding his breath, but he could feel his chest was still rising and falling.

What the hell has happened to me? he internally screamed.

Brian didn't feel anything apart from of his own body, so he didn't know if he was touching something or not. Besides seeing, hearing and noticing himself move, he could also still feel emotions — fear being the most prominent right now.

He was a spectator as his own body exited the train and walked up the stairs. His vision swayed back and forth with each step as he left the station. But, he had no awareness of where he was heading.

It didn't take long for Brian to figure out that he was without a doubt at an airport, but he wasn't sure at which one specifically. His head turned from left to right, providing him a glimpse around at the check-in desks for the various airlines. There were hundreds of people quickly moving about. People headed for security to board their flights, while many others had just exited a plane. His body started walking towards a group of small shops in the back right corner of the entryway. Patrons passed in front of him, blocking his vision, but then he spotted the menacing phantom on his right. It hung there above the ground, slowly swaying in place like a flag in a gentle breeze. Other people were walking around its hovering presence. Against his will, he turned and started walking straight for the shadow.

As Brian drew closer, he noticed the hovering darkness had moved and was now between a clothing and shoe rack. A long black arm extended out of the spectral mass and pointed to a Hawaiian shirt hanging on the rack. It then pointed to a pair of flip-flops on the adjacent one. The shadow then drifted towards the little checkout stand.

His body went and stood where the darkened mass had just been, between the two racks. He watched as the mass floated over to the counter and outstretched its tentacle-like arm. When the long black finger touched the counter, it suddenly exploded. The cash drawer flew open and money shot up into the air. The glass candy jars in front of the register shattered, sending candy and gum balls sprawling across the terminal.

He witnessed everyone turning their attention to the register. Suddenly his arms shot out and grabbed the Hawaiian shirt off the rack and quickly put it on. He watched as his hands quickly reached out again to grab the flip-flops. His arms gave the sandals a tug, breaking the little plastic ring that held them together, and he felt his head accelerate forwards as his body bent over. He watched as his feet slipped into the shoes. While everyone else's eyes were on the clerk, watching him scurry to pick up his money up off the floor. Brian's body turned and left the store.

The foreboding shadow figure floated past him like a cop going to block an intersection for a precession. It weaved in and around people as it moved. He could see it was heading towards the ticket counter. Brian knew he wouldn't be able to buy a ticket since he had no money nor his I.D, which he would need to make it through security and to board a flight.

He kept his eye on the ticket counter, searching for that dark shadowy thing. He hated it. It scared him. It felt like death to him.

The line at the counter snaked through a maze of black dividers and had at least sixty people in it. Brian thought, *If I get in that line, I must do whatever I can to stop my body from getting a ticket and boarding a plane.* He knew deep down inside that he was sick. He knew he was contaminated with something that, with every breath he took, was infecting everyone around him. Inside he started crying when a mother and father walked past him with their two small children, knowing they had all just caught his virus.

Suddenly his body turned away from the ticket line. *Thank God,* he said to himself, feeling relieved that he would not be boarding a flight and spreading his contagion.

Just as quickly as he felt relieved however, he suddenly felt even worse as he noticed his body was now heading towards the boarding pass kiosk. The shadowy dark figure hovered next to it, now resembling the silhouette of a man. It reminded him of one of those black, wooden statues that people put in their yards, usually near a tree, that looks like a farmer smoking a pipe.

He stepped up to the machine and the silhouette leaned up against the kiosk. The machine beeped and the screen flashed like a strobe light in a haunted house. It then made a weird revving sound and spit out a boarding pass with his name on it. His arm reached out and grabbed the ticket. He was able to see it in his hand, but couldn't read the printed destination since his eyes were not looking down.

Hopefully this will all end in a few minutes, Brian said to himself assuming there was no way his body would make it through security without an I.D.

He continued to watch as his body turned and started walking away towards the other side of the entryway, where he was able to see a large sign on the far wall for a security checkpoint.

He made his way through the hordes of people and could feel his lungs taking in breaths and exhaling the invisible, deadly poison.

Brian screamed at the top of his lungs, begging people to turn the other way and run, but they couldn't hear him. They walked past his body, and as they breathed in his exhaled air, they all unknowingly doomed themselves to a horrible death.

Again he tried to stop his body from moving, but he could do nothing. He frantically tried to reach out and grab someone as they passed, to no avail. He was just a witness to whatever was going to happen next.

Why? Brian screamed.

He let himself sink into the blackness of his body. The only light visible was that from his eyes high above. He couldn't watch anymore. He could no longer stand bearing witness to people around him as they instantly started coughing after walking past him.

Brian could tell his body stopped and knew he was in line for security. He stood back up and looked through his eyes again, and could see there were three other people in front of him. One was an older woman with a walker and another was her husband, who was assisting her by putting her purse on the belt for the x-ray machine. The third person was a young woman who was searching for her I.D. in her wallet.

"Please have your ticket and I.D. ready," the big burly TSA officer said as he looked down the line of passengers.

This is it. I have no I.D. There's going to be a flurry of guards here in a minute to escort me to a secure room, because I don't have my I.D.

The older woman and her husband passed through the metal detector, and the younger woman found her I.D. just as she stepped up to the TSA officer. He scribbled something on her ticket, handed it back to the young woman and waved her through.

"Next," the security guard said.

His body stepped up to the metal detector with his arm outstretched with the ticket.

This is it, Brian repeated to himself. *I have no I.D.! Pull me out of line!* he shouted from inside himself.

He was staring at the big massive TSA officer, who looked down at the ticket and noticed there was no I.D.

Come on! Stop me! he shouted.

Just as the officer was about to look up, Brian noticed the menacing black shadow thingy right behind him. The thing reached out its arm and its long, foreboding, black finger curled out until it touched the officer on the shoulder.

The officer instantly felt an unbearable pain in his stomach, as if it were about to explode. His face turned bright red and sweat began to form on his brow. Suddenly, a low growling sound came from his stomach, and he doubled over as burning liquid began to rise in his throat. The man's insides felt like they were on fire, and he could actually feel his esophagus disintegrating, as stomach acid and bile forced their way up through his system. The acid entirely ate away at the lining in his throat, followed by the blood vessels beneath the lining's surface. The security officer reached up to his neck and grasped at it as if he was choking. A look of sheer terror washed over the large man's face as the blood vessels behind his throat burst, and he suddenly felt a rush of blood down his throat. He tried gasping for air but only managed to inhale blood as it poured into his lungs. He was swallowing the blood he wasn't inhaling, and a button on his shirt popped off as his blood-filled belly began to distend. As the man fell to the ground from the lack of oxygen, Brian's arm reached out and took the ticket from the dying officer's hand.

In that quick moment, he was finally able to read the destination — his possessed body was bound for London.

No! No! No! Brian shouted as he body passed through security. No one had taken notice; other passengers and TSA officers ran over to assist the man who now lay on the ground with blood pouring from his mouth.

Chapter 10

Thursday, October 29th
7:08 P.M.

Stanley McKnight's flight landed several days ago. He had made his rounds to the local farms meeting their owners, families and farm hands. The company he worked for sold farm machinery and equipment, and he was out surveying his clients to see if they were pleased with the new equipment he had sold them a few months prior, before the season was set to start. It was company policy to travel and meet with the clients to assess their level of satisfaction for its products. Feedback was important.

He listened carefully to the farmers describe what features they liked as well as those they did not. The company thrived over the past few years because of a key decision to sit down and actively listen to clients. Board members found that this particular business practice gave their clients a more personal connection with the company, and, as word of the company's reputation spread, the number of loyal customers increased. Furthermore, the feedback the company received allowed its engineers to develop options for its equipment's features and modifications, targeting the specific needs of each individual client. Both tactics ensured that costs for such features would be paid for tenfold in the long run, as clients were willing to pay more to get what suited their needs, rather than pay less for something that did not.

Stanley loved his clients — they were some of the nicest people on the face of the planet and they were always hospitable.

He was currently staying at the Holiday Inn, the same hotel he always utilized when he traveled to Nebraska on business. With a busy day scheduled ahead, he felt it best to conduct his routine call to his wife earlier rather than later so he could get some rest. Stanley spoke with her every night from whichever hotel room in whichever part of the country to which he was assigned. He hated being away from Carol, but the job paid well. They were financially stable at the moment, while many others were not. During the height of the country's prosperity several years back, he and his wife were flat broke. They barely had enough money for food and their bills. Stanley found it ironic that when the country started to spin financially downward, they began to prosper.

"Stan, how are you feeling?" Carol asked.

"I feel fine," he answered somewhat defensively. She always worried about him too much. "Why? Do I sound sick?"

"No, but have you seen the news lately? There's a terrible sickness going around."

"It's probably just the flu."

"No, they say this is some sort of virus and that it's spreading very quickly. They're reporting that hundreds of people are infected and are flooding area hospitals."

"Really?" he said with surprise. "I haven't heard anything. Then again, I haven't been getting back to the hotel until real late at night. Hold on, hon; I'll put the TV on." He reached across the hotel bed, grabbed the remote and pressed the "on" button.

"Put on the cable news—they're doing continuous coverage," she instructed.

"Wait a sec. I don't know what channels are what out here." Stanley continued rapidly flicking the "channel up" button until he found one of the major news stations. He suddenly blinked in disbelief as he saw footage shot earlier in the day from New York City. People were running in the streets. Some had on white masks covering their faces, like the ones he used when he sanded the walls before painting. Others held garments to their faces so that only their eyes were exposed. The ticker at the bottom of the screen read, "Hundreds infected in New York City and Boston."

"Oh my God! When did this start?" he asked.

"The story broke this afternoon while I was getting ready to leave work."

Stanley's heart skipped a beat as a worrisome thought came to mind. "Does anybody at home have it?"

"No, but I still thought it best to come straight home instead of going to my parents for dinner."

He exhaled the breath that he hadn't realized he'd been holding. "Good. I want you to call in tomorrow, too. Boston isn't that far from us. People from your work could have been in the city today and you'd never know until it was too late. Best to just stay home until it passes."

"What about you?" Carol asked. "Are you going to come home?"

"I have an appointment in the morning with the Johnsons and my flight's not scheduled to leave until seven tomorrow night."

"Can't you see if you can catch a flight out tonight?" she pleaded with more than a hint of concern in her voice.

"Honey, the Johnsons are my biggest client. I can't skip out on them. Plus, Mrs. Johnson always has a big breakfast waiting for me when I get there," he tried to joke, hoping to alleviate her anxiety.

"Okay," she sighed, "but call me when you get back to the hotel room tomorrow."

"I'll call you as soon as I get in. I love you!"

"I love you too," Carol said, as if she were afraid she'd never get the chance to do so again.

Stanley hung up the phone, sat on the end of the bed

and watched the news coverage for a few minutes longer. Once the station started repeating the same footage, he decided to hop in the shower and get ready for bed, reminding himself that he had to get up early.

He finished drying off in front of the TV, which was still showing the same footage as earlier. Then, after putting on his pj's, he knelt next to the bed to say his prayers. He prayed for his wife and thanked God for bringing her into his life. Carol changed him into a better man and brought him out of the darkness he had found himself in years back. He also prayed for a safe journey to the Johnsons' farm and a safe flight home. Finally, Stanley ended his prayers by asking God to watch over the people of New York and Boston and then climbed into bed and fell asleep with the TV still on.

Chapter 11

Thursday, October 29th
8:14 P.M.

When Drew returned to his hotel room, he poured himself a drink. He shot it down and repeated the process several times. Then he sat on the edge of the bed and opened the box of pictures his mother had left to him. There were pictures from when he was first born to when he graduated high school. When he saw a picture of his father, he took a long swig of his drink as more memories came flooding back. He remembered his mother wiping away his tears after another one of his father's physical rants. He remembered asking his mother why she just didn't leave him, to which his mother sadly replied, "It isn't that easy for a mother."

He now understood what that meant. His mother didn't make enough money to get her own place, and she had no family around to help her out. She was all alone. He remembered her kicking his father out on several occasions after finding out he had cheated on her, but always letting him back in eventually, because she needed the money. There were weekends when his father wouldn't come home, probably because he was out banging some other woman. And, when Drew had asked his mother, "Where's dad?" she replied, "I don't care as long as he's not here." He felt the same way and hoped wherever he was he'd just stay there.

Drew rummaged through more of the photos and came across one where the angel's kiss on his forehead was predominant. Being raised Irish Catholic, his mother was very religious and believed in God. Drew had a birthmark on his forehead that would become raised when he was either angry or scared. He chuckled to himself as he thought back to what his mother had told him: that he was blessed. An angel kissed his forehead when he was born and he had a guardian angel watching over him. He always dismissed this. Either his guardian angel sucked or there wasn't one, because of all the shit he endured at the hands of his father. There was no angel. No one had saved him from that bastard.

He swallowed hard and felt the tears coming as he looked at a picture of himself and his sister. He didn't know where she was or if she was even alive anymore. He remembered the day she kissed him goodbye and told him she loved him, then was gone for good.

He poured himself another drink, took a long swig, picked up the box of pictures and chucked it across the room. The box slammed into the wall and pictures went everywhere. Some came pouring down like rain and others floated down like an early November snow. A picture of when he and Annabelle had first started dating landed on the floor in front of him.

He reached down and picked up the picture with one hand while holding his drink in the other. He stared at the picture and hung his head low. *What have I become?* he thought, reflecting on his life. With little hope, he looked at his phone on the bed, but he still had no missed calls.

Looking at the picture reminded him of when he and Annabelle first started dating. They had met through a mutual friend, Maggie, who arranged a double date. They had hit it off from the start. The conversation came easy and the time flew by. Annabelle invited the group back to her house for drinks. They sat for hours, listening to music and talking. Drew remembered how much he liked Annabelle on their first date and how, when it was time to leave, he didn't want to go, having enjoyed her company. Their friends went to wait in the car and give them a moment alone. He remembered being so nervous. It had been a while since he had been on a date—he had given up on the dating scene after one too many bad experiences. Drew smiled when he thought back to that day...

Halfway home, Maggie received a text from Annabelle. Shocked, she let out a gasp.

"What is it?" Maggie's husband John asked as he drove.

"Drew, did you forget to do something?" Maggie teased.

Perplexed by the question, Drew answered, "No, what do you mean?"

"You liked Annabelle, right?" she pried.

"I did. A lot." A reddish tint colored his cheeks.

"Then why didn't you ask her for her number?"

"You forgot to ask for her number?" John said and laughed.

Drew's eyes went wide with realization. "Aw shit! You know, Maggie, I was so nervous, I forgot to ask." If he had a Sharpie, he would've told Maggie to write "Idiot" on his forehead.

"Don't worry. She liked you too, so I just texted you her number."

He couldn't wait to get home and call Annabelle. But as soon as he was about to dial her number, he became nervous again, fearing he would come off as desperate, so he decided to call her the next day after work.

That whole day at work, all he could do was think about Annabelle. How beautiful she looked with her long, brown hair and those stunning eyes. For someone very confident in himself when it came to most things, talking to women was not one of his strong suits. Yet he had been able to talk to her like he'd never been able to converse with another woman before.

When he got home from work, he mustered up enough nerve to call her, and from that moment on they spoke every day. Before long they were spending every free minute with each other. They went on many dates to the beach, several concerts, and different expos. They would curl up on the couch together, watching movies and listening to music for hours. And they would lay in bed and talk for hours after making passionate love to one another. He was in love and when he told her, she told him she loved him too.

Drew was the happiest he had ever been. He thought his life was finally complete. That is, until he heard the words: "You're going to be a daddy."

He couldn't remember the last time he had cried tears of joy, but, right then, they streamed down his face.

Drew went out and bought Annabelle an engagement ring, and they were married before Stephanie arrived that winter.

Everything was going so well, and he finally had the family he always wanted.

Before long he started wondering when the other shoe was going to drop and when his Irish Luck would start to catch up to him. And there came a point when Drew started doing something he had never done before — he started thinking about death.

Death was nothing new to him — he dealt with it every day — but he never questioned his own mortality. Soon his mind raced, and it was all he could think about. Question after question arose in his mind. *Who will take care of my family? Will I live long enough it to be able to walk my daughter down the aisle?* He also feared for Annabelle and his daughter. *What would I do if something happened to them?* Work had started becoming very stressful and it seemed like the world was going crazy. He was responding to more domestic violence calls and murders than he could ever remember. It seemed like his life was spinning downward.

Soon he went from drinking socially to drinking every day. He found that drinking shut off all of the stress, and the questions swirling in his head. It made the visions of the horrific things he saw every day at work fade away and allowed him to sleep...

Now here he sat in a hotel room, separated from his wife, staring into a half-emptied glass, and wondering if he was becoming like his father, something he vowed never to become.

He peered into the glass for a few minutes longer before bringing it up to his mouth, tilting the bottom up and swallowing down the last of the bottle.

Chapter 12

Kendra used a wet wipe to clean her cooch as the john in the hotel bathroom relieved his bladder. As she pulled up her panties, she heard the constant stream of his urine turn into drips, followed by the sound of the toilet flushing. She pulled up her sweatpants and was clasping her bra when he came out of the bathroom, holding a small mirror with lines of cocaine on it.

"Want another hit before I get out of here?" he asked as he approached her.

"Oh, yeah I do," she said with a smile as she sat on the bed, taking the mirror in one hand and cupping the man's groin with the other. "The two things I love most: sex and coke."

She used the rolled up hundred dollar bill – her payment for allowing him to fuck her – and snorted both lines, then flipped her head back and held her nose. She loved that feeling, the rush from the cocaine.

"Good stuff," he commented.

"Oh yeah, makes me want to fuck again," she said seductively as she leaned into his crotch and playfully bit at it.

"I can't," he replied, taking a step back. "I have to get home to my wife. She's already called me twice."

"No problem. You know where to find me if you want me, baby."

"Let me get your number," he said as he took the mirror from her. "My wife is flying out of town next weekend to visit her parents in California." He brought the mirror up to his mouth and licked up the remaining powder.

"Your phone," she said with her hand out.

After he reached into his pants pocket, pulled out his phone and handed it to her, she quickly typed into it and tossed it back to him.

"Keith?" he asked upon checking what she had entered. "You're name is Keith? I thought it was Kendra?"

"It is, silly. I put Keith just in case your wife is a snoopy wife." She gave him a wink.

"Good thinking," he said as he put his phone back in his pocket, tucked in his shirt and headed for the door. She walked over to the window and watched him climb into his truck and back out.

Watching him leave made her think back to when she was a child. Her step-father would leave after bringing his friends over and letting them have their way with her. She never forgot how she screamed out in pain, as the large bulky men violently penetrated her. The thought of those sweaty, massive, and out-of-shape men climbing on top of her and smothering her with their weight sent shivers down her spine. She had cried and begged for them to stop, but they never did—not until they repeatedly groaned and their bodies shook. She remembered her addict mother all drugged-up on the couch, caring less about what happened to her daughter and more concerned about getting high. Kendra prayed to God to make it stop, but He never answered. When she was eleven, she started stealing from her mother's stash, using the drugs to cope with the constant sexual abuse.

Once the man's truck was gone, she went into the bathroom to wash up, and to brush her teeth to get the taste of his cock out of her mouth. She looked in the mirror and fixed her dirty-blond hair, which was everywhere, and pulled out her makeup from her purse to touch up her eyeliner, darkening the lids around her green eyes, making them stand out. Over time she got used to the constant compliments on how beautiful her eyes were. Men told her she had "fuck-me" eyes — she hated it at first, but now used it to her advantage. After dolling herself back up, she unrolled the hundred-dollar bill, flattened it out and put it in her purse along with her makeup, then pulled out her phone to check the time. It was a little after nine, and she didn't have to start her shift at the club until ten.

Kendra arrived at the club a few minutes early. She walked in and put her things down at her little vanity that the club provided. Out front the music thumped. When one of the girls did one of those mind-blowing tricks on the pole, the cheer of men drowned out the music. Kendra preferred the front stage to the pole, because she could use her fifteen minute solo to shake her ass and spread her lips for the men in the front row. They always tipped in tens and twenties when she spread her legs wide.

She knew that men would pay to see a woman like her — someone they couldn't have. Men who had obviously never had a woman at all would pay even more. While she was up on stage, she would spot them out in the crowd. Once she got down, she'd make a beeline for them. She'd shake her tits in their faces and ask if they wanted a private dance out back. If they accepted, she'd escort them to a secluded area outside, where she'd offer them a hand job for twenty bucks, a blow job for fifty, or "one hell of a ride," as she put it, for a hundred. It wasn't a common practice for strip clubs to allow touching, but she made a deal with the owner to give him twenty-five percent of what she made.

Most of the time the men would be too drunk to get their dicks hard. Or, being out in public would keep them from getting an erection. Some were so embarrassed about not being able to get it up, they paid her anyway, making it an easy score. Some would get upset and create a scene, but over time she learned to steer clear of those types. But for the others, she'd whisper in their ear not to worry. "It's okay baby. Next time," she'd soothe to make them feel better, knowing they would never come back. They would pay her, and probably go home relieved that they couldn't perform. Most of them were married and were out for a good time with their friends—the heat of the moment made them do something rash. Most of them probably woke up thankful for whiskey dick. In a small way, she hoped it made them appreciate their wives. After all, she picked these men knowing exactly what would happen. Easy money.

She finished getting dressed and stood at the curtain waiting to be announced.

"Gentlemen, please give a warm welcome to our next performer! She's sexy! She's sassy! She's sizzling, and it's going to get hot in here because she brings a little bit of Hell to the stage. Please welcome, Sin!" announced the DJ.

Chapter 13

Brian's body sat directly in the middle of the plane. He had pulled back inside himself and sat in his own blackened inner Hell and wept, thinking of all the people he had infected. And of all the people they went on to infect in turn.

What did they do to me? he asked himself as he thought back to his time at the Lumpton Treatment Center. *I knew there was a reason for that airlock and why they kept injecting me. I can't believe Nurse Robin lied to me.*

Is this it? he began to wonder. *Am I dead? Does everyone retract into themselves when they die, or am I being punished?*

Brian had lost all sense of time. He knew the flight to London was a long one, but he figured they must be getting close to landing.

When he first boarded the plane, there was much commotion as people spoke and stored their luggage. The other passengers had continued to converse until the plane lunged down the runway. Once in the air, however, it grew quiet. Some people put on their headphones and listened to music, while others watched the TV's. He observed the passengers as they all became entranced in their own little world of electronic devices.

About two hours into the flight, Brian had heard the first cough, followed by a sniffle. Little by little, he had noticed more and more passengers bringing their hands to their mouths, covering their coughing. Eventually, several passengers had gotten out of their seats and headed to the bathroom to get toilet paper for their noses, while others had flagged down the flight attendant, requesting facial tissues.

When Brian couldn't stand it anymore, he had retreated into himself. He couldn't stomach watching everyone's health deteriorating at such a rate. The plane was a flying incubator. Remembering his old roommate Howard at the treatment center, and the coughing that had grown worse, he knew what came next—everyone on the plane would be dead before tomorrow.

He sat in the darkness of himself, wishing he would wake up from this nightmare. At some point he heard something strange within the cabin, like the sound of rustling plastic, and stood back up to look out of his eyes. He could see the flight attendants going up and down the aisle with trash bags, collecting a plethora of dirty tissues from the passengers. A moment later the pilot came on and announced they were beginning their descent into London.

1:37 A.M.

Brian's plane touched down and taxied over to the gate. All 347 passengers, including three babies and five toddlers, were infected with the sickness and would soon die. On the inside he wept for the little ones. *It wasn't fair*, he thought, *Why did God grant them life only to take them now? They never had a chance! What a waste of life!* He felt his body stand up once the plane stopped at the gate. The door of the plane opened and the infected air rushed into the airport. A breeze brushed past many others who waited to board aircrafts bound for all parts of Europe and Asia. His body exited the plane headed for the front door of the lobby. The shadowy black figure was there to greet him when his body hailed a taxi. He watched it drift through the taxi's front door as his body opened the back and climbed in.

"Where to?" asked the taxi driver, reaching up to set the meter.

The driver reached for the meter and just as he touched it, the ominous figure in the front seat touched it too. Sparks went flying and the driver's body shook as a powerful current ran through his body and caused his eyeballs to pop out of his head. The smell of burning flesh filled the taxi as the car shot out from the airport curbside and headed towards the London Eye.

The autonomous taxi stopped on the side of the Thames River, and Brian stepped out into a mass of tourists. The large Ferris wheel attracts millions of visitors each year, but today it would send thousands to their deaths.

Brian's body made it through the hordes of people and stumbled towards the queue.

Chapter 14

After Kendra's shift ended, she walked out of the strip club and into the parking lot, yawned, got in her car and drove back to her plush, one-bedroom apartment. She lived on the top floor, which looked out over the Orlando strip, and she would be home in plenty of time to relax and watch the sun rise.

With the johns in the early evening and then late nights at the club, Kendra was pulling in close to two-thousand dollars a day. The first day of work basically paid for the cheap motel she used for the johns, and it paid the owner of the club for a month. Each day after was all profit—cash profit, close to thirty-six thousand dollars a month, almost half a million dollars a year. She laughed at the thought of getting paid that much money to do the two things she loved so much—having sex and doing drugs. And the men usually provided the latter for free.

Some of the girls at the club would cry after their shifts. Men putting their hands on them and asking to fuck them didn't go over very well with most of the women. "Sister, you're in the sex business," she would tell them when they complained, "so deal with it or leave. You keep turning the other cheek and coming back because the money is so good." They didn't like taking their clothes off for money, but it paid the bills and provided extra spending cash, so the clothes came off.

Kendra thought of it as supply and demand. The men demanded it, so she supplied it. She learned from a young age what men wanted, having developed breasts when she was only eleven, and she noticed how men looked at her. She watched other women and realized that if she showed a little skin and gave the men a little attention, they would basically do what she wanted them to do—within reason.

She discovered that if she gave the men their deep-down desires, they would do anything for her. It was easy—the men would tell her what they wanted, and she would provide it. Men are simple creatures who, unlike women, will tell you exactly what they want. They wouldn't beat around the bush or make her guess. They would just whisper in her ear what they wanted and they all wanted the same thing: for her to touch their cocks and to put them inside her. They wanted to get off. The faster the better. The faster she was, the faster she could get to the next erect cock, and then the next. Each one was worth money.

At first she went for the alpha males—the big, strong men who knew what they wanted. But that took time, and she wanted to capitalize and make real money quickly. She soon discovered that if she went after the geeks and awkward men—men who most likely had never been with a woman or were married to some fat cow—it was easy money. They wanted to be with a beautiful, sexy woman but didn't know how. She would come onto them, and they would instantly fold. Supply and demand.

Most would agree to go out back, because a piece of them wanted it, but they didn't know what to do once the time came to perform. She'd have them sit down and then she'd straddle them, rubbing her big, soft tits and hard nipples all over their faces while she sucked and gently bit their earlobes. Within seconds they would be hard as a rock and then they would shutter as she reached down and grabbed their cocks. That was all it took. They would speckle the inside of their underwear with their hot load. No mess and no clean up required for her.

Kendra made herself a stiff drink and stood looking out of her apartment window at the city below. The memory she had earlier about her step-father and his friends reminded her why she got into this business. The drugs had clouded her mind and she had forgotten she was doing all of this for a better life. Lacking an education, this was the only way she knew how to make money. She dreamed of owning a farm with the mountains off in the distance, and of living the rest of her life away from the hustle and bustle of the city — far away from the sex and drugs. She even imagined having children someday and envisioned them growing up on the farm, far away from the city life and all the shit that came with it.

The sun was just starting to rise and vanquish the darkness of the night. Kendra undressed, dropped her clothes on the floor, walked into the bathroom and turned on the shower. She reached behind the curtain, adjusted the temperature and hopped in. It was soothing to let the warm water wash away the stench and nastiness the men had left behind. When finally clean, she stepped out of the shower and dried off. The cool air-conditioning caused goose bumps to form all over her body. She wrapped herself in her long plush robe and walked back out into the living room, where she gazed out of the window as the city slowly came to life. Kendra enjoyed this time of day. Traffic slowly filled the streets and most of the city lights were off as the sun rose above the Earth. Off in the distance, was the steady stream of planes departing and arriving. Once the glory of dawn settled her mind, she finished her drink and climbed into bed.

Chapter 15

Friday, October 30th
4:00 A.M.

Stanley awoke to the blasting of his alarm. *Four o'clock already*, he thought as he rolled over and flicked off the buzzer. He rubbed his lower back, which always hurt from sleeping on cheap hotel room beds, then grabbed his bottle of pills and proceeded to pop a few into his mouth. *I swear, I'm getting addicted to these*, he thought while taking a sip of water to wash them down. Remembering the phone conversation with Carol the night before, he sat up and turned on the TV to watch the news for any updates on the virus before getting ready for his long drive out to the Johnsons' farm. With little time to spare however, he continued to follow his usual morning routine after turning the volume up. From what he could tell as he busied himself, though all reporters remained on the topic of the unknown disease, there didn't seem to be anything new on the matter.

Stanley finished getting dressed and brushing his teeth, then grabbed the keys to the rental car off the nightstand. He took one last moment to stare at the TV before finally shutting it off and heading out to begin his two-hour drive. Several minutes after he had left, the news channel he'd been watching aired breaking news — the first few people who had contracted the sickness had died.

Drew's alarm went off, waking him from his alcohol-induced sleep. He reached for the phone, shut off the alarm and checked to see if Annabelle had called. Still no texts or voicemails. Already he was missing his wife and little girl, particularly when he thought of the way

Stephanie called out *Daddy* when she saw him and how she came running to him with the widest smile, showing her little teeth. Moments he'd taken for granted before. Moments that occurred only recently, yet he was now well aware of their sudden absence, especially as he lay there in a strange place, far from home.

He sat up, turned and put his feet on the carpeted floor. The arch of his foot landed right on one of the many photos scattered across the room. Reaching down, he pulled it off of his foot and examined it. It was a picture of him and his mother, her arm around his shoulder while they posed in front of the house he grew up in. He must've been about ten years old, and he smiled at the thought of a time when his mother was vibrant and full of life. After several seconds down Memory Lane, with a heavy heart, Drew got up and quickly picked up all of the pictures and put them back into the box.

Once he finished getting showered and dressed, he noticed it was now 4:15 a.m., and that he had a little less than two hours before his flight was scheduled to leave. Regardless, he grabbed his bag along with the box of pictures and made his way downstairs to the lobby to check out.

The young woman behind the counter who had checked him in yesterday stood behind the desk wearing a white dust mask. *That's kind of odd*, he thought to himself. As he slid his room key and credit card to her across the desk, he couldn't help but ask,

"What's up with the mask?"

"Have you not seen the news?" she said, with that pompous attitude common among so many Millennials. "There's a sickness going around!"

She handed him back his credit card and receipt.

"Probably just another case of bird flu or something. Some people go crazy and think the end of the world is at hand, just because the media reports on a single case," he said as he turned and walked away.

Drew exited the lobby and stepped outside where the warm, muggy Florida air met him. He didn't look forward to going back to Massachusetts and facing the coming winter. One of his friends at work was a novice meteorologist, who on his free time studied the weather and even used his vacation time to go on storm chasing expeditions. He had recently told Drew that he predicted a brutal winter.

He put his bag and box of pictures in the backseat and climbed into the rental car, where he tried calling Annabelle again. This time it rang six times before going to voicemail. Now he was starting to grow frustrated. *What the hell! Answer the damn phone!*

4:53 A.M.

Bill Johnson awoke the same time every morning, a few minutes before his alarm set for 5:00 a.m. would sound off. He climbed out of bed, put on his shirt and pants, then pulled on his socks and boots and headed downstairs where he grabbed his jacket off the kitchen chair and set out to the barn to start his daily ritual of feeding the animals. The routine was always the same: the screen door slamming shut behind him, sliding open the big barn door and switching on the lights, then pitching hay into the pens for the animals to eat. Running a farm and harvesting corn took strenuous effort and a lot of time. As a boy he had wanted a different life, but shortly after high school, when his father passed away and left him the farm, he found himself following in his daddy's footsteps.

As he tossed hay into each stable he thought about the questions he had for Stanley regarding the new pipe puller and attachment blade he wanted to purchase. Last year he bought some new land just on the outskirts of his property. Virgin soil, he was told would produce the best crops of any season. He had cleared the land during the winter and wanted to plant new crops for the following year, but he needed to irrigate the land first. He made the attempt a few weeks back, but his old pipe puller broke down several times. Now pressed for time, Bill would have to start planting the crops for this season soon if he wanted to harvest them in time to bring them to market.

The virgin soil would have to wait until the end of the season for him to try again, but he wanted to be ready. One of his neighbors told him about a new attachment blade for the pipe puller, which was used to pull the irrigation pipe under the ground, that was supposedly almost impossible to break. With virgin soil he never knew what he would find under the surface, so unbreakable sounded good to him.

5:03 A.M.

Drew returned the rental car, picked up his plane ticket using one of the kiosks and made his way over to the security checkpoint. His head was pounding from drinking last night, and he hoped the line for security would not be too long. Once he reached the security line, there seemed to be a lot of tension in the air and a heightened TSA presence. *Another terrorist attack?* he wondered.

He was surprised, though, when he made it through security pretty quickly. As he headed towards his gate, he stopped at a little shop and bought a packet of aspirin and a bottle of water, deciding he should straighten himself out before returning home. *Hopefully Annabelle won't still be so mad and I can stay in the house,* he prayed as he dumped the pills into his mouth, opened the bottle of water and washed the medication down. *I can't believe she called me an alcoholic. Yeah, I've been drinking more and more lately but work has been really stressful with all the overdoses and shootings. Speaking of drinks, I should try and get one on the plane and cure this hangover before I get home.*

Drew walked from the little shop towards the tram that would take him out to the terminal. While waiting for the next available shuttle, he noticed everyone was engaged in their phones with somewhat of a shared frantic demeanor. He pulled out his phone again and looked at the screen — still no call or text from Annabelle. The tram arrived and he boarded it for the short ride to the terminal. As the tram doors opened, he observed everyone exiting flocked over to a TV mounted on a nearby wall, joining the massive group of people who had already formed under the glowing screen.

Curiously, he started to make his way over to see what all the commotion was when his phone buzzed in his pocket. Hoping it was Annabelle, Drew instantly pulled it from his pocket, but his hopes were dashed by a store's text letting him know he could "Save 20% Today on Men's Apparel!" Grinding his teeth, he jammed the phone back in his pocket, made his way to the terminal and took a seat, suddenly no longer concerned with whatever was happening in the world. His own world was fucked anyway; why should he care about anyone else's?

He sat in the hard, uncomfortable chair waiting for them to announce the plane was boarding. Again, almost as if on auto-drive, he pulled his phone from his pocket and stared at it with eyes that bored into the black screen, as if he could somehow will Annabelle to call or text before he got on the plane. *If I don't talk to her before this flight, watch it probably crash*, he bet.

The airport was packed, but it was eerily quiet. The crowd huddled beneath the TV was at least six people deep. The volume was off and the closed captions were on, though the set was too far away for Drew to read, but no one was talking. The only sound were giggles coming from the woman working behind the boarding counter. There was a man standing there in a three-piece suit, flirting with her, his black hair combed back. The man pulled the cigarette from behind his ear and tapped it on the counter. He whispered something to the woman, causing her to giggle again before looking down at her chart. The businessman then tapped the cigarette again on the counter and replaced it behind his ear. The young lady peeked up with blushed cheeks and then looked back down. It sounded like he was trying to get in her pants, or get her phone number at least. He kept his hand on the counter, and she reached up and put her own hand on top of his. Just then, the phone on the back wall rang, and a look of disdain washed over her face when she had to move away from him to answer it. After a brief conversation, the woman hung up the phone and hurriedly stepped away from the man.

The man in the three-piece suit turned and looked around, until he noticed a tall brunette sitting by herself, wearing a sundress with her long crossed legs stretching out in front of her while she read a book. Drew watched as the businessman made his way over to the empty seat next to the woman, sat down and immediately started flirting with her. She glanced up from her book with a stare that at first said *please stop bothering me*. But it didn't take long before the woman in the sundress looked the man up and down and smiled. He stuck out his hand and she reached for it, then he proceeded to kiss the back of her hand. She too reddened, pulling up her shoulders as she smiled.

Drew was a lot of things, but a player wasn't one of them. He found it fake—people pretending to be someone they were not, just to get someone to like them. Or, in this guy's case, probably to get some action.

The woman behind the counter returned and announced over the PA system that they would start boarding the plane now. The hordes of people in front of the TV's started to break up and those with seats on that flight started to make their way towards the counter to board.

Drew boarded the plane for his return flight home. He put his bag in the compartment above his seat, which was just behind the wing, and plopped down. Some passengers took their own seats, while others milled about placing their bags in the overhead compartments. The stale, compartmentalized air of the cabin replaced the warm Florida air. He sat quietly, turning his gaze out the window, watching the ground crew tend to their duties. His head was pounding and felt fuzzy—*I'm going to need a drink to clear this head of mine.* Turning in his seat, he looked over his right shoulder and got the flight attendant's attention. She was a beautiful woman with long brown hair. As she approached, he asked her for a rum and coke. The attractive attendant apologetically informed him they weren't allowed to serve drinks until they were off the ground, but when she saw he looked like he needed one, she said, "I'll try and get one for you before we depart."

He turned back around to find the man in the three-piece suit standing in the aisle staring at him. *Kind of early to be drinking isn't it?* The man said with his eyes as he sat down next to him, put on his seat belt and started to play with the TV in the seatback in front of him.

Chapter 16

Friday, October 30th
5:57 A.M.

Glen Daniels woke up to the sound of his work phone's buzzing. It had been doing so all morning but that was nothing new. He was one of the lead anchors for the local news outlet, so he was accustomed to his phone constantly going off. Instead of answering it however, he stayed in bed, questioning his life.

He was up late unpacking the night before. Glen had taken a week off to move into his new apartment after his wife kicked him out of the house. He knew he shouldn't have slept with the new intern Amber—she didn't seem quite right in the head. And she turned out to be one of those girls that couldn't just go out for a few drinks and have one night of fun with no strings attached. Glen could tell she was going to be trouble the minute he had climbed out of her bed. Amber had told him she had a good time and asked if they could go out again. She clearly didn't understand the concept of a one-night stand. The poor girl thought he liked her. Glen liked her in the *I want to have sex with you way*, but he didn't like her in the *I want to leave my wife for you* sort of way.

"Sure," he had replied as he put his shoes on. A few years ago, he had been with a young woman like her, who was looking for love and clinging to attention. Both were attractive women but neither had boyfriends, which was a plus because they could use their place to sleep together, instead of renting a place. It would be hard to explain another hotel room charge on the credit card statement to his wife. Just like the last girl, who had also worked with him, Amber would bring him coffee and shower him with attention. His co-workers had questioned him about her clingy behavior, and soon word started to spread through the station of an affair between the news anchor and an intern.

He laughed it off and said he thought she was just hoping for a good recommendation from him when she finished her internship. He joked that he would write her the best reference letter just to get rid of her. In the meantime, he'd take the free coffee and ego boost while she was there.

When the intern before Amber had professed her love for him and asked him to leave his wife for her, Glen lucked out. He was offered a position as lead anchor for another network in Cincinnati, where he worked now. He told the young woman that once he was situated in Ohio at the new network, he would try and get her a position there with him. He had no intention of honoring this promise and was glad she would be out of his life.

This time around, though, he had no such luck. Amber became pregnant and when he started ignoring her, she contacted his wife. This wasn't the first time Glen had an affair, but it was the last time, his wife said. She told him to leave and that she would be filing for divorce.

Glen technically didn't request the week off—he was more or less told to stay away from the office while HR looked into the situation. The news channel didn't want to deal with bad press, especially when it came to their lead evening anchor. There seemed to be a lot of news anchors across the nation getting into trouble lately, for one thing or another.

He rolled over trying to go back to sleep, but his new mattress wasn't very comfortable. *It just needs to be broken in with a few good lays*, he thought. There were always women throwing themselves at him, wherever he went. There's something about being on TV that made women want to climb into bed with him, which he didn't mind, nor did he refuse. He had grown used to it. Back at his prior news station, once he made anchor, women started approaching him in restaurants and in the grocery store. They were practically throwing themselves at him. Eventually he couldn't resist. He met a few of them after work for drinks, which lead straight to renting a hotel room for the night.

His wife was a nurse who worked nights in the ER at one of the local city hospitals. He took advantage of the time she spent at work to sleep with admiring fans of his. Glen believed he still loved and respected his wife. He wasn't looking for a relationship, he was just trying to make up for his nonexistent sex life. And, he wasn't disrespecting her by having sex in their bed — he had been renting hotel rooms from the beginning.

He had come home early one morning and was surprised to see his wife's car in the driveway. He walked in and found Sandra, sitting at the kitchen table, crying uncontrollably, with a used condom wrapper on the table. Sandra told him she had found it in his pants pocket while she was doing laundry a few weeks back. He tried to play it off and said he picked it up off the front yard, and that some kid must have dropped it.

"Really?" she snapped.

"Really!" he replied.

"Then how do you explain this?" she yelled as she pulled out their credit card statement and slid it across the table.

Glen sat there stunned. He didn't know what to say and was trying to come up with something when Sandra spoke.

"Don't even bother to lie," she said as she wiped away her tears.

He sat still, racking his brain and trying to come up with a valid excuse.

"I was sitting right here when I opened that bill. I couldn't believe how high it was. I almost fell out of the chair," Sandra said as she picked the statement up and shook it. I told myself this can't be right, so I called the credit card company to find out why the balance was so high." Tears started streaming down her face again as she continued, "I didn't believe the customer service representative—he had to put his manager on to verify that the charges were correct. He said that they were accrued two or three times a week over the course of a few months at a hotel downtown.

Glen thought he almost came up with a good explanation, but there was no excuse to get him out of what she said next.

"So I took a week off and didn't tell you. I acted like I went to work, but I actually went and parked downtown across from the hotel. And, do you know what I saw?" she asked.

He said nothing, petrified of what she was going to say next.

"That's right—you know!" She nearly screamed.

His eyes widened and he could feel his face becoming flushed.

"I saw you pull in, park and get out with some young twenty-something blond girl." Tears continued to run down Sandra's cheeks as she described what she saw. "I watched you stroll into the hotel hand in hand. I watched you let go of her hand to open the door for her, and as she walked through, I watched you give her a slap on her ass. I watched her toss her hair over her shoulder," Sandra mimicked tossing her hair over her shoulder. "Then that whore stuck up her ass, asking for another spanking, which you so gratefully supplied. How could you do this to me?" she sobbed uncontrollably.

"Sandra, I have a problem," he said.

"Oh you have a big problem, Glen! How could you do this to me?" she asked again.

"I'm addicted to sex."

Sandra just laughed through her tears.

"No, really. I'm addicted to sex. I can't help myself."

They sat for hours and talked. He explained that she had done nothing wrong and that he was a sex addict. He told her that he always used protection, which she believed because she had found the condom wrapper recently.

Glen told her that he loved her, that it was just sex, and that he didn't have any feelings for the women. He offered to get help. After they talked, Sandra actually felt bad for him. She knew that she was never home when he was and that they had not had sex in years. His wife even started to blame herself. Finally, she agreed not to leave him, and they began to look into finding a place for him to go and treat his sexual addiction.

They found a center that dealt with sex addiction out in Arizona, which worked best because no one would recognize him there. He was famous, but only locally. They signed him up and Sandra took the flight out West with him to show her support. They spent the night in a hotel, and the following morning he checked into the treatment center while Sandra flew back home.

Glen really didn't care if he got help or not. He wasn't even remorseful. He got caught and figured this was his cheapest option. If he didn't go for help, Sandra would have left him and taken half of everything if not more. He liked his lifestyle, so in the interest of self-preservation, he opted to go get treatment for his "sexual addiction".

He lay there in his new apartment on that uncomfortable mattress, thinking of all the women he missed out on because of his so-called treatment. If he had just told his wife he didn't want to change his lifestyle and that he wanted to keep hooking up with younger women, he could have been on his own a hell of a lot sooner.

BUZZ. BUZZ. BUZZ. His phone persisted on his nightstand. Realizing, between the new mattress and his phone constantly going off, that he wasn't going to get any sleep. Glen rolled over and grabbed his cell... and was shocked as he read the top story: "Sickness kills hundreds in New York City, Boston and other parts of New England." He scrolled through the report. He couldn't believe he was sidelined during a story like this.

Chapter 17

Friday, October 30th
6:04 A.M.

Stanley drove his small rental car, listening to a CD from his collection that he brought with him every trip. It was music that he loved because it reminded him of home. The songs took his mind away from the loneliness and kept it active as he drove countless miles from farm to farm.

He arrived at the Johnsons' farm and pulled up the driveway. It was still mostly dark out, but the sun was starting to rise on the horizon. He parked the rental car in the circular driveway in front of the white farm-house. Before he was out of the car, Bill Johnson was there to greet him.

"Good morning, Stanley," Bill said with his hand outstretched.

"Good morning, Bill," he said, shaking Bill's hand. "All the times I've been here and every time I'm stunned by its beauty," Stanley said, slapping Bill on the shoulder as he scanned the vast openness.

"Come on in—Maureen should have breakfast on the table."

"Don't take this the wrong way, but her breakfast is the best part of the whole trip."

"You know, you're not the first person to say that." Both men began to laugh.

They made their way towards the house and entered in through the side door of the kitchen. Stanley greeted Maureen with a hug and a kiss on the cheek and they shared pleasantries. After Bill's two boys came down and greeted him, they all sat down at the kitchen table and held each other's outstretched hands for morning prayer.

He loved the fact the Johnsons still said grace before every meal, something that, over the years, other families had dropped from their daily ritual.

"As usual, an outstanding feast," he said when he had finished eating.

Maureen lowered her head, trying to hide the fact she was blushing. "Why thank you, Stanley."

After breakfast, Bill took him for a tour of the land he just purchased and showed him where he wanted to plant the new crop of corn. "I love coming here in the morning," Bill said as he stopped the truck, got out, and started up a slight incline.

Stanley opened his door and stepped out. The rich smell of the soil filled his nostrils. He took a deep breath, savoring the scent of the earth, then turned and saw Bill standing on the top of the small hill, his body a silhouette before the rising sun. He walked up the slope, and the moist soil from the night's dew clung to his shoes.

"Absolutely beautiful," Stanley said, looking out over the vast openness of the new field that lay beyond.

"Indeed. A beautiful sight created by God," Bill said.

"And this is all virgin land? It's never seen crops?" Stanley asked.

"Nope. Just what God has grown here," Bill replied.

"Reminds me of a story I heard," Stanley said. "Years back I met an old farmer out in Ohio who had a large patch of land he never sowed. When I asked him about it, he told me a story that was passed down through his family. He said back in the 1930's during the Dust Bowl, his family had lost everything except for a patch of virgin soil. All of their crop had died and their fields wouldn't grow a thing. This old farmer told me that, out of desperation, they sowed the virgin soil, and it happened to produce the largest crops they had ever seen. So afterwards, his family bought another parcel of virgin land and never used it. He said they were saving it… just in case."

"Oh, wow," Bill commented.

"Just think," Stanley added. "If there's ever a great famine, you'll be able to grow crop." He slapped Bill on the shoulder.

Bill turned and looked back at the corn stalks of the current field. The sun's rays glistened off the water from the irrigation system as it sprayed the corn fields, casting them in a golden brilliance that stretched across the horizon. He stood there for a minute, wondering if he should leave the land the way it was and hold off sowing seeds.

After a few peaceful moments of enjoying the view, Stanley spoke, "Shall we get back to business?"

Both men climbed back into the truck and headed for the barn.

"I'm looking for a new pipe puller," Bill informed, "but I want the same make I have now. I also want to know if you carry that new blade I've heard about that is supposedly impossible to break?"

"I think we do. I'll just have to check the catalog when we get back."

The red barn in the distance was dwarfed by the white farm-house, but it steadily grew larger as they approached. Bill stopped the truck in front of its huge, sliding, doors. The boys had both open and were tending to their daily chores.

"I'll go pull the pipe puller out of the barn so you can get a good look at it in the sunlight," Bill said.

"Sounds good," Stanly acknowledged. "While you're doing that, I'll go grab the catalogs and order forms out of the car."

Stanley returned a few minutes later, looked at the model of the pipe puller and flipped through the catalog.

"I've got good news and great news," he said, looking up from the catalogs. "We carry that attachment and it is compatible with the new machine you want. Plus, we now sell the irrigation pipe, the fittings, along with everything else you will need."

"Really!" Bill said. "That's good to hear!"

"Now for the great news: if you buy more than fifty coils of irrigation pipe—are you ready for this?—I can give you fifty percent off."

"Wow, Fifty percent off! I'll take a hundred coils."

"And the attachment is twenty percent off as well."

"I knew there was a reason I liked you so much," Bill smiled. "What do you say we go back in the house and fill out the order form?"

"Sounds good."

"Man, this is turning out to be a great day," Bill said as they made their way towards the house.

"Yes, it is," Stanley agreed, thinking he could be back to the hotel in a few hours, make it to the airport before noon, and be home for dinner that same night.

As both men stepped through the front door, they suddenly could feel something in the air. As the screen door slammed behind them, Maureen cried out for Bill. Without hesitating, Bill ran into the living room and stopped. Maureen was sitting on the couch with her eyes glued to the television. "You won't believe what's happening," she said.

"What? What is it?" Stanley asked, having followed Bill. The news channel was showing footage from earlier in New York.

"Is it about the sickness? Has it spread?" he asked.

"The anchor is saying that several states are reporting the disease," Maureen answered, never taking her eyes from the TV, "and the death toll is staggering!"

"Did they say what it is?" Bill asked.

"They're not sure. Everyone that tries to experiment on it has died."

"Holy shit," Bill exclaimed, taking a seat.

Maureen broke her gaze away from the TV and glanced over at her husband, not accustomed to hearing him swear and then asked, "Are you guys done yet?"

"Stanley here is going to save us a boat-load of money, and we're getting a great deal. We just need to fill out the paperwork," Bill replied.

"Well, you better get going because they just announced the FAA might be shutting down the airports soon."

"What?" Stanley asked taking a step closer to the TV.

Chapter 18

Friday, October 30th
6:15 A.M.

Drew was about to pull out his phone to see if Annabelle had called or texted when something caught his attention outside the small, oval window. He looked out at the luggage being towed over to the plane followed by a small swarm of men that ran over and began loading the suitcases and travel bags of various sizes and colors. He then turned his attention to the fuel truck that pulled up and watched as the crew hopped out. One of the men went to the back of the fuel truck and began dragging the long snake-like fuel line over to the plane. The other man ran under the aircraft, presumably to remove the fuel cap, and then a minute later reappeared and ran back to help the other crew member drag the line.

He looked back down at his lap and pulled his phone out of his pocket and up to his ear, again giving in to his newly compulsive behavior and trying Annabelle for what seemed like the hundredth time. As the phone rang, he glanced up and saw a young lady assisting an elderly woman down the cramped aisle.

"I think this is our row, Grandma," the younger of the two said as she pointed to the seats in front of him. The older woman reminded him of his mother.

Drew heard Annabelle's voice in his ear and went to speak when he realized it was just her voicemail again. He hung up the phone and opened up his text messages and typed: *My mom passed away. I just boarded my flight back to Boston. Can we talk when I get home, please? I love you.* Shoving the phone back in his pocket, he directed his gaze up again and saw the older woman looking at him as her granddaughter was placing a small carry-on bag in the storage bin above the seats. She smiled when his eyes met hers. He politely returned the smile, then looked to his right to see that the man in the three-piece suit was eyeing the young woman up and down like she was a piece of meat on display at a butcher's shop. Drew's smile instantly faded into a grimace. The businessman noticed the look of disgust on his face, but he merely responded with an arrogant smirk, especially since, just at that same moment, the flight attendant returned with his drink.

Drew understood all too well what the man's smirk implied. It was as if the asshole's expression itself had a voice of its own: *Judge not, buddy. Lest ye be judged.*

The businessman's smirk widened into a full smile when the flight attendant reached across him, her bosom brushing past his face as she handed the drink to Drew.

"Looks like I have the best seat in the house today," the man said with a wink.

Drew made eye contact with the flight attendant and watched as she rolled her eyes at the comment.

"Thank you," he said taking the drink from her.

She smiled and replied, "You're welcome, but you'll have to finish it before we take off."

"I will."

Just as she handed the drink to him, a voice came over the loudspeaker asking for all flight attendants to come to the front of the plane.

The man in the three-piece suit leaned to his right and watched the flight attendant as she walked back down the aisle. He whispered to himself, "Man, I'd tap that!" before turning back to Drew, who merely shook his head again.

The horndog said nothing, but that same smirk with its own voice returned. Drew could almost hear it laughing, *Go ahead and disapprove. I dare ya. All that'll do is label you a fucking hypocrite.* As if to confirm what his smirk insinuated, horndog winked at Drew, nodding to the alcoholic drink in his hand and tapping the cigarette behind his own ear. His point made, he then turned his attention back to the TV in front of him. He started pushing buttons on his arm rest, trying to get the screen to work.

Drew got horndog's message loud and clear. He figured the guy tapped his own cigarette to also show that he himself was not one to judge, so Drew shouldn't either. Everyone had vices. Instead of turning his nose at others for theirs, he realized he should reflect on his own, especially since it had started to ruin his life. Shamefully, he stared at the drink in his hand. *If it wasn't for my wife and daughter, my life would suck. Now I have nothing to go back to. Annabelle kicked me out and won't even return my calls. All for what? A stupid drink.* Annabelle's words ringing in his head: "You're a fucking alcoholic!"

Why can't I stop? He could feel the anger welling up inside him as he clenched his fist. His eyes began filling with tears.

I need to stop, but it's so fucking hard. Drinking is the only thing that makes me feel comfortable in my own skin. I hate myself. I'm a useless piece of shit. I'd probably make everyone's life better if I just died. What's the point of living? I screw everything up.

Tears started to run down his face.

I have nothing to go back to — a job that under-pays me, a wife that doesn't want me. I'll probably never get to see my daughter again. I just wish Annabelle would answer, so I can say I'm sorry. What happened to me? I used to be a good man. Now I'm just bitter and hateful. People always tell me I'm a good guy but I don't see it. All I see is a failure. I can't even stand looking at the person in the mirror. I need to drink to cope. I need to drink to live. It's the only peace I'm granted. "Stop drinking," she says, but it's the only thing that makes me whole. I know I've never asked you for help before, God, but please help me now. I'm not one to ask for help and I know others need you more than I do, but I want to be there for my little girl. I want her to grow up knowing her daddy and to know I was a good man. Make me the man I should be – that I can be.

He looked down at the drink in front of him.

I need to call Annabelle and tell her I will change. I will stop drinking. I will be a better husband and a great daddy for our little girl. He reached into his pocket, pulled out his phone and dialed Annabelle's number again. He intently waited for the phone to ring, hoping to hear her voice on the other end. Suddenly there was a loud beep followed by a message: "All circuits are busy. Please try your call later."

"What the fuck?" he said, pulling the phone away from his ear and looking at it. He dialed the correct number. Suddenly a loud gasp filled the plane. Several passengers were pointing to the TV's in the back of the seats in front of them. Drew started scanning the cabin as he redialed the phone. Again, he received the same message: "All circuits are busy. Please try your call later."

The man in the three-piece suit started cursing and punching the TV in front of him trying to get it to work. He tried waving to the flight attendant who looked at him but didn't seem to care. She had a shocked look on her face as she and the other flight attendants talked frantically to one another.

The businessman reached across Drew and started pushing the buttons aggressively on his armrest for the TV.

"What are you doing?" Drew asked.

"I need to see how bad it is back home."

"What?" Drew replied.

"The sickness and all the death up North."

"What are you talking about?" Drew said, wiping the remaining tears away, hoping the man didn't see them.

"You haven't heard? There's a sickness going around and the death toll is getting pretty bad."

"No, I didn't hear."

"It started in New York and spread to Boston, Chicago, and this morning I heard Los Angeles had cases too. I'm surprised they're letting us fly back. There was talk the FAA might be grounding all flights."

"Really?!"

"Yeah. Put on your TV — mine's not working."

Drew turned his attention to the small screen built into the back of the seat in front of him. He put his hand on the arm rest and changed the channel from the picture of his plane smack dab in the middle of Florida to the live feed from NBC in New York. His eyes widened as his brain registered what he saw on the screen: people in New York were dragging countless sheet-covered bodies out into the streets.

He fumbled, found his head phones and plugged them into the auxiliary port. The live feed bounced from the news anchor back in the studio to the street-level camera crew. The cameraman panned around and Drew's mouth dropped open as he saw the corpses of both adults and children scattered everywhere. He and the other viewers near him watched a man put down the body of a little child. The mother ran down the front stairs after him, pulling on her hair and screaming.

He couldn't bear the thought of putting his own daughter's lifeless body out on the curb and quickly tried to shake the vision from his mind.

Loud gasps filled the plane as others watched in horror while the news unfolded. "I can't believe what I'm seeing," said the anchor, sitting in his chair in the studio as the camera closed in on the woman and her small child.

A loud commotion at the front of the plane broke his attention away from the small TV. He looked up and saw the flight attendant arguing with passengers trying to board the plane. Others noticed the commotion and rose to their feet.

"May I have your attention please," announced a voice over the plane's loudspeaker, cutting into the news audio. Passengers looked around in panic, trying to figure out what was going on.

"We've received word that all flights have been canceled at this time. We have to ask you all to exit the plane." Gasps and shouts came from the passengers. "Once we have determined the current situation, we'll have you board the plane again," said the flight attendant with a hint of doubt in her voice. Some people instantly got out of their seats, grabbed their luggage from the overhead compartment and headed for the front of the plane. They bunched up by the cabin door, while others sat in their seats, waiting until the aisle was clear enough to exit.

Drew remained in his seat watching as some passengers exited the plane, while others made their way up the main aisle, when the older woman in front of him sneezed. The man standing in the aisle next to her row quickly pointed at her and screamed, "She has the sickness!"

Instantly the plane was filled with cries and shrieks as the passengers who were already standing started pushing those in front of them in the aisle towards the open door at the front. Those still sitting quickly rose to their feet and started shoving, punching and clawing as they tried in desperation to escape the confines of their rows and toward the exit.

Drew stood up quickly and looked for a way out, the move yanking the headphones from his head. He caught a glimpse of the older woman in front of him who was now holding her chest. The young woman assisting her turned and looked at him. "She doesn't have the sickness. She just sneezed!"

With the moblike mentality having overtaken the frightened passengers, the younger woman was knocked off her feet and forced into her grandmother who fell down between the seats. The older woman's body began to tremble and shake as her hands clutched at her chest. Drew looked down into her eyes and could see the fear behind them.

The man in the three-piece suit watched everything unfold. When the old woman fell, he turned and looked at Drew and then reached over and grabbed what remained of his drink from the tray. He shot it down in one gulp, then dropped the cup to the floor and snatched up Drew's headphones so he could continue listening to the news coverage.

Drew saw people throwing fists and elbows at each other as they fought to open the emergency hatch a few rows up. He glanced to his right and saw the businessman just standing there watching TV with a shocked look of horror covering his face. He turned to his left and looked out the small window, watching those who had exited the emergency door running down the wing of the plane, jumping off and then falling to the ground.

Members of the ground-crew squinted at the plane trying to figure out what was going on. They could hear the screams coming from inside the aircraft.

"Must be a terrorist!" one of them shouted.

"Help them!" cried out another.

One of the biggest crew members went over to try and catch people as they leapt off the wing. The man falling, though, was afraid that everyone was infected, so when he came down, he kicked the ground crew member right in the face. The big guy's nose instantly broke, and blood poured out. Another ground crew member grabbed one of the giant wrenches used to fix the plane and chased the passenger who had jumped off the plane. When he caught up to him, the crewman started bludgeoning the man with the wrench, thinking he was a terrorist trying to escape. The man fell to the ground, turned over onto his back and tried to scurry away, but the ground crew member was too fast. He swung the huge wrench over his head and brought it down with such a fury that the man's head split wide open, popping like a zit.

It was total confusion. When another man who had jumped off the plane saw his fellow passenger killed, he thought the ground crew members were trying to keep the passengers on the aircraft. He ran up behind the ground crew member holding the wrench and swung his briefcase at him, hitting the wrench-wielding man square in the back of the head. The wrench flew from his hand as he fell to the ground and the papers from the man's briefcase scattered everywhere as the passenger ran off. All of this happening in just a few seconds.

One of the ground crew members refueling the plane watched the events unfold in disbelief. He took his hand off the lever for the fuel pump, ran to the front of the truck, and jumped into the cab, fearing there was a bomb on the plane that might explode. A puff of black smoke shot from the truck's exhaust as he started the engine. Suddenly the small puff of smoke turned into to a straight-up out stream as the truck raced away from the plane. The fuel line's hose, which was still connected, looked like a snake zipping across the ground and uncoiling into a straight line. When the entire length of the hose was finally unrolled, the truck briefly slowed and then yanked the fuel line off the plane, shaking the aircraft.

The people who had successfully jumped off the plane were now running towards the terminal, but turned and tried to jump onto the truck as it raced away. Two men grabbed onto the driver's side step. One of the men was able to get his arm into the window and snatch the steering wheel. The truck swerved back and forth as the driver fought with the man trying to get into the cab.

The man on the other side of the truck had jumped onto the running boards. He was steadying himself when he realized that the vehicle was racing towards the terminal, and that neither of the other men was paying attention. The man decided to jump off the truck instead of riding a large, flammable vehicle into a building at a high rate of speed, then curled up into a ball and hit the ground hard, tearing his shirt and scraping his knees and elbows on impact. He got to his feet and dusted himself off, then turned to watch the truck speed away—he noticed the fuel line, zipping behind the truck. He heard the metal connector at the end of the hose skipping across the tarmac and turned just as the metal end bounced. It came up off the ground and struck him in the head, the force of the impact tossing his bloodied, fuel-covered body like a ragdoll.

Fuel was now pouring out of the plane and pooling where the fuel line had detached.

Suddenly the fuel truck crashed into the terminal just beneath the window where a mass of the people were watching what was going on outside. The truck hit the building with such force that the back end came up off the ground, ejecting both men from the truck like they had been fired from a cannon.

Drew's eyes widened as sparks started shooting from the truck and the fuel caught fire. Within seconds flames engulfed the vehicle and thick, black smoke plumed upwards. His heart skipped a beat as fire raced up the line of fuel that led from the truck to the plane. Frantically, he searched for a way out, but people still bunched up by the exits, fighting to get off the plane.

Suddenly the truck exploded. The shockwave from the blast reached the plane, violently rocking it, knocking Drew off of his feet.

Chapter 19

Friday, October 30th
6:38 A.M.

Kendra awoke to the sound of a large explosion off in the distance that rattled her apartment windows. Half asleep, she grabbed one of the throw pillows on her bed and covered her eyes from the sunlight that crept in. When she had just started to fall back to sleep again, a larger and louder explosion shook her whole apartment, causing her to jump out of bed in a fright. She ran to the window and pulled the blinds up, where off in the distance she could see thick black smoke billowing up from the Orlando airport.

Holy shit, a plane must have crashed, she thought as she hurried back to her bed and grabbed the remote for the 64" TV that hung on the wall. She turned it on and flipped to the local news channel. After a quick trip to the bathroom, she came out to start her coffee maker and walked back to the window. The fire at the airport looked like it was spreading and growing in intensity. Hoping for the local news to shed some light on the matter, she went back to the TV to check for any footage regarding a plane crash in Orlando, but she was confused when instead, her screen displayed a live feed of New York. Particularly of people running around in a panic and, more disturbing, what looked like bodies wrapped in sheets and bags lining the streets of the Big Apple. She turned the volume up and heard that the sickness was spreading. The anchor directed viewers to stay indoors, and to stay away from other people.

The news anchor then put his hand up to his ear, shook his head up and down, and then turned his attention back to the monitor and said, "We have breaking news coming out of Orlando, Florida. It appears that a plane has crashed at the airport." The still-image above the anchor's right shoulder switched from a shot of New York City to that of MCO, the Orlando International Airport. "We're also receiving word that it may have been a fuel truck that crashed into the terminal," the anchor said as he put his hand up to his ear and shook his head up and down again. "We'll have our reports confirmed in just a few moments as we're about to have access to video footage of the scene there."

An idea came to Kendra as she rushed back to her window and looked out toward the direction of the airport. Off in the distance she could see the dense cloud of smoke continue to pile straight up into the air. She grabbed her telescope, pointed it towards the airport, and scanned the horizon until, after a few seconds of searching, she found the plume of smoke and followed it down to the plane that was on fire. She could just make out the remains of the fuel truck that had crashed into the terminal.

The plane had somehow ended up on its side, the fuselage running across the ground with the wing of the plane facing upward. She looked at it twice because the way the wreckage looked, with the burning terminal behind it, almost made it appear as if the plane was an upside down cross being consumed by fire.

Chapter 20

Friday, October 30th
7:05 A.M.

Annabelle woke up feeling a little rested, but she could definitely still have used a few more hours' sleep. Regardless, she went into the kitchen and made herself a cup of coffee — her favorite drink next to a margarita, then went and sat on her mother's couch, still in her PJ's — it was something she hadn't done since a child. Almost as if on autopilot, as it was part of her normal daily routine, her hand gripped the remote to turn the TV on to the local news channel. Within seconds, her groggy mind came to full attention when it registered what her eyes witnessed. The news was reporting a deadly sickness spreading across the state and that people were infected all across the region. They were announcing which towns had confirmed cases of the unknown virus. She gasped when she saw Stanton on the list.

"Oh, you're awake," Susan said, hearing the TV on in the living room as she came up the stairs from doing laundry.

"Mom, did you see this?" she said, turning towards her mother.

"No," Susan replied as she put her laundry basket down. "I try not to watch the news anymore since your father passed away. It's just too depressing."

Before Annabelle could relay the details given from the news report, Stephanie started crying from her room, indicating she was ready to be let out of her crib.

"I'll get her," Susan offered, turning to head down the hall before even finishing her sentence.

Annabelle turned her focus back to the TV and read the ticker across the bottom of the screen that now stated several infected people in New York have been confirmed dead.

"Mommy! Mommy!" she heard along with the pitter-patter of little feet running down the hallway. When her daughter reached her, Anabelle scooped up Stephanie and gave her a big hug and kiss.

"Good morning, my darling. Mommy loves you," she said, giving her daughter kisses on the cheek.

"Mommy boo boo," Stephanie said pointing to the makeup that had streamed down Annabelle's face.

Susan came into the room behind Stephanie and looked at Annabelle. "I thought for sure you would have come out of your room yesterday, but since you didn't, I figured it was pretty bad between you and Drew."

"It is," Annabelle admitted. "He really needs to quit drinking. I told him I wanted a divorce."

"Divorce!" Stephanie repeated.

"I'm sorry, honey," Susan said in a noticeably lower volume. "We should talk more when there aren't little ears around." She paused and then asked, "How's his mom?

"I don't know — I haven't spoken with him."

"I really like her," Susan commented as she checked her watch. "I may not be her son's biggest fan, no doubt about that, but she is such a nice woman. Breakfast?"

"Not right now, thank you though."

"Well, if you get hungry, you know where to find everything. I'm going to run to the store and grab a few things. I'll be back shortly."

"Mom, I don't think you should go," Annabelle said with concern. "The news is saying there's a highly contagious sickness going around and people are dying from it. They even reported several people here in Stanton have it."

"The news is so full of itself," Susan scoffed, waving Annabelle off with one hand. "Some pharmaceutical company is probably trying to sell flu medicine and trumped up people being sick so they can sell their product. It's stuff like this that drove your dad crazy. God bless his soul." She made the sign of the cross over her heart.

Annabelle knew her mother wouldn't change her mind, so it was pointless to argue with the woman, but she figured she would try anyway. "Please don't go, Mom. What if you catch this sickness and bring it back here and infect your granddaughter?"

"Oh please, Annabelle," Susan said as she picked up her car keys off the table by the front door and headed out.

"Breakfast, Mommy?" Stephanie asked.

She went into the kitchen and cut up a banana and some fresh fruit, which her mother always had plenty of, then situated Stephanie in her booster seat and served her breakfast before grabbing her phone from the bedroom.

Picking up her phone from the nightstand, she saw there more missed calls and texts from Drew. She dreaded calling him back; it was going to be the same conversation they always had after a night of his drinking, and she knew nothing was going to change. Annabelle figured she should at least call him back to find out about his mother. Besides, it would be ideal to talk while Susan was out of the house in order to avoid her listening in on the conversation. She was getting ready to call Drew when she heard the front door open unexpectedly.

"Mom, is that you?" she shouted down the hall.

"Yes dear," her mother shouted back.

"That was fast," she said as she made her way back down the hallway.

"I couldn't get into the center of town because the police have all the roads blocked off," Susan explained, climbing up the foyer stairs.

"See, I told you mom. That's a little much for a pharmaceutical company to just sell flu medicine."

"I agree," Susan said with a nod as she walked past her, grabbing the cordless phone off the receiver and dialing.

"Who are you calling?" Annabelle asked.

"Patti," Susan replied as she held the phone up to her ear. "Her brother is the Town Selectman. She'll know what's going on."

Annabelle could hear the phone ring and then click when Patti picked up.

"Hi, Patti? It's Susan. How are you?"

Annabelle couldn't decipher what Patti was saying, but her mother always repeated what people said to her over the phone.

"No way! There are seventy-seven cases here in Stanton?"

Annabelle mouthed the number seventy-seven to herself in disbelief — it seemed pretty high for such a small town.

"They think the people caught it from someone on a bus or train out of New York?"

She knew from years of listening to her mom what was coming next.

"I've always said this town should never have allowed the commuter rail through Stanton."

And there it was. The line her mother had used for years, ever since the little McCarthy kid had been struck and killed by the train some eighteen years prior.

There was a pause as Patti spoke. Annabelle waited for her mother to repeat back the information.

"So they brought men in with HAZMAT suits to check the train cars and busses, and the houses of people who have been infected. And, did you say they quarantined the patients up the street at the hospital?"

Annabelle thought about the local hospital that was just less than three miles up the road.

She turned her attention to the TV and couldn't believe what she was seeing on the news. The media was reporting on a new development about big trucks that were being brought into New York City. The live video displayed men in big, white chemical suits climbing out of the trucks, heaving bodies draped in white sheets up to other men, in the same suits, who began stacking the bodies on top of each other. She felt nauseous as she watched.

"Where's the dignity?" Susan said, startling Annabelle who had not heard her mother finish her phone call.

"The news reported they are taking the bodies and dumping them in huge pits, Annabelle said. "They're setting them on fire."

"I'm glad I wasn't able to make it into town," Susan admitted. "Otherwise I could have caught the sickness and brought it home with me."

"I know, Mom. Remember I tried to stop you from going?"

"Well I just did an inventory and we have plenty of food. The fridge and freezer up here are stocked, and so is the freezer in the basement."

Just pray we don't lose power, Annabelle thought.

"Have you heard from Drew?" Susan asked.

Annabelle remembered seeing a text message from him and grabbed her phone. She opened and read the message from Drew: *My Mom passed away. I just boarded my flight back to Boston. Can we talk when I get home, please? I love you.*

Oh Drew, I'm sorry, she thought. After recently losing her own father, she knew what he was going through. Memories of her father came fluttering back. She remembered how he was such a strong man who had principles and beliefs and how he never wavered. She loved her daddy the same way her daughter loved Drew. She thought back to when she and Drew first started dating and how he reminded her so much of her dad. She also remembered back to when her father died, how supportive he was, and that he didn't drink at all during that period.

I should call him, she thought as she dialed his number and put the phone up against her ear.

She looked back up at the TV as the phone rang in her ear. The news anchor put his hand up to his headset, shook his head up and down, then looked back at the monitor and said, "We have breaking news out of Florida that a plane has crashed."

The footage switched from the shot of the HAZMAT crew in New York to Orlando International Airport. "It appears that a plane has exploded at the terminal while refueling." He put his hand up to his ear and shook his head up and down again. "I just received word that there is video footage of what happened at the Orlando airport."

The phone, still pressed up against her ear, was on its third ring when the scene cut from the anchor to a cell phone video of a plane sitting in front of a terminal being refueled. Suddenly the emergency exit above the wing swung open and a big, yellow slide shot out from the side of the plane.

The person holding the camera ran right over to the terminal window and zoomed in on the plane that was right outside the window. The video panned to the right, capturing the shocked faces of the passengers inside the plane. As the camera kept panning she thought she saw Drew's face looking out from one of the windows of the plane. Whoever recorded the video panned back to the door above the wing as a couple of men jumped down from it. It appeared that one of the men who jumped off the wing attacked a member of the ground crew, but the angle the video was shot from was blocked by the fuel truck. The camera moved again and caught one of the men who worked on the fuel truck as he jumped into the front seat of the truck and started to drive away. The video captured two of the men who had jumped off the wing now climbing onto the fuel truck's running boards. It panned again to follow the fuel truck racing off and tearing the fuel line abruptly from the plane. She saw fuel pouring out of the aircraft before leaving the camera's view as it followed the speeding truck.

Annabelle was so mesmerized by what she was watching that she didn't even hear the ringing in her ear turn to Drew's voicemail greeting.

The video then showed the fuel truck racing towards a different terminal with the torn off fuel line in tow. One of the men who had previously climbed onto the truck now leapt off onto the ground.

She gasped as the fuel line bounced and came up off the ground, striking the man in the head and tossing him like a rag doll.

The camera followed the truck until it crashed into another terminal and caught fire. Then it slowly turned back towards the way it had come, following the fire that was now consuming the fuel on the ground that led to the plane.

"No! No! No!" she shouted as the fire raced towards her husband's plane.

The camera turned back to film the inside of the terminal, catching dozens of people pressed up against the windows, watching the events outside. Suddenly, the video started swinging from left to right as the person holding the camera took off running, trying to get as far away as possible.

"Drew!" she screamed and fell to her knees as the force of the explosion threw the person holding the camera to the ground. The cellphone slid across the floor.

The now-still camera caught shards of glass and debris raining down. Thick black smoke rapidly filled the terminal, enveloping the camera, and finally the only thing on the screen was blackness.

The anchor came back on said, "We're receiving word that the plane that exploded was bound for Boston.

Chapter 21

Friday, October 30th
8:05 A.M.

A slight warm breeze blew across Drew's face, waking him from his unconscious state. With each passing gust, he could hear what sounded like the rustling of grass. Though gathering his bearings took effort, the notion that he was lying on his back slowly registered in his mind. He tried to open his eyes, but they fluttered and squinted to the point where they almost shut themselves again, for the sun was blinding, not to mention warm—a little too much to bear for someone used to the gloomy, harsh winters of Massachusetts. His head hurt something fierce, and for a moment he assumed it was from another hangover, but as the fogginess of his mind cleared, his memory of the plane, the chaos, and finally the explosion returned. Fearing he sustained an injury, Drew reached up and touched the center of his forehead, right where his angel's kiss was. He pulled his hand away and looked at it, expecting to see blood, but there was nothing there. Exhaling a sigh of relief, he lay there for a minute watching the puffy white clouds wisp by, when suddenly thick heavy smoke engulfed him, causing him to choke and gag as it drifted past.

What the hell happened? Drew wondered as he slowly sat up and rolled over onto one side. He held himself up on his elbow and scanned the area. By the looks of it, he was still at the airport in a field just off the runway. At first he couldn't recall how he had gotten there, but as he rubbed his throbbing temples, the recent events started coming back to him little by little. He remembered the flight attendant talking over the plane's loudspeaker, the fuel truck crashing into the terminal, and the shockwave rocking the plane.

He scanned the area, and became horrified when he noticed lifeless bodies, and body parts, scattered everywhere. Calming his nerves by reminding himself it wasn't the first time he'd been exposed to such horrors, he got to his knees and slowly forced his way to his feet. For a minute, Drew was sure that the pain in his head was so intense he was going to throw up. Reaching up to his forehead again, his angel's kiss felt puffy and pronounced. He rubbed it and the pain quickly subsided.

After a more thorough search around the area, he saw that two other planes had collided on the runway. As best he could figure, the smoke from the fire in the terminal that the fuel truck had crashed into, must have blocked visibility on the runways, causing the two planes trying to land at the same time to wreck. All that was left was two burned-out shells of planes, both of which had dense, dark clouds pouring up from them. He quickly realized, though, that something was odd – there were no firetrucks, no firemen dragging hoses to contain the fire or save lives. No one. Everyone appeared dead.

He stood in the open field just off the terminal, trying to figure out how everything had gone so wrong. Gazing at the crashed fuel truck up against the burning terminal, more of the sequence of events came to him as he remembered the flight attendant on the PA, people fighting, the old woman holding her chest. And the sickness. *The sickness caused all this*, he thought to himself.

Drew turned and saw another plane leaning up against the terminal. It looked like the force of the shockwave from the exploding fuel truck had sent pieces of the truck flying everywhere. A large chunk must have careened across the tarmac and struck the back landing gears, shearing them off the plane. Fire from the exploded truck had then raced up the trail of spilled jet fuel, following the snake-like pattern towards the plane. Within seconds the flames had reached the aircraft and leapt up the fuel as it leaked from the side. He remembered the violent explosion. The force was so strong that it lifted the back of the plane off the ground and thrust it up against the terminal. The plane was now resting on its wing. The rear end of the aircraft had been shredded and dangled down, resembling an upside down cross.

How the hell did I survive that? he asked himself, suddenly realizing that the plane was the one he had been on. He stood there for a moment in disbelief before setting off towards the front of the wreckage. When he got to the plane, he looked up and saw the pilot's lifeless body hanging halfway out of the cockpit window. The emergency exit behind the cockpit was open and the yellow slide that had been deployed looked awkward, upside-down and deflated, flapping in the breeze. Sections of the plane had large, gaping holes in them, and the areas around the holes were charred. Seats were smoldering, some still with bodies strapped in them. He stopped when he noticed the dead bodies up in the windows of the terminal. *I don't know what happened here, but I need to get far away from this place,* he thought.

Drew was stumbling away from the terminal and heading back towards where he had come from when he thought of his phone. He reached into his pocket and only found his car keys. *The phone must have come out of my pocket during the explosion.* He instantly felt lost without it, his lifeline home, and he frantically patted himself down to check if it was tangled in his clothes. A wave of relief washed over him as he finally found it in his opposite pocket. He remembered putting it there because he didn't want to elbow the man sitting next to him on the plane.

Drew was used to seeing death and destruction as part of his job. His training would always take over and he dealt with the emotional aftermath later. But what he just felt when he thought he lost his phone was worse than surviving the explosion.

Now Drew was making his way through the open field, which was scattered with body parts. He stopped and searched the horizon when he suddenly saw someone moving and trying to get up off the grass. It was the man in the three-piece suit, crawling on all fours, trying to figure out what had happened. Drew called out to him, "Hey!"

The man started looking around while his hands searched his body for any injury.

"Over here!" Drew shouted.

The man turned around in circles before finally spotting Drew waving to him.

"What the hell happened?" asked the businessman once Drew had made his way to him.

"That fuel truck crashed into the terminal and our plane blew up," Drew replied.

The man looked around at all of the bodies on the ground, the crashed fuel truck and the plane on its side leaning against the terminal.

"How the hell did we survive that?"

"Not a fucking clue!" answered Drew.

"Are they dead?"

"They're all dead," Drew said with a shaky voice, "So far you're the only other survivor I've come across."

"What's the last thing you remember?" the man asked as he reached up behind his ear searching for his cigarette. "Not about the fuel truck, but what was on the TV?" He patted his pockets, felt something, reached inside and pulled out a pack of cigarettes.

"I remember seeing people bringing bodies covered with sheets out to the street in New York," Drew replied with a look of surprise on his face at the fact the man's cigarette box hadn't been crushed.

The man looked down, "Holy shit! Look at that. Something finally lived up to its reputation," he said pointing to the tiny print on the cigarette box that read "crush proof box." Surprisingly they both laughed.

The man opened the box and took out a cigarette, put it in between his lips and lit the end. He breathed in deep and blew out smoke rings. He stood there and smoked the cigarette to the filter, before dropping it on the ground.

"What do you remember?" asked Drew.

"You don't want to know what I saw," the man in the crumpled three-piece suit said as he pulled out another cigarette and lit it.

"What about the news?" Drew clarified.

The man took another long drag and said, "They were saying that people were getting sick and that at first it appeared like the common cold, but then they soon developed black painful spots all over their bodies, followed by this thick yellowish-green mucus that formed in their lungs and caused them to drown in it."

"Sounds like the Black Plague."

"They said that, too. They said they've tried everything on it, but nothing seems to work." He paused to take another haul of his cigarette. "What's worse, it's reported to be highly communicable and can be passed from one person to another just by breathing."

"No shit?"

"No shit!" replied the man as he dropped the cigarette butt and pulled yet another one out of the pack, lighting up again.

"What else did they say?"

"It was hard to hear, because everyone was going bat-shit crazy on the plane, but the anchor said for everyone to avoid other people and to find seclusion until the sickness passes. He also said something like this could take weeks to end, but since it has such a high mortality rate, it probably won't last long because it will run out of people to infect."

"Well, since all of these people are already dead, I guess we don't have to worry about catching the sickness from them," Drew said pointing around as he laughed uncomfortably.

"I guess not," the man said as he took another drag, not sure what to think of that comment.

"Sorry, I tend to laugh in the midst of bad situations. It's something I picked up in the Marines and working as an EMT up in Boston."

"I get it, man. I live in Boston, so I can only imagine what you guys deal with. Sometimes you just have to laugh at the shit or you'll go crazy."

Drew started laughing uncontrollably and choked, "Yeah, like being in a field surrounded by dead bodies." He doubled over with laughter. It was a coping mechanism, just like alcohol, but laughing would have to do for now.

The man continued to smoke, chuckled and said, "I guess so."

They stood there for a few minutes before the man in the three-piece suit asked, "So what do we do now?"

"We find a car and start driving home, because flying home is clearly not an option any longer."

The man looked around the area and replied, "Clearly." Both men laughed this time.

"I'd say we head back past the terminal and try and find a car, but we're more apt to run into people that way.

If what the news is saying is true, we should avoid anyone else so we don't get sick."

"Speaking of being sick, do you think we're already infected?"

"No, what makes you ask?" replied Drew.

"Well the news said you can catch it just from breathing and the old lady sitting on the plane in front of us was sneezing."

Drew remembered her sneezing and falling in between the seats after the man in the aisle had knocked the younger woman down. He remembered the younger woman announcing her grandmother wasn't sick, that she had just sneezed. "No, I think she just happened to sneeze at the wrong time."

"Well if I'm infected then you're infected too, and vice versa."

"I guess time will tell."

The man in the three-piece suit took out another cigarette and lit it, then looked at Drew. "I know. I smoke a lot when I'm stressed out. It's my laughing."

Drew nodded in understanding, then scanned the airport until he determined that the only place that appeared safe — and probably didn't have many people — was directly across from them.

"There," he said as he pointed to the fence and tree line on the other side of the runway. "I say we hop that fence and try to find a vehicle."

"Sounds like a plan to me," the man agreed as he tossed the cigarette butt to the ground.

The two started their way across the runway towards the open field and the fence beyond.

"Hey, what's your name?" Drew asked as they made their way across the runway and into the open field.

"Brad. How about yours?"

"Drew."

They reached out and shook hands as they made their way closer to the fence. Drew glanced back over his shoulder at the airport — the thick, billowing smoke rising up — and shook his head in awe that he had survived. He noticed people starting to mill about in the terminal.

As they continued on their way across the open field, the shorter grass gave way to longer blade. Beyond the field was the fence, followed by a dense forest.

When they reached the airport's perimeter fence, they saw that it was old and rusty and didn't appear as if it could their weight. They looked up and down the fence, searching for a stronger section to climb, but it all looked the same.

"Screw it," Drew said and grabbed the fence, scaled up it and dropped down to the other side.

Brad followed right behind him, cursing when the toe of his shoe became stuck and got scuffed up from finding a toehold on the fence.

Once on the other side, they walked a little farther before making their way to an access road used strictly by airport personnel that circled the backside of the airport.

"Which way?" asked Brad.

Drew looked to the sky and saw the sun still rising from the east. He knew that they would ultimately have to head north to make it home, so he turned left onto the road and began walking.

As they walked, Drew's thoughts turned to his wife and daughter back in Massachusetts and to how he was going to get back to them. He pulled his phone out of his pocket and hit redial, but was instantly met with the "all circuits are busy" message. His mind started racing, running through all sorts of scenarios, and he couldn't help but envision both Annabelle and Stephanie wrapped up in a sheet on the side of the road like the many bodies on the news. Unable to bear the thought of losing his mother, wife and daughter, all in the same week, he tried without success to think of something else.

They're fine, he tried to convince himself. *Annabelle is at her mom's. The phones in Boston probably aren't working is all. They're fine.*

Drew and Brad had walked several hundred yards when they spotted a little white shack up ahead with a small white pickup truck out front. As he approached the building, he noticed that it had large lightbulbs hanging off the sides of it. Drew realized they were replacement bulbs for the lights that ran along the side of the runway, used to assist pilots during night landings. He walked up to the truck and looked at the small bubble light on its roof. It reminded him of a gum ball machine. He tried to open the truck's doors, but they were locked.

"Do you want to go in or stay out here and watch for other people?" he asked, looking back and forth between Brad and the door to the shack.

"I'll stand watch out here," Brad replied.

Drew nodded his head, walked up to the front door of the shack and turned the knob. To his surprise, the door swung opened and he stepped in. Once inside, he noticed a small desk against the back wall. Above it was a map of the airport and the surrounding grounds, and the rest of the walls were covered with tools and parts used to fix the runway light fixtures. Drew walked over and searched the desk until he found a set of keys under some paperwork. There was also a stained wooden box about the size of a shoebox with the words "Critter Killer" written on it. He flipped open the box and found a black 9mm Berretta. His lips curled into a half-smile as he picked up the weapon and thought back to his time in the Marines. The Barretta was the military's standard issue pistol, and he was thankful, not only to have found a weapon which he might need in these uncertain times, but also that it happened to be one with which he was already familiar. He almost couldn't believe his luck as he pressed the magazine release and let the clip slide half-way out, noting that it was fully-loaded, then used his palm to slap it back up. Then he pulled back the slide to expose the brass shell inside, indicating there was a round in the chamber and ready to shoot. After he checked to make sure the safety was on, he lifted up the back of his shirt and tucked the gun into the small of his back.

Drew continued searching the confines of the shack and found a small first aid kit in the dingy bathroom. After taking a piss and checking his head in the mirror to verify he hadn't suffered any major injuries when knocked unconscious, he went back outside and told Brad there was a bathroom inside if he needed to use it.

While Brad went inside to relieve himself, Drew checked the truck and used the key to unlock it. He climbed in, stuck the keys in the ignition and turned the key. Again, he gave thanks to Lady Luck when it fired right up. As the engine ran idle, he checked his immediate surroundings and found a flashlight in the glove box and a road map above the passenger visor, the latter of which he unfolded and put in his lap. He then turned the radio on and held the tune button down, searching for a channel, but it was just as he suspected...

Brad opened the passenger door, climbed inside and asked, "Anything on the radio?"

"Nothing," Drew sighed with a hint of dismay.

"Really? No Emergency Broadcast System message?"

"Nope. Just static."

"Oh man. That's bad. That's like...*really* bad.

"Look," Drew said, forcing a weak and unconvincing smile, "maybe it's not. I mean, the antenna on this thing could just be broken is all."

"Yeah," Brad returned a smile just as wavering. "Probably just the antenna."

Coping method or not, no laughter came this time.

Though a chill ran up his spine from the dismal silence that suddenly filled the cab, Drew, being accustomed to emergencies, forced his focus back into working order. "Hey, do you know how to read a map?"

"A little."

"Good. Find us a way out of here." He handed the map to Brad, then put the truck into drive and took off.

Brad was adequate enough with navigating to direct Drew off the airport grounds via a bumpy, little access road Brad had found on the map. It was a dirt road that ran through a large section of trees, and as they followed along, thick, dense grass grew along the side. Soon thereafter, they exited the trees and passed through an open gate in the fence line that led into a wide-open field, where Drew could see a road up ahead. He tried to avoid the bumps but he seemed to hit every one of them as the truck was constantly bouncing and shaking.

"Take a left onto that road up there," Brad said as he folded down the map and pointed up ahead.

Drew had a wide view of the airport's main road as he approached and could see that there were no cars coming in either direction, so he didn't even bother to slow down as he took the turn. The truck bounced one last time as it turned onto the pavement and then smoothened out.

Drew gunned it on the open pavement, hitting seventy miles an hour. They could see a break in the trees coming up on his side of the road—it was the end of the runway.

"Holy shit! Look at that," Drew exclaimed as they passed the end of the runway, giving them a clear view to the airport terminal. Heavy black smoke wafted up from several buildings now.

Seconds later they reached the other side of the opening where thick, dense trees blocked their view once again. They drove a few minutes in silence before Brad spoke, "So what now?"

"We drive home. We can get there quickly if we take turns driving."

"Do you think this little truck will make it that far?"

"If not, we'll grab something else and continue on."

"We're going to avoid people, correct?" asked Brad with a sound of uncertainty in his voice.

"Hell yeah, especially if what you said is true. I'm avoiding everyone."

"Okay, good."

"One thing though: we're going to have to take I-95, which could be heavy with traffic, especially as we pass major cities, but it's our most direct route home. Either that or Route 1."

"Route 1 goes through towns and has stop lights the whole way," Brad commented.

"Yeah," Drew agreed. "Either way there'll be a lot of people around."

Brad thought for a moment before chiming in. "My vote's for 95. At least that way we won't be stuck at a red light where someone might try to force their way into the truck."

Drew nodded. "And on the interstate, everyone else *should* be in their own vehicles, so we won't be breathing the same air as anyone who might be infected."

"Let's be sure to keep our windows up just in case," Brad added with a nervous laugh.

"Right. Okay, I-95 it is. See if you can find it on that map. The sooner we do, the sooner we get home."

Brad unfolded the map, expanding his view of the state of Florida. He found Interstate 95 and moved his fingers tracing a path to where they were. "Okay, keep driving another mile or so and then take State Road 528. That will lead us straight to 95."

As Drew acknowledged, he glanced at the display panel in front of him and whispered a curse under his breath when he noticed the familiar "E" was lit. "If you see a gas station let me know," he said.

"Will do."

After several minutes of silence Brad felt the need to pass the time. "So… an EMT. That can't be an easy job. I don't know how you deal with all that you see."

"It has its days. What do you do? I'm guessing your job requires travel since you were dressed in business attire at the airport."

"Yeah, well, I wanted to look my best. I was meeting with some of the higher-ups at NASA."

"You work for NASA?" Drew asked with an excited voice.

"Not directly. I work for a company contracted by NASA. They sent me down here for the launch of the their new spacecraft, which just brought astronauts up to the space station the other day."

"Wow! That's pretty cool."

"Yeah, I guess it is," Brad said as he opened his cigarette box, which was now empty. He looked back up and pointed to a gas station up on the right.

Drew pulled off the road and up next to the pump. Once he exited the truck and found the gas cap, he inserted his credit card into the slot on the pump and held his breath, hoping the current national crisis had not yet affected the everyday necessities of society like electronic payment transactions. When the prompt to select his fuel grade and begin pumping blinked on the display, Drew exhaled with relief, making a mental note to find an ATM and take out as much cash as he could before it was too late.

Brad got out as well and went for the front doors of the gas station, but found they were locked. He looked into the window and could see a young kid, probably eighteen or nineteen years old, looking back out at him suspiciously.

"Hey, let me in. I want to buy a pack of cigarettes," Brad said.

The kid shook his head indicating no and motioned with his hand for Brad to leave.

Brad pulled out his wallet, reached inside and pulled out a crisp one-hundred dollar bill. "I'll give you a hundred dollars for a pack of smokes."

The young clerk shook his head no again.

Exasperated, Brad pulled out another crisp bill. "I'll give you two hundred dollars for a pack of smokes."

The kid liked the idea of earning double his weekly paycheck and figured these guys weren't sick since they were still alive. He pointed to the far end of building, where Brad looked and saw one of those safety drawers that protect night-shift clerks from would-be robbers was built into the side of the wall.

Brad met the kid in front of the safety drawer and pointed to the pack of cigarettes he wanted. The kid grabbed a pack and threw them into the drawer, then pushed a lever that opened the drawer to him. Brad grabbed the pack of cigarettes and put in a single hundred dollar bill. The kid banged on the window and shook the lever, causing the drawer to shake. He pointed to the other hundred still in Brad's hand.

Having filled the tank completely, Drew hung up the nozzle and turned his attention to the exchange between Brad and the clerk behind the glass.

"One hundred a pack, kid," Brad said, waving the cash in front of the window. "Throw in another if you want this."

The kid pulled back the drawer, removed the hundred dollar bill and tossed in two more packs of smokes before pushing the drawer back out to Brad.

Brad reached in and fished out the two packs of cigarettes and contemplated turning around and walking away, keeping the hundred bucks. The clerk, sensing that Brad was going to stiff him and walk away started pounding on the window. Brad dropped the bill in, but when he looked up, the little punk was flipping him off, so he shot his hand into the drawer and snatched the money back out before the kid could pull the lever. He started walking, away as the clerk continued pounding on the window furiously, but then for the hell of it, he looked back at the window, held up to display the cigarettes and the cash in one hand, and flipped the kid off with the other.

Drew banged on the side of the truck and started laughing out loud as Brad approached, laughing as well. Then he turned back around and made the gesture of jerking off to the kid in the store as Drew climbed into the truck.

"I can't believe you just paid a hundred bucks for three packs of smokes," Drew said when Brad opened the passenger door.

"I would have paid a hundred bucks a pack. I can't live without my cigarettes, even though they'll probably be the death of me." Brad kept the door open, but stayed outside of the truck as he opened a pack and tugged out a cigarette with his teeth and lit it, not before carelessly tossing the wrapper to the ground. He took about three long hauls off the cigarette before flicking it in the opposite direction of the pumps and climbing into the truck.

Just as Brad's door closed, Drew saw the sun's reflection off the store door as it opened in the passenger-side mirror. He was shifting his eyes to look out of the rearview mirror so that he could see if anyone came outside, when suddenly there was a loud bang and glass shattered everywhere. Almost instantly, Drew felt something warm on his cheek that had the consistency of pudding. He reached up, touched his face and pulled his hand away to see something gray and gooey on his hand. Brad's body was slumped over, and a huge chunk of his head was missing.

Another gunshot boomed causing the rest of the back window to shatter and fall in, and there was now a large hole in the front windshield. Glass was still raining down as a third shot rang out. The truck shook as the bullet tore through the dashboard and embedded itself into the engine block.

Drew leaned into the door, and as he pulled on the handle to open it, he went spilling out onto the ground. There was another loud bang and the driver's door window and mirror blew apart, and thousands of glass fragments fell on top of him and the surrounding pavement. He shielded his face from the downpour of glass, then reached into the small of his back and pulled out the 9mm Beretta.

"Teach you to rob me, old man!" the young clerk yelled as he fired another shot, which hit the gas pump above where Drew was crouching.

The kid had a revolver grasped with both hands and pointed it straight out in front of him as he slowly made his way around the back of the truck, hoping to catch Drew lying on the ground, expecting to find him crawling around the front of the truck and onto the passenger side like he saw in the movies. To his surprise, his quarry wasn't there, so he quickly turned around and ran to the back of the truck. But, Drew wasn't in front of the vehicle either. The kid stood there for a second trying to figure out where he had gone.

"Looking for me?" shouted Drew.

The young clerk looked up and caught Drew out of the corner of his eye, crouched down next to the far side of the convenience store. He started to raise his gun to shoot again when Drew flipped the safety off with his thumb and squeezed the trigger twice. Both rounds found their mark and tore into the clerk's chest, knocking him to the ground.

Drew stood up and, with his weapon still aimed at the kid, walked over to check if he was still alive.

"You idiot!" Drew shouted. "You got killed over a pack of smokes, really?"

He picked up the silver .38 snub nose revolver that had gone flying when the kid got shot and tucked it into his waistband, then went to check on Brad, but he knew he was dead.

With a sudden need to calm his nerves, Drew walked shakily to the front of the store and entered, scanning down the row of coolers until he found the one with the big beer sign above it.

Chapter 22

Commander William Johanson and Science Officer Sean Fitzgerald were enjoying their third day aboard the International Space Station. William, known to his friends as Willy, was used to tight spaces from being frequently cramped in the cockpit of fighter jets. The space station was actually a welcomed relief in size. Sean was having a harder time adjusting to the tight quarters and was beginning to feel a little claustrophobic. Although he prepared for it during his training, the real thing was far more difficult to tolerate. But as long as he was near a window and could look out to see the earth below, he managed well enough. He loved watching the different continents zoom by below. Traveling almost 250 miles above the Earth and at the incredible speed of 17,000 miles an hour made for quite the view.

Willy had just finished his breakfast and was getting ready for the scheduled 9:00 a.m. video conference with Mission Control while Sean read over their itinerary for the day. They both sat huddled together in front of the tiny screen and watched as Frank Harvey's face replaced the NASA logo. Frank looked like he was catching a cold—his eyes were watering and he kept wiping his nose with a tissue.

"Hey, Frank," Willy greeted.

"Good morning, Commander," said Frank sounding nasally and congested.

"You got a cold, Frank?" Sean asked.

"Yeah, you look like crap. You should be home in bed," added Willy.

"There's some sort of bad cold going around down here, probably the flu. I guess it's pretty bad up North though. So, how are you guys doing up there?"

"Not too bad," Willy replied.

"We've got one hell of a view up here," Sean said.

"I'm glad you're enjoying it. Should we get to the itinerary?"

"Sure," both Willy and Sean said.

Frank held up a clipboard, looked at it closely. He started rubbing his eyes as if he was having trouble seeing. Suddenly Frank sneezed and long yellowish-green goop came shooting out of his nose, landing on the camera lens and blocking part of the astronaut's view.

"Frank, you need to wipe off the camera lens, we can't see you," Willy said with a laugh.

A minute or two passed and Frank still had not wiped off the lens, nor had he spoken. The snot had started to slide down the camera lens a little, and they could see what appeared to be Frank's shoulder slowly coming towards the screen.

"Frank! You okay buddy?" Willy asked.

Both Willy and Sean watched Frank's body fall towards the lens and his face smash into the camera.

"Frank!" Sean shouted.

Both men watched as yellowish-green froth poured from Frank's nose and mouth.

"Frank! Frank!" Willy yelled just as the communication cut out.

Chapter 23

Glen tried calling the station to see if they needed an extra hand covering the story, but his calls went unanswered. He turned on the TV and switched the channel to the news station he worked for. He was surprised to see his old co-worker Bethany Rogers at the national news WTFH headline desk. They had worked together years ago, back when he was sleeping with the first intern at his previous job. He wondered how bad it was out there, if his news station had to hand off their broadcast to the national news agency.

Bethany didn't look well. She looked weak for someone who, he remembered, worked out twice a day, and who hardly had an ounce of body fat. His prior coworker sat slumped over to one side in the anchor chair. Glen remembered her always sitting up straight, with her back arched and her bust out. The news was the news, but who was delivering the news is what kept viewers watching. Like all anchors, Bethany understood this and used every weapon in her arsenal. When he worked with her, she was what he called a triple threat. She was smart as a whip, quick on her feet, and drop-dead gorgeous, having high, well-defined cheek bones and long, silky blond hair. The woman sitting in the anchor chair was Bethany, but it did not look like Bethany. Her face was sunken in and her hair was unkempt. It looked like her death was imminent. She kept coughing on the air, which was a big no-no in the industry, but what else could she do? She was dying and everyone watching at home knew it.

The station replayed a clip from yesterday — patients had been pouring into the nearby hospitals from all over the area, trying to find some kind of help to ease their suffering, but nothing the doctors did seemed to help. The hospital eventually had to turn patients away because it did not have enough beds and was running low on supplies. Bethany was there on site, reporting on the overcrowding. She wore a white mask that looked more like a respirator from a hardware store than a medical mask, while she interviewed several nurses and patients, all of whom looked sick.

The woman in the replayed news clip from yesterday looked like the Bethany that Glen remembered. It was highly discomforting to see just how quickly she had deteriorated in so little time. *That little white mask clearly didn't work*, Glen thought to himself.

Glen never cared for her and still didn't, even as he lay in bed watching her slowly die on national television. He had tried to sleep with her once, but she just laughed him off. She was a very stuck-up woman who walked around like her shit didn't stink. He couldn't stand her, but damn he wanted to have his way with her. She was one of those women who knew she was beautiful and flaunted it, even to other women. She wore tight shirts with an old-school bra that allowed her hard nipples to poke against her shirt for all to see. He couldn't stand those new push-up bras that were packed with padding — they just looked down right foolish. He figured women probably wore them to make their breasts look bigger, but he loved natural breasts of all sizes and enjoyed seeing hard nipples poking at him. That was probably the only thing Glen did like about Bethany.

Bethany sat at the news anchor desk swaying back and forth in her seat, staring off into space. No one was looking at her breasts today. Instead, viewers were probably waiting to see if she would either fall out of her seat or die in it. Glen, and all of the other viewers gasped as they witnessed small black marks form on Bethany's face while she gave what would be her final report on live TV.

9:33 A.M.

Chris Hughes, the new News Director at WTFH, stood in the production booth, unsure of what to do. This was his first director gig, and he didn't want to screw it up. He was contemplating going to commercial and calling an ambulance for Bethany when the red phone next to him started to ring. Chris knew there was only one person who would be calling the red phone and dreaded picking it up.

When he was given a tour of the production booth on his first day last week, he was told that if the red phone ever rang, he better answer it before the third ring if he wanted to keep his job. But he was also told that the red phone would never ring so no need to worry. He had been informed that only one person had the number for the red phone, and that was the station owner, Mr. Matthews. The other employees of the station, including the management, told him that the owner was a miserable, mean old man. Apparently, years ago, Mr. Matthews had come home early one day and found his wife in bed with another man, and that she left him and took half of his money with her. Shortly after the divorce, he became the lonely, miserable man he was today who only cared about one thing—the bottom line. Mr. Matthews didn't care about any individual story, but understood that certain stories drove his bottom line.

Chris had met Mr. Matthews briefly in the hall last week. The only thing the owner said to him was, "Don't fuck up!"

He reached across the control board and picked up the phone on the second ring.

"You best not pan away from her or it will be the last thing you do here at WTFH. Do you understand me?" Mr. Matthews asked.

"Yes sir. I understand."

"I don't care if that dumb twat dies on the air. Hopefully she does. It will be great for ratings. You stay on her until the end of the broadcast. Got it?"

"Yes sir."

"No commercials. If she dies, she dies on the air."

"I understand sir."

"You better!" he barked, and then the line went dead.

Chris stood, nearly paralyzed for a moment, processing what he just heard and said to himself, *Wow, what a heartless prick!*

He took a deep breath, reached out and pushed the talk button on the control board labeled "cameraman" and began to speak, "Derek, I need you to stay on Bethany, no matter what happens."

"Are you serious? She's falling apart!"

"I know, but I just received a call from Mr. Matthews telling me if we don't stay on Bethany, we'll be fired."

"Are you kidding me?"

"I wish I was. And no commercial breaks either."

"Jesus! He *wants* her to die on TV doesn't he?"

"I'm pretty sure he does."

"That's fucked up."

"I know, but I need my job, so please stay on her."

"Okay, I'll stay on Bethany."

Derek sighed in disgust. "Copy that. But Chris, what do we do if she does die?"

"I don't know. I'm hoping she'll make it until the end of the broadcast."

Just then Bethany lurched in her seat. Her body went rigid and she fell forwards, smashing her face into the anchor's desk. Her right cheek and shoulder were holding her onto the desk. Blood poured from a gash in her nose, which broke on impact and ran across the desk. David, her co-anchor pushed away from the desk and threw up his hands. The wheels on his chair launched him backwards several feet.

Bethany lifted her left hand and brought it up to her face, trying to stop the blood pouring from her nose. Her arm swung like a puppet's attached to a string. Her hand flopped onto the desk, splashing blood everywhere. She slowly tried to lift her head up off the desk.

"David, go assist her," Chris said into his earpiece.

David got up out of his chair and went over to her.

"Bethany! Are you okay?" David said as he put both hands on her shoulders and pulled her back from the table, sitting her upright. As Bethany's head came up off the table, her blond hair dragged through the pool of blood. Strands of her hair were soaked in blood, and they clung to her face. Blood dripped from her chin like an IV bag hanging from a pole on a fast drip.

David started to turn her chair towards him when she suddenly coughed, spraying blood all over him. David stood there in shock. Bethany's blood was in his mouth, and he could taste the warmth and saltiness of it.

David started spitting onto the floor and was on the verge of throwing up when Bethany's body started to tremble in his hands. He and the viewers watched her eyes roll up into her head. Her body went limp and yellowish-green pus started oozing from her mouth and nose, mixing with her blood.

David released Bethany's shoulders and jumped back. Her body went limp and fell forwards, and her head bounced off the desk with a loud *THUMP*. Her body hung there on the desk for a moment and slowly started sliding in the pool of crimson blood, then it slipped off the desk and out of sight from the camera. There was another loud *THUMP* when her corpse hit the floor.

Chris had had enough and reached over to press the button, ending the live feed. As he terminated the signal, another member in the control room pressed a few buttons to broadcast commercials.

Just then the red phone in the booth began to ring again.

Chris picked up the phone and held it to his ear, expecting to be screamed at and told to pack his belongings and get out.

"That was incredible! Is she dead?" Mr. Matthews asked.

"I don't know, sir."

"Find out."

Chris peered out the control booth window into the newsroom and saw most of the cast and crew standing over Bethany. "Is she alive?" he asked upon pressing the speaker button.

David was dry heaving with his hands on his knees, but was able to shake his head no.

Derek left his position behind the camera and went to check on Bethany. He knelt down next to her lifeless body and felt her wrist searching for a pulse. Blood slowly wept from the gash on the bridge of her nose and pooled on the floor next to her. Yellowish-green pus oozed from her mouth and nostrils, which gave off a foul odor. He kept his fingertips pressed against her wrist and counted off sixty seconds in his head. Nothing. He slowly moved his fingers, trying to find a pulse like he was taught last spring when he took a CPR course. Still nothing. He looked at her chest to see if it was rising and falling. Nothing. In his CPR class, he had been taught to put his ear next to the victims mouth and listen for any sounds of breathing, but he was not going anywhere near the retched pus oozing from her mouth.

Derek stood up and looked into the control booth window at Chris who was holding his hands up and mouthing, "Anything?" Derek shook his head no.

One of the assistants in the control booth tried calling 911, but received a message that all circuits were busy.

Chris took off his headset and was wondering what to do next when the red phone rang again.

"Yes, sir," Chris said as he answered the phone.

"Are you alone?" Mr. Matthews asked.

"Yes," he answered as he looked around the empty control room.

"I'm going to ask you a few obscure questions."

"Okay," Chris said with a certain type curiosity in his voice.

"Are you married or have a girlfriend?"

"No," Chis replied, not sure what the questions were about.

"Do you have any loved ones here in the city?"

"No, all of my family is back in Seattle."

"Now this is very important. Think back—have you had any contact with Bethany since she returned from that story she did at the hospital?"

"No," Chris answered. "She came right in and went straight to the anchor desk because she came in late. Makeup went to her to get her ready for the broadcast."

"I want you to use the intercom and ask the crew to drag Bethany's body out of the newsroom and out into the lobby. Tell them you made contact with 911 and that the paramedics are on their way. You're also to instruct them all to leave after they drag her body out, and that you will be out in a minute to meet the paramedics, that you are just getting the file on Bethany. Tell them now," Mr. Matthews said.

Chis pressed the intercom button and told the crew exactly what Mr. Matthews had said.

"Done," Chris said into the phone receiver as he released the intercom button.

"Once they leave, I want you to hit the automatic lock button to seal off the newsroom."

Chris watched as the crew dragged Bethany's body out into the lobby. Derek turned and looked back at him, and motioned for him to come.

Chris pushed the intercom button again and said, "I'm still on the phone with 911. I'll be right out," he said and then released the intercom button.

Derek waved goodbye and walked out. Once the door closed, Chris scanned the newsroom making sure no one was left behind and hit the auto-lock button for the doors to the newsroom.

"Done," Chris repeated.

"Are they all gone?"

"Yes sir. What is this all about?" Chris asked.

"I'm a bit of a survivalist, and I have enough supplies up here in my suite to last a month or more for two people. You just bought yourself a ticket to survival. See, when the dust settles, most of the people we know will be dead, and you and I will be the only ones left with the knowledge of how to run a news agency. I want you to leave the control room, lock the door behind you and take the back elevator to the fifty-eighth floor. Enter pound-eight-eight-four on the control panel, and that will grant you access to the top floor." Mr. Matthew's then hung up without waiting for Chris's reply.

Chapter 24

Friday, October 30th
9:40 A.M.

Stanley parked out back of the hotel, used his electronic key to gain entry, made his way up to his room, and flicked on the TV. The news was still running the same footage he had seen at the Johnsons' farm. He flipped up through several channels and stopped when his eyes caught hold of an unbelievable sight—a news anchor was covered in blood with black sores on her face and yellowish-green pus coming out of her nose and mouth. Taking a step back from the TV's horrible image, he covered his mouth in shock. The woman had just died on national TV.

Stanley picked up the hotel phone and tried to call home, but he instantly received an "all circuits are busy" message.

"Damn!" he shouted, slamming the phone down. He quickly picked it up again and dialed his wife's cell phone number. Again, he received the same automated message.

9:43 A.M.

Downstairs, the manager and two housekeepers stood next to the vending machine while a third removed sheets from the linen closet. All four of them kept sneezing as they waited to load up their carts.

"I knew I shouldn't have used that pen the man from New York used to check in last night," the manager complained. "I totally watched him wipe his nose with his fingers before he touched it. Now I probably have whatever he has."

Within minutes, all four women felt lethargic. Their heads were pounding, and the inside of their throats felt like they had just swallowed razor blades. The manager sneezed and sent yellowish-green snot flying.

"Gross! Cover your nose," one of the housekeepers said as she wiped the fine mist of snot off her arm.

9:45 A.M.

Stanley grabbed his suitcase, placed it on the bed and rounded up his loose clothes. He ran into the bathroom, gathered up all his toiletries and stuffed them into his suitcase. Suddenly, he felt afraid as an inexplicable chill filled the room, and he got the strangest notion that an unearthly presence was with him. Though his unexpected feeling defied all logic, he couldn't help but to instinctively stop what he was doing to look around.

Movement out of the corner of his eye.

He could've sworn he was hallucinating, but a dark, minacious figure glided across the room towards the bed. The form passed right in front of him. He was only able to move his eyes as his body was paralyzed with fear, and he watched as the form floated across the room and disappeared into the wall. His body jerked and he snapped himself free from terror's grip, quickly grabbing his suitcase, then bolting for the door. Stanley made his way down the hall while his mind raced. *It was just a shadow and nothing more. You freaked yourself out over a shadow.* But the fact that his legs continued to hurry proved he had not convinced himself.

He reached the elevator and hit the call button. In a minute the elevator doors opened, and he wasted no time stepping inside and pushing the button for the lobby. As he waited impatiently, his eyes widened and goosebumps formed on his arms when he caught sight of the ominous figure moving down the hall, closing in on the elevator.

"Jesus! Come on!" he shouted as he frantically pressed the button for the lobby over and over again. The dark shadowy figure was within mere feet of the elevator when the doors finally closed. Stanley felt a wave of relief wash over him as the elevator descended. The doors opened, and he walked briskly towards the front desk, constantly looking back over his shoulder. When he arrived at the front desk there was no one there to check him out. *Figures!* he nearly mumbled as he glanced around, looking for the girl who worked behind the counter. He saw a little silver bell on the counter and gave it a tap while continuing to check over his shoulder down the hallway, towards the elevator. He reached into his pocket, took out his rental car key and held it in his left hand, wanting to be ready to bolt if that shadowy thingy came back.

With every second that passed, a sense of urgency increased tenfold in Stanley's bones. Fighting off panic with every fiber of his willpower, he reached up and tapped the bell repeatedly. He stepped away from the counter to check the elevator again when he noticed a TV mounted on the wall in the dining area to his left. A shocked look washed over his face when he looked at the screen and saw the sheet-covered bodies lining the streets of New York City.

What the hell is going on? He said to himself as he turned back towards the still-vacant counter. Refusing to wait any longer, he plopped his key card next to the bell, grabbed his belongings, and made a beeline for the front door, daring one more glance behind his shoulder to make sure that creepy shadow thing wasn't following him. Given the current national crisis, he was certain the hotel staff would understand his skipping out. And if they didn't, they could hash it out with him once the world returned to normal. Besides, they had his credit card on file.

As Stanley made his way through the parking lot toward his rental car, he glanced over when he passed by the side entrance door, then suddenly stopped. It took his brain a second to process what his eyes saw. He slowly approached the door, staring through the bottom pane of glass at the pair of white-stockinged legs lying on the floor inside. Pressing his face to the window, he cupped his hands around his eyes, blocking the sun's glare.

His brain finally caught up with his eyes, and he let out a gasp. Two housekeeping staff members and the manager were lying on the floor near the base of the stairs. Their bodies were covered with black marks, and a yellowish-green froth ran down their cheeks and pooled on the floor. The manager's eyes were cold, lifeless and appeared glassed over. The warm, gentle smile she had greeted him with upon his arrival was gone and had been replaced with a look that showed she had suffered an agonizing death.

It's spreading, he thought. Just then he noticed the baleful shadowy thing gliding down the stairs towards him, and his legs automatically backed away from the glass.

With his heart was pounding with dread, Stanley turned and sprinted for his rental car. He had no time to open the trunk, so he flung open the driver's door and threw his suitcase into the passenger seat as he jumped in. He started the car, put it in drive and pushed down on the accelerator as hard as he could. The tires squealed as he shot out of the parking spot, almost hitting the vehicle parked across from him.

He glanced in the rearview mirror and saw the dreadful thing float right through the hotel door and out into the parking lot behind him.

"Come on baby!" Stanley screamed as he again pushed the accelerator to the floor. The engine roared and he felt the car come to life as he raced towards the entrance. He barely touched the brakes as he rounded the corner, exiting the hotel parking lot. All four tires squealed, trying to stay on the ground as he sped through the turn. The highway entrance was a hundred yards up on the left, and he kept his foot on the accelerator until he reached the intersection, where he turned the wheel as he jammed the brakes, causing the back end of the car to swing around. Then, like a professional racer, he stomped on the accelerator and launched up the highway's on-ramp.

He looked in the rearview mirror again and let out a sigh of relief when he saw there was nothing behind him. After thanking God that the menacing shadow apparently gave up its pursuit, he shot onto the highway and started laughing at the movie-stuntman driving he had just pulled off.

Stanley was cruising eastbound down the highway when he remembered the terrible reports on the news. Though he would have preferred his custom selection of music more than anything right now, updates on the country's status unfortunately took precedence. As soon as he turned on the radio and switched it from CD to FM, he heard the electronic voice of the Emergency Broadcast System announcing a national pandemic emergency had been declared.

My God, he thought as he looked down at the radio.

Stanley looked back up just in time to hit the brakes, using both feet to stomp down and causing the rental's engine to pitch down as the brakes locked up. The car jostled and shook as the tires caught on the pavement, leaving rubber trails fused to the road, and its front end was inches from the stopped vehicle in front of him.

Traffic had come to a halt because there was a bad wreck up ahead on the opposite side of the highway. One of the vehicles had caught fire, and red flames danced and licked at the bottom of the thick, billowing black smoke that spiraling into the air for all to see.

That's not good, Stanley said to himself as he noticed a body that had been ejected from the crash, lying in the middle of the road on his side of the highway a few cars up.

He got out of the rental car and made his way towards the mangled body in the road to see if there was anything he could do to help him or her. As he approached, he noticed it was a blond-haired woman lying in the road wearing a yellow dress. Stanley quickened his pace towards her, until he was close enough to realize her forehead had been split open, and he quickly grew nauseous at the sight of exposed brain matter, not to mention the woman's eyeball that was hanging out of its socket, resting in a pool of blood.

Turning and covering his mouth in an effort to stop himself from vomiting, he moved hastily over to the Jersey barrier that separated the highway. There was a white hardtop convertible with its rear-end completely smashed up. It had come to rest against the barrier and had a large hole in the windshield where the woman in the yellow dress had apparently been ejected.

He hopped over the barrier and rushed towards the other cars involved in the accident. The one that was on fire must have slammed into the back of the white convertible—its front-end was caved in. It looked as if it had spun around before it came to a stop in the center lane. Fire engulfed the entire front of the car, including the driver who was still in the vehicle, and the back tires were hissing from the intense heat.

There was nothing he could do. Seeing the driver had long since burned to death, Stanley turned and headed for the two cars farther back with minimal damage.

"Those poor people!" someone shouted.

"It's that blue car's fault! They just stopped in the middle of the road," someone else shouted and pointed to the blue automobile.

Stanley advanced towards the blue car and could see right away that the driver was slumped over the wheel. As he approached the car, he was startled by an explosion which sent a large chunk of debris sailing past him. He turned around and saw a large fireball rising from the back of the car on fire. *Gas tank must have exploded*, he thought, then turned and picked up his pace until he reached the blue car, hoping its driver was not yet beyond help like the others.

"Hey, are you alright?" Stanley shouted through the closed window of the driver's side door.

The driver did not move.

"Hey, you okay?" he repeated more loudly, this time banging on the window. Just as he reached to open the door, he noticed the driver, a young woman, was covered with black marks all over her face, and a yellowish-green pus ran from her mouth. He quickly retracted his hand, and at the same time noticed a small boy restrained in a car seat. The boy was also covered with black marks and had yellowish-green froth coming from his mouth.

Stanley was slowly backing away from the car when he saw the forbidding shadowy thing from earlier on the other side. It was staring at him and pointed at him as if it wanted him dead. He turned and stumbled, but was able to catch himself, and immediately broke out in a full sprint across the highway back the way he had come, until he reached his rental car.

He wanted to take a moment to catch his breath as his lungs were on fire but he couldn't stop, knowing in his heart the otherworldly phantom was somehow connected to this plague, and fearing it would kill him like it had the others. He started up the rental and put it into reverse. The tires squealed again as the car flew backwards, and he drove several hundred yards in reverse before slowing down and doing a three-point turn. With a death grip on the steering wheel, he sped back the way he had come, hoping there would be no more oncoming traffic since he was driving the wrong way up the highway. But he had only driven a mile or two before he found an emergency vehicle turn off resting in the middle of the divided highway.

Once he piloted the car back onto the correct side, he floored it, having little to worry about other vehicles since he was now ahead of the accident that had completely blocked all traffic.

What do I do? he thought to himself. He grabbed his cell phone and tried calling home again. "All circuits are busy," again.

The Johnsons, he thought. *I'll go back to the Johnsons.*

10:23 A.M.

Stanley turned down the same driveway he had pulled out of roughly four hours ago. The Johnsons' house had never looked so welcoming.

Bill was in the barn cleaning out the stables when he heard the car turn onto the gravel driveway. He walked over to the barn door, putting his hand to his brow to block the sun and to get a better view. Maureen had come onto the porch also having been alarmed by the aggressive sound of the approaching vehicle.

The car came to a sliding halt, and the driver's side door swung open.

"Stan, what are you doing back here?" asked Bill, as he walked over with concern for the man.

Maureen came off the porch and, standing closer to Stanley, instantly noticed the cell phone in his hand and the worried look on his face. "What's wrong?" she asked.

"The sickness is here," Stanley said.

"What do you mean, the sickness is here?" Bill asked.

"Back at the hotel, the housekeepers were all dead. They were covered with those black marks and stuff was oozing from their mouths."

"Are you serious?" Bill asked.

"Yes, and then there was a bad accident out on the highway and there were bodies in the road," Stanley said. Maureen gasped and covered her mouth. "And there was another car with a mother and her small child still strapped into the car seat. Both of them were dead and covered with those black marks." Tears rolled down his face.

Maureen went to give him a hug and console him, but Bill reached out and grabbed her arm, pulling her back. She turned and looked at her husband who had never grabbed her like that before.

"Stan, how do we know you're not infected if you saw those bodies?" Bill asked.

Maureen, now knowing why he prevented her from consoling Stan, took a step back.

"I saw the housekeepers through the glass door, and the people in the cars still had their windows up," Stanley said.

"You said you saw bodies lying in the road. You could have been infected by them," Bill said.

"I don't think I was close enough to them to get infected. I was a good twenty to thirty yards away."

"Are you sure?" Maureen asked.

"Yes," replied Stanley hoping he wasn't infected.

Maureen looked down at Stanley's cell phone in his hand, which reminded him to tell them about the phones.

"I tried calling my wife at home, but the call won't go through. All I get is an 'all circuits are busy' message. Same goes for her cell phone too."

"Let's try our phone," Maureen said.

She hurried into the house, the screen door slamming shut behind her, then proceeded into the kitchen, lifted the phone off the receiver and put it up to her ear. No dial tone. She clicked the button, but nothing—the line was dead.

"Well?" asked Bill as Maureen approached.

"Nothing. Not even a dial tone."

"What is the news saying?" Stanley asked.

"Let's go check," Bill said.

"Is it safe?" Maureen asked as he nodded her head towards Stanley.

"We'll just have to put our trust in the Lord," Bill replied and they all walked up to the house.

Once inside, Bill walked into the living room and turned on the TV.

The three of them stood there, staring dumbfounded at the Emergency Alert System on the screen with only the eerie, foreboding buzzing that accompanied it, which told them more than any news reported could at this point.

Chapter 25

Annabelle sat on the couch and cried uncontrollably. She couldn't get her last image of Drew, his face in the window of the plane before it blew up, out of her mind. Outside, the dark and gloomy weather of late October matched the mood inside the house.

"I can't believe he's gone," she said through the tears.

"At least it was quick and he didn't suffer, honey," Susan said.

"He did suffer though," Annabelle replied.

"You don't know that," Susan said trying to reassure her daughter.

"But I do!" Annabelle said as she held out her cell phone.

"What do you mean?" Susan asked confused.

"I made Drew suffer by not answering his texts or calls. He tried calling me from the plane." More tears streamed down her face. "How do I tell Stephanie her daddy is gone?"

Then, as if to add insult to injury, Stephanie came bumbling around the corner. "Daddy! Daddy!" Upon hearing his name.

Annabelle lost it and stuck her face into the seat cushion of the couch and sobbed.

Susan went and found another box of tissues since the one she kept in the living room was now empty. When she returned, she placed the new box on the couch armrest and began to rub her daughter's back to console her.

Annabelle sat up and grabbed a tissue, then wiped the tears away. Susan pulled her daughter into her chest and kissed the top of her head.

"The worst part is the last message I sent him. I told him I wanted a divorce," she said as she reached out and grabbed another tissue.

Susan reached down and gave her another kiss on top of her head, brushing the bangs out of her daughter's eyes.

Her chest started heaving again and the tears came streaming back as she said, "And the last thing Drew texted me was that he loved me."

6:18 P.M.

"Goddammit!" Susan said as things flew out of the junk drawer in the kitchen. She had just put the flashlight in there last week, after using it to find the back of her earring that had rolled under the fridge.

"Mom, are you sure it's in there?" Annabelle asked.

"Yes, I'm sure," Susan said as her hand grasped the cylindrical object and pulled it out, then flicked the switch and filled the kitchen with light.

"Do you still have the box of emergency candles in the hallway closet?"

"Yes, dear," Susan said as she made her way down the hallway, the light swaying side to side with each step.

Susan pulled out the box of candles, put it on the kitchen table and went back to the junk drawer to find the matches.

"Mom, I can do it," Annabelle said as her mother struck a match.

Susan lit the candle, and then handed the box of matches to Annabelle. "Light a few more while I go try and figure out the generator."

"You have a generator?" Annabelle asked surprised.

"Yes, your father insisted we get one after the terrible ice storm a few years back, when we were without power for over a week."

"I remember that storm," Annabelle recalled. "I lost most of the trees in my yard from that one."

"Your father had someone deliver the generator and set it up," Susan went on. "It sits out back behind the house, under a covered area, and the men who installed it hooked it up to the house somehow. Your father showed me how to use it. I'm just supposed to turn a switch and push a button."

"That's it? That sounds pretty easy," Annabelle said.

"Oh and add gas. Your father was a stickler for running out of gas. There's enough full gas canisters in the garage to last us over a week. Hopefully it still works. Be right back." She went downstairs and left through the back door.

Within a few minutes later, the lights flickered and came back on, followed by the television several seconds later. Susan had a satellite dish that allowed them to continue watching TV even though the power was out in the town.

Annabelle stood and watched the coverage in complete disbelief. The news was showing bodies out by the side of the road in every town, city and state. They showed a map of the United States that indicated every state now reported cases of the virus.

Even more distressing, the ticker on the bottom of the screen was reiterating an updated message that there was a ban on all travel until further notice, and anyone seen traveling would be shot on site.

She sat on the couch, put her head in her hands and thought, *How are we going to survive this?*

Chapter 26

Saturday, October 31st
6:34 A.M.

Drew woke up on the floor of the convenience store, surrounded by empty beer bottles and cans. It appeared he had tried stacking the empty cans up like a pyramid, but didn't remember doing so. He didn't remember drinking that many beers either, but the empties were all there on the floor. A slight but distinct smell of urine invaded his nostrils, which was weird because, after quickly checking himself, he had not pissed himself in the night, though he needed to go at the moment quite badly. He started up the main aisle and was heading for the front door when he noticed the unpleasant odor was getting stronger.

He looked down when he heard the splatter of water under his foot and saw that he was standing in a puddle of urine. *I must have been so drunk last night that I walked over here and pissed all over the floor,* he thought. Drew tiptoed through the urine and, as he approached the door, he noticed the sun was just starting to come up over the horizon. Stepping outside to answer Mother Nature's call, he saw that the young kid was still lying in the parking lot motionless. *What the hell made that kid come out of the store shooting like it was the O.K. Corral? Did he really snap over two packs of cigarettes?* Drew felt bad, but it was either him or the kid. *Sorry kid.*

Once finished he went back inside and gathered a few supplies to take with him, sorting them on the counter next to the register. While searching behind the counter, he found the box of shells for the clerk's .38 snub nose revolver. He reloaded the pistol, tucked it into his front waistband, then filled his pockets with shells. Next, he found some plastic bags behind the counter and loaded a few up with food supplies and water. Lastly, though hesitating slightly, he grabbed the little round plastic container filled with tiny bottles of booze and dumped them into a separate plastic bag. *A few for the road,* he thought as he gathered up his bags and exited the store.

Drew strode past the pickup truck where Brad's body lay slumped over, and suddenly all the wild and unlikely events that occurred the day before filled his mind: the airline passengers quickly turning into a mindless mob, followed by the explosion at the airport, and now one of the two survivors getting his brains shot out over a pack of cigarettes. It was hard to believe just how much had gone to shit so quickly. Staring at Brad's remains while reflecting on the past twenty-four hours, Drew noticed it was uncannily quiet, save for the gentle breeze rustling through the nearby trees and the circling swarm of flies that had descended upon the two fresh corpses. *The world is no longer the place it was yesterday*, he thought to himself as he checked both pistols, then placed the .38 in his front pocket and the 9mm tucked in his back waistband. He took one last moment of silence out of respect for Brad and his short-lived friendship with him, and then set out on his way up the road on foot.

He had hiked about three-quarters of a mile, and was approaching the on-ramp for State Road 528, when he noticed a large retail store to his right with a sign in the window announcing a sale on camping gear. *Jackpot*, he silently cheered as he cut across the parking lot towards the front door. He tried to look in through a window, but couldn't see anything because the glare from the sun on the window was so bright.

The world has changed, Drew reminded himself, not wishing to end up like Brad. He put the plastic bags down, reached behind into his waistband and pulled out the 9mm handgun, then gently pushed open the front door, taking a few stealthy steps inside to let his eyes adjust from the bright Florida sun to the darker interior of the store. He remained motionless with the gun out in front of his body, looking and listening for any noises.

Once his sight adjusted, he slowly started moving towards the sporting goods section in the back corner of the store, cautiously looking up and down every aisle, not wanting to be caught off guard again. Not even halfway into the store, the unmistakable stench of death and decay made its presence known. Forcing back a gag, he pulled a shirt off one of the clothing racks and held it to his face. He could see the fishing poles sticking up from the sporting goods section and knew he was close. After passing a few more aisles, he finally saw the sign for the guns and picked up his pace towards it.

Drew turned the corner, and even though the large glass cabinets filled with rifles on his left were what he had been searching for, his eyes instead became focused on the dead employee, now finding where the smell was coming from. There was a blood trail that led down the aisle to where the employee lay with a gunshot wound in his back. It appeared that someone, or more likely a group of someones, had smashed the glass counter and had stolen the handguns and ammo before killing the store employee with them.

He couldn't care less about the handguns—the rifles were what he was after. He wanted to be able to reach out and touch someone from a long distance with the rifle, if need be, before that someone could get close enough to touch him.

Drew needed to find a way into the cabinets to get the rifles out. He contemplated searching the dead store employee for the cabinet key, but figured the smell would get even worse when he got closer. He walked around into the next aisle and found the right tool for the job. Tucking the 9mm in the small of his back, he grabbed an aluminum baseball bat from a nearby shelf and headed back to the rifle cabinet. It took a couple swings, but the glass finally broke.

He reached in and grabbed the pump action 12-gauge shotgun and an AR-15—the civilian version of the military's M-16, then broke a smaller cabinet to retrieve some ammo, where he also found a scope for the rifle, which would certainly enable him to reach out and touch someone. The shotgun, not so much, but it was ideal for any possible close encounters, and it had a hell of a lot more stopping power than the 9mm.

Drew noticed a lawn-furniture display with a table, chairs and umbrella setup. He carried the weapons and ammo over and placed them on the table, then sat down and proceeded to load the shotgun. Once finished, he pumped and chambered a round making it ready to fire, then carried it with him to the front of the store and back outside. Within a minute or two he returned inside, now carrying the plastic bags he'd left, and brought them back to the table. It was time for a drink.

He needed a hair of the dog today. He never knew why, but having another drink always seemed to cure his hangover. Drew pounded down the drink and began loading the magazine for the rifle. He made another when he started to feel that sharp pain in his left side again, which, as of late, always came whenever he downed hard alcohol. His solution: have another drink to dull the pain, which is what he did.

He was feeling pretty good for eight in the morning and went to pull another small bottle of booze from the plastic bag when it ripped. *Well, I can't carry it like that*, he thought as he grabbed the shotgun and went in search of a backpack to carry his supplies.

Drew quickly found the hiking section and selected a pack with a metal frame that would allow him to carry more weight. The pack reminded him again of his days in the service, and he suddenly realized the high likelihood that he'd have to travel on foot from this point forward. *No way the roads will be clear during a shitstorm like this.* Understanding how fortune favors the prepared, he made a quick mental checklist of all necessities, then went on a shopping spree.

Drew got himself into a routine in which he would grab any and all items that he would need for the long trek home, until the pack was full, then bring them to the table and stack them up. His idea was to sort everything, then start separating what was essential from what he felt he could do without. So far he had for his potential inventory a down sleeping bag and a rolled-up foam mat, in case he had to sleep on the ground, a pair of high quality hiking sneakers, several pairs of socks, some sport-style with moisture absorbency and some wool ones for warmth, synthetic underwear, a waterproof poncho and rain slacks, a compass, and a Swiss Army Knife. There was still plenty more to gather, and he had to remind himself to leave room for food.

He was about to search for a good first aid kit when he felt a chill in the air that caused goose bumps to form on his skin. For some reason, be it instinct or some sixth sense he was unaware of, Drew turned back in the direction of the table and immediately saw it. His grip tightened on the shotgun and he placed his finger on the trigger. There appeared to be a dark, shadowy humanoid thing of some sort near the table, except it seemed to be moving in a very non-human way.

He inched a little farther before stopping to watch the figure. An arm appeared from the shadow and Drew's eyes widened as long black finger type things curled out.

The plastic bag crinkled as the thing's fingers entered the bag. The hand retracted, holding one of the little bottles of booze. The shadow seemed to be studying the bottle. The thing's hand turned over and a bottle rolled out of its hand and fell back into the bag.

Drew was mesmerized. He didn't know what he was looking at, but his heart was racing with fear inside his chest, and the angel's kiss on his forehead started to throb. Drew watched as the menacing looking figure then picked up the glass he had been drinking out of earlier. The figure brought the glass up to where its face would have been, as if it was smelling the contents of the cup.

Deep down inside, Drew felt something he hadn't felt in quite a while—rage. It was the type of rage he had carried around for years for his father. The type of rage that kept him warm on cold nights. The type of rage that, combined with his training to run towards danger as a Marine and EMT, set off a storm inside him.

"Hey! What the fuck are you doing?" he yelled as he advanced towards the dark figure. The thing looked up and dropped the glass it was holding, letting it bounce off the table and shatter upon the floor. Drew shouldered the butt of the shotgun, pointing it at the figure as he continued towards it.

A funny thing would happen to Drew during intense or scary situations. His blood pressure and heart rate would drop, his mind would focus on what needed to be done, and he would do it. He was known to take action in the face of fear, whereas most others were crippled by it.

He stopped, took a stance and leaned into the shotgun, unsure if what he was seeing was real, or if it was the booze or his subconscious messing with him from the events of the last few days. "If I'm going crazy, I'm going out with a bang," he said out loud as he looked down the barrel, aimed it at the unnatural figure and squeezed the trigger.

Drew was ready for the kickback, having braced himself, but the sound of the shotgun going off inside the store was deafening. If he hadn't seen it, he wouldn't have believed it. The shotgun slug tore right through the shadowy figure. But it disappeared like a puff of smoke and was gone. The items on the shelf behind the display table and chairs exploded, scattering items everywhere.

Drew remained motionless at first, unable to determine if what he just saw was his imagination or if he had just come face to face with death itself. He also wondered if he should quit drinking or drink more after this inexplicable encounter, but, unlike the first, that was a question he could answer, which he did so when he reached into the plastic bag on the table, took out a nip, twisted off the cap and downed it.

After several consecutive drinks, he concluded it was all in his head. There was no other logical explanation. Besides, he had more immediate problems to solve, especially when his stomach grumbled.

After collecting further necessary items commonly utilized for long-distance backpacking, Drew found the food section of the store, gathered non-perishables and then loaded his pack with all of his supplies. He searched the gun cases again and found slings for both the shotgun and rifle. Then he put on the pack, adjusted the straps and finally slung the weapons over his shoulder. Before heading for the exit, he grabbed an atlas off an end cap of the checkout line. It was going to be a long way home.

After countless miles heading east on State Road 528, his legs and back were starting to hurt from carrying all the extra weight. He thought to himself, *I'm not twenty anymore,* as he wiped sweat from his brow. The hot Florida sun was unrelenting and was worsened by the black asphalt. He could already feel the back of his neck starting to burn, and he cursed at himself for not thinking to grab sunblock. All the booze from earlier was now working against him, and he had already consumed all of the water he brought with him. In an attempt to get his mind off his thirst and the pain, he started to think about the sickness and wondered how far it had spread. Everyone must've been dead or hiding—he hadn't seen a single person since he shot the kid back at the convenience store.

A smile flashed upon his face when finally came upon a sign that said "Interstate 95, 1 Mile." Once he got on I-95, he was welcomed by another sign for a rest area up ahead.

Chapter 27

Saturday, October 31th
11:05 A.M.

Cass and Greg enjoyed the nice fall day, sitting down on the little beach by the cabin. Shawn and Renell were inside, lying on the sectional, enjoying each other's bodies while drinking and smoking pot. Jim and Jessica were on their way back to the campus to get Jim's car and to stop for more beers and a pizza.

"This is so relaxing, I could do this all day long," Cass said. "I dread finding a job after college and working forty hours a week."

"Babe, we won't be working after college," Greg laughed. "We can do whatever we want."

"How will we survive?" she asked as she folded down her bikini top and applied more sunscreen to her breasts.

"My father's rich. He'll probably give us a house if we get married after college."

"You want to get married?" Cass asked with excitement in her voice.

"Sure, babe. Why not?"

"Well, it's something we never discussed," she said.

"We're discussing it now. You're not like the other girls at school. All they want to do is get a job and become successful. They want to spend every minute studying and working. College was made for partying and doing nothing. It's not my fault their parents aren't rich, and they have to work for the rest of their lives."

"I know," Cass agreed. "I think my parents paid for me to come here just to get me out of the house. My mother was always complaining I didn't help out around the house. I mean really — why should I pick up their house? It's not mine."

"See, you get it," Greg said. "Why should we have to do those things when we have the money to pay someone else to do it? After we're married and my dad gives us a house, we'll get a maid, and she can do all the cleaning. We can lay in bed all day, go to the beach or to the movies and do what we want or do nothing at all."

"I knew there was a reason I loved you," she said, happy she found a man who wouldn't make her clean the house and do chores like her parents did.

"I love you too, babe," he replied.

She turned in her chair, leaned over and gave Greg a long, passionate kiss, and reached over and placed her hand on his crotch.

Their romantic moment was cut short when they heard shouting coming from the cabin. Cass stood up, used the back of her hand to wipe her mouth and then dusted off her knees. Greg adjusted his shorts and got up out of his seat. When more shouting came from the cabin, they looked at each other and both hurried up the dirt path to the cabin.

Cass was the first through the door and saw Shawn and Renell sitting on the large sectional with perplexed looks on their faces.

"What's wrong?" Cass asked.

"We need to leave now!" Jim shouted from the back room.

"Did he say we need to leave?" Greg asked.

"Jim, what's wrong?" Cass repeated.

"Where's the pizza?" Shawn asked, clearly too stoned to comprehend what was going on.

"Did you hear Jim? We need to leave now!" Jessica screamed from the back room as she threw her belongings into a bag.

"Why?" asked Greg as he walked over to the fridge and took out the last beer.

"Jim, what's going on?" Cass asked more loudly, growing frustrated by her previous failed attempts to get an answer out of him.

Jim walked over to Greg, grabbed the beer from his hand and slammed it down on the table, "Everyone's dead, that's why!" Jim shouted.

"Wait, who's dead?" asked Cass.

"Everyone back at school," Jessica cried hysterically.

"There are bodies everywhere," Jim said as he rushed into the small bedroom and started packing his belongings.

"Wait, are you serious?" Cass asked.

"Yes, I'm fucking serious! You can stay if you want to, but Jessica and I are leaving," Jim said.

Jessica went to the other side of the bed and finished packing up her belongings.

"How did they all die?" Cass asked still confused as to what was going on.

"We don't know, but there were bodies all over campus," Jessica said.

"Are you coming?" Jim shouted.

Cass stood there for a moment, thinking Jim was never one for practical jokes and was usually the most serious one of the group. She turned to Greg and said, "Go pack your stuff. If Jim says we need to leave, we need to leave."

Cass took off running into her room and started packing up her things.

"Wait, are we leaving?" asked Shawn.

"Put the bong down and pack your shit," Jim ordered, his eyes almost bulging out of his head.

11:25 A.M.

Pieces of their belongings were hanging out of their bags. Clothing kept getting caught on small protruding branches of the shrubs and underbrush as they ran down the path towards Jim's car. When they'd arrived, Jim had driven over the grass and parked right at the entrance of the path. Now, he popped open the trunk, and everyone threw in their bags. The six of them were used to taking Jim's car off campus and had found the best way to cram six people into the little car.

Everyone quickly jammed in, and Jim hit the gas. The spinning tires tore up the grass, spitting it everywhere, and the ass end of the car fishtailed across the open area until they reached the road. The car lunged as the spinning tires caught on the pavement.

Jim straightened out and gunned the gas, and the car took off down the road, its ass end hanging low with all the extra weight.

The first building they passed was the science lab. There were two bodies lying at the base of the stairs.

"Oh my God!" screamed Renell when she saw the bodies.

"Jim, speed up!" Jessica said, knowing they were about to pass the cafeteria where most of the bodies were. Jim stepped on the gas, but had to slow down for the speed bump, fearing he would break something if he drove too fast.

Cass was looking out the window closest to the cafeteria when they drove by. She let out an audible gasp when she saw all the bodies everywhere. She looked into the big windows next to the cafeteria's front door and noticed a large pile of bodies crowded there.

"What the hell happened?" asked Shawn as they drove past.

"Do you think it was a gunman?" asked Cass.

"I don't know," Jim said, "But I'm not stopping to ask."

"What's going on!" Renell screamed and started crying.

Jim made it past the last speed bump and stepped on the gas, heading for the main road into town.

3:52 P.M.

Jim kept his foot pressed hard on the accelerator, and the car shook as it went over every bump. They weren't sure what had happened to everyone back at school, but they each had their own theory.

Greg said he thought it could have been a gunman on the loose. Renell believed it was food poisoning in the cafeteria food because she swore the food tasted funny the last few days. Shawn agreed with her, since all the bodies they saw were in and around the cafe. Jim said he was with Greg and thought it was a gunman since there had been so many shootings on college campuses lately.

Cass and Jessica both agreed it had to have been a terrorist attack. "They probably used chemical weapons or something," Jessica said. "Cass and I learned all about how terror attacks have increased across the globe when we did our research paper for Mr. Stapleton's class."

"Check to see if there's someone following us," Jim said, trying to see out of his rearview mirror, which was damn near impossible with six people crammed into his tiny car.

"I think I see a car way back there, Jim," Cass said, arching her neck to see out the back window.

Jim pushed harder on the gas pedal, but it was already to the floor. His small vehicle wasn't made to hold the weight of six people.

"Are they still there?" Jim asked, knowing he couldn't gain any more speed.

Cass shifted on Greg's lap, allowing her to get a better view out the back window.

"I think you lost them. I don't see them anymore," Cass said with a good view of the road behind them.

"Wait, where are all the other cars?" Renell asked as she adjusted her seat on Shawn's bony knees.

Both Jim and Greg instantly started looking for other cars but didn't see any.

"Where the hell are all the other cars?" Jim said as he slammed his fist down on the steering wheel.

"Well, like, if it was a school shooting, like, wouldn't everyone evacuate?" Renell said.

"True! True!" Shawn said, "Maybe they all evacuated."

"Where are all the police cars then?" asked Cass.

Silence filled the car while each of them again pondered what had happened.

"So what do we do now?" Cass asked.

"Jim, take I-95 South up here. We'll head to my dad's beach house in Florida," Greg said.

"Okay," Jim said. He saw the sign for I-95 South up ahead and, once they cleared on the on-ramp, Jim floored it again, forcing the tiny engine to whine under the strain of the six-person load.

They drove for miles not seeing a single car, but that was normal for that stretch of road.

Suddenly it felt like the car was losing power.

"Jim, why are we slowing down?" Cass asked. Jim looked down at the gas gauge and saw the needle was on E.

Chapter 28

By the fourth day, world governments had collapsed and time as it was known had stopped. Washington, DC, like most other large cities, had a high death toll, most of them government workers. Professionals with invaluable knowledge and experience were among the dead. The sickness spread without discrimination. Poor people, rich people, people from the middle class—no one was safe. The plague spread at an incalculable pace and was estimated that between 25−30 million had died in the first three days in the U.S. alone. Ten percent of the nation's population was now gone. Billions were dead worldwide.

The government implemented the Emergency Broadcast System, and a recorded message was put on a constant loop. News agencies closed and went off the air. Most of the nation's reporters were the first to die, right behind health care professionals. As usual, the reporters and camera crews had arrived on scene to broadcast the events as they unfolded, in most cases interviewing the sick and dying. Many returned to the stations after being out in the field, infecting most of their colleagues. By the second day, most television and radio stations were shut down.

Many fire departments were now just empty buildings since almost every firefighter across the country had been infected by sick patients. Calls came into every firehouse across the country. The sickness had spread so far and so fast, it was beating media coverage. At first it was reported to be isolated to the Northeast only, but soon the heart of the country had infected patients, followed by the West Coast. Within hours it had spread to all four points of the nation.

Public transportation had shut down. Buses and trains were soon littered with corpses and stopped running. People were trapped with no way home. Drivers who had not been infected abandoned their buses—they were pulling over, opening the doors, getting out and walking away. Trains went screaming by stations, not stopping to pick up or drop off passengers. The conductors wanted to get back to get their own cars and return home.

Workers at power plants walked off their jobs, leaving the stations unmanned with no one to regulate the power running through the lines. And when people racing to get home drove like crazed lunatics, crashing into poles and knocking out power, neighborhoods across the country were left in the dark. All of the linemen had gone home, leaving no one to fix downed power lines. Buildings caught fire and quickly spread to adjacent structures, then spread further still, since there were no firefighters to man the apparatus. Whole neighborhoods and city blocks burned to the ground.

The looting didn't last long. Soon people started avoiding each other as the fear of catching the sickness outweighed the need to loot. Survivors were warned to stay away from the bodies of the sick and dying.

The Pentagon tried to put the National Guard into the major cities to enforce martial law, but a large population of the troops became infected. Many died before they even reached the cities, and the rest abandoned their posts.

Distribution of goods came to a screeching halt. Truck drivers didn't show up to pick up their cargo, which didn't matter because the warehouse workers didn't show up for loading. Supplies weren't being delivered. Food that was on grocery store shelves sat spoiling, because people feared venturing out with all of the dead and decomposing bodies everywhere. They would either have to live on what they had stockpiled in their pantries or risk catching the sickness. Fear crippled the living.

The forward progression of time had ended, and the countdown to extinction had begun.

Chapter 29

Kendra could hear people crying and screaming out for help from the apartments below, but she didn't dare open her door. She had gone grocery shopping the other day in preparation of her week off from work. That was a luxury of the business she was in, making enough money that she could take one week off every month. After working so many long hours during the other three, she needed that time to recover. Normally, Kendra would use her week to lock herself away in her apartment and simply veg, catch up on TV shows, and sleep. But without that time off, she would never get the opportunity to enjoy her place or the spectacular view, nor would she last long in her line of work.

She kept the news on until it went off the air. The only thing on the TV now was the Emergency Alert System's constantly looping message. When she could no longer stand the electronic voice, she hit the mute button but left the television on, just in case.

Eventually the screams and crying below faded away, but were replaced by someone walking back and forth down the hall banging on doors. "Anyone home?" the voice shouted. It sounded like the young man one floor below, who lived with his rich parents. She thought his name was Hector. He was always trying to sell her something whenever she would go out in the middle of the day. He was one of those types who wanted to work, but never had a job. He just tried to peddle stuff he had probably stolen. She had asked him once where he got the things he was selling to which he replied, "I found them." She knew he was lying when he tried to sell her a nice ceramic vase that the woman in Apartment 508 had reported stolen after her apartment had been broken into months ago.

Kendra checked the deadbolt on the front door and latched the chain. She didn't trust Hector, and there was a frightening aggressiveness in his voice that plucked the strings of her female instincts, warning her that extra caution may be in order. Retrieving her purse from the kitchen island, she reached in for her handgun she had purchased for protection. In her line of work, it was pretty much a requirement. As she pulled the gun out, a small bag of cocaine slipped from her purse and fell to the floor. One of the guys from the club had it given to her the other night.

I've got nothing but time to kill, she thought, especially since Hector's voice grew more distant, indicating he was heading in the opposite direction, so her nerves relaxed a bit. As she dumped out a little bit of cocaine onto the onyx countertop, she opened a drawer and grabbed a butter knife to make a long thin line. Then she picked up a little coffee stirrer with which she sniffed the coke all at once.

Feeling energized, she made herself some scrambled eggs and wheat toast, then sat down at the table next to the window that overlooked Orlando. The city looked dead. There were cars everywhere, but none were moving. It looked like a scene from a horror movie about the end of the world. She went over to her telescope and started scanning the city, barely able to believe what the lens was showing her.

From way up high, they looked like little dots on the street or bags of trash. But once she looked through the telescope she saw that they were not bags of trash, but people. Dead people. Some were covered with sheets or tarps while others were exposed for anyone to see.

She stepped back from the telescope and moved to the window sill, wanting to look down and see if there were any bodies lining the street below. When she pressed her forehead against the window and looked down. She instantly spotted movement below. Two men exited the apartment building across from hers and rolled a woman's body out into the street like she was a piece of trash. One of the men stood there and wiped his nose before heading back inside. Kendra was standing on her tippy toes, trying to see the front entrance of her apartment building below. She slid her forehead to the left and saw a pile of bodies out front. She couldn't believe it. It was like watching the news on TV, but out of her window instead.

As she looked back to the right she saw someone walking. She was still on her tippy toes, which along with the balls of her feet were starting to cramp up. But she wanted to see who was down there. She could tell it was a man and then recognized it was Hector, carrying a plastic bag. She watched as he went over to the stack of dead bodies and started going through their pockets. He took rings off their fingers and watches off their wrists and put all of the loot into the shopping bag. Once he finished rummaging through the dead, he headed back towards the apartment building entrance directly below and disappeared from her view.

She put her heels down, wiggled her toes shaking off the cramps, and went back to the telescope to continue scanning the city. The airport off in the distance showed that a little thin line of smoke had replaced the once thick black cloud. Whatever had been burning was almost out now, she realized.

Kendra sat on the couch, the coke finally wearing off, and fear, along with the realization of what was happening started to settle in. She found herself holding her knees up to her chest, rocking herself and thinking, *What am I going to do? Everyone outside is dead. How will I survive? I'll run out of food and starve.* She released her legs from her chest and shot them out in front of her, stood up and bolted for the pantry, feeling a little relief when she verified she had approximately two weeks' supply of food. She was thankful she constantly went grocery shopping hungry, which always made her buy more, because she now had a decent stockpile that she would probably need.

Just when her anxiety began to settle, however, she heard the banging on her door.

"Let me in!"

It was Hector. He was back.

Kendra froze in place, trying not to make a sound, hoping he would go away.

"I know you're home. Let me in!" cried the voice on the other side of the door. She ran into the kitchen and grabbed the gun off the island. The pounding turned into kicking, and she could hear the wood splitting on the door.

She tip-toed out of the kitchen with the gun out in front of her, aiming at the door and praying the chain would hold.

Hector was now screaming for her to let him in and started using his shoulder to try and force the door open.

She stood there shaking. The gun was wobbling all over the place, and she could feel sweat dripping down her back. Her adrenaline was pumping.

"Let me in!" Hector shouted again.

"I have a gun. Go away!" Kendra yelled.

"Let me in, you fucking slut!"

She used her right thumb and pulled the hammer back on the handgun.

"Let me in, you bitch! I'm gonna take a free piece of what you charge everyone else for."

"Oh no, you're not! I have a gun and I'll use it," she warned again.

"I'm coming for you!"

She knew it was Hector, but he sounded different, like he was congested. Holding a defensive position about five feet back from the door, Kendra shifted to her right so if it opened a little he would see her with the gun.

Hector gave the door another heave with his shoulder and the wooden molding shattered, only the chain now staying his advance. She could see him through the few inches-wide gap as he slammed himself against the open door with his shoulder, trying to break the chain.

Kendra remembered her gun training course and she took a wide stance and a deep breath. She was taught to only put her finger on the trigger if she intended to shoot, and at this moment, her intentions were clear.

Hector looked up trying to see what was keeping the door from opening. When he lifted his head, she saw his face was covered with black sores, and yellow pus was dripping from his mouth and nose. He looked from the chain to Kendra. They made eye contact for a split second before she pulled the trigger. The sound of the gun going off startled her and made her jump, but she quickly recovered and refocused her eyes on her target. Hector was now slumped on the floor against the door, a hole where his right eye used to be and his brains splattered all across the hallway wall.

Chapter 30

Drew continued up Interstate 95 and could see the rest area up ahead. As he approached, he noticed a small stone building with vending machines next to the front entrance and a single empty car out front. It wasn't a full-service rest area with chain restaurants and shops, but the kind that just had restrooms off the main lobby, along with several little stands containing tourist pamphlets.

He decided to err on the side of caution and circled the building, looking into the windows to make sure it was empty, not forgetting Brad's misfortune. After confirming all was clear, he returned to the front and stood in front of the two vending machines. One had a glass front that housed snacks and candy while the other was a soda machine. He used the butt of the shotgun to break the glass that kept the snacks safely locked away.

Years back, Drew had watched a delivery man fill a soda machine. The man twisted the locking mechanism, which seemed to take forever to lock. He was amazed at how long it took to lock up cans and bottles of carbonated flavored sugar water.

He took a few steps back and shouldered the shotgun, aiming the barrel at the soda machine's lock. He pulled the trigger and the shotgun slug disintegrated the lock. The door wobbled as it flung open, and cans of soda came twirling out, spewing soda everywhere as pieces of the machine pierced the pressurized cans.

He was about to set the shotgun down to load up his pack with snacks and sodas when he heard footsteps behind him. As if on instinct, he raised his weapon and simultaneously spun around on his knee until his eyes fixed on a man walking cautiously towards him up the main path.

"Whoa pal!" Drew said, pointing the shotgun at the newcomer.

"Don't shoot!" the man cried, raising his hands in a disarming gesture. "I'm just thirsty and wanted something to drink."

"Where did you come from?" Drew asked, studying the stranger who appeared to be about middle-aged and was wearing a blue polo shirt, khaki shorts and a black baseball hat.

"I was sitting over there in my car," the man said as he removed his hat, exposing his brown, ear-length hair, which was soaked with sweat. "I've been here since I ran out of gas the other day, and you're the first person I've seen since then."

"You armed?" asked Drew

"No."

"Sick?" He suddenly realized that these two questions, "Armed? Sick?" would most likely become the new standard greeting among any survivors like himself, who would happen upon each other during their travels.

"Gosh I hope not," the man replied. "At least I don't think so. I don't have any symptoms, and I haven't been in contact with anyone for quite a while. They say it spreads fast, so I'm guessing if I'd caught it from someone, I'd be dead by now.

"Turn around slowly," Drew said and moved the barrel of the shotgun in a small circle.

The man slowly turned around and exposed his back, which was drenched with sweat. Both his shirt and pants were sticking to him and sweat was running down his legs. Drew knew if the man had a weapon hidden in his back the sweat covered shirt would have clung to it, making it stick out like a sore thumb. He also knew that if the stranger were infected, he would have those reported black sores or yellow pus. Drew breathed a sigh of relief when he appeared disease-free; not even so much as a sniffle.

"You can turn back around," he said.

As the man turned around his eyes gazed past Drew with the shotgun and straight to the soda vending machine; another sign that his reason for approaching was genuine.

Drew lowered the shotgun. "Come up here and grab yourself a drink," he said as he backed away, allowing the man up the front steps and over to the machine.

The man scurried up the stairs and over to the blown-open soda machine. He searched through the vertical rows of soda until he found the row filled with water, pulled out two bottles and moved back to the stairs to sit down. Twisting off the cap of one of the bottles, he started sucking down water greedily, drinking about half the bottle in one gulp, and then dumped the rest on his head.

Drew held back a chuckle as he watched the cool water stream down the man's face and back. "Thirsty?" he asked sarcastically.

"Yes I am," the man said, wiping his face.

"I would have never guessed," Drew said with that Boston sarcastic tone of his.

"Thank God you came along. You're my guardian angel," the man said as he opened the second bottle of water and started gulping it down.

"I'm Drew. What's your name?"

"Hi Drew, I'm Steve," he replied wiping his mouth with the back of his hand. "Are you from Boston? Because I sense a Boston accent."

"I am. It's kinda hard to hide it," Drew said accentuating the *aaaarrr* in "hard" and then asked, "Where are you from?" trying to find an accent in his voice.

"I'm from Maine, a little over an hour north of Boston."

"Really?"

"Yup, born and raised."

Drew hesitated for a moment, then with some reluctance said, "I'm heading home, if you want to travel together…"

"Oh, that would be great. There's an old saying that there's safety in numbers."

Drew began to chuckle and said, "Unless someone has the sickness."

Steve was taking a sip of water and spit it out in a fit of laughter. "I guess they'll have to change that saying," he said once he finished laughing.

"So what the hell were you doing down here?" Drew asked.

"I was a speaker at a conference."

"Oh really, what on?"

"Drug addiction, alcohol dependency, and God."

"Oh," Drew said as he headed over to the soda machine to fill his pack with drinks.

"With God on your side you can overcome anything," Steve said getting up and following Drew.

"I bet," Drew said and thought to himself, *What the hell did I just get myself into?*

Drew finished filling his pack with snacks and drinks and said, "I'm ready to head out whenever you are."

"Let me just grab my bag out of my car."

"You have a bag?" Drew asked.

"Yeah."

"Well go grab it so we can fill it with snacks and drinks. I'm not carrying all of this for both of us." His accent was fully emphasized now, accompanied by that locally famous Boston sarcasm.

Steve returned with a small brown knapsack, and Drew motioned for him to hand it over. He opened the knapsack and found a change of clothes, Bible, prayer book and a picture of two little blond-haired boys.

"Those are my boys," Steve said with a hint of remorse in his voice. "I haven't seen them since my wife kicked me out."

Drew looked up from the picture and thought of his current situation: how he missed his little girl and wished he could see her right now.

"God willing, they're still alive," Steve added.

"God willing," Drew repeated and hoped the same for Annabelle and his little girl.

They loaded up Steve's knapsack with as many snacks and drinks as they could cram into it and started out down the ramp, back onto I-95.

Chapter 31

Kendra was scared. She didn't know what to do and didn't want to get sick. She tried pushing the door closed, but the way Hector's body slumped down after she shot him had caused his shoulder to become wedged between the door and the doorjamb, preventing her from closing it. She had also tried to pull the door open and break the chain, but she just didn't have enough strength. She even attempted to use a broom handle to push him away from the door, but his body seemed to just absorb the handle and would not move.

Kendra searched her apartment, hoping to find something to help her remove Hector's body from the door. She looked in her closet and grabbed a few scarves to wrap around her face so she wouldn't have to breathe in the growing stench. She climbed down on all fours and started pulling things out from underneath her bed: shoes, a storage bin for her summer clothes and an old wooden box she had forgotten about. The box was similar to a shoebox, but bigger. It was her party box. She always kept it stocked, never knowing when she might throw a large bash. She removed the top of the box, exposing a smorgasbord of drugs. The contents included a few eight balls of cocaine, along with tiny little bags of heroin, spoons, lighters, syringes, crack wrapped in tinfoil, crack pipes, and large cigars that she had removed the tobacco from and replaced it with weed and a sprinkle of cocaine for an added kick. There was also a few bottles of pills and some LSD. She sat staring at the large array of narcotics, enough to last her over a month, before replacing the cover and sliding it back under the bed.

Kendra put layers of clothes on and covered her face the best she could. She tied the scarves so that she could still see and finally dared to try pushing Hector away from the door. She pushed with all her might, but his body would not budge. As she continued her struggle, yellowish-green pus started pouring out from his mouth and mixed with the blood from the gunshot wound that had begun to pool on the floor. Kendra's foot slipped on the bodily substances and she fell hard, hitting the back of her head on the floor. The way she landed, her legs and butt were covered in blood and the yellow stuff that was once Hector's insides. She jumped up and quickly removed the scarves from her face, along with the makeshift protective garments, gagging and vomiting as she felt his bodily fluids seep through her clothes and onto her skin. She then proceeded to strip off her clothes, tossing them onto his body to cover it. Panic setting in, she ran to the bathroom and threw up again in the toilet before taking a shower to remove what was once Hector.

Kendra got out of the shower and stood by her bedroom door, trying to figure out how to remove the body from her apartment before it would start to decompose and smell even worse. Out of ideas, she sat on the bed and began to cry.

Chapter 32

Drew was back in his kitchen, sitting at the head of the table, his usual spot. He watched as his wife slammed dishes down onto the counter and could tell she was mad—very mad. She turned towards him, pointing at him. Her mouth going a mile a minute and her face flashing pure anger, but he could not hear a word of what she was saying. He could feel his head spinning and he grabbed hold of the table, trying to stop himself from falling. It felt like someone was shaking him, trying to force him to fall off his chair. His wife was still screaming at him, or so he thought. His head felt very cloudy and he couldn't think straight. Tightening his grip, as the feeling of being shaken intensified. He was able to hold on as he focused in on his wife and what she was saying. Annabelle slowly reached up, grabbed the back of the chair, leaned forward and screamed at him. Her words came out slow and clear. This time he could hear her, "You're a fucking alcoholic!"

SLAP! Drew was stunned—a stinging sensation engulfed the left side of his face. He opened his eyes to find Steve inches from his him, poised to slap him again. He saw Steve's arm start to swing and muscle memory from his time in the service kicked in. Drew shot up his forearm, blocking the strike.

He could tell Steve was yelling at him, but he felt like he was in a fish bowl. Steve's first slap caught him more in the ear than cheek, stunning his hearing.

Steve was shocked by Drew's responsiveness. One minute he was dead to the world and the next he was blocking his slap and on his feet in seconds. He was actually impressed and scared at the same time.

"What the fuck are you hitting me for?" Drew yelled with a drawn back fist ready to strike, the smell of booze permeating from him.

"Look!" Steve shouted, pointing at the road.

Drew noticed a tire near his feet and as he turned to his right, he was shocked to find debris all over the road and that a car had crashed within feet of him. The guardrail was sheared off right up to where he had been sleeping.

"Holy shit!" Drew exclaimed.

"You almost got killed," Steve said.

Drew assessed the scene before him. "The driver must have been cruising at a high speed when he saw all of the parked cars at the last minute," he concluded after a few minutes of studying the wreck. "None of the cars have tail or break lights on, so the parked cars must have seemed to come out of nowhere."

Drew scanned the area and could tell that the car had bounced off the guardrail on the other side of the road and crashed into the one right next to him. He went over to the vehicle and looked through the windows, but there was no one inside the vehicle and the windshield had a big gaping hole in it.

Drew moved around to the other side of the car to see if he could find the driver. He peeped inside the car again to make sure the driver wasn't stuffed under the dashboard, knowing from experience that could happen. He peered at the large hole in the window and went over to where the guardrail had been, looking down the embankment. Halfway down the hill, he spotted the driver's body resting at the base of a tree.

Steve came around the car and stood next to him. "Is that the driver down there?"

"Yup."

"Should we go check on him?"

"Nope."

"Nope? Why not? He could still be alive."

"I've seen enough of these types of accidents and he isn't alive. Even if he were, there's absolutely nothing we can do for him. He'll probably need to be med-flighted to a trauma center and well, we know that ain't gonna happen."

"So you're just going to let him die?"

"I'm telling you, he's already dead. That bell has been rung and you can't unring it."

"Jesus, Drew!"

"What? You sound like I made them bounce off one guardrail and plow into this one!"

"How do you know he didn't fall asleep?" Steve protested. "If he was asleep, he could have survived the crash. I've heard stories of how people survived bad car accidents because they were asleep."

"Kinda like drunk drivers who slam into a minivan and kill a whole family yet walk away?" Drew retorted.

"Yes, like that I guess."

"You see that hole in the windshield?" Drew said, pointing.

"Yes."

"That hole was created as the driver's body was launched through the windshield. There was enough force from the crash to actually cause the person down there to travel through that solid object." Drew used his fist to pound on the glass showing how strong it was. "Then his body kept going and by the looks of it slammed into that tree right there. Then his body fell, what a good twenty feet?" He leaned over the guardrail, trying to figure out the height. "And then ended up against the base of that tree." Steve became still, a shocked look formed on his face.

"So that's why I know there's nothing we can do for him," Drew said.

"Can I get my Bible and say a prayer for that person down there?"

"Of course you can."

Steve walked over to his pack and grabbed his Bible. When he returned, he flipped open his Bible and began to read,

Then they cried to the Lord in their trouble, and he delivered them from their distress. He made the storm be still, and the waves of the sea were hushed. Then they were glad that the waters were quiet, and he brought them to their desired haven. Psalm 107:28-30

Steve made the sign of the cross and turned around. He was surprised to find Drew standing behind him with his head bowed in prayer—he didn't think Drew was religious.

After a moment of silence, the two companions retrieved their packs and they set out down the road, neither one speaking for some time.

Chapter 33

Willy and Sean tried for days to reestablish the lost signal with Mission Control but had been unsuccessful since witnessing the inexplicable horror that occurred during their daily itinerary briefing with Frank a few days ago.

"What the hell is going on down there?" asked Sean who had his face pressed against the window again. It was still the only thing that helped him fight the claustrophobia. He didn't know why he was having such a hard time dealing with it. It came in waves—there were days he could move around the space station and it didn't bother him, but then there were other days where it became debilitating. He kept his forehead against the glass and watched for hours as the world spun far below. Every ninety minutes, they circled the Earth, and Sean watched as night descended upon the Eastern seaboard of the United States.

Something looks different, Sean thought to himself as Boston and New York began to pass.

Willy tried everything he could think of to contact Mission Control. He used every communication device on board the space station but no signal came through.

"Either we passed through a solar flare and burned out all of our communications, or something is going on down there on Earth," Willy said as he slammed his fist against the communication panel.

Eighty-five minutes had passed, and they were coming up on Boston and New York again in just a few minutes. Sean checked his watch as the minutes passed by, yet he saw nothing below but blackness. Soon he saw the darkness give way to the Rocky Mountains basked in sunlight, followed by the shoreline of the West Coast of the United States.

He set his watch alarm again, but this time he would have Willy come look out the window as well.

The minutes ticked by and Sean called out to Willy, "Hey, do you have a minute?"

"What's up?" Willy asked, tired of playing with the communication systems. He set it to pick up anything being broadcast and made his way over to Sean.

"I saw something on our last revolution and I want you to take a look and make sure I'm not crazy. Can you go over to the other window and look down at the Earth?" Sean asked.

Willy, unsure of what he was talking about, headed over to the other window that looked down on the Earth and looked out. He saw the boot of Italy and watched as Europe passed by.

"We're about to cross over the Atlantic Ocean, headed for Boston and New York," Sean said.

"Yes, I know our flight path," Willy groaned.

"Just watch," Sean replied.

The minutes ticked past and soon the darkness gave way to the sun setting on the California coast.

Suddenly it dawned on Willy as he studied the landmass that was North America.

"Sean, did I just not see what I think I didn't see?"

"So it's not just me. You didn't see any city lights either."

"No. It's completely dark. Sean, what the hell happened down there?"

Suddenly the communications system picked up on a transmission coming from Earth. Both men gingerly floated over to the monitor which had received a television broadcast. It lasted only moments before they were out of range and the screen turned back to the white snowy noise, but it had revealed enough. Both men looked at each other in disbelief at what they had just seen.

Chapter 34

The sun was high overhead, beating down on them as they walked on a stretch of highway that had become congested with abandoned vehicles. Doors were left opened. Cars looked like their drivers had tried to turn around, but could not with the heavy congestion. They passed an SUV with both the driver's door and back door left open, and a small stuffed teddy bear lay on the ground beneath the latter. The seatbelts dangled out of the door from the car seat. It appeared as if the occupants tried to get out in a hurry, the keys still in the ignition.

"Check the vehicles for anything useful," Drew said.

They both scavenged the vehicles for food or drinks.

Drew hopped in and out of the various cars, trying to see if anyone had shut off the engine before leaving the keys behind, hoping to find one with the battery not completely drained. *Something must have really spooked these people for them to have left their cars running*, he thought to himself.

He finally found a pickup truck with the keys still in the ignition, but the driver had turned the vehicle off before exiting. After turning the key and pumping the gas pedal, the engine came to life, and Drew immediately turned on the radio. Only the sound of static filled the cab. He turned the knob on the radio, searching for a signal, scanning through all the frequencies twice, but the only report he could pick up on a couple of the major channels was a recorded emergency broadcast message, advising everyone to take shelter and avoid other people. *What the hell?* he thought. *People have to eventually venture out of their homes.*

"Hey!"

Drew exited the vehicle and saw Steve about ten cars up, waving his arms to get his attention.

"Hey! I think I found what scared everyone away," Steve shouted.

As Drew approached, he was hit with the most foul smell on earth. He knew right away what it was as his countless rides in a Boston ambulance accustomed him to the smell of a decomposing body. As he drew closer, he could hear the sounds of hundreds of flies buzzing around, feasting on the corpse.

Steve had moved to the far left lane and was bent over with his hands on his knees gasping for air and holding back the urge to puke. It's a smell that, once it gets in your nose, is hard to get rid of, and it's a smell you'll never forget.

"Don't go near it! It could be contagious!" Steve shouted.

Drew contemplated what Steve had said, but figured the virus needed a living host to survive in, and well, this wasn't a living host. In fact, the man lying on the road, he could tell, appeared to have died quite a few days ago.

Drew studied the body, what was left of it anyway, and noticed there were black spots on the arms, neck and face. There was a dried pool of some sort of yellowish-green substance next to the body's mouth.

"Looks like he had the sickness and got out of his car," he surmised, "which spooked everyone else to the point they abandoned their vehicles."

"How awful," said Steve.

"Yup. Nothing we can do. Let's keep moving."

Steve pulled out his Bible and recited the same verse as earlier, then made the sign of the cross.

Drew watched him from the other side of the highway and thought, *At least he's consistent.*

In total they had found three bottles of water, a half open pack of cigarettes with a lighter, binoculars and a wallet with $147 dollars in it. Drew took the money and left the wallet. *Money might come in handy the farther north we go.*

About an hour later, they came to a point where I-95 passed over a small town, giving them a bird's eye view of the intersection below. To the left of the interstate, there was a gas station next to a liquor store. Both stores shared the same parking lot. To the right, there was another gas station and a bank. Drew instantly knew which side he was going to.

They crouched down on the left side of I-95 and looked out over the buildings, watching for any movement or sign of life. Drew used the binoculars to search each car and look into the windows of each of the businesses. There were two cars parked in front of the liquor store and a car in front of one of the gas pumps. He noticed a body slummed over the steering wheel of the car at the gas pump and watched for a few minutes for any movement, but didn't see any.

"Let's cross over and check the other side," Drew said and started for the opposite side of the interstate.

After they had crossed over the highway divider, again Drew scanned each window of the bank through the binoculars and counted three cars in the parking lot. He then focused his view on the gas station. "Damn it!" he said, spotting a body lying in the doorway of the gas station. He scanned the gas pumps and counted four cars in the parking lot with two more bodies inside them.

"What did you see?" asked Steve.

"There are three bodies down there," Drew said and pointed to where they were.

"So, let's go down to the left side and avoid the car with the body in it," Steve said.

"The problem is we can't tell if there's anyone else down there who might be sick as well. We don't know when those people died. They could have just recently keeled over, and someone else who is infected could still be down there. All they need to do is breathe on you, and you're done."

"Are we going to have to stay away from people forever?"

"Probably not," Drew replied. "Something like this virus that is so lethal usually dies off quickly, because it has such a high mortality rate. If people hunker down like the government suggested, it should pass quickly."

"Really? That's good news," Steve said.

"But I could be wrong too, and that's why we need to avoid people for now. But the sickness needs a host to survive and spread, so the more time that passes, the more likely the sickness will be gone."

"Well, I say we pass on going down there then," Steve suggested.

"But we need supplies," Drew countered.

They waited several hours, but never saw anything or anyone move down below.

"Okay," Drew began, cutting the silence. "The sun has started to set, which will affect the visibility of anyone down there as their eyes have to constantly adjust to the diminishing light. It will affect us as well, but it works to our advantage since we're expecting to see someone and they're not." He checked Steve's pack, making sure nothing would make too much noise alerting anyone of their arrival.

"We're going to do a slow jog, okay?" he advised. Steve nodded in understanding. "Keep your left hand on my right shoulder at all times so I know where you are. If you see someone, squeeze my shoulder twice to slow down," He handed Steve his pack. "If anyone's down there, and the situation gets ugly, we can head back here under the cover of darkness."

Drew had gone over the use of clock positions and taught Steve how to orient himself to match his spot when calling out locations. He had been out of the Marines for a long time, but some things stick with you, and the ability to orientate himself was one of them.

"Ready?" Drew asked.

"Ready," answered Steve.

Drew set out on a slow trot down the off-ramp with the AR-15 shouldered and ready to shoot any threat. Within a minute they were down the ramp and heading for the middle of the two parking lots. He kept his eye on the front of both buildings while scanning the gas pumps. Steering to the right of the gas pumps, they hurried up along the left side of the gas station. Drew fixed his gaze straight ahead while using his peripheral vision to check the side of the liquor store to his left as they moved towards the back of the building where he conducted a thorough scan of the area. They came to the end of the building and he quickly stuck his head out and glanced behind the gas station. No one there. He turned the corner with Steve in tow, and they continued to circle the entire store until they came back to the front.

"Wait here," Drew said as he went inside to clear the building.

Steve crouched low in his spot, hoping no one was inside the gas station, because he knew Drew would probably kill them out of reflex. Yet he couldn't help being impressed with him again. It was like watching a machine work, the way he cleared the area.

After only a few minutes, Drew exited the gas station. "Nothing of use," he said and motioned for Steve to get behind him again. His plan after checking the gas station was to go directly to the liquor store.

Steve got behind him and squeezed his shoulder once, indicating he was ready. Drew took off in another trot, and within seconds they had crossed over to the liquor store.

Drew indicated for Steve to wait outside again and pushed on the front, surprised to find it was unlocked. He entered the building, leaving Steve alone in the parking lot. The sun had set, and it was starting to become dark.

He found the checkout counter and used his hands to search the top of it. The first thing he felt was a set of keys which he put into his front pocket, hoping they were for the car parked out front. Then he continued searching the counter until his hands found what he was looking for, and he flashed a smile upon his hunch being right. With the quivering hands of an addict, he set right away to dumping his treasure basket of nips into the backpack.

Drew had entered the liquor store for one reason, and one reason only, but he knew he had to come out with something other than alcohol, or he'd have to face Steve's disapproval. Not that he would blame the guy. Risking their lives to satisfy his habit, one that had ruined his marriage, was foolish, he knew. But at the same time, their lives were already at risk since the whole world was going to hell in a handbasket. So, on the chance that he might be going there too, he might as fill the handbasket with booze and satisfy his cravings. Regardless, to save face, he searched the rest of the store, flailing his arms out in front of himself like a blind person and smiled again when he came across a stand of potato chips. *See, Steve?* He planned his upcoming defense in his head as he grabbed a few bags and headed for the exit. *I was looking for food and I found some. So what if I took a couple drinks as well?*

Steve could no longer see the gas station through the darkness. He wondered if it was actually that dark out, or if it was just from his eyes trying to adjust to the diminishing light like Drew had said. Either way, he was getting nervous because the darkness thickened as each second ticked by.

Suddenly there was a bright flash of light and a loud beep of a car horn, causing him to scream as he dropped to the ground.

Drew exited the store with his hand outstretched in front of him pushing the buttons on the car fob. There was another flash of light followed by the loud car horn.

"What the fuck are you doing on the ground?" Drew asked as the headlights illuminated the area around the car.

"That just scared the heck out of me," Steve said, getting up and dusting himself off.

Drew slipped off his backpack and gently put it down in the backseat, hoping the newly collected bottles of booze wouldn't clink together alerting Steve to their presence.

"What took you so long?" Steve asked wiping more sand off the front of his shirt.

"It was dark in there, but I found these," he replied as he tossed two bags of chips to Steve. Then he dangled the keys. "And these on the front counter."

"Where to then?" asked Steve.

This car won't do us much good on the interstate, but since we need more supplies, I suggest we follow this town road out front here and see where it leads us."

"Agreed," Steve replied.

They both hopped in, and Drew started up the car, noticing it had three-quarters of a tank of gas. They set off down the dark road and drove for miles, but they were greeted by nothing but open farm land along the way. Soon weariness was upon them both, growing stronger until they decided it was time to stop for the night and rest.

Chapter 35

They had passed a few cars the next day, and unlike the interstate, which was cluttered with vehicles that served only as obstacles, the country road on which they now drove was navigable, the cars they passed were mostly still in operation by their owners. Every time they came upon an oncoming vehicle, both drivers would pull farther to the right side of the road and speed up, as if they feared the sickness would jump from one moving car to another. Every now and then they would spot a car that had stopped and there was someone slumped over against the wheel, but there was still enough room on the road to maneuver around them. One of the cars had a dog in it that was barking and scratching at the windows as they passed by. *Poor dog*, Steve thought, *It will probably starve to death in the car*. He wanted to stop and let the dog out, but doing so would mean exposing themselves to the virus.

Drew kept a watchful eye on the gas gauge and when they came to a group of cars he stopped and siphon gas from their tanks. After an hour they were back on their way.

They had traveled a good portion of the day, keeping in mind to bear north as much as possible, and believed they were somewhere near the Georgia line.

"I say we stop and find a place to sleep tonight and have a bite to eat," Drew said.

"Don't you want to keep going?" asked Steve.

"No, I'm worried about driving into one of those parked cars at night. There'll be no warning of brake lights, and constantly trying to avoid abandoned cars all over the road is going to prove quite stressful."

"Yeah, I don't want to drive into a car in the middle of the night," Steve said.

"If one of us got hurt it would really suck because even if we could find a hospital, I'm betting it would be full of dead bodies."

"Good point," Steve agreed. "I guess stopping for the night is our best option then."

Drew drove until they came to a crossroads, and he turned right onto a road that was narrower and not so well kempt as the previous, promising a better chance they would not be disturbed during the night. They continued for about a mile and pulled over to the strip of dirt on the side. The sun was setting in the West, which backlit a farm house off in the distance that sat right in the middle of a big open field. Steve couldn't wait to get out and stretch his legs, which were beginning to cramp up from sharing the passenger seat with the rifle and shotgun.

Billy and his mother Betty-Sue sat on his bed, passing the time by throwing crumpled up pieces of paper into a wastebasket. Imagining he was a big star basketball player who had just seconds on the clock to make the game winning shot, he rose up on the balls of his feet and raised his arms above his head when he noticed car headlights turning onto the side street off in the distance.

"Momma look! There's a car over on Jacobs Lane."

Betty-Sue stood up and went over to the window where she saw the car off in the distance and, with still enough daylight, could make out the two men who exited it. She reached up and quickly shut off the light.

She hurried downstairs to tell her husband Henry, about the men outside and found her mother and father looking out the living room window.

"Is that a car out there?" asked her father.

"Mom! Dad! Get away from the window!" Betty-Sue said as she reached the bottom of the stairs.

Henry heard the commotion and met her in the living room. "What's going on?"

"There's a car out on Jacobs Lane and two men got out," she said as she pointed towards the window. Henry walked cautiously over to the window and saw the interior car light come on, exposing two men who appeared to remove something from the backseat.

Suddenly they could hear heavy footsteps above them as Billy came running out of his room and raced down the stairs.

"Momma! Momma! Two men got out," Billy said as he came to a sudden stop and crouched down next to his father, pressing his face against the window.

"We saw them too," his father said. "Back away now, son."

"What are they doing?" Billy asked, obeying his father's orders.

"I don't know—probably just need a place to sleep for the night, I'd say."

"We should go say hi!"

"Absolutely not, Billy," Betty-Sue said.

"We don't know who they are, or if they're sick," Grandma said as she now sat in her comfy chair next to her husband Gus.

Henry's three brothers Dave, Arthur and Ralph all made their way it into the room to see what all the commotion was about.

"What's going on out there?" asked Dave.

Drew walked over to the cluster of trees just off the side of the road and found enough branches to make a small fire to warm up their dinner.

Steve put the packs next to the fire like Drew had shown him and pulled out the cans of food, along with the pans needed to heat up their meal.

Drew stood watch and every few seconds he would turn a little. He completed a full circle in less than a minute. He was watching out for other people,—not wanting anyone sneaking up on them, and as he directed his stare toward the farm house in the distance, he wondered if the people inside would be a problem.

Steve came over and stood next to Drew, looking in the same direction.

"Do you want to go over and check it out?" Steve asked, "It might be nice to sleep in an actual bed tonight."

"No," replied Drew.

"No? Just like that?" Steve said.

"Yup."

"You didn't even entertain the thought."

"Nope."

"Why not?"

"Because there are people in that house."

"How do you know? There isn't even a light on."

"Because I saw a woman in the window when we parked."

"Really?"

"Yup."

"But there's no lights on."

"There was."

"Maybe she saw us park and didn't want us to come and ask for assistance if we saw the light on."

"Maybe."

"Are you sure you saw a woman?"

"I'm sure."

"Okay."

"I'll stand watch if you want to cook dinner."

Steve turned and started to walk away, but stopped and looked back at the house, wondering if there was anyone else in there. And why Drew was acting strange.

Drew continued slowly turning in place, constantly checking a 360-degree circle. The tall grass on either side of the road made it hard to see, which in turn made it harder for anyone to see them.

"Billy, help Grandma and Grandpa to bed," Henry said.

Billy left his position near the window and headed to help his grandpa into his bedroom, which was adjacent to the kitchen. He returned and grabbed Grandma's hand, startling her.

"It's just me, Grandma," Billy said.

"Help me to bed dear," replied Grandma.

He helped her up and out of the chair and handed her her cane. He then walked with her to her room where Grandpa was already sound asleep and snoring.

When he returned to the living room, he could see the through the window that a small fire had been started behind the car, illuminating it. Billy wanted to get a better view and ran upstairs to his bedroom. As he entered, he flicked on his light out of habit, which filled his room along with the hallway and spilled down the stairs.

"Billy! Turn off that light!" his father shouted.

Somewhat frightened by his blunder, but still curious as a child can be, he quickly ran over and shut the light off, but then went back over to the window.

Henry called his brothers into the living room to come up with a plan—the men parked over on Jacobs Lane could have possibly seen the light come on. He asked them to get their rifles and keep them with them at all times, just in case the men decided to come and investigate. Ralph suggested they take turns staying awake to make sure the men didn't try to come over and get into the house during the middle of the night.

Drew had just turned to face the farmhouse when he saw the light in the upstairs window come on. He thought he heard faint shouting before the light went out again.

He waited until he could hear Steve snoring before going into his backpack, wanting to be sure he had fallen asleep. He made his way to the back of the packs, lined up just the way he had shown Steve, making it easier for him to get the bottle of vodka he had stashed. The bottle seemed to be calling him all day, and nightfall couldn't come soon enough. All he could think about was having a drink. Even when his mind had to think of something else, it always came back to the booze. He loved how it made him feel. It relaxed him. It made him feel complete.

He got the bottle out of his pack and could already taste the vodka in his mouth, which started salivating, craving the liquid much like a dog sitting patiently, waiting for scraps to fall off its master's plate.

He was worried Steve would hear the commotion when he had unzipped the pack and pulled out the bottle, so he had moved as stealthily as possible, slowly opening the zipper inch by inch, the worst way to pull off a bandage. This had become a nightly ritual for Drew. He'd take out a bottle of booze and disappear for a little while, then come back without it and fall asleep.

He found a darkened area among the little grove of trees and went to the backside. Sleep was hard to come by with the worry of getting home. But soon he would be able to forget all of his worries — the bottle promised it.

He leaned up against the biggest tree within the far side of the grove and twisted off the cap before bringing the bottle to his mouth and taking a big gulp. He felt its warmth seep down his throat and coat his innards. Soon that same warmth enveloped him into the relaxed state he'd yearned for. All of his problems washed away for a minute. He took another swig and then another. Half the bottle was gone already, but Drew needed his brain to stop. Besides the booze, all he could think about was his family back home and hoped they were alright. The anxiety of not knowing made it worse. The only cure to shut off his brain was to drink, so drink he did. He chugged the rest, put the cap back on and tossed the useless bottle into the tall grass before leaving the cover of the grove and making his way back to the fire. Now relaxed, the booze doing its job, he sat down in front of his pack and leaned back, resting against the bag. He closed his eyes and that constant worry in his head finally died down. Soon the worries would be completely gone, and sleep would come. He knew he would only get a couple hours before the sun came up, but some sleep was better than none.

Steve woke in the middle of the night with a sore back and realized he had to relieve himself. Once done, he climbed into the backseat of the car figuring that it had to be better than the hard ground. And he wouldn't wake up covered in dew.

The next morning, just as the sun was coming up, Billy awoke and went to his bedroom window to look outside. The car was still there on Jacobs Lane, but the fire was no longer burning. He slipped on his jeans and sneakers and opened his window, then climbed out onto the roof and slid down the downspout.

Billy made his way through the tall cornstalks until he reached the road right across from the car parked on Jacobs Lane.

He slowly made his way over to the car and peaked inside. A man was curled up in the backseat sleeping. He made his way to the front of the car, wanting to see what was on the other side. As he treaded along the pavement, his feet stepped in a sandy spot on the road, causing the sand to crunch under his shoes.

Drew heard someone creeping towards the car and slowly opened his eyes. The sun was blinding and didn't help his pounding head. It only intensified his hangover. He squinted, trying to block out the sun and could barely make out a pair of shoes underneath the car on the far side. Placing one hand on his rifle and pulling it closer to himself, he positioned the stock under his arm so that all he had to do was raise the barrel and shoot. He moved his finger to the trigger guard preparing to fire, then opened his eyes just enough to see, giving the illusion he was still asleep.

Drew was surprised to see a young boy come around the front of the car. Immediately relaxing his grip on the rifle, he watched as the boy checked out the area and figured he probably came from the farmhouse, curious as to who was parked out across from his home.

Drew opened his eyes and looked at the boy, who seemed startled at first until Drew smiled and winked at him. He quickly looked the kid up and down and, seeing no signs of the virus, determined it was alright that he was near the camp. The boy awkwardly stood there and waved hi.

"I'm Drew. What's your name?"

"Billy."

"Hi Billy. It's a pleasure to meet you."

Billy stood there and waved again.

"What are you doing out so early?" Drew asked.

Billy just shrugged his shoulders.

"Couldn't sleep?" Drew asked.

Billy nodded his head no.

"Do you live over at that farmhouse?"

"Yes sir."

"Are you hungry, Billy?"

Billy's eyes lit up as he shook his head yes.

"I'll make us something quick to eat," Drew said as he rose to his feet.

Twenty minutes later Billy was sitting crisscross applesauce next to Drew as he finished his orange. Steve woke up and hung his head out the back window of his makeshift bed.

Billy told them how they had cows—lots of cows—and chickens and pigs. He went on about how they have corn and that they grew hay, which they sold to local farmers and used it to feed their own animals as well.

"Do you have power?" Drew asked.

"Solar panels and the old windmill."

"Do you have a pump out back for water?"

"Yes sir."

"Do you think your mom and dad would mind if we filled up our water bottles?"

"I don't think they'll mind."

"Perfect, because we're getting low on water," Steve said.

"Real quick question though, Billy," Drew cut in as gently as possible. "Is anyone at your house sick?"

Billy shook his head. "No sir. Daddy said a lot of people were sick though, so we had Grandma and Grandpa come over, and some of my uncles too. And we stayed here. No one's left the farm for days because Daddy didn't want any of us getting sick from other people."

"Sounds like it's safe to me," Steve commented.

Drew nodded. "Your dad was right to keep all of you here, Billy. Do your parents know you came out here?"

Billy hesitated before looking down shamefully. "No," he admitted.

"Well, I think your father would be very upset if he knew you were here talking to us. You know, it's dangerous to sneak out when travelers are passing by. Lucky for you, we're not sick, but the next person might be, so you need to be more careful, okay?"

Billy nodded, keeping his gaze to the ground.

Drew stepped to his pack and pulled out a candy bar he had retrieved from the vending machine. "Here, kid," he offered. "This is all yours if you can promise me you won't leave your house again the next time strangers come around."

When Billy happily agreed, Drew tossed him the snack, then stepped closer to Steve as the boy sat down and enjoyed his treat.

"I'm not sure about this," Drew whispered to Steve. "His parents will probably be pissed when they see their son out here with us. Chances are they'll assume the worst, and we could have trouble on our hands. Might be a good idea to send the kid back home and get on the road before they realize he's gone."

Steve nodded subtly. "You're right," he replied just as quietly, "but this area is pretty devoid of convenience stores and such. I'm not sure where else we'll find water, and we're gonna need some soon."

Drew thought for a moment. His head still throbbed; making a clear decision proved difficult. "Okay. We'll have to play this smart. Give the folks a reason not to shoot us if they're armed."

They started packing up and within five minutes they were ready to go.

"We can give you a ride over to your house if you'd like," Drew offered. Maybe we can talk to your dad for you so he won't get too angry with you for sneaking out."

"Sure!" Billy replied, wiping a smudge of chocolate from his lips.

Henry woke up to the faint sound of the car door closing off in the distance. He got up, slipped on his pants and shirt and headed downstairs.

Arthur and Ralph were already downstairs when Henry came down. The three men were all looking out the window.

"It sounds like they're packing up," said Ralph.

Betty-Sue woke up to the sound of the men talking and got up out of bed, got dressed and headed downstairs as well. Dave came out of his room at the bottom of the stairs just as Betty-Sue was coming down.

"The car's moving," Ralph said as he stood in front of the window.

They all watched from the windows as the car did a U-turn and started to head back to the main road. They watched the car approach the intersection and turned right.

"They're coming this way!" shouted Arthur.

They all moved to the front of the house to get a better view of the car as it drove by. But it didn't drive by—it turned into their driveway and was now approaching the house slowly.

"Grab your guns, boys!" yelled Henry as he grabbed his shotgun and made his way out the front door.

Drew slammed on the brakes as he saw the four men rush out of the front door, all holding guns. He rolled his window down and slowly put his hands out. He reached out and opened the door from the outside and slid out of the car with both of his hands raised.

"This is our land, and we're asking you kindly to leave," Henry said.

"Yes sir," Drew began. "Were just camping along the road for the night and had no intention on coming any closer to your home, but we had a little situation this morning that-"

"Fuck! Billy's in their car!" Ralph yelled.

All of the men raised their guns and pointed them at Drew.

"Billy! Billy!" Betty-Sue screamed when she heard Ralph yell and immediately came running out onto the front porch.

Henry turned his head as his wife came running out screaming their sons name.

"Whoa! Whoa!" Drew shouted.

"What are you doing with my boy?" Henry asked.

"That's what I'm trying to explain, sir," Drew answered, speaking quickly. "Billy came over to us this morning. I think he was curious."

"Get him out of that car now!" Henry ordered.

"Yes sir. That's exactly why we're here. We know how dangerous these times are, so we wanted to get him back home safely and make sure he didn't run off anywhere else. It's the only reason he's in our car in the first-"

Henry pumped his shotgun, the familiar but intimidating sound echoed in the nearby field. "Let my son out now! Boy, don't make me say it again!"

Drew kept his arms up but turned his head and made eye contact with Steve and said as calmly as possible, "Let Billy out."

Billy got out of the car and walked up to the porch. His mother came running over to him. "Did they hurt you? Did they touch you?" she asked.

"No mama. They made me breakfast," Billy replied.

"Listen, we don't want any trouble," Drew assured them. "We drove your son back here because he came over to us, I swear."

"Billy, did you sneak out of the house again?" Henry asked while pointing his shotgun at Drew.

"Yes, Daddy."

Henry lowered his shotgun. "Dammit, Billy! I've half a mind to tan your hide! Do you know how dangerous that was? These fellas could've been infected with the sickness! Then you could've gotten us all killed!" He turned his attention back to the strangers and raised his shotgun again. "You boys ain't sick, are ya?"

Drew raised his hands back up in response. "No, sir. We're not sick. You can see that, can't you? If we were, we'd be dead by now, or we'd have the symptoms at least."

The men on the porch lowered their weapons, realizing Drew and Steve appeared healthy. "Listen," Drew began in a softer tone that was pleading in nature, "you've got a good kid there. He scared the hell out of us this morning when he came around the front of our car, but he was very polite and just wanted to see what we were up to. But I told him the same as you, that he shouldn't go outside when strangers are nearby."

"It's true, Daddy," Billy said, wishing to defend his new friends. "He gave me a candy bar for promising not to sneak out again."

Henry raised an eyebrow at Drew. "You gave my boy sugar early in the morning?"

Drew shrugged. "Figured it was a good bargain as long as he keeps his promise. You'll keep your promise, right Billy?"

The kid nodded. "Yes sir."

Henry unexpectedly stifled a chuckle. "Son," he addressed Billy, "first you sneak out of the house. Then you take candy from strangers. Boy we got some lessons to teach you. Polite, maybe. Common sense? Definitely lacking in that department. Get inside and wash up while I figure out what extra chores to give you."

Billy hung his head but obeyed his father and hurried into the house with Betty-Sue close on his heels.

With the tension now easing, Drew cut in, changing the subject. "We can't get any radio stations to come in. Have you heard how bad it is?"

"Last we heard it was around fifty dead," Henry said.

"Fifty thousand?" Drew asked.

"No, fifty *million* in the U.S. alone."

"Holy shit!" Drew said leaning against the hood of the car, stunned by the number.

"Where are you from?" Henry asked.

"I'm from Boston."

"That's what I figured given your accent," Henry said.

Drew turned and pointed at the windshield and said, "Steve's from Maine. We're trying to get home."

Steve got out and stood to the side of the car.

"What are you boys doing down here?" Henry asked.

Drew explained his mother's passing and how Steve was at a conference when the sickness hit.

"News said it started up in New York and spread to Boston. Both areas had large death tolls."

Steve put his hand up to his mouth and crouched down as if he was going to be sick and said, "I'm sorry, did you say fifty million dead?"

"I did, according to the last news update I saw."

"When was that?"

"A week back."

Steve stood back up, turned to Drew and said, "We need to get home now!"

"He's right," Henry agreed. "I appreciate what you did, talking to Billy about staying inside, and making sure he got straight home, but you boys have a long road ahead of you. Best if you get going before things get worse... if they can *get* any worse.

Drew nodded. "Thanks for understanding, but seeing as how we went through all the trouble, can you possibly spare some water? I hate to ask, but our jugs are nearly empty, and as bad as things are, we don't know how far we'll have to go before we'll be able to refill."

Well played, Steve thought to himself.

"Dave, go get their water jugs and fill them up out back," Henry ordered.

Dave handed his brother his shotgun and walked down off the porch towards the car.

"We have one jug in the front and a couple in the backseat," Steve told him.

Dave opened the back door first and was about to grab the water jugs on the seat when he stopped short and jumped back. "Guns! They have guns!"

The men on the porch once again raised their weapons and pointed them at the two men.

"Whoa! We have them for protection, just like you. Drew said, shooting his hands in the air as quickly as the firearms were raised. He himself had determined not long ago the new standard greeting between strangers, and he silently cursed himself for forgetting to mention their weapons beforehand when Henry asked if they were sick. "We mean you no harm. We're just asking for some water and we'll be on our way."

Henry let out a sigh and lowered his weapon, followed by his brothers. "Dave, go get the water so these men can be on their way."

The two northerners relaxed as well. Drew couldn't blame the men for being so on edge. It was, after all, a new world. One in which no one could be too careful. No one could trust anyone. No matter how innocent they appeared.

Dave grabbed the jug from the front seat and made his way around back to fill the jugs from the pump.

"You planning on driving all the way back?" asked Henry.

"Yes sir," both Drew and Steve replied in unison.

"Good luck, because you'll need it."

"Why's that?" asked Drew.

"The news had been reporting fuel shortages and that there's no power up north. Seems everyone has barricaded themselves indoors until whatever this sickness is passes."

"Really?" Steve asked shakily.

"Yeah, and they say the highways are all clogged with abandoned cars. Some people left them and went home. Some people died in their cars while sitting in traffic."

Steve turned to Drew, "What are we going to do?"

"We'll find a way Steve. Don't worry."

"Don't worry! My God! Apparently we can't drive home because of all the cars clogging the highways and even if we could get through, there'll be no gas for us to use to get home!"

"Steve, calm down!"

"Oh dear Lord, please grant us protection and a means to get home," Steve said.

"Oh great, here we go again with the whole God thing," Drew replied.

"We need God. He'll get us home."

"I think God gave up on us and that's how we got here," Drew said with that tone of his.

"Shut up! You're still probably drunk from last night. I heard you sneak off and drink your booze. You snore something horrible when you drink and all you did last night was snore."

Drew noticed that everyone was looking at him. Just then Dave came around the corner with the jugs of water.

Chapter 36

Kendra's inability to remove the rotten carcass from her doorway was starting to affect her. She finished off the small bag of cocaine, figuring it would help, but it didn't. She couldn't stand being trapped with a decomposing corpse in her apartment. Who could, for that matter? But adding to the fact she had shot and killed the man didn't sit well with her conscience. She tried to justify it by telling herself Hector was breaking in and would have killed her. She even recognized the logic that she did him a favor by ending his life quickly before he truly started to suffer from the sickness, but that didn't help much.

She couldn't shake the memory. Her mind repeatedly played back that exact moment of looking down her outstretched arms as she aimed the gun at Hector. The feel of the trigger on her index finger and the frighteningly small amount of pressure she had to apply. The loud bang and the force of the kickback when the gun went off. She felt like she was going to be sick as she thought back to the sight of his head snapping back when the bullet tore through his head. His pulverized brain exited the back of his head in chunks, and a fine mist had landed on the hallway wall with a distinct wet slop sound. His brain looked like an artist had tossed paint onto a canvas, like the ones you see at a city fair. Kendra shot her hands up to her head and applied pressure to her temples, trying to stop the visual of Hector's body as it crumpled in her doorway. She grabbed handfuls of her hair and started tugging. Pain coursed across her scalp, but it did not stop the memory that came next—the one that haunted her the most. The blank look on his face as his body lay there with blood gushing from the large gaping hole in the back of his head.

She cursed, wishing there was something she could do, needing something to take her mind off of poor Hector and his missing chunks of skull and brain matter lying in her doorway.

Kendra's arm tinged as she thought how great a hit of heroin would be right then, and suddenly she remembered the stash of drugs under her bed.

She slowly moved from the middle of the living room towards her room as the drugs practically called to her from underneath the bed. They whispered to her like they had years ago. It was a constant whisper only she could hear.

She leaned against her bedroom doorjamb staring at her bed, and a small part of her was trying to ignore the calling as she knew the substance would only consume her, but her only other option was to go back to thinking about and dealing with Hector's body. At least the drugs would make her forget all about him.

Her body was remembering how wonderful it felt when she first took the drug. The thrill of chasing it, trying to find that initial feeling and getting it to last as long as it did like the first time. Knowing that every time she used it the feeling lasted less and less made her chase it even more. She had to have it. Soon the drugs under the bed were consuming her thoughts. It was her *only* thought. The dead man in her door and all of the hundreds and thousands of dead out in the city no longer existed or mattered. The drugs were talking to her, calling her name. The whisper became a voice with weight. It seemed to have a purpose. It wanted her. It needed her. Her old addiction had resurfaced. She thought she had been able to keep it under control but, in light of the current situation, she could no longer fight off the temptation.

Kendra found herself sitting on the bed bent over, trying to fight the urge to pull the wooden box back out. She had forgotten about the party stash until this morning. Having worked so many hours and getting her drugs for free left little need for it. She only used coke and weed, steering clear of the hard drugs. A while back she found she had been spending so much money on the hard drugs that she would soon have to work just to support her habit. The drugs had been slowly killing her, and if she wanted that farm with the mountains off in the distance she would have to give them up, so she had checked herself into a rehab. After a tough struggle she had finally kicked the hard drugs.

Kendra curled up her fists and held them to her eyes, rubbing against them with the heels of her palms. She found herself rocking back and forth, something she only did when she used heroin. Her body was remembering.

There came a point in which she couldn't fight herself any longer. It was all too much. Reaching under the bed and sliding out the wooden box, she removed the cover and pulled out the paraphernalia needed to get a fix.

Kendra heated the heroin up on a spoon using a lighter. Once it started to melt and boil, she used the syringe to suck it up off the spoon. She tied the elastic band around her bicep, found a vein, stuck the needle in and pushed the syringe plunger.

The rush was immediate. It hit her like a ton of bricks. She leaned back, putting her head on the pillow. Her body shivered as it took in the foreign substance. While she lay there, the needle pulsed rapidly with every beat of her rushing heart. Her mind went from clear to a beautiful white. It was like being tangled in fresh, clean sheets, hanging from a clothesline on a warm summer day. Everywhere was white. It encompassed her. All of the noise and thoughts in her head had ceased, and she loved every second of it.

The ominous figure made its way down the hall, towards the body slumped in the apartment door, which was only being held open by the weight against the security chain. The otherworldly entity slipped in through the small opening and drifted across the floor as if dancing in the breeze, then made its way into Kendra's room. It stopped at the end of her bed and continued to dance like a sheet, a sheet of death.

Suddenly the bedroom air became frigid and felt like someone had opened a window on a cold winter's night.

The white sheets that seemed to be encompassing Kendra quickly started to fade and lose their brightness. They became pale and dirty as the warmth faded, and the newly formed stains began to spread and become darker as the cold crept in. The sheets had gone from flowing around her to constricting her, tightening. The feeling of euphoria was replaced with fear. She had no control and could do nothing to prevent the sheets from rolling her up like a joint. Suddenly unable to move, all she could do was be part of the moment. Be part of her own death. The sheets kept tightening, crushing her chest.

Her breathing became labored and her pulse slowed. The needle protruding from her arm now twitched every few seconds with the beat of her slowly dying heart. Kendra's eyes squinted open and she saw the noxious shadowy figure at the end of her bed and then her eyes rolled into the back of her head.

The actual sheets below her on the bed were soaked in sweat. In her mind, she tried to fight the coming darkness but it was useless. She was being swallowed by a black hole. The heroin had gone from giving her so much pleasure, making her feel invincible, to now sucking the life out of her. Little bubbles of spit started to form on the inside of her mouth with every exhale, which had now become almost nonexistent. In a few moments, she would be like Hector and the millions of other people who had perished in the past few days. There was no one to save her. The end was near.

A death rattle escaped her lifeless body, and the slowly ticking needle in her arm no longer twitched.

Chapter 37

They left the farmhouse and headed east. The main road would bring them into the center of town, which Henry said had been closed off since the sickness hit and that they would have to travel east and pick up another road to make it around the town. Drew knew Henry had told them the name of the road, but he had also marked it on the map he gave them to ensure they wouldn't forget. It made Drew think of how many other towns and cities they might come to that could be blocked off to the public, and he wondered if it was even possible to get home. *We're in the middle of nowhere where the sickness hasn't even affected that many people and all of the small hick towns' roads have been sealed off.*

It was to be expected though, he realized. If a town is lucky enough to exist in Bumblefuck-Nowhere America, isolated enough where its residents have little opportunity to travel in and out, that town would be disease free. And the best way for the people living there to keep it that way would be to barricade themselves in and everyone else out.

Henry also warned that there were reports of such towns forming a watch rotation, where those on duty would shoot strangers if they tried to enter their borders. Everyone feared the sickness. Most people stayed home and huddled with their families, waiting for any news or updates and praying their loved ones were alive and uninfected.

Drew started thinking about Steve and how he had called him out about his drinking in front of those people back on the farm. It reminded him of his wife, always nagging him not to drink too much when they went out. Of course he never listened, and they'd get into a fight, and he'd wake up and apologize. It got to the point she would just say, "What's the point of wasting my breath? You're just going to drink again tonight, and we'll repeat this all over again tomorrow."

He could see they were approaching an intersection and needed to know which way to go. He turned to ask Steve where they were on the map, but he had fallen asleep in the backseat. He told Drew he didn't like guns and didn't like sitting next to them in the front, which was just fine with Drew. In the event that he needed to grab the AR-15 in a hurry, he wouldn't have to worry about Steve being in the way.

"Steve, grab the map and see where we are!" Drew shouted, waking Steve.

"Huh?" Steve looked up and wiped the drool from his chin. He shifted in his seat and his Bible slid from his lap onto the floor.

"The map — where are we?" Drew repeated.

"I think we're on Main Street and we passed Grove Street a while back on the right," Drew said, trying to help Steve locate their position on the map as he fumbled it open, still not quite awake.

Steve rotated the map, looking at it blankly and turning it again. Drew thought he even saw him flip the map over when he glanced in the rearview mirror.

"Do you know how to read a map?" he asked suspiciously.

"Yeah, sort of," Steve replied as he bent over to pick up his Bible.

"Sort of?" Drew asked while looking at Steve in the mirror. Drew took his eyes off the road again and focused on Steve through the mirror. "You're killing me, man. Look, find Main Street and trace your finger east until-"

CRACK! The car shook and Drew jammed on the brakes as hard as he could, causing the nose of the car to dive forwards as it came to a careening stop. Steve went flying forwards, slamming into the back of the front seat.

"What was that?" Steve shouted, rubbing his forehead.

Drew sat still for a moment, staring out the front window, then, without speaking, quickly put the car in reverse, backing the car up slowly.

"What happened? Did we hit something?" asked Steve as he looked around the car. Suddenly, he noticed a small opening in the windshield. "Holy crap! Is that a bullet hole?"

"Yup," said Drew as he continued driving backwards cautiously.

Off in the distance there were cars blocking both sides of the road and men with guns leaning across the hoods of the cars pointing their weapons at them.

"That bullet went through the middle of the front and right through the back windshield!" Steve said with a shaky voice after finding the identical hole behind him. "Thank Jesus neither of us was hit! He was watching over us."

Drew nodded his head, keeping the car in reverse until he was certain they were out of range of the townspeople.

"What are we going to do?" Steve asked, still trying to calm his nerves.

"Gosh, I don't know, Steve," Drew replied impatiently. "But it looks like we just might have to find a way around, crazy as that sounds."

Steve felt a tinge of irritation at Drew's sarcasm. "Well excuse me, Rambo! In case it hasn't occurred to you, I've never had a gun pointed at me until this past week, and this is the first time I've ever been shot at. So forgive me if I can't think straight right now."

"You're right. I'm sorry." Drew commented more softly, ditching the cynical tone. "But something tells me you'll have to get used to it, with the way the world is now."

He backed up to the nearest intersection and did a quick three-point turn. "I was afraid of this."

"What?" asked Steve.

"What Henry said," Drew answered. "That all of these towns would be closed off.

"So how far do you think we'll have to go to get around?"

"I'm not sure," Drew admitted. "Look, I saw a sign not too far back for I-95. Maybe we should try that again," Drew said.

"Didn't Henry also say that the highways were all clogged?"

"We haven't even gone a few miles and we've already turned around twice," Drew debated. "I say we take I-95 and see how bad it is. Even if we can get another twenty miles that would be great." Steve appeared apprehensive when he glanced in the rearview mirror. "Hey, it beats getting shot at, right?"

That seemed good enough for Steve. "Okay. Head back to I-95," he said.

After they followed the signs and returned to the interstate, they drove for about twenty minutes before a specific chime came from the console. It was a gentle sound, but it was enough to get both men's attention, and they quickly noticed that, simultaneously with the ding, the light indicating an almost empty gas tank had appeared on the dashboard.

Steve bowed his head and clasped his hands together in prayer, "Dear Lord, please lead us to safety. Thank you Heavenly Father."

They drove on for another twenty minutes before the car started to sputter and died. The power steering pump turned off, making it hard to steer the car.

The car coasted along before coming to a stop in the middle of nowhere.

"I guess we're hoofing it," Drew said.

"Yeah," Steve grumbled. "But it'll be a hell of a long time if we have to hoof it all the way to Boston."

"I know, but even if we had a full tank and plenty of gas cans to spare, how much farther would we have gotten before hitting another cluster of abandoned vehicles? I'm pretty sure we'd be hoofing it eventually anyway."

Steve agreed and they exited the car with their supplies, packing everything up the best they could. Once all was situated, they began the hike.

They walked the lonely open highway for miles. *So far so good*, Drew thought to himself as Steve wasn't complaining yet.

Dusk was upon them when Drew decided to call it a night. They started a small fire to heat up the canned soup they had. It wasn't much but it was better than nothing. Drew extinguished the fire once they finished cooking as he didn't want to draw unexpected visitors in the middle of the night.

They put their packs up against the guardrail and settled in. Drew knew it wouldn't be long before Steve would be out cold since the long walk carrying the heavy pack would grant him a good night's sleep.

His mind had been going non-stop all day, worrying about all sorts of threats. Trying to get home was proving harder than it should be. He couldn't stop thinking about his wife and little girl. *Are they OK? Did they survive? Did I lose my whole family in less than a week? I need a drink. I can't believe that bullet missed us earlier. I should have gotten out and fired back. No, we were outnumbered. We would have lost for sure. Besides, they were just protecting their territory.*

His brain was in overload and he couldn't take it. He needed a drink to slow it down before it exploded inside his head. He needed a drink now.

Unzipping his pack and reaching down to the bottom, he felt the small cylindrical bottles and pulled a few out. The moonlight illuminated the bottles, the "Peppermint Schnapps" label clearly visible. He zipped up his pack and started walking a little down the road before twisting off the top and downing the first bottle. He enjoyed the taste of Peppermint Schnapps and how the alcohol took effect almost instantly. As he finished each tiny bottle, Drew could feel his thoughts dying down and his tension fading away. He continued walking, flinging the bottles over the guardrail as he emptied them down his throat, until they were all gone.

When he returned, Steve was sitting up drawing circles in the sand with a stick.

"You okay?" he asked.

"Yeah, why?"

"I noticed you left with several little bottles and returned with none. And your cheeks are all flushed."

"What's your problem?"

"I don't have a problem, but I think you do."

"A problem with what?"

"Drinking."

"Oh you mean with all that's going on—all the death and trying to get back home, which is over a thousand miles away by the way, and now we have no car, never mind the fact we were shot at earlier today. Then, add in not knowing if our families are alive or not. You don't think all that doesn't warrant a drink? Is that what you're telling me?"

"Yeah, it warrants a drink."

"Thank you!"

"But it doesn't warrant you drinking six or seven of those little bottles in the span of from here to there and back," Steve said pointing to the spot Drew turned around and starting walking back.

"Unless you want to wake up all bruised and bleeding, I suggest you shut the fuck up right now, you little fucking pussy. Go read your fucking Bible and preach to someone else."

"So you're an angry drunk with a potty mouth."

Drew took a step closer and bent over with a closed fist ready to punch Steve in the face.

"Alright, alright, I'll shut up."

Drew grabbed his pack and moved it further down the road. He leaned up against the guardrail and closed his eyes and thought to himself, *What the fuck is that guy's problem*? He felt his body relaxing, and the non-stop racing in his mind was finally starting to slow down. The Peppermint Schnapps was kicking in. Soon he was sound asleep, snoring like he was trying to raise the dead.

Drew woke up with a stiff back from sleeping up against his pack. He looked over at Steve who was reading his Bible. Without saying a word, he stood up and went to relieve himself on the other side of the guardrail. He was still pissed at Steve's comments from the night before, and he hadn't forgotten that he had called him out in front of Henry and his family back at the farmhouse.

When he returned, Steve had pulled out a few granola bars and a bottle of water and set them on top of his pack for him to have for breakfast.

"Thank you," Drew said, picking up a granola bar and opening it.

"You're welcome," Steve said as he ate his own bar.

"Once we're done eating, we'll head out. Hopefully we can find some supplies today," Drew said as he uncapped his water and took a swig.

They finished breakfast in silence. Drew put on his pack, walked a few paces and stopped to wait for Steve.

Steve stood up, cinched his pack closed, swung it over his shoulder and started following. When Drew heard his footsteps, he began walking again, staying in front of Steve the whole rest of the day.

They walked through lunch but finally stopped as the sun started to set. Drew reached in and pulled out two packs of beef jerky. He threw one to Steve as he took his pack off and set it down.

"How are you doing?" Steve asked as he opened the bag of jerky.

"Fine. You?"

"Good. Do you want to discuss your drinking?"

"Are you on this again? What the fuck is your problem? Why do you keep bringing this up? I'm growing tired of it."

"Can we be honest?" Steve asked.

"Yeah. I honestly don't want to talk about it because I don't have a problem."

"Yes, you do and I know it. I bet your family knows it too."

Drew stood up, anger washing over him. "We're done with this conversation."

"Don't you want to know how I know?"

"It's simple. You saw me drink a couple times and you think I have a problem."

"I know you have a problem because I used to be just like you. So I know. I remember pounding drinks to achieve the buzz faster, sometimes allowing for more time between drinks to keep the buzz steady, just like you do. The average person doesn't drink the way we do. And if they did, they sure as hell don't bounce back like we do the next morning, or at least the way you do. That comes with practice. A lot of practice."

Drew just stood there staring at Steve.

"You know I'm right. I bet you were a late afternoon or early evening drinker who drank late into the night. You had to work, so drinking in the daytime was out of the question. That only left the afternoon and evening. I bet you started out with beer and switched to liquor. That old saying, beer before liquor makes you sicker, I assume didn't apply to you. You'd done enough drinking of both that your stomach became used to mixing them. You learned that shooting beers would give you a buzz quickly, but that you couldn't keep pounding beers all night. Your stomach can't hold that much liquid. So you switched to liquor. I bet you made a strong drink and pounded that after the beers. It helped you keep the buzz, but with a little extra push."

Drew just stared at him. It was like Steve had just summed up every night of the last two and a half years of his life.

"I can tell by the way you're looking at me that I'm right. But what you don't know, because you haven't reached that point yet — and you might never — is that sooner or later you'll start chasing something else. I started smoking pot to achieve a new high because the booze was doing a number on my stomach."

Drew had reached that point. A few months back, his stomach had started bothering him whenever he drank. So he drank even more to make the pain go away.

"Then I tried cocaine and, wow, that took me to another level and I loved it. But eventually I needed something more. A friend was using heroin and said it was like being next to God. Next thing I knew I had lost everything in my life. I lost my house. Then my wife and kids. I lost everything including my teeth, which had turned black and fallen out. There came a point when I started stealing from my friends and family just to get my next fix. I stole and sold large TV's for pennies on the dollar just to get more drugs. I completely ruined my life. And at the end of it all, I had no one.

"I OD'd the last time I used. One of the people I was squatting with called 911 and the paramedics hit me with some Narcan. I was pissed when I came out of it since they had killed my buzz. They put me on the stretcher and brought me to the E.R.. There was a nurse there who was brutally honest with me and told me if I didn't do anything to change my life, the next time I used I'd probably die."

Drew just sat there listening. He could easily see Steve's story becoming that of his own life.

"Then the nurse did the best and worst thing— she brought me a mirror. I saw how bad I was. I knew my teeth had fallen out because I had basically pulled them out myself, but to actually see... I couldn't believe that was me in the mirror. I was disgusted by myself. That was my rock bottom. I lost it and started balling my eyes out. I told the nurse I wanted to change. I told her I wanted my life back. She consoled me and said she would help me if I truly wanted to change my life. I did. She found me a rehab center that accepted me the next day. I did pretty well at first because I wanted to be there. I wanted to change. But it was hard. I was with a bunch of people just like me— all addicts. There were people there from all walks of life. Addiction knows no social barriers. The worst thing about addiction is that you're addicted. Some people call it a disease and others call it an addiction. I guess either way it doesn't really matter what you call it because once it has a hold of you, nothing matters except getting high. But I guess it's important if they're going to find a way to break people of it."

Drew enjoyed listening to Steve tell him his story. He could relate.

"Like I said, I did well at first but all of these people who had been in the rehab were dropping out. They couldn't take it. Some left and ended up coming back and others left, used again and died. Seeing people who had time under their belts leave with all of this confidence about themselves and how they weren't going to use again, only to return defeated. . . . I was afraid of that. I had already lost so much and the only thing I had left to lose was my life, and I knew that if I used again I would die. I still feel that way to this very day. But I was afraid to die. My life was the one and only thing I hadn't lost to the drugs, so I was determined to hold onto to that one thing, if nothing else. Trust me—it's been a constant struggle since the world turned. But I found God in rehab, and He's helped me make it through. I'm here today because of Him. He wants me to succeed. He wants me to stay clean and sober, and I think He wants me to help you stay clean and sober."

"Why did you roll your eyes?" asked Steve.

"Nothing."

"No, you rolled your eyes. Why?" Steve asked.

"Because I no longer believe in God the way you do."

"But you believed in God once before though, right?"

"Yes," Drew replied.

"What made you lose your belief?"

"What I saw day in and day out from doing my job," Drew said.

"What did you see?" asked Steve.

"Death."

"But death is part of life."

"Are you fucking kidding me? Okay, tell that to a mother whose little daughter fell down a flight of stairs and broke her neck because someone forgot to close a child gate. Tell that to a parent of a child who was snatched off the street, raped and murdered by some fucking sicko. Tell that to the inner-city parents of a child who was playing in a park and was shot for no reason by some punk ass kid with a gun. Where was God then? You tell me! Go tell those families that! Those aren't just stories in the paper or on the news the next day. Those are faces of the dead that are burned into every police officer, firefighter and EMT who tried to help those people in the aftermath. The ones who have to deal with it. Who try with all their might to save everyone. So for you to say death is part of life, well you don't have the faces of the dead burned into your memory like we all do."

Steve remained silent, not knowing what to say.

"Tell that to the millions of people who have died in from the sickness."

Drew got up and walked straight over to his backpack, where he pulled out another tiny bottle of Peppermint Schnapps. He twisted off the top and swallowed down the contents in one big gulp. He looked up and saw Steve was still staring at him. Drew held out the bottle and nodded his head, "You want some?"

Steve shook his head and turned around. He couldn't watch Drew drink himself to oblivion.

The next morning Steve had breakfast ready when Drew woke up. He made him a plate and brought it over to him.

"Thank you," Drew acknowledged as he accepted the plate.

"You're welcome."

Drew reached for his bottle of water and took a long pull, almost draining it.

"Do you drink all drinks that fast?" Steve asked.

"Yeah, for the most part, except soda. The bubbles start to burn going down."

"I didn't mean to make you upset last night."

"I know. But you were right. I do drink a lot. My wife left me the day the sickness started because of my drinking."

"I'm sorry."

"It's not your fault. It's mine."

"I know it's not my fault, but I'm sorry because I've been there before. Losing everything. It really sucks, but you can fix it."

"Fix it how?"

"Gosh, I don't know, Drew. But it looks like you may have to stop drinking, crazy as that sounds."

Drew glanced up at Steve to see he was smirking at him as he gave him a wink. "Easier said than done," he replied without sharing Steve's humor. "I've tried stopping before and I only lasted a week."

"It's hard, but it can be done," Steve said, also in a more serious tone. "Trust me. It can be done."

"How long have you been sober?"

"Three years to the day of the sickness."

"Really?"

"Really. So I took the fact that I'm still alive to mean that I'm doing something right. And I think it has a lot to do with this," Steve said she he shook the Bible in his right hand. "If I'm still alive after all I've done, it must mean God has a purpose for me, and my work's not finished."

"That again," Drew said with a tone.

"It's part of it but not all of it. Actually it came later. Before, it was just me focusing on staying clean. I joined AA, which was a huge help. They have a motto: "One day at a time." The only day you need to worry about is today, and you only need to focus on staying sober that day."

Drew had a lot of respect for all that Steve had been through, but that didn't mean that Steve was right about everything, especially about God. *Because if there is a God, I think He gave up on us.*

Chapter 38

The minacious, dark figure made its way around to the side of the bed. It stopped, tilted its head and looked at her. Kendra had been a beautiful woman. A woman no more, though. She had started to cross to the other side. The figure moved closer to her foot, which hung off the bed. It reached out its long black finger and touched her toe. A spark jumped and cracked like the way a static charge jumps when you touch something metal after walking across a carpeted floor. The same charge that is in everyone's heart, making it pump.

It waited, not for life to fill her body, but for death. Her life was being drained. It would fill it back up with death. Death it could control. Life it could not. God made life and gave it free will. No one could change free will. Therefore, no one could control life. Once someone died, that life could be replaced with death.

The figure needed to time it just right, or a piece of her former life would be trapped in her shell of a body, which would cause Kendra and her body to be in a constant inner struggle for control. It needed to capture her soul once the life was gone from her body. For one to live trapped within both life and death was not the way. Both would be too much to bear.

Once her life had been completely drained, the figure touched her before her soul could escape. It filled her with death. Death was his area. Death was its to control, as life was God's.

It waited. At first nothing happened. Kendra just lay there motionless. Suddenly the needle in her arm twitched. There was a pause, and then the needle twitched again, slowly gaining speed and swinging back and forth like a pendulum as each heart beat ticked away.

A loud gasping sound came from her body as she sucked air into her lungs. Her chest expanded like a balloon filling and her back arched. Strands of her hair clung to the dampness on her forehead. Her eyes, no longer green but now black as death, shot open exposing them to the new world.

Kendra's body sat up. She body could feel the presence of her new master in the room. It controlled her body. It owned her soul. She looked at the hovering baleful figure that had now started to resemble a silhouette of a man and could feel its power and energy. In its presence, she felt like she did when she first pushed the plunger on the needle, releasing the heroin into her veins for the first time all those years ago. She felt connected. The feeling of being wrapped in warm white sheets had been replaced with the cold of the black sheets. That feeling of being suffocated was constant. At first her body fought it, but then quickly embraced it. She sat on the edge of the bed adjusting to her new life. The world of color had been replaced with a one of gray. Everything had the look of a brewing thunderstorm. A dark and dreary look. The color of the world was gone.

Follow me, she heard a voice whisper as the figure turned and moved out of her bedroom. She stood up and followed it into the living room and towards Hector's lifeless body. Kendra no longer felt remorse or guilt over shooting him. Her guilt replaced with pleasure. She thought back to pulling the trigger, watching his head snap back as the bullet entered his right eye and slamming out the back of his head. She found herself smiling, now suddenly enjoying the memory of killing him. *He was nothing more than just a liar and a thief and he deserved to die,* she thought to herself.

It made its way through the opening in the door and into the hallway where it waited for her to follow.

Before, she was afraid of catching the sickness from Hector. Now she somehow knew that no sickness could affect her. Nothing could kill her now. Nothing but the sinister dark figure in the hallway. She tried the door, but her small frame did not have the strength to move his corpse.

Kendra's arm reached up and grabbed the door frame with one hand and the door with the other, using them for leverage. She planted her right foot between his neck and shoulder and began to push. Slowly the lifeless corpse started sliding and wiggling in the piss and excrement that had been released from his body. She pushed hard enough to where she could close the door a little and undo the chain. The door flung open, and his head fell, hitting the floor. Blood, pus and gray brain matter oozed from the bullet hole where his right eye used to be and pooled on the hallway carpet.

Kendra followed her new master down the hall and through the door to the stairs. She loved the new sense of freedom. Freedom from guilt. Freedom from fear. But somewhere deep inside her reanimated form, a tiny piece of Kendra screamed.

Chapter 39

Stanley sat at the Johnsons' kitchen table wondering how he was going to get home. The airports were closed. The roads were clogged with accidents, which meant that buses weren't running, and the trains were probably shut down as well. To top it off, all this sitting wasn't helping his back. He had surgery a few months ago and he was in terrible pain if he sat or stood for too long.

The surgery was a failure and the only thing that seemed to help him were the pills. He couldn't remember what they were called or if he had the generic brand, but all he knew was they helped with the pain. But on the downside, they bound him up pretty badly, so he needed to take another medicine with them to help him poop.

Stanley reached into his bag, pulled out his pill bottle, opened the cover and looked in. He had used almost half the bottle and he had picked up the prescription just before he left. *Seems like I have to take more and more of these damn pills to help quell the pain in my back.*

Bill walked into the kitchen and leaned up against the sink.

"Any luck?" Bill asked, nodding towards the phone on the table.

"None," Stanley replied despondently. "I can't even get a dial tone now. How could this have happened?" He rolled the pill bottle in his hands.

"I don't know."

"Anything on the TV?"

"No. It's all static now and has been for a couple hours."

"I hope my wife is okay."

"She's probably fine," Bill said and attempted a smile.

"I hope so," Stanley said as the pill bottle fell out of his hands and bounced off the hardwood floor.

"What's up with the pills? I've noticed you're popping them quite often. You okay?"

"Oh these," Stanley said while shaking the bottle. "These are my pain meds. I had surgery on my back a few months ago and all of this driving around isn't helping it heal. Plus, I think I'm pretty tense from the stress of all that's going on, and that's making it worse."

"You should be careful with those," Bill warned. "Dan Haskins lives a few doors down, well *used* to live a few doors down. He got his hand stuck in a combine and had to have surgery to repair it, and the doctors gave him some painkillers too. I guess he got hooked on them and overdosed. His thirteen-year-old son found him after school one day while his mother was out grocery shopping."

"Oh wow. I'm sorry," Stanley said.

"You should get off of those as soon as possible. They're not good for you."

Stan understood Bill was trying to be helpful and showing concern, which he appreciated, but now wasn't a good time with all his other worries. "Is there anything I can do to help out around here?" he asked trying to change the conversation.

"We've finished our chores for today but you're more than welcome to join us tomorrow morning."

"You tell me a time and I'll be up."

"We usually start around five thirty."

"Okay, I'll be ready."

"Try and get some sleep tonight and hopefully the phones will be back up tomorrow."

"Thank you, Bill. Thank you for your hospitality. I truly appreciate it."

"It's our pleasure." And with that Bill turned and walked into the other room and up the stairs.

Stanley made his way to the guest bedroom which was off the back of the kitchen. It had a bed and nightstands on each side, with a light on the right one.

He emptied his pockets and put his cell phone, car keys, wallet and bottle of pills on the left side nightstand, then changed into his pj's and climbed into bed. The crisp sheets were a welcome amenity after the long day.

He grabbed his cell phone and tried calling home again. There was a dial tone, which gave him hope. He dialed his wife's cell phone number hoping it would ring and that she would pick up. But instead he heard the same message, "All circuits are busy."

Stanley wondered what Carol was doing. Was she safe? Was she even alive? God he hoped so. Hopefully Bill was right and the phones would be working the next day. He set his alarm on his phone, placed it back on the nightstand, and rested his head on the pillow.

As he lay there he could hear this faint whisper. He couldn't make out what it was saying. It was like a whisper from another room.

He had an impulse and reached for the pill bottle. It seemed like the painkillers were calling to him, as if the whispers were coming from the pill bottle. Stanley picked up the bottle and was about to open the cover when he remembered the conversation he had just had with Bill. *These things are starting to becoming a crutch,* he thought. He willed himself not to open it and put the pill bottle back down. The whispers ceased. Stanley rolled over and turned off the light.

Chapter 40

Drew and Steve pushed on through the intense heat that rose up from the blacktop. Little by little they were becoming more dehydrated as they continued on. Drew could feel his organs screaming for water. They walked several more miles before coming to an exit where luckily there was a gas station a few hundred yards up on the left.

Steve started to make his way around to the right side of the building like Drew had shown him a while back in order to scope it out for any possible threats and means of egress for once they got inside. He turned to check and caught Drew out of the corner of his eye, walking straight up three concrete steps and to the glass front door.

Drew had started to become slow and lethargic. He knew he needed water and fast. The heat and the weight of the pack were doing him in. He pushed, then pulled on the front door, but it was locked and wouldn't budge. He leaned back and gave the door a swift kick, but all it did was shake, and he was so weak and exhausted that he nearly stumbled and lost his balance when putting his foot back down.

"Let me help," Steve said as he started towards Drew.

Drew turned his head, looked at Steve and then back at the door. He then took a step back.

Finally, he'll let me help him, Steve thought.

Drew took another step back, unslung the shotgun, pumped it and fired it pointblank into the door. The blast sent glass and pieces of the metal frame flying everywhere.

"Jesus, Drew!" Steve shouted as he covered his eyes.

"It's open," Drew said as he pulled the pulverized door open and walked in.

Steve rushed in behind him and was surprised to watch Drew just walk to the back of the store and open one of the cooler doors without even checking to make sure the place was empty..

Deciding it was time to step up and assume his role, Steve rushed from one side of the store to the other, checking the four little aisles, making sure no one was in the store, then walked over and joined Drew at the back of the store.

"What the hell were you thinking?" yelled Steve.

Drew had a gallon of water pressed up against his lips and was drinking feverishly from it. Water ran down around his mouth, down his chin and onto his shirt. He was sucking so hard the plastic jug started to collapse in on itself and made a crushing sound with every gulp. Steve watched in amazement—Drew had downed half a gallon already and was still going. He finished three-quarters of the gallon before he stopped and switched from sucking water to sucking air.

He turned and put his back against the cooler door and slid down until his ass hit the floor, then he began drinking more water.

The cooler stopped working a week ago and the water wasn't cold but it didn't matter to Drew. It was wet and for something having no taste, it was delicious.

"Dehydrated huh?" Steve commented. It was more of a statement then a question.

Drew just moved his eyes and glared at Steve, because he knew what was coming next.

"Just another reason to quit drinking," he added.

Drew just groaned.

"I've noticed you get angry when you don't drink too, which means there's an underlying problem that is exacerbated when you drink."

"Are you back on this again?" Drew moaned.

"Well most drunks just get the shakes and the DT's when they go too long without a drink, but man you get really angry. I was expecting you to get the shakes, but you never did. You're more like the little engine that could with a fire that never goes out. And I rarely see you with a hangover for the amount of alcohol you drink."

"Jealous?"

"No. But if I drank as much as you do, I'd be down and out for a week with one hell of a hangover. But not you. You're the first one awake and the last one asleep. It's almost as if alcohol doesn't affect you, other than get you drunk of course."

"Practice. It comes from lots of practice."

"There's a name for it and it's called a high-functioning alcoholic. Are you seriously proud of that? Are you proud of how much you can drink and how belligerent you can get?"

"No."

"Because it seems like alcohol turns on your inner asshole. So there's an underlying problem somewhere."

"Didn't your mother ever tell you that if you don't have anything nice to say then don't say anything at all?"

They both sat there for a few minutes, an uncomfortable silence between them.

But in the silence, a realization crept into Drew's conscience as he stared at the floor, and before long he could feel the tears welling up in his eyes.

"What have I done?" Drew said in a voice just above a whisper.

"It's okay," Steve said.

"No, it's not. I lost everything. I lost my wife. My little girl, my beautiful little girl. I wasn't there for her."

"It will be okay."

Drew looked up. "How can you say that? All I cared about was drinking. I should have spent more time with them. All my little girl will remember is having a drunk for a daddy. I should have been a better husband. I was so selfish."

"Yes you were, but you can fix it."

"How can I fix it? They're probably dead."

"Don't think that way."

"I should have been there for them, to protect them. But instead my wife left me because I drank too much and become an asshole when I do. And now they're probably dead."

Tears ran down his cheeks and fell into his lap. Two little wet spots formed on his blue jeans, one on each thigh.

Steve reached over and grabbed Drew's shoulder and pulled him over to him. Drew's chest heaved up and down as he cried.

"It's going to be okay," Steve said again.

"Why do you keep saying that? How do you know it will be okay?"

"I don't know, but I feel it. Don't you feel it too?"

Drew continued to weep more uncontrollably.

"I'm such an asshole. I let my drinking ruin everything," Drew said as snot hung from his nose.

"We're going to make our way home and find your family. Find my family," Steve said.

"Annabelle kept telling me to quit drinking or she'd leave me. She always called me a jerk when I drank and told me her family felt the same way. She was so ashamed. I made my own wife and daughter ashamed of me. What kind of man am I?"

"You're a man who made a mistake."

"It was more than just a mistake."

"Okay, a man who kept making the same mistake over and over again."

Drew suddenly chuckled through his sniffling, and a smile flashed across his face as he saw the humor in what Steve said, but then the smile turned to a frown. He knew that making the same mistake over and over again made those who loved him miserable.

"Drew, listen to me."

"Okay."

"Listen real good. We're going to rest here tonight and get you hydrated, and tomorrow morning we're going to head north and find our families. They're still alive—I feel it."

Drew shook his head, "I feel it too."

"You're done drinking. No more. Do you understand?"

Drew shook his head again.

"I know it's going to be hard. Your mind will work against you. It will make you want to drink. It will make you think you need a drink. It will become so bad, that all you'll be able to do is think about drinking. I've been there, and it sucks. It really sucks. It's so hard to shut off your brain."

"It is hard. I've wanted to stop before, but the bottle calls my name. My body craves it. I'm addicted. You're right—my mind keeps thinking about drinking. I would think about how once I had my first drink, all of my problems would wash away. But looking back, all of my problems really started when I drank. I'd run my mouth and become belligerent. I wouldn't care what I said or who I said it to. My wife would always say I was full of such anger when I drank. She said it was as if I became a different man, that she hated me drinking. And I would tell her I would stop, but the very next night I'd stop at the packie and buy more booze. She'd make me promise not to drink, but when I started drinking again she'd tell me I had promised. It was like I couldn't control myself. Looking back, it really *was* like I became a different person. A person no one seemed to like except me. I liked the way I felt. But it was false. I want a drink right now and to stop talking about it."

"Have a drink."

Drew sat up with a puzzled look on his face, "Have a drink? Really?"

"If you want a drink, have one. But be warned, if you take that drink, you'll become that man again. That angry, full-of-hate man who only cares for himself. How is that man going to find his family? He isn't, that's how."

"You're right," Drew said as he took another drink of water.

"We all make mistakes and then we pay for them. You're paying for it now, my friend."

"Karma is a bitch."

"Yes it is. But you need to learn from your mistakes and not repeat them again. But trust me—you'll make a mistake. Learn and move on."

"But how do I silence that voice in my head telling me to have a drink?"

"Easy—you treat it like a child. You repeatedly keep telling it no. Tell yourself you can drink whenever you want, except you can't drink today and tell yourself that every day. Soon the voice will learn. But it will always be there. It will be like that annoying fly at a restaurant when you're out to eat. It will pop up and buzz around for a second, just long enough to annoy you and make you lose your focus, but then it will disappear. But then it will be back again, and this time you'll swat at it and miss and it will disappear again. But you know that annoying little black fly will be back again, and it will be all you can think of. You've stopped listening to the person at the other side of the table. You're constantly searching for that little black fly. Now when it returns again, this time you'll stop mid-sentence, mid-forkful or chew and focus all of your attention on it and try to kill it. But you don't kill it. All you managed to do was knock your utensils onto the floor and tip over your drink and cover the table in liquid, which will disrupt everyone else at your table and get the attention of everyone in the restaurant. You let some small little thing completely disrupt your meal.

That little voice is just like that little black fly. First it makes you lose focus. Then it makes you focus on it until you are consumed by it. You're no longer focused on life. You're only focused on what that little voice is saying, and it's telling you to have a drink.

And then you have made a complete fool of yourself. Ignore the fly, the voice, and they'll go away."

"You're a wise man Steve."

"I learned the hard way too, except my little black bug was a hornet and my drink was heroin."

The sunlight crept in through a little square window on the east sidewall and made its way across the floor until it was smack dab in Steve's face, waking him. He had slept well. And he was glad he was able to finally talk to Drew about his drinking the night before and that he was receptive. He just hoped Drew had really listened.

Steve opened his eyes, expecting to see Drew slumped over in the corner where he fell asleep last night but he was not there. Steve instantly thought he must have gotten up in the middle of the night, had gotten drunk, and couldn't find his way back.

He scurried to his feet and searched the store. Drew was nowhere to be found. He went to the front door and pulled it open. His heart raced when he saw Drew's pack lying out in the middle of the parking lot. Steve pushed himself out through the mangled door and ran out into the parking lot, turning in a semicircle, searching for Drew.

"Dammit!" Steve screamed.

"What?" he heard from behind him.

Steve turned and saw that Drew was sitting on a box next to the front door.

"Oh, there you are," Steve said.

"Did you think I left?"

"Well . . . I wasn't sure after our discussion last night."

"No, I didn't leave to go and find a drink," Drew assured him. "I've been up since dawn though, thanks to my bladder. Apparently it can only hold so much water."

"Well you did drink quite a bit," Steve replied. "Water that is."

"And some dummy didn't put the cover back on the water, so it got knocked over in the middle of the night and my pack got wet. Hence why it's in the middle of the parking lot, drying in the sun."

Steve tried to think back if he knocked over his water or not and chuckled once he realized Drew was talking about himself. *He definitely has a different sense of humor*, Steve thought.

"So sitting out here, I realized something. I keep seeing that metaphoric black fly you mentioned last night in every store we pass. It seems every place down here sells booze, and we keep passing stores when we're on the these side streets and main roads. But when we're on the highway, we keep running into trouble."

Steve nodded in agreement.

"A mile or so back that way," Drew said pointing down the road, "We crossed some train tracks that got me thinking."

"Okay," Steve said.

"I grabbed this atlas from a store a while back, and it has rail lines indicated on it. I figure we could walk the tracks and stay out of sight, be away from people and not pass any more stores selling booze. Avoid that proverbial black fly."

"I like your thinking," Steve agreed. "We can move undetected and probably make good time. Fewer decomposing bodies will be nice, too."

They ate breakfast and loaded up on supplies. Drew found a unique item on the back shelf of the little store, a handheld water purifier. It had a tube and pump which turned most water into clean drinking water. *We can most defiantly use this on our way*, he thought. He packed it up along with bottled water and left his booze behind. Once ready, they set out to find the train tracks they had passed.

"Where the heck do you think we are?" asked Steve as they walked the train tracks heading north. Drew just shrugged his shoulders as they pressed on. *The sun was up early as usual this morning*, Steve thought, *but not earlier than Drew*. If it wasn't for watching him fall asleep so fast, he would never have guessed Drew slept. Steve tossed and turned every night trying to fall asleep, yet Drew was out like a light in under a minute. *Not fair. I'm so exhausted at the end of the day, but I can't fall asleep.*

The sun was now directly overhead and baking down on them. Steve was happy they had decided to walk the train tracks. They hardly saw anyone or any dead and decomposing bodies.

Out of nowhere, a strong wind blew in from the south against their backs. The wind carried leaves and debris that danced down the tracks. Drew turned and saw the sky had turned black. A storm was approaching.

Up ahead, about a half mile down the tracks, there appeared to be an old abandoned mill of some sort. As they grew closer, they could see a long loading dock that faced the tracks. At some point, the train must have stopped there to pick up and drop off supplies before running them up and down the line.

As they approached, Drew could see a church steeple rising up above the treetops along with an old looking brick building beyond the mill.

The wind had really started to pick up now, and the black clouds were whipping past above.

"Storm's coming!" yelled Steve.

No shit genius, Drew wanted to say as he nodded his head in agreement. Instead, he remained cordial and simply replied, "We should try and take cover inside the old mill."

The wood siding on the building was old, and the elements had washed it a storm-gray over time.

Drew walked over to the loading dock and pounded on the dock, testing the integrity of the wood. He didn't want to hop up onto it and fall through the flooring. The wood was old, but it was strong. He jumped up and walked over to the old sliding door. It had a rusted metal latch that kept it closed and he thought it would disintegrate just by touching it. He used his thumb to press down on the thumb latch. It didn't budge. He grabbed the handle and lifted up, pressing the latch again using both thumbs. The latch broke and fell to the floor with a clang. Drew leaned to his right and pulled on the door. It opened a few inches before the handle broke which caused him to stumble and almost fall.

Steve laughed.

"Just my luck. Both the latch and handle broke," Drew said now visibly upset. He grabbed the door and heaved it open. The heavy door slid across its old track and crashed into the sidewall, and then started making its way back towards Drew.

He put out his hands to stop the door from slamming into them.

CRACK! A bolt of lightning crashed high above and then thunder exploded above them.

Drew and Steve made their way inside just as the sky opened up and the rain came down in buckets.

"Stay with me," Drew told Steve as they walked farther into the old mill.

The main area was huge and had an old skylight window that might've normally let some light in, but the thick storm clouds outside currently kept the area rather dim. There were several smaller, office type rooms off to each side of the main one.

Drew made his way over to the rooms on the right side. They were empty except for a few newspapers and old clothes in the corner. They made their way back across to the other side. As they approached, he noticed a light coming from the room on the far right. They moved cautiously over to the room, where inside they found a man lying on a few newspapers with an oil lamp next to him that was turned down low.

There was a foul smell in the air. It wasn't as bad as a decomposing body, but it was pretty bad. Drew knew what it was right away: human shit.

Both Drew and Steve stood there for a minute, staring at the man. His shirt was off and he was so thin and covered with some sort of rash. The light from the lamp illuminated the man's ribcage. His skin was sunken to his ribs and looked like it was shrink-wrapped onto him like the way Drew shrink-wrapped his windows back home during the winter. The long piece of plastic would stick to the window when the heat from the hairdryer was applied to it.

Keeping their eyes on the body before them, not yet noticing any signs of the sickness, but not wanting to take chances, they started inching closer, when the man stirred and rolled over. His back was worse than his front. The skin was so tight it had started to split and bleed.

"He's alive!" Steve whispered.

Drew turned and flashed him a look that said, *Dur! Dead people don't roll over.*

"Does he have the sickness?" Steve asked.

Just then the man started to mumble but they couldn't make out what he was saying.

Outside the storm intensified. The lightning was impressive as it cracked and streaked across the sky. The thunder boomed and rolled, making the building shake.

Both Drew and Steve looked to the ceiling. The sound was so loud it felt like the roof had been torn off.

They looked back down at the skinny man who had now rolled back over, his white eyes staring back at them. The man reached out and grabbed the small brown paper bag in front of him and pulled it into his chest before scurrying across the floor into the corner.

Both Drew and Steve looked at each other again with unsureness and then turned their attention back toward the skinny man.

The skinny man leaned forwards and yelled, "You can't have them! They're mine!" and pulled the brown paper bag up under his chin, crossing his forearms over it.

"Trust me, pal. We don't want whatever it is you've got," Drew said.

The man just tilted his head as if he didn't understand Drew.

"Are you sick?" Steve asked.

"Sick?" The man said as if he was a parrot.

Drew turned his head to Steve, "He's fucking sick alright, but not with the virus. He's a pill popper."

Steve looked at the poor soul of a man in the corner who was covered in his own vomit and feces. "How do you know he's a pill popper?"

"Pill poppers usually have a loss of appetite and can develop a rash, hence him being so skinny and red all over," Drew said pointing at the man. "They also can get confused, and this boy is clearly confused. He's covered in his own vomit and shit, and it looks like he's been pissing in those plastic bottles over there."

The skinny man kept looking around as if other people were in the room and he barely made eye contact with Drew or Steve.

"We should help him," Steve said.

"There's clearly no helping this kid."

"Can't you help him? You're an EMT."

"Are you kidding me? He needs an emergency room and a detox center, and we're in the middle of nowhere. Plus, he'll be dead in a day or two if not sooner."

"Don't you have any compassion?" Steve said, making it sound more like a statement than a question.

Drew was about to answer, when the skinny man, reached into the bag, pulled out a handful of pills, and tossed them into his mouth. He then leaned over and grabbed one of the bottles filled with his urine, twisted off the cap and took a long pull from it, washing down the pills.

"Yeah, there's no helping this kid," Drew said as he turned and walked out of the room and headed across the main area, back towards the rooms on the other side.

Steve came shuffling behind him. "So there's nothing we can do for him?"

"I can go put a bullet in his head and end his suffering."

A look of disbelief came over Steve's face. "How can you say that? I thought you saved people? I thought you were a good man?"

"Because it's what's needed to end his misery. I did save people. I guess I'm not a good man anymore though," Drew answered as he dropped his backpack up against the wall.

"I can't believe you! You disgust me!" Steve said as he turned to walk out of the room when a streak of lightning cracked across the sky, lighting the main room and illuminating the dark shadowy figure standing in the corner, followed by another rolling volley of thunder as Steve walked out.

"What the fuck do you want from me?" Drew yelled as he knelt down and started pulling things out of his pack.

Twenty minutes had passed when Drew decided to go check on Steve. He checked the other rooms first, but when he couldn't find him, he reentered the skinny man's room and found Steve kneeling over the man. Drew respected him for wanting to help this unfortunate soul, but there was no helping him.

The way Steve was kneeling and positioned in front of the oil lamp, the light backlit him, giving him the appearance of an angel, like those depicted in the stained glass windows of a church.

Drew stood in the doorway and bowed his head as Steve began to pray over the man.

"Merciful Lord of life, I lift up my heart to You in my suffering and ask for Your comforting help. I know that You would withhold the thorns of this life if I could attain eternal life without them. So I throw myself on Your mercy, resigning myself to this suffering. Grant me the grace to bear it and to offer it in union with Your sufferings. No matter what suffering may come my way, let me trust in You."

"Steve," Drew interrupted when he noticed Steve drawing the sign of the cross on the man's forehead, "don't make contact with him. In his confused state, he could attack you."

Steve turned and looked at Drew with a somber face, and Drew noticed Steve had his prayer book in his hand and his Bible on the floor next to him. "It's okay," he replied softly. "He died a few minutes ago," Steve said.

Drew walked over to Steve and put his hand on his shoulder, "I'm sorry."

"At least someone was with him when he passed," Steve said.

Drew squeezed Steve's shoulder and then patted him on the head.

"How did you know he was going to die?" Steve asked, wiping away tears.

"Because I've seen enough people just like him—not to this extreme obviously—and this is how they look just before we get the call that they've overdosed. Plus we know just by the address when the call comes in since most of them are frequent fliers. Sometimes it's the person's first time using and they end up overdosing. Total surprise to the family. But with someone like this kid, the family is expecting it. It was only a matter of time—I assume that probably wasn't his first handful of pills he popped today."

He paused for a moment, the silence only itching away at him to speak further. "It's not that I don't have compassion, you know. I just... in my line of work..."

"You start to get numb to it. I know."

Drew sighed with a hint of guilt. "Yeah."

Steve hesitated. "And I didn't mean to lash out at you. It's just that, with this kid dying because of his addiction...with my own history..."

"It hits a soft spot. I get it."

"Yeah," Steve agreed. "But more than that too. I mean, aren't you worried this could be us?"

"What?" Drew asked with a tone in his voice.

"We'll we're both addicts, so this could be us someday."

"Umm. . . .I've never popped pills a day in my life. I'll admit, I love my booze but pill popping was never on my list of kicks to try."

Steve looked back down at the man, "But you could have easily killed yourself, or worse a family, when you drove drunk."

"Touché."

"Do you think he wanted to die and that's why he popped a handful of pills?" Steve asked as he flipped through his Bible.

"I don't know," Drew said shaking his head. "I don't know if everyone he loved died from the sickness so he just wanted to die, or if he was an addict before the sickness. I tend to believe he was an addict before the sickness and was jonesing for a fix after the sickness hit. And I bet he broke into a pharmacy, found the pills he was looking for and dumped them all into the bag. He probably grabbed every bottle located around the pills he was looking for and dumped them in too. I bet the pharmacy probably kept the laxative next to the opiates and this poor bastard was popping just as many laxatives as pain pills, hence him covered in his own shit. People who take opiates are usually prescribed a laxative because the pills make them constipated."

"Really?"

"Really."

"Wow! He would just take pills that he didn't know what they were?"

"Steve, if you knew what these kids are doing," Drew said as he made his way over to the opposite corner and sat down. "Kids will raid their parents' medicine cabinet and take any pills that are in a prescription bottle. Then they'll meet up with their friends and combine all of their pills in a bowl and start popping them."

"They will just take whatever they find?"

"Yup, and kids will pop anything from high blood pressure medication to pain killers," Drew said as he picked up a newspaper lying in the corner. "Steeling and mixing their parents' meds are the most convenient way for them to get high, and they don't stop to think about how dangerous that is." He looked at the date, which was over a month ago, and read the top story about a bad accident out on I-95 that tied up traffic for hours. It said it was one of the worst traffic nightmares in decades. *Oh yeah, well it's worse now – it's a permanent parking lot*, he thought and dropped the paper back down into the corner.

Once Steve finished, Drew got up and started to walk out. "I'm going to catch a nap in the other room. I can't stand that smell of shit in here. Hopefully the storm will end soon and we can be on our way."

The dark, otherworldly figure had hid in the corner after claiming another life. It watched how the men interacted with each other. It studied them, then moved on.

Chapter 41

The storm ended sometime in the middle of the night while both men caught up on some much-needed sleep. After breakfast they headed back out onto the tracks. Even though they knew the trains were not running, they still had the fear that a large freight train would come barreling down the tracks towards them.

At the same time, however, they felt like children walking on the track trying to see who could stay on the longest. "If your foot touches the ground you lose," Drew said with his arms out to his side, trying to balance himself. The two grown men laughed like they had not a care in the world. Once that got boring, they started another game. "You can only step on the railroad ties and nothing else," Steve said.

Drew was more than happy to play since it took away from the boredom. Soon they were racing each other. They competed to see who could go the fastest without stepping off the ties.

The miles passed by, and Drew realized he was glad he had Steve with him. He wasn't fond of the guy at first, but he had grown on him. He would have never guessed Steve for someone who used heroin. *I guess it's true what they say,* he thought. *Addiction knows no social boundaries.*

Drew was starting to recognize that he may indeed have a drinking problem. He started thinking back on his life and how alcohol has been a part of it since he was eighteen. After going into the Marines, his drinking really picked up to the point of affecting his life. It started out simple at first. He and his friends would get their hands on some beer, and after two bottles he had a buzz. He had instantly fallen in love with that feeling: turning off his brain and making his problems disappear for a little while.

At the time, all of his friends were drinking or smoking pot. He tried pot himself, but it just put him to sleep and he didn't find it enjoyable. But beer — now that was something else. As kids they drank whatever they could get their hands on. One of his friends had an older brother who would buy them beer. He and his friends would pool their money together and get the cheapest beer they could buy. Taste didn't matter back then, only the buzz. Hell, that's all that mattered, otherwise they would have just bought a soda and saved themselves all that money and hassle.

It was new and they enjoyed the experience. Drew and his friends would have parties in the woods and collect money from people to buy more beer for the next party. They'd have a large bonfire and invite kids from all over the neighborhood. Sometimes they'd even hide the beer in the woods and drink it warm. Most of his friends hated it, but he didn't mind. He thought it gave him a buzz quicker and that was what he was after.

Drew had a friend whose parents would go away every now and then, so they'd have a party there, though it wasn't the same as the get-togethers in the woods because they couldn't invite as many people to the house. It wasn't perfect, but it worked.

Then came the barrooms once he was out of the Marines. This was when the drinking started to turn into a problem. He'd finish work on Friday, go and cash his check, then and hit the bar. He'd return on Saturday and Sunday and wake up penniless on Monday. The problem worsened when he had to borrow money from his boss for gas to get him through the week, and soon thereafter his bills started to pile up.

He then decided to change careers and enrolled in an EMT course. Drew did well in the class and enjoyed it. He was looking forward to the thrill. Soon he finished the course and found a job working for a local ambulance service before taking a job working in Boston. The work suited him well, but he enjoyed the adrenaline rush more. His training prepared him for most of the calls and he, like all other EMT's, winged it at times, improvising when needed, as each situation was different.

The training prepared him to handle the blood, gore and carnage and how to save someone's life, but it did not train him for home. Dealing with the faces of the dead, the screams of loved ones and the gasps of the dying were never things one could get used to.

Soon the drinking was no longer for the buzz, but to drown out the screams, to make the faces go away, to sleep. Everyone handles what they see differently. Some talk about it, others turn inward, and others self-medicate.

Looking back now, he wished he'd handled it differently. The industry does a lot to help prevent self-medicating and has special stress debriefings, but they only work if you partake. His pride was too big to swallow back then, and admitting something bothered him was a sign of weakness in his mind. He carried that weight alone, plus the added weight of his childhood. But all that weight had a cost.

"You're an alcoholic!" his wife had called him the last time he saw her. *She's right*, he thought, *I am an alcoholic*.

Suddenly Steve put his arm on his shoulder startling him, "Are you okay? You seem pretty quiet."

"Yeah, just thinking," Drew said.

"Anything good?"

"About my life and my drinking," Drew replied. "My wife called me an alcoholic and told me she wanted a divorce the last time I saw her. So no, nothing good."

"Really? I'm sorry."

"How did you get clean?" Drew asked.

"First I needed to acknowledge that I had a problem. Do you have a problem?"

"I think I do," Drew replied.

"You think?"

Drew looked down and kicked a rock that bounced off the train track and went flying into the woods. "No, I do have a problem with drinking. What now?"

"Well, I enrolled in a program and they helped me through it. They educated me about addiction and what I could do to try and stop it."

"Try and stop it?" Drew repeated.

"It's not a proven science, but it helps if you want to quit."

"I guess I'm screwed since there're no more programs."

Steve put his hand on Drew's shoulder, and both men stopped and faced each other. "Drew, it's not about the program. It's about you wanting to stop. To beat your addiction. If you want to stop, you can."

"Addiction. I never considered myself an addict."

"Well in your case it would be an alcoholic. You're an alcoholic. I'm an addict."

"I am. I'm an alcoholic," Drew admitted.

"Welcome to the first step, my friend."

They had been walking the tracks for the better part of the morning with the sun overhead in the sky, unrelentingly beating down on them. Both were drenched in sweat. Drew opened his bottle of water and drank the last sip. The water was piss-warm, but it went down.

As they continued, the vegetation became sparse, and Drew noticed he could see the interstate on his right. He looked at the atlas and saw that I-95 and the tracks ran parallel to each other.

"Look, buildings," Steve said as he pointed through an opening in the vegetation.

Drew stopped and saw, just beyond a car sitting on the interstate, the buildings on that far side, just as Steve had said.

"Let's go see if we can find some water and a shady spot to sit down for a while," Drew suggested as he adjusted his pack and wiped the sweat from his brow.

"Sounds good to me," Steve said.

They turned and exited the tracks, heading through the small scrub brush and up the slight embankment. Drew checked to his right where he saw nothing except vast open road. He turned left and scanned the perimeter around the car they had spotted from the tracks, surprised to suddenly notice two people sitting on the hood. One of them was lying back, sunning herself.

Drew quickly reached down and grabbed the butt of the shotgun that hung on his right shoulder. With his right hand he pulled up on the back of the butt with so much force, he caused the barrel to spin behind him and swing up in front of him. He reached out with his left hand, caught the pump action part of the barrel and shouldered the weapon all in one smooth motion.

Before Drew could get his feet on the solid ground of the asphalt, Steve lost his footing and let out a weird moan as he fell and hit the ground.

The two people sitting on the hood of the car, a young man and woman, both turned toward the noise and spotted Drew. The young man slid off the hood and stood up while the young woman slid off the hood and crouched down behind the car.

"Whoa! Don't shoot!" the young man shouted as he raised his arms into the air.

"Please don't shoot us, mister!" pleaded the girl crouched behind the car.

"Who's out there?" came a voice from inside the car.

"Greg, stay down!" said the kid who had just gotten off the hood.

"Out of the car now!" Drew ordered.

The kid at the front of the car remained still, and Drew could hear the people in the back of the car whispering.

"Now!" shouted Drew as he pumped the shotgun. He wasn't taking any chances of stumbling upon another road block and getting shot at again.

Steve stayed low to the ground, figuring it was the best place for him if bullets started flying.

Drew watched as two heads popped up and down in the backseat. The back door slowly opened, and a young shirtless man stepped out, buttoned his shorts and tried to cover his erection with his hands.

He motioned with the barrel of the shotgun for the young man to raise his hands and then shouted,

"Whoever else is in there better come out with their hands up."

The young man looked down seeing he still had an erection and looked back at Drew.

"Up!" Drew said again, this time not only motioning with the barrel of the shotgun but with his head as well.

The kid slowly raised his hands, his face becoming red with humiliation.

"Person in the backseat, this is the last time I'm going to tell you. Get out!" Drew shouted.

A young woman stuck her feet out the door and scooched her way out and stood up, her naked breasts joggled as she raised her arms above her head. In her left hand she held her shirt.

"Young lady, put your shirt on," Drew said.

Steve shot his head up to try and get a view of the girl's boobs, but she had already slipped on her shirt.

Drew quickly glanced over his shoulder. "Steve, get up," he said quietly as if his compadre's behavior was embarrassing him. Steve stood up and moved to the right of Drew out on the asphalt of I-95.

"The four of you over there," Drew said using the shotgun to point where he wanted the kids to go and stand.

Once the kids complied, he told Steve to go check the car for any weapons. Steve quickly moved towards the car and poked his head inside but saw no weapons. He stood back up and signaled Drew by shaking his head.

"Nothing at all?" Drew shouted to Steve.

Steve double-checked inside the car. After a few short seconds he shouted back, "Just two bags."

"Search them. But be careful!"

"Hey, those are our bags!" the girl who had originally crouched down behind the hood of the car said.

"Relax!" Drew yelled back. "We're not taking your shit, we're just checking to see if you have any weapons."

"We don't have any guns," said the girl.

Steve searched the bags, but all he found were clothes. He stood back up and shook his head again.

Drew lowered the shotgun and slowly walked towards the group of kids. "What the hell are you doing out here in the middle of nowhere?"

"We ran out of gas trying to get away," the young man from the backseat said.

"Away from what?" Steve asked.

"From whatever killed everyone back at our college," the girl who had put on her shirt said.

"The sickness?" Drew asked.

"Is that what it is?" the same girl asked.

"Yeah, and you're lucky you ran out of gas or you would have eventually driven right into a road block, and they would have shot you on sight."

"No way!" said the kid who had been sitting on the hood of the car.

"Well, I'm Drew and that's Steve over there," and nodded his head towards Steve who waved.

"I'm Shawn and this is my girlfriend Renell," said the young man who had been sitting on the hood of the car.

"And I'm Cassandra," said naked-boobie girl, "but you can call me Cass. And this is my boyfriend Greg."

"So you guys ran out of gas and just decided to stay in the middle of nowhere?" asked Drew.

"No, our other friends Jim and Jessica went to find gas and water," Greg answered.

"Kid," Drew explained, "the power's out everywhere. No electricity means the gas pumps won't work."

The kids all looked at each other like they didn't understand how gas pumps work. Drew turned and looked at Steve with this "Can you believe these idiots?" look on his face.

"So you had six people in this tiny car?" Steve asked.

The students told Drew and Steve about the cabin they had found and how they took off after seeing all of the bodies at the college campus. They waited a while longer until Jim and Jessica returned. Drew already couldn't stand these kids, just from their story. He could tell they were lazy and completely worthless, but Steve seemed smitten with them.

Chapter 42

Drew couldn't believe it. How the hell did they become babysitters to this bunch of worthless twenty-one year-olds? He suspected the moment they came upon them in the road the other day that they were going to become a problem. The only one of them that was any good was Jim, and that was because he told him about the liquor store that was two streets over. Drew kept telling himself, *You can drink whenever you want, but you just can't drink today.* Just like Steve had taught him. It was getting harder, especially with those damn lazy kids around. All they did was sit around and drink and fuck. At least when he was a kid, he worked during the day, and only drank and fucked at night.

Drew got up early to go gather firewood and told Steve he was going to look for food in the area. He took out some of the non-essentials and left them next to Steve's pack. Steve had started acting differently since coming across the kids, watching over them like a father figure. He tried to get them to slow down on the drinking, but they were college kids. What did he expect? They laughed and made fun of him, yet he tried harder to get them to stop. Drew felt in some way that Steve was trying to get them to like him.

The previous day, Drew had asked the kids nicely to help pull their weight, but all they did was laugh at him, which infuriated him further. They were too lazy to gather firewood or bring back food for him and Steve. That kid Jim went out and found food with his snooty little bitchy girlfriend Jessica, but only brought back enough for him and his friends. And then had the gall to question Drew why he didn't bring enough back for them later on that day. He couldn't believe it when Steve decided to get involved and take their side. He wanted to leave them behind and continue home, but Steve felt it best to stay and help get the kids situated.

Drew left camp and set out to find the grocery store he heard the kids talking about—the one they had only grabbed enough food for themselves from.

"Fucking brats," Drew said out loud as he walked away, not caring if they heard him or not. That one kid Greg had a smart mouth on him, but all it would take was a good bitch-slap and he'd shut right the hell up. If there was one thing he couldn't stand it was lazy people who didn't help out and expected someone else to do everything for them. He thought back to his father, *Even though that asshole's teachings were way off, he still taught me the meaning of hard work.* His Spidey-sense started going off in the back of his head and knew he was heading for trouble with those kids.

As he walked, that proverbial little black fly, as Steve called it, popped into his head.

Drew made his way down the ravine, crossed over the first street and then headed to the second per Jim's instructions. The whole time he was walking, he knew he should be keeping an eye out for people, but his mind started racing and all he could think about was finding a drink. For some reason, he started thinking about his favorite chair at home that he liked to sit and drink in. He thought about how he should be miles from here and on his way home, but those damn, needy punks had slowed him down. They were dead weight and prevented him from doing what he needed to do. Hell, if Steve wanted to take care of them so much, he could stay behind with them. "Fuck them," he said out loud and could feel the anger building inside himself.

Drew turned the corner and walked into the parking lot. He looked up at the signs above each establishment and saw that the liquor store was to the right. At the far end of the strip mall there was a grocery store — probably a chain — with a name he had never heard before. He noticed several cars in the otherwise-desolate parking lot. Each one had a body slumped over the steering wheel.

He was so consumed with the thought of the kids that he was on autopilot, totally forgetting about the grocery store and instead heading over towards the front door with a sign that read "Pete's Convenience and Liquor Store." Drew pulled the already-busted door open and walked in.

Once inside, he went straight to the beer section, opened the fridge door and took out a six pack. He pulled a bottle out, twisted the cap off and then took a long swig. The beer was still cool, but not cold. The power must have cut off some time ago so the bottles just started to get warm, but Drew didn't care.

He pounded the six-pack of bottles within minutes. He loved shooting the beers and feeling the calm wash over him. The only downfall was the constant pissing, but hey, there was the buzz to keep him going.

Next, he found a rack of chips, pulled off a bag and munched away, one chip after the other. The salt tasted good. It made him want another beer.

After his quick snack, Drew walked up to the register where they kept the pint bottles of alcohol. He found the Peppermint Schnapps and counted only six pints, which he put into his backpack. On the counter there was a tub filled with little plastic nip bottles, each filled with about an ounce and a half of alcohol — the equivalent of a shot in most barrooms. The tub was basically filled with flavored vodka: vanilla, cherry, raspberry and watermelon. He dumped the whole tub into his backpack as well. There were a few left that wouldn't fit, so he stuffed those into his pant pockets.

He walked out of the liquor store and, remembering the grocery store, headed to the far end of the plaza. The glass was missing from the front window and there were at least four or five bodies in the store that he could see. Some had the black sores on them while others appeared to have been shot dead. He tried to imagine what it was like when the sickness broke out. People must have panicked and headed straight to the grocery stores to stock up. Some of the people in the store must have gotten sick and others probably tried to loot the place, only to be met with a barrage of gunfire. Possibly the store clerk or a police officer dispatched to the area.

Drew poked his head into the store, but couldn't stay in there for very long. The smell of the decaying bodies was just too overwhelming. And the power was off, so anything that could have spoiled probably had, adding to the disturbing odor. For the most part, the shelves looked empty anyway.

The beers had now run their course through his system, and he needed to take a piss. He walked over to the corner of the store and unzipped his fly, letting it rain down on the green blades of grass and ants below.

Drew turned around and saw an old woman walking down the road. She was in her nightgown and talking to herself. Dried blood stains covered her forehead and the side of her face, with some spots having dripped onto her clothing. He noticed that she was barefoot, but it didn't seem to bother her.

His mind started racing again. He thought about how good the buzz felt, and how the warm beer had tasted so delicious. He told himself he needed to get back, but that voice inside his head kept telling him he should get another drink.

What's one more drink? he asked himself.

No, I can't. I have to get back.

No one will know. Plus who cares if they do? You're a grown man, enjoying a nice drink.

He carried on the conversation in his head until he realized he had walked back into the liquor store and was standing in front of the beer fridge, pulling out another six pack.

Chapter 43

Stanley awoke to the sound of his alarm going off. He reached and grabbed the phone to silence it, and as he did he knocked the pill bottle to the floor. For a moment, he laid his head back down on the pillow, realizing he felt relaxed for once. Surprisingly, he felt like he had gotten a good-night's sleep, in spite of all that was going on. But the normal, daily worries slowly began to replace the placidity of his surroundings as his mind became more awake with each passing second, and he reached for his cell phone again to try dialing Carol.

He sat straight up when her phone rang, and his heart started to race.

"Pick up! Please pick up!" he said out loud.

The phone rang six, seven, eight times and then went dead.

"What?" he thought as he turned the phone over, looking at it and seeing that the call had ended.

He quickly hit the redial button. Again the phone rang multiple times before going dead.

Stanley jumped out of bed and went to his suitcase, pulled out his clothes and got dressed.

If the phones are working, then she might be okay, he thought as he closed up his suitcase. *Only one way to find out for sure.*

He went out into the kitchen and found Maureen standing at the stove cooking breakfast and Bill sitting at the table drinking coffee.

"Are you ready to help out with some chores?" Bill asked.

"I tried calling my wife and the phone actually rang," Stanley announced. "Things must be getting better if the phones are working."

Maureen walked over to the phone on the wall and picked up the receiver, holding it to her ear. A smile washed over her face. "There's a dial tone."

She hung up the phone, ran into the living room, and turned on the TV. The Emergency Alert System message was gone and had been replaced by the words, "Please Stand By."

"He's right—things are getting better," she said excitedly.

"Let's not jump to conclusions," Bill said.

"But the phone is working and the message on the TV has changed! It means people are working to fix things," Maureen replied.

"Wait," Bill protested. "We need to wait and see what is going on."

"I can't wait. I need to get home," Stanley said.

"Stan, think about it before you venture out there again. The other day, you said it was pretty bad out there."

"It was. But maybe it's not as bad as it was now that the phones are back. Plus you never lost power. If things were getting worse your power probably would have gone out."

"Maybe," Bill admitted, "but we haven't gotten any updates yet. The roads could still be blocked for all we know."

"But if they are fixing the phone lines, then they are probably removing the wrecks from the highways."

"Stan, please. I think you should wait one more day. Or at least until a news report comes in on the TV."

"I can't. What if my wife is hurt? She needs me. I can't leave her all alone."

"How are you going to get home?" Bill asked.

"I'll drive as far as I can, and then walk the rest of the way if I have to."

"You're welcome to stay," Maureen said.

"I appreciate it, but I must get back home," Stanley persisted. With his mind made up, he went for his suitcase and brought it out to the rental car.

Within minutes he was ready to go, and he returned to the front porch where he met Maureen to thank her for her hospitality and kindness. She gave him a hug and kiss on the cheek, "Be careful please."

"I will."

The screen door shut and they both turned around to see Bill walking out with a rifle in his hands. "I can't stop you from going, but I insist you take these," he said as he handed Stanley the rifle, then pulled out a 9mm handgun.

"Are you sure?"

"Yes, I'm sure. In fact, my conscience will rest a little better knowing yo have them. "

"Don't worry. He has plenty of guns," Maureen said.

"Take them," Bill nearly ordered, "because you never know what you're going to run into out there. We live in a pretty rural area, but who knows how bad the suburban and urban areas will be."

He put the weapons in the car and then turned around and gave Maureen another hug before seating himself in the driver's seat and shutting the car door and starting the engine.

Bill leaned forward and rested his forearms on the door where the window had been retracted into, and he shook Stanley's hand through the opening. "Remember, you can always come back."

Stanley gripped his hand firmly, then turned to him with a melancholy expression on his face. "Bill, listen," he spoke just above a whisper in a monotone voice. "Hold off on that virgin soil as long as you can. Who knows what's coming next, but if things really don't get better, it just might be your best chance for surviving this."

Bill gave him a quizzical look at first, but then nodded slowly in agreement before stepping back away from the car. Stanley gave him one last smile that reflected fearfulness, though he was attempting a reassuring one, then drove off into the unknown.

Chapter 44

Glen had locked himself in his apartment ever since all the television stations had gone off the air. Now low on food, he was worried how he was going to survive, especially without power, and he reluctantly resigned to the fact he would need to venture out to find food if he wanted to live. But he still didn't know what to expect on the other side of his apartment door.

He wished he could watch the news and find out what was happening out there. The last thing he had seen was Bethany dying on live TV. *What a horrible way to go. I hope that never happens to me*, he thought to himself.

Glen had just started to fall asleep after physically accosting himself. He had a stack of porn magazines under his bed and, with nothing better to do, had tried breaking his record of masturbating eight times in a single day. His penis was rubbed raw and it burned every time he peed. He couldn't help it. He was addicted to the feeling of ejaculating.

The phone's ringing woke him up. Surprised that it was even working again, he reached over and grabbed for it, fumbling to look at who was calling.

"Hello," Glen said rubbing his eyes.

"Is this Glen Daniels?" asked an older voice.

"Yes. Who's calling?"

"This is Mr. Matthews, owner of WTFH in New York."

Upon hearing the old man's name—which everyone in the business knew—Glen sat up and asked, "How are you calling me?"

"I have a satellite phone. Do you want a job?"

"I'm sorry?" asked Glen, not sure what he heard.

"A job. Do you want a job being lead anchor here at WTFH?"

"I'd love to work for you, sir."

"Get your ass here to New York City as fast as you can, then."

"What about the sickness?" Glen asked.

"We're hearing at the news desk that the sickness has run its course and has just about completely stopped."

"That's good news," Glen replied.

"It is. I need you here at once, ready at the anchor desk for when the power comes back on," the voice said, and then the line became all-static and went dead.

Glen sat there for a moment processing what had just happened. He looked down at his cell phone, which now only had two percent battery left. *Wow, another few minutes and I would never have received that call*, Glen thought.

He stood there for a minute contemplating whether or not he should go. New York was over five-hundred miles away, which was an eight-hour drive. He had filled his gas tank the day he moved, so he didn't need to worry about trying to fill up before heading out. Furthermore, his car averaged thirty-two miles per gallon on the highway and his tank held sixteen gallons, so he could make it roughly 512 miles. If he got the car up to speed and tried to coast, he might just be able to make it. And worst case, maybe he would have to walk the last ten to twenty miles to the studio. Glen had been to the WFTH studio several times before. At the start of his career, he had applied for jobs there, but unfortunately was turned down. At any rate, he could find his way there once he reached the city, whether by car or on foot. He knew that hiking that far was a risk, but he also knew that most people didn't get a second chance in life. And it now looked like his second chance could lead him to becoming the face of the new world. That was most definitely worth the risk.

He packed his suitcase with his best suits and ties and stashed the rest of his non-perishable food in a plastic bag. Figuring it best to wait until dawn, he set the two items by the front door, then climbed back into bed. He didn't know what he would have to deal with once he left his apartment, but he figured dealing with it rested and in the light would be better than dealing with it tired and in the dark.

He woke at first light and quickly got dressed, then gulped down the last can of noodle soup for breakfast. With a makeshift mask of an old sweatshirt around his face, he walked over to the front door and unlocked it. Glen hesitated a minute, building up the nerve to open the door, realizing there would be no reversing his actions if crossing the threshold turned out to be a mistake. After a few deep breaths, he finally grabbed the doorknob and slowly twisted. The wooden door let out a small squeak as he pulled it open, but only silence followed, as if the rest of the complex had been deserted. The deed now done, the point of no return passed, he grabbed his suitcase and plastic bag of food and exited his apartment.

Glen made it to his car and thankfully didn't see anyone, living or dead. He had his key ready and got right into his car and started it up. Slamming his door shut, he threw the suitcase into the backseat and removed his makeshift mask as he quickly put the car in reverse. As he backed out of the parking spot, he stopped when he noticed movement over at the entrance to his apartment building that he had called home for a short duration. Squinting, his eyes suddenly focused on what looked like a shadow of a person slowly approaching his car down the walkway. The air around him somehow began to grow cold, and the leather on the steering wheel creaked as Glen's hands tightened around it. His heart raced as he watched the dark figure's arm rise up. Long black fingers curled out and pointed towards the parking lot exit.

His hair tussled as if there was a slight breeze in the car that passed over his forehead and cheeks. As the unnatural gust passed his ears, he could have sworn he heard the word, *Go!* His eyes widened when he realized the voice was coming from the dark shadowy figure. Another breeze swirled inside the car and he heard the word, *Now*. Glen thought he was going to shit his pants when the dark shadowy figure's arm moved and pointed at him. The pages of the note pad he kept on his dashboard started to flutter, and the cold breeze suddenly intensified around his face and ears as he heard the word, *You* followed by, *New York*.

That was it. Glen had experienced enough. He slammed the car into drive, stomped on the gas, and the car shot out of the parking lot.

Chapter 45

Drew returned to the campsite with his buzz in full swing, feeling really good. He had drunken a few of the nips on the way back and was actually surprised he could remember where the camp was. As he stumbled over to Steve and sat down, a cool breeze blew through camp, rustling the tree leaves. Under a nearby tree stood the dark shadowy figure, hidden by the shade.

Steve stared at Drew and could tell he was drunk, not only by his clumsy gait, but more so by the smell of booze that emanated from him.

"You've been drinking," Steve accused with a clearly disapproving tone.

"A little," Drew said as he held out his hand and pressed his index finger towards his thumb but left a little gap.

Steve's face nearly reddened. "I can't believe you! I thought you weren't going to drink again."

The kids were sitting across from them and started laughing.

"Look! Steve's his little bitch," Greg joshed with a snort.

"Really, I can't believe you," Steve said.

Drew rose back on his feet with a bit of effort. "What are you, my fucking wife?"

"Sit down," Steve ordered.

The laughter from the others intensified. "Why don't you go over behind the trees and kiss and make up?" Jim teased.

Drew turned toward them with fury in his eyes. How dare these punk ass kids talk to him that way?

"Someone getting mad?" Cass taunted through her giggling.

"Fuck you, you dumb fucking cunt!" snarled Drew. "The only thing you're good for is lying on your back with your legs spread open. You fucking cum dumpster!"

The kids stopped laughing sensing Drew's anger. But Greg couldn't sit there and let him talk to his girlfriend like that. "What good are you? You're just a drunk!" he yelled.

Drew had had just about enough of these little twats. He could tell his top was about to blow and told himself, *Fuck it –I'll, let them have it.*

"Listen to me, you little fucking worthless piece of shit, you daddy's boy. I heard you talking. You live off your daddy and can't do shit for yourself. Hell, all you've done since I've met you is sit on your ass and expect others to wait on you. Good luck to you in this new world, you fucking pussy!"

"What new world, old man?" Greg retorted. "It's the same world. Nothing's changed."

"Really? What the hell are you doing sitting here with me then? Why aren't you at home, sucking on your daddy's balls and getting everything you want?"

"Don't talk to my boyfriend that way!" Cass shouted.

"Or what?" Drew snapped back. "What are you going to do? You're as fucking worthless as he is. I haven't seen you get up off your ass and do a single thing to help out either. Thinking about it, the only thing I have seen you do is take off your clothes, you fucking whore. Hell, when we first met, you were naked and sucking on his tiny prick. And I bet you'd suck his dick real good in hopes of a free ride. Shit, I bet you'd fuck his old man in order to never have to do any work."

Greg turned and looked at Cass as if he had suspected the same thing.

"Enough!" Steve shouted.

"Enough is right," Drew said. "Fuck these kids. Not one of them has contributed. Not one of them went to get firewood or start a fire. Shit, they didn't even put wood on the fire as it was dying down. They just let it die."

"Drew, enough!" Steve repeated more forcefully.

"They don't cook or clean up. They just expect us to do it like we're their fucking slaves!" Drew thought back to his childhood, and an anger washed over his face that frightened Steve. "I'm no one's fucking slave and never will be!" Drew shouted.

"Get out of here old man!" Greg yelled.

"Yeah, leave you drunk!" yelled Cass.

"You're lucky we don't kick your ass!" Shawn shouted.

"Fucking try, you pussy, and see what happens!" Drew said as he clenched his fists and took a step closer towards Shawn who scurried back.

"Alright, Drew. Time for you to leave," Steve said, stepping between the two.

"You want me to leave?" Drew asked.

"Yeah! Leave old man!" Renell shouted.

Drew turned and flipped her the bird.

"Leave, Drew," Steve said again.

Drew stormed over to his pack and put it on. He grabbed the rifle and shotgun and slung them over his shoulder and turned to walk away, but Steve suddenly scurried after him.

"Drew, calm down. You can stay. Just go over and apologize and tell them you've had too much to drink." He put his hand on Drew's shoulder. "This is just one of those mistakes I told you about that would happen. We can get past it. You just need to sober up is all."

"Get your fucking hands off me," Drew yelled as he gave Steve a look that terrified him.

Steve removed his hand from Drew's shoulder and calmly said, "Just go over and apologize."

"I will do no such thing."

"Come on, Drew."

"All these kids will do is use you, and they'll get you killed, Steve. The world has changed and is no longer safe, and I know it's only going to get worse, a lot worse."

"But they need our help," Steve pleaded.

"They don't need your help," Drew argued. "They need you to do everything for them. If they haven't learned how to do for themselves yet, they're in for a rude wake-up call."

"Get him out of here, Steve," Greg yelled.

"Go fuck yourself!" Drew said.

"Enough, Drew!" Steve said.

"That's right, Steve," Drew agreed. "Enough. Grab your pack. Come on, we're leaving."

Steve walked over to his pack and just stood there.

"Be strong, Steve!" Shawn yelled.

Drew took a few steps, stopped and turned around. "You coming?"

Steve looked down, then over to the kids and back to Drew and shook his head no.

"Good-bye Steve," Drew said then turned and walked away.

Steve took a few steps and stopped.

"You did the right thing, Steve," Greg said.

"Yeah, don't feel bad, Steve," Cass said, "He's just a drunken asshole."

The sun had started to set on the horizon, and Steve watched Drew walk the desolate stretch of highway alone. He turned to look at the kids and then looked back at Drew. But he was gone, and his silhouette had disappeared.

"Steve, we're going to need some firewood," Renell said.

"Steve, what are you making us for dinner?" asked Cass.

"We need more water too," Greg said.

Jesus, Drew was right. What did I just do? Steve asked himself.

Chapter 46

Drew awoke just off the side of the road. His clothes were damp from the morning dew that had formed on everything. He sat up and instantly pressed the palm of his hand to his forehead, which was pounding. This was one hell of a hangover. Turning his pack around and removing the bottle of aspirin from the back pocket, he popped three pills into his mouth and washed them down with a gulp of water.

What the hell did I do last night? Drew asked himself as the recent events came flooding back. *I shouldn't have had those drinks yesterday. I'm such an idiot. Yet again someone good in my life has walked away because of my drinking. I'm such a fucking idiot! When am I going to learn? No wonder Annabelle left me — I would have left me too.*

He put on his backpack and tightened up the straps, then hopped over the guardrail, heading in the direction from which he had come, back towards the camp. Gray clouds hung in the air and it looked like rain.

The world has changed and you must change too, if you are to survive. You're going to go back and find Steve, apologize to him for the way you acted, ask for forgiveness and never drink again, Drew told himself.

As he walked, his mind automatically reflected back on how everything had gone from bad to worse.

First, Annabelle left me because of my drinking, then my mother died, just before the world is infected with some sort of deadly plague. The plane I'm on explodes and the only other person who survived the explosion is shot and killed over a pack of cigarettes. I find a decent person who tries to help me, but who ends up kicking me out because of my drinking. And oh yeah, there's that group of worthless kids who don't seem to want to do a damn thing other than sit around and drink and fuck and will probably get the decent guy killed.

Drew could feel a spark ignite deep inside him. It was something he hadn't felt since his father was alive. He could feel a warmth wash over him, just as it did when he was a kid, and he felt himself walking taller, his hangover somehow dissipating.

I will not let this world beat me. No matter what it throws at me, I will overcome it. I'm going to get Steve and go home and find Annabelle and Stephanie. I will never drink again. I will do what needs to be done to survive and protect the ones I love, and I will not let anyone or anything stop me. As he continued on his way, the gray clouds parted, the sun appeared and shone brightly upon him. A slight breeze caressed him, causing goosebumps to form on his arms. The fire inside him began to burn and it felt good to be alive.

He was thinking of what to say to Steve when he would reach the camp. He decided to start with, *I'm sorry.*

As Drew crested the top of a hill, he could see a plume of smoke rising from the area where he had left Steve and the kids. *Well, it looks like they managed to start a fire,* he said to himself. As he grew closer to the campsite, though, he could hear shouting from the kids followed by gunshots.

I didn't leave them a gun, Drew thought as the warmth that had engulfed him was instantly swallowed by a wave of panic and a sense of urgency. Before he could even begin to run however, he saw Steve come running out of the tree line up ahead, followed by four armed men.

Chapter 47

Steve's thoughts faded as he leaned over the guardrail. The whack to the head had done some serious damage to the top side of his head. Blood streamed from the wound and started filling his right eye and seeping into his mouth. The warmth and saltiness of it made him want to vomit. His face held a strange, confused look, and he felt tired, having a hard time trying to get his body to do what he wanted it to do. Even his thoughts of what to do next became slow and lethargic.

Steve! Steve! Drew cried to himself as his heart raced. He ran full sprint towards the four, unknown men that were now standing over Steve, removing the shotgun from his shoulder. He had no idea what the strangers wanted from Steve, nor did he care. All he cared about at the moment was that they had just attacked his friend.

In a confused daze, Steve could make out something coming from off to his left. Suddenly his body shook, reacting to the loud booms.

As Drew approached, he shouldered the shotgun, aimed and fired at the assailant standing over Steve. The round hit with precision, the shotgun slug disintegrating the man's ribcage, and bone fragments tore through his heart and lungs, which sprayed all over the galvanized guardrail as they exited his chest. The man was dead before he even hit the ground. A fine mist rained down on Steve just before the corpse landed next to him.

Drew slid the pump action and chambered another round just as the other strangers turned towards him. He quickly aimed at the next man nearest to Steve and fired again, point blank to his target's face which exploded like a cherry bomb filled with blood, cartilage, and bone. The force of the impact lifted him airborne and dropped him next to his lifeless friend.

The third man pulled a knife out from behind him and charged at Drew, who immediately aimed the barrel down and fired. The slug hit the attacker's right knee, which instantly shattered to pieces. Chunks of bone and cartilage went flying in a vapor of red, and the round severed the leg at the knee. The man went sprawling mid-stride as his missing limb went one direction and his body went the other. He sat up screaming as he grabbed the stump and leaned back, lifting the bloody mass up in an effort to stop the profuse bleeding while sucking in deep breaths of air in between screams of pain.

Drew was now walking quickly and noticed the fourth man had taken off running. He looked at Steve and saw him clutching at his head while blood seeped through his fingers and ran down his face. His condition looked awful, but Drew was relieved to see his friend was alive. He pumped the shotgun again as he approached the man with the severed leg.

The man let go of his stump and raised his hands, begging for mercy. He cried out in agony as his stump hit the ground.

"Please mister, no!" he pleaded, seeing the anger that covered Drew's face.

"You want to attack unarmed people, you piece of shit?" Drew said as he lowered the shotgun and aimed it at the man's chest.

"Please, no!"

As Drew passed, he fired the shotgun into the

man's chest. The slug went right through his body, imbedding itself in the pavement beneath him. Blood and chunks sprayed up onto the barrel of the shotgun, as well as onto the sleeve of Drew's coat.

Three down and one to go, he thought, watching the last man run down the side of the highway.

He glanced down when he reached Steve, who had a large chunk of skin torn from his scalp that hung from his head. At first glimpse, he thought it was a toupee that had been partially blown off and couldn't help but chuckle to himself.

"Steve, are you alright?" Drew asked in a calm voice.

"He took my backpack!" Steve cried out with a shaking voice. "My family pictures...my kids..."

Drew understood. He knew how he'd feel if he lost his own pictures of his wife and daughter, his last worldly possessions. Plus, he knew what needed to be done. He couldn't allow that man to escape, only to come back with others.

Looking down the highway, Drew estimated that the would-be assailant was roughly two hundred and fifty yards away, but had slowed to a slight jog. He put the shotgun down next to Steve and took the AR-15 off his other shoulder, then sprinted down the road, trying to close the gap between himself and the retreating man. Once satisfied with the distance, he stopped, got down on one knee and brought the butt of the AR-15 into his shoulder.

He leaned into the scope and sighted in on his target, then aligned the crosshairs with the middle of the man's back. The assailant was still a good football field down the road, but Drew remembered his training in the Marines, and took a deep breath before squeezing the trigger.

Boom! The crack of the muzzle reverberated through the trees.

Drew watched through the scope as his quarry came to a sliding halt. Steve's backpack went careening off the side of the road when the man fell. He waited for a moment, then saw his target down the road try to get up. He could see the white stuffing that lined his coat protruding on his right shoulder where the bullet had entered. Suspecting these men were part of a larger group, Drew knew that he could not allow any of them to live, lest they come back seeking vengeance and taking everything they had from them. He understood deep inside that the world had already changed, and that he better change too if he wanted to survive. And he knew what would come next for society. The strong would take from the weak. People would be forced into slavery, forced to work for those who would assume control, or they would die if they refused. He would not allow that to happen to anyone he knew or loved.

Drew took another deep breath. The late fall air felt cool as it passed down his throat. He aimed the crosshairs on the middle of the man's head, let out his breath and squeezed the trigger. Again the loud crack of the muzzle rang through the desolate trees.

He turned and started walking back towards Steve, who had propped himself up against the guardrail next to the innards of the first man he shot.

"Are you okay, Steve?"

"Yeah, I fine. Juss took a bad knock onna head," Steve replied, though his words were slightly slurred.

A knock on the head? It looks like they tried to knock it off, Drew thought. He held up his index finger.

"Steve, I need you to look at my finger. Follow it with your eyes."

Steve did as he asked, doing the best he could to move his eyes from side to side along with Drew's finger.

"I'll s'vive," Steve assured as Drew knelt by his side. But Drew, dere's notta lotta time."

"Just hold still and try not to talk," Drew interrupted. "I've got to check you out and try to patch you up."

Steve held his head and watched as Drew quickly retrieved his pack and set it down beside him, then started to rummage through it. He had so much to tell, but his thoughts were fuzzy. Trying to get a clean sentence out seemed like a handful.

Drew pulled out a slew of bandages and other medical supplies, along with a small flashlight and a brown bottle of hydrogen peroxide. "Move your hand and let me see," he said.

"How bad's it look?"

"A flap of skin, but it's not as bad as I thought," Drew answered as he clicked on the flashlight and shined it into his friend's eyes, one at a time. "Looks like you also might have a slight concussion, but nothing too serious." He matched the bandages to the size of the wound. "Alright, Steve. I'm going to pour some hydrogen peroxide on your head. We don't want any of it running into your eyes, so you need to keep them shut for me."

"Okay. Zit gonna sting?"

"Like a bastard."

Steve braced himself and waited for the stinging feeling.

Drew empathized, remembering all too well the

feeling of the cool wetness followed by that painful sensation. He thought back to the hundreds of times his mother had treated his cuts and scrapes as a child.

"Gotta listen t'me, Drew," Steve tried to explain.

"Hold that thought a sec," Drew said as he poured the liquid on the wound, and the peroxide instantly started bubbling over the area. The cool substance ran down Steve's forehead and along the side of each nostril, washing away the blood from his face as it ran off his chin.

Steve grimaced when the twinge from the peroxide instantly set in.

Drew lifted up the flap of skin and poured more hydrogen peroxide around the entire area, wanting to make sure it didn't get infected.

"Blow on it," Steve yipped as his head was really stinging now.

"What?" Drew asked.

"Blow on it. My mother used to blow on the cut after cleaning it to help take the sting out."

"Steve, this is more than just a scrape after a bicycle fall," Drew said with an awkward laugh. But he remembered his own mother blowing on his cuts as well, and though it did little to help with the physical healing of the wounds, he understood that there was a positive effect, if only psychologically. And after the traumatic experience Steve clearly just went through, the familiarity of a mother's touch was not that tall of an order. In the old world, Steve wouldn't have had a chance in hell of Drew blowing on his head. But since the world had changed, so had Drew who knelt in the middle of Interstate 95 giving into his friend's request to help ease his pain.

After a few minutes, Drew placed the bandage on Steve's head the best he could, but his hair hindered it from covering the entire wound. He figured a little air would probably help it heal faster anyway.

Walking back over to his pack and pulling out his canteen and a few napkins, he poured some water on the napkins and handed them to Steve. "Here, wipe down your face."

"Thank you," Steve said as he took the wet napkins and began wiping the blood away. Drew noticed, with relief, that his friend was speaking a bit more clearly, further supporting his assessment that the concussion was mild, and that the blow to Steve's head mostly made him lethargic once his adrenaline died down. Apparently the intense stinging sensation from the ointment brought back his alertness, if only a little bit.

"Now just sit tight for a minute. I'll go get your backpack."

"No!" Steve shouted as he grabbed Drew's wrist with more sternness than Drew would have expected in his condition. "Listen. I've been trying to tell you but I was too much in a daze before, we've got to go back to the camp now!"

In the thick of all that had just occurred, between the battle with the four assailants and the worry for his friend's condition, Drew hadn't the time to dwell on finding out just what had transpired during his absence that led up to such.

"Steve, what happened?"

"We were ambushed," Steve replied as tears suddenly ran down his face. "Oh God, Drew. It was awful!"

"By these men, right?" Drew asked while

pointing towards the guardrail.

"Yes. But there were other men too. I was gathering firewood, and when I came back…" He tried to stand, but stumbled from a fresh wave of dizziness.

"What, Steve?" Drew said forcefully while shaking him gently. "What happened when you got back?"

"Help me up, Drew," Steve said, grabbing Drew's shoulders for support.

"Steve," Drew replied just as sternly. "You need to rest. Tell me what happened and I'll go take care of it, but you're not in any condition to-"

"They're dead, Drew," Steve interrupted, his voice suddenly calm, though the tears continued to fall. "Greg, Shawn, Jim…all the boys are dead. Those men shot them. But the girls might still be alive. So we need to go back and save them if we can. And I'll be damned if I'm letting you leave me here. Now help me the hell up."

For the first time since Drew first met him, a fire that he was familiar with seemed to burn inside Steve's eyes. It was a fire that he knew better than to feed. He nodded slowly, then helped his friend to his feet.

Chapter 48

Drew made his way back through the woods as quickly as possible with the AR-15 slung over his shoulder, but Steve struggled to follow. He was slowing them down, no doubt, but Drew was also glad he insisted on coming with him. If there were more enemies to deal with, especially enemies with weapons, having backup evened the odds a bit. Regardless, he had reason to worry. Steve's head injury could have impaired his judgement, and though he was apprehensive, even nervous when giving him the shotgun, he couldn't let him go into unknown dangers unarmed. Before they headed back towards the camp, Drew had probably reminded Steve to keep the shotgun slung over his shoulder about twenty times, and, if things got hot to make sure Drew was not directly in front of him if he needed to use the thing.

"Okay, you went for firewood and then what?" Drew asked. He figured the best way to prevent Steve from becoming lethargic again was to keep him talking.

"When I was walking back, I heard shouting. I thought the kids were arguing with each other, but as I got closer I could see that Greg was arguing with a man holding a gun."

Damn fool, Drew thought with pity. *Should've kept his mouth shut.*

"I watched as the men forced the kids onto their knees," Steve continued, his voice becoming slightly hysterical as he recounted the horrors he bore witness to. "The man you shot, the one who tried to run off with my backpack, he raped Jessica."

Drew could feel his blood begin to boil and was thankful he blew that asshole's brains out the front of his head. He quickened his pace upon hearing this, hoping that Steve would forgive him for both the physical and emotional burden he was putting on him. "Then what happened? Keep talking, Steve. No matter how terrible it is. And keep breathing."

"Greg got real mouthy with them and they shot him in the head. Cass screamed and started crying. One of the other men tried to rape her."

Drew shook his head in disbelief as they hurried. He had hoped he was wrong about the world changing, but clearly he was right. "Then what?"

Steve forced his voice through his labored breathing and crying as he continued, "They started tearing the clothes off Jessica. Jim and Shawn tried stopping them, but they shot them both in the head too."

"Jesus."

"Jesus is right," Steve said and suddenly stopped, too distraught to continue. Drew stopped as well and turned to face him. "I hope he can forgive me for the coward I am." Fresh tears of shame flowed down freely.

"What are you talking about, man?"

Steve took deep breaths, trying to regain his stamina. "I just stood there, Drew. Too paralyzed with fear to do anything but hide and watch. But when they shot the last of the three boys, I couldn't help it. I just shouted 'Stop!' out loud, giving away my position. When they turned their attention to me, I took off running as fast as I could. All I could think about was trying to find you." His sobs intensified. "Because you're brave, Drew. And I'm... just a pussy. You were right."

They were wasting precious seconds, but Drew understood that it would be foolish to run into armed men out of breath, and from what he could tell, Steve needed the break. And much more.

He put his hand on Steve's shoulder. "You're not a pussy, Steve. I'm sorry I ever said that. What you are is incredibly smart. There was no way you could've done anything. These men were armed and you had nothing. If you tried to stop them all you would've done was gotten killed, and then I wouldn't be here to help you. Then what chance would the girls have? Because you ran for help, you got those men to chase you. Your choices just might have saved them."

"And if they're already dead, them my choices only got them killed."

Drew's half smile of encouragement faded. "These men were armed and you had nothing," he repeated. "That was *my* fault. I'm the one who left you without a gun. Those boys' deaths, and whatever has happened to the girls, that's on me. If anyone needs Jesus' forgiveness, it's me." He dropped his hand from Steve's shoulder realizing how much damage his selfishness had caused.

Again a small spark of fire lit in Steve's eyes, again at a most unexpected moment. "No, Drew," he said as if he hadn't been crying just seconds before. "This is no one's fault but those savages who attacked us. This is on them, and only them."

Drew looked up from the ground, suddenly inspired by his friend's voice. "Then let's go get the fuckers and save the girls."

They soon passed a large cluster of white birch trees Drew remembered seeing when they had first

319

come this way the day before, and he knew they were close to the camp. He always loved the way the white bark stood out against the green and brown of the other trees. It reminded him of himself and how he felt different.

He had always loved white birch trees, but there seemed to be fewer of them over the years. He remembered hearing something a few years back about a fungus or something that was killing them all off back up in New England.

They crept through the woods trying to be as quiet as possible, but Steve didn't move so silently. It seemed like he was stepping on every downed branch, causing that distinct *SNAP* sound repeatedly. In a forest where the acoustics were amplified, it might as well have been thunderbolts.

As they moved through the trees, Drew could see the base of the fire. It was just now smoldering. Not seeing anyone around, he turned to Steve and told him to wait there and that he would go up and investigate. Steve acknowledged with a nod of his head.

Drew continued on, closing in on the campfire. At first glance he thought the kids were sleeping, but from Steve's telling, he knew they were not.

He crept up to the base of the fire and was taken aback by what he saw. The three boys had been killed execution style, and two of the girls lay naked with their legs spread open. He walked over to the first body and saw it was Jessica. He suspected right away, that, like Greg, her mouth probably got her killed. Renell's corpse was next to Jessica's. Her bra was the only article of clothing left on her, while the rest of their garments lay scattered about. Drew scanned the area for Cass, but she was missing.

He thought whoever killed the kids probably took Cass with them as a trophy. Jessica probably tried to fight, and if so, they would've wanted nothing to do with her, so they did the worst thing they could possibly do to a woman. It looked like when they were done with her, they shot her in both breasts. The left breast gunshot probably hit her heart, killing her instantly.

He never cared for Jessica, but that was a horrible way to go. First to be victimized, and then gunned down like a dog.

Drew was startled as Steve snuck up behind him. He turned and noticed a look wash over his friend's face at the sight of the tragedy.

Instantly, Steve lowered his head and let his tears fall freely, Unable to control himself. He had befriended these young kids, and to find them dead was heart-wrenching. He clenched his fists, his knuckles whitening.

Drew put his hand on Steve's shoulder. "If you hadn't left, you would be laying right here next to them," he reminded him softly.

"I know," Steve acknowledged in a shaky whisper. "We need to bury them."

Drew quickly scanned the area.

"We need to bury them, Drew," Steve repeated, this time with a little more composure.

"We'll come back later and bury them."

Steve's breathing intensified as he tweaked out an audible, "Why?"

Drew turned and faced the fire. "Steve the fire isn't even completely out yet," he explained. "Whoever killed them could still be in the area. We'll come back later if we can, but for now we need to move."

"But what about animals?" Steve asked.

"That fucking whack on the head really did you in. What do you think happens to them when we bury them? Bugs and small critters will eat at theme there too, you know."

"You really have no sympathy, do you?"

The accusation almost set Drew off. "No sympathy? Are you kidding?" He took a small step towards Steve. "What about the fucking animals. Here's a question for you: What about Cass, Steve?"

Steve's eyes widened with realization.

"She's not here, which means she might still be alive. We waste time burying the dead, we might have to dig one more grave than we need to. Have you thought about that?"

Steve lowered his head again. "You're right, Drew. I'm sorry."

Drew turned away to investigate the scene again. "No sympathy," he grumbled.

"I'm sorry, I said. You're right, okay? Let's just get going so we can find Cass."

Suddenly, Drew heard someone running up behind them. With incredible reflexes he spun, dropped to one knee and brought the rifle up to his shoulder ready to kill whoever was coming at them. He tracked the sound of the movement with the muzzle, ready to fire, but luckily withheld his shot, for it was Cass running towards them, appearing in a flash as if conjured when her name was spoken.

Steve stood stunned, but only momentarily before he took off running to meet Cassandra. The two met with a long embrace and plenty of tears.

"Oh my God! Are you okay?" Steve asked.

Cass just shook her head up and down as it was

pressed up against Steve's chest.

Drew walked up to them and rubbed Cass's head. She looked up from Steve's chest with an expression of sheer terror in her eyes. Drew's heart sank at that moment. He held her head steady to face him, keeping her from observing the gruesome scene of her murdered friends.

Cass was twenty years young. She was forced to witness things that most adults don't see, forced to watch as her boyfriend and his friends were shot execution style, forced to watch as her two best friends were raped and murdered. Forced to grow up in the worst way imaginable. Drew could tell by her eyes that she had changed.

Drew continued to look into her eyes and saw that she finally understood why Drew was the way he was. And her own eyes told Drew that, going forward, she would listen to him no matter what.

Their embrace didn't last long. Cass expressed with desperation that they needed to get as far away from the campsite as possible. With no debates from either men, they walked with much speed back towards the interstate.

As they hurried, Steve couldn't help but ask if the men who held her hostage had hurt her. "No," she responded in a wavering voice. "They were going to do to me what they did to Jess and Renell, but they didn't get a chance."

"How so?" Steve asked.

"Gunshots," she replied. "There were gunshots in the distance. When they heard that, one of the men said something about needing to go back."

Drew and Steve gave each other a quick glance. They knew the gunshots she referred to were from the battle on the highway. "How many men?" Drew pressed.

"Three," Cass said. "They forced me to go with them, and we walked for a long while. With each step I became more terrified. I thought for sure that, once I got to wherever they were taking me, they'd never let me leave. It got to the point where I just couldn't take it anymore, and I collapsed... and I... urinated." She began to cry as she recounted the traumatic experience.

"It's okay, Cass," Steve assured her. "You don't have to talk about it."

"Steve's right," Drew added. "You escaped and that's all that matters. But can you tell us if they're chasing you? We need to know if we should be ready for them to come up from behind us."

Cass took a few breaths to calm herself as best she could. "I don't think so," she finally answered. "After I fell, one of them pulled me to my feet but he got grossed out when he realized I had pissed myself. He called me names and spat on me while the other two men, who were several feet in front of us started laughing at him. The man loosened his grip on me a little, probably because he didn't want to get pee on himself, then there was this noise just ahead of us."

"A noise?" Steve repeated wanting to make sure he heard her right.

"It was just a deer that took off from the commotion, but it caused the men to turn and look. The man who was holding me by the arms was also distracted, and I just got this strange feeling. Like I just knew that was my moment to act. Because that deer should've run off long before we got close to it, with all the noise those men were making. But for some reason it didn't run until we were only a few feet away from it. I know it sounds weird, but I just got this crazy idea that the deer purposefully waited for the men to get closer so it could distract them, as if it did that to give me a chance to get out of there."

"The Lord works in mysterious ways," Steve commented.

"Anyway, while the man who held my arms was distracted, I elbowed him in the stomach as hard as I could. He let go and took off as fast as I could."

"And they didn't chase you?" Drew asked, surprised.

"They did for a little while," Cass replied, "because I heard their footsteps and their voices cursing at me. But I just kept running and didn't look back. The woods were pretty thick, and I think that helped me gain distance from them, since they were pretty big men, and I'm much smaller. But I knew they had stopped chasing me because I tripped. When that happened I was sure they'd be on top of me in a second and start hurting me... or worse. I was so scared... too scared to even get up. Whatever courage that came into me when I escaped was gone, and I just laid there crying, waiting for their hands to grab ahold of me. But they never did. I finally dared to turn over and look back, and I didn't see or hear them anymore."

"They must've decided it was better to hurry back to wherever they planned on taking you," Drew said, almost as if he were talking to himself pensively.

"I got up," Cass continued, "Then kept running in the direction that I thought was toward the highway. But soon I could hear your voices. I wanted to scream for you, but I was still not convinced they had stopped following me, and I didn't want them to know where I was. So I just ran toward your voices.

Thank God I found you!" Her sobbing resumed.

Steve put a supportive arm around her, assuring her that she was both strong and brave. "We better hurry and get as far away from here as we can," he said to Drew.

"I agree," Drew said, quickening his pace, "but first we need to go back to the bodies of the men I killed."

"What the hell for?"

"We need to get as much intel on these men as we can. And we need to hide the bodies."

"But Drew," Steve protested, "won't that take time? Time that we should be using to get farther away?"

"Yeah, but something tells me these guys are going to want to know what happened to their friends. It'll only take us a few minutes to dump the bodies down the embankment off the side of the road. But then it will take those men much longer to find them. We waste a little bit of time in order to delay them a greater amount of time."

Steve and Cass remained silent as they followed behind Drew, who could feel their uneasiness with his idea. "Hey, look on the bright side," he said as he turned and gave a smirk. "At least you can get your backpack while we're there."

Chapter 49

Within minutes, thanks to their hurried pace, they were back on the highway. The horrid scene remained as Drew and Steve had left it, with only small swarms of flies and buzzards circling overhead as an addition to the setting. The sense of urgency pasting thickly to his bones, Drew set to work dragging the four bodies towards the guardrail at the edge of the highway in order to push them over the embankment, careful not to touch any of their open wounds.

Steve had retrieved his backpack and sat down nearby with his back against the rail, pulling out the photos of his family he had stored in one of the compartments. He fixed his eyes on his favorite of the small stack, one from a few years back. He had taken his family to the local mall and had the portrait done just after the Fourth of July weekend. He held the picture up to his face and started to cry softly.

Cass stood next to Steve and placed a gentle hand on his shoulder as he wept, but her eyes remained distant, a blank expression on her face.

Drew did not mind that his two companions did not help with the "clean-up." Both had been through enough. Hell, *he* had been through enough, but at least he hadn't suffered a mild concussion or stood on the brink of shock after watching all of his friends get murdered in front of him.

Before lifting the bodies over the guardrail, he checked each one, somewhat distraught when all he found was a black .45 in the jacket pocket of the man who had stolen Steve's pack, along with a handful of ammo.

"Cass?" he called to the girl, who just turned her head towards him with that lack of expression. "The three men who tried to kidnap you... do you remember if they had anything on them?"

"What do you mean?" she asked more calmly than Drew was comfortable with.

"Like, were they wearing packs or any gear?"

Cass shook her head slowly. "No. Just... guns."

Steve had already gotten himself together, wiped his eyes and nose one last time, then got up, almost falling back over. Dizziness was returning now that his adrenaline had subsided, and he had to put a hand on the guardrail to steady himself. With some effort, he managed to make his way next to Drew. "What's on your mind?" he asked his friend softly, as if he realized that whatever Drew was thinking, he didn't want to share with Cass, for fear of making her hysterical.

"You were right about getting as far away from here as possible," Drew answered. "As soon as we're done here, we've got to push on for as long as we can."

"You really think they'll come looking for us?"

Drew nodded. "Wouldn't you want to know what happened to your four friends if you were one of them? Also, these guys aren't travelers like us. They couldn't get far without supplies, and they have nothing on them. No food, water, any of that shit. Which means they're holed up somewhere. Wherever they were taking Cass, it's their base of operations."

"But there are only three of them left."

"I wouldn't bet on that," Drew revealed. "Something tells me there are more of them."

"Why do you think so?" Steve wondered.

"A hunch. Think about it. Seven guys attack the

kids. Four of them gave chase to you, leaving three of them to do what they please with Cass after killing the rest. Then they hear the gunshots when I killed these four fucks. They clearly must've suspected their friends encountered trouble, so why wouldn't they come to their aid? Why try to head back to wherever their hideout is?"

Steve nodded. "They were already armed, so it's not like they would have to go back for weapons."

"Which means they most likely went for backup. I'm almost certain there are definitely more then three. A fuck-load more."

Steve pressed his hand against his head where the bandage was wrapped, trying to soothe the ache he began to feel. "I don't get it," he said, still just above a whisper after double-checking to make sure Cass was not within earshot of them. "How could there be such a large group of men with such evil intentions? Like there was some sort of murderer-rapist convention or something?"

"Facebook?" Drew tried to joke.

Steve didn't laugh. "I mean, how can you be so sure that there's a large number of them?"

"I'm not positive," Drew admitted, "but when they attacked you guys, they did it without fear. They had no worry of any consequences for their actions, as inhumane as they were. That tells me they were confident. Confident because they have a large group. And that large group, having established themselves somewhere, probably an abandoned facility nearby, has gotten it into their heads that this is their turf. Which means they're sure to come looking for the trespassers who brought trouble to their kind."

A quick moment of silence followed, and in

that silence came a growing sense of foreboding. "Let me help you get these bodies down the embankment," Steve finally said, his voice a bit shaky with trepidation.

"No, sir. No heavy lifting for you. EMT's orders." Drew immediately set to work, making sure Steve did not assist.

"Fine," Steve said. He knew he was feeling feint, and that if he tried to help and passed out, he would be putting both of his friends in danger. "Tell me what you want me to do."

"Best thing for you," Drew said with a grunt as he lifted the second boy over the guardrail and gave it a forceful shove, "is to get Cass and start heading north now." He wiped a bit of sweat from his brow and took a few heavy breaths before speaking again. "Since you're both going to move more slowly than normal, given your conditions, I'll catch up in no time."

Steve nodded and did as asked while Drew started on the third corpse, but not before handing Steve the .45 he had confiscated. Once all four had been rolled down the embankment, he said a little prayer asking God to forgive their sins, as well as his own, though he only killed because he had to.

As far as Drew was concerned, if it came down to them or him, he would always choose himself. Ever since he was a young man, he always found himself in hairy situations. He always thought they more or less always seemed to find him. No matter how bad the situation was, however, he always found a way through it and came out unscathed. He called it the BLGL syndrome. Bad luck put him in the situation, and good luck always got him out. Curse of the Irish, he called it.

By the time he had finished the work, he could see that Steve and Cass had only gotten about three hundred yards ahead of him. He didn't expect them to get very far at all, and their head start made little difference, but he thought it best to give Steve something to do that made him feel useful.

After a few minutes of jogging lightly, not wanting to over exert himself with his pack on, he caught up to his companions. When they greeted him, he could tell that Cass was still in shock from what had happened, but she was responsive to his directions and able to pull her own weight. Still, Drew hated seeing her like that, and an anger simmered inside him at the thought of what those men had done to the kids. He hadn't felt that kind of anger since his father was alive.

Instead of continuing forward, Drew suggested they cross over the median and onto the northbound side of Interstate 95. He now hoped that if the men that had attacked the group were to be giving chase, that they would follow the first side of the interstate they came to, which would be the southbound one. He was thankful that both sides of this particular section of I-95 were divided by a median that was approximately three lanes wide, and thickly covered with trees and brush, blocking any sight between the north and southbound routes.

Still, taking extra precaution, Drew had them cross over to the far side of the northbound route and into the tree line, wanting to be out of sight if the group did happen to cross over as well. He knew a confrontation would end badly for him and his two companions. Steve's gait had become more of a ogre's trudge. He was in no condition to fight, and Cass was brutally traumatized. Furthermore, he didn't know the strength size of the other group. But if his hunch was right, they would have a hell of a lot more than three men to deal with. Possibly a fuck-load, as he had described to Steve.

They traveled until dusk. The sun was setting behind the trees when Drew decided to stop. He still wanted sunlight to be able to find a strategic place to camp.

There would be no fire that night; a cold meal would have to do. They forced Cass to eat as she just sat on a small rock staring at the ground.

"Come on, Steve. Let's put her to bed," Drew said.

They rolled out Drew's sleeping bag and helped her climb inside. Drew kept a close eye on her as they did so, his worry clearly showing on his face. Fortunately, she was sound asleep within minutes.

"Hey, I'll take the first watch," whispered Steve, trying not to wake Cass.

Drew shook his head in refusal. 'You need your rest after taking that blow to the head," he whispered back. "I'll take the first watch." Drew said with the hint of a whisper.

"You're going to stay up all night, aren't you?" asked Steve.

Drew just looked at him.

Steve found his answer in Drew's eyes. He knew it was useless to argue with the man. Plus, Drew was right—the knock on his head had made him more weary than he was comfortable with. He may not have been as knowledgeable of a survivalist as his friend, but he was wise enough to know, and mature enough to admit, that his reaction-time had slowed.

Steve walked over to his pack and was starting

to pull out his sleeping bag when Drew spoke, "Steve, sleep with Cass tonight. It's going to get cold and you can keep each other warm with your body heat."

Steve put his pack down and approached Cass's sleeping bag. Just before he climbed in Drew stopped him and said, "Tonight, you sleep with the gun."

Steve lifted up his shirt exposing the handle of the .45 drew had handed to him earlier. "Finally, a step ahead of you," he said and fell asleep moments after.

Drew checked the shotgun and the AR-15, making sure both were loaded before the darkness fully engulfed them. If they were attacked, he wouldn't have time to reload.

He sat up against a tree hoping they wouldn't be discovered in the middle of the night. It would be hard to fight off s force of unknown numbers in the darkness, but the darkness also worked to their advantage. They would be hard to find in the pitch black of night, especially since, to their unusual luck, the sky was overcast with clouds, blocking out the light of the moon. He tried to keep himself awake by going over various military tactics in his head, but it was a struggle to keep his eyes open after such a long day…

Chapter 50

Sleep had taken him home to where he was playing with Stephanie and kissing his wife. In this happy place he felt safe, with no constant fear of the unknown. Right then, he was embraced by Annabelle and it had been so peaceful. She had forgiven him, and they were moving on with their lives, together.

But when he had heard people shouting, he felt an anger begin to rise within himself as the disruption somehow caused his wife and daughter to fade away, and the feeling of love was replaced with that too familiar fear. His eyes had fluttered open and he had found himself resting against the tree...

His eyes darted from left to right scanning and counting. A tree trunk partially blocked his view, so he leaned his head to the right to see past it and counted again. Both times he came up with the same number, six flashlights and two torches. "Great. It's a fuck-load alright." With his mind racing uncontrollably he pondered whether he should stay put or move, hoping that maybe they would just continue past, but deep down inside he knew that wouldn't happen. He contemplated running, but he couldn't abandon Steve and Cass. Besides, it wasn't in his nature to run. All he knew was he needed a plan and fast.

Out on the highway the dark shadowy figure had now taken on a more human form. It still looked like a shadow of a man, but it now had red, sinister, glowing eyes. It had found a weak-minded man at a couples' retreat and put him in control. He was the type of man that didn't mind hurting others to get what he wanted, and what he wanted was power.

The shadow man, as Chad the leader called it, pointed its long black talon towards the left side of the road just before the guardrail.

There! Chad heard as if it were a whisper on the wind. Somehow, he understood that only he could see and hear the thing. He turned back towards his men and nodded with his head indicating that he wanted them to check out the area beyond the guardrail.

Drew promised not to drink, but what he was about to do required one, if not several. With his eyes focused on the highway he reached into his bag and searched its contents. His fingers found a tiny bottle amongst all the larger ones and he pulled it out. In one swift motion he brought the small bottle up to his lips and placed the cap into his mouth, clamped down with his teeth and twisted the cap. Four faint snaps indicated the cover was free. The cap sailed into the darkness of the night after he spit it out. He dumped the contents into his mouth and swallowed. It tasted delicious. Dropping the bottle to his side, he reached into the bag and this time he pulled out a pint. After snapping the cover free, he took a long swig. It burned going down, but it felt good, like an old friend coming to visit after being gone for so long. Within seconds the bottle was empty.

Leaning back against the base of the tree, he listened to the voices that carried in the darkness. As he drank, he thought back to the sound discipline training he received in the Marines. Back then he could sneak up on just about anyone, something he could still do to this day.

He sat and watched as the group of men came

to a stop. The torches danced and flickered and illuminated an eerie shadow that moved amongst them. Drew thought back to the sporting goods store and the thing that scoped out his drink. It looked different somehow. Then it dawned on him, it was the same thing he had seen, only now it had red sinister glowing eyes.

Drew reached into the bag and grabbed another bottle. Instantly by the taste he knew it was Peppermint Schnapps. With a few gulps he downed the first half of the contents. Pausing, he took a deep breath, and pounded the rest.

Sitting there, he allowed the alcohol to work its magic. It wasn't a magical potion, but the way it turned off the constant thoughts running through his head made it feel like such.

Drew felt his inner demon awakening as his body consumed the alcohol, as if it lived off of booze. Now it was free. Closing his eyes for a minute, he found himself in a memory.

His little arms and legs flailed as waves crashed over his face and the salt water filled his mouth and nose. The coldness took his breath away and he clutched frantically through the liquid, searching for something solid to hold onto, anything.

A hundred yards away he heard his father's voice from the boat. "Swim boy, before the sharks get you!" followed by laughter. Swallowing water, he went under and everything turned black. Then he found himself back in his childhood home. It never felt like home, but more like a house of horrors. Fear encompassed him when he heard his father's heavy breathing behind him, and before he could turn around, those massive hands grabbed him from behind and pulled him in tightly against his father's large gut. The stench of those fingers filled his nostrils before they pinched them closed, and then his father's palm pressed hard against his mouth, shutting off his air supply. Struggling to break free from that powerful grasp in an effort to breathe just made it worse. Fear followed by impending doom, which overtook him as everything went black again.

Drew opened his eyes and the memory began to fade, but it was always there, reminding him that Hell does exist on earth. Over the years he learned how to control it when the horrible memories of his childhood came flooding back. Now instead of the fear that he felt as a child, he felt anger. Rage. It rose from deep within him and it brought the answer to his current problem. He knew what he had to do.

Reaching into his bag he felt for another bottle and his fingers found one. The booze in his system started to run its course and his nerves began to calm, his mind started to clear.

He counted the flashlights and torches again and came up with the same number. *They brought a small fucking army*, Drew thought to himself. *Well, the best defense is a good offense.*

Tossing the bottle into the darkness, it landed on a patch of ferns with a soft clunk. Drew had an idea, a dangerous one.

Picking up the rifle, he slid the bolt back, chambering a round, then grabbed another pint and slipped it into his back pocket before stealthily making his way towards Steve and Cass.

Drew knelt down next to Steve, gently shaking him.

Steve's eyes opened merely half-mast, his head

still pounding from the blows he had taken earlier.

"Shhh, I don't know how, but they found us. They're out on the highway. Running's not an option anymore. We need to end this."

Steve could smell the booze on Drew's breath. *No point in arguing over it now*, he thought. Remembering what had happened to the kids, he realized there was nothing he could do but hope and pray that Drew could stop them, because if not, he and Cass would suffer the same fate as Greg and the others.

Just then, yelling came from the highway.

"We're coming for you boy!" Chad shouted into the darkness as his men gathered behind him. "Come out now and we'll make your death quick. Make us find you and you'll die slow, real slow." He waited a moment, listening for any movement.

Drew looked around at his surroundings and had an idea. "I'm going to cover you guys in leaves. Don't come out until I get back. Okay?"

Steve nodded that he understood.

Drew quickly grabbed armfuls of dried, dead leaves that littered the ground and began covering the sleeping bag. Once sufficiently covered, he placed a few branches on top for added concealment and then grabbed both weapons before heading towards the highway.

"Time's up," Chad yelled. "We're coming in to find you and kill you."

The dark shadowy thing slipped into the tree line, and Chad turned and signaled for his men to bring up the rear as he made his way into the woods, following the apparition.

Sensing the dark figure's urgency, Chad turned and looked back at the group. "Hurry up back there," he said looking at the last man in the group.

Grant Bailey followed up the rear of the men on the highway and knew Chad was talking to him. He hated Chad and he hated carrying the torch too. The heat that it gave off scared him and he had visions of his hair catching on fire. *What am I doing out here in the middle of nowhere?* he asked himself, and wishing he had never gone on that couple's retreat and wondered if catching the sickness would have been better than being someone's slave.

"Hey boss!" one of the men yelled.

"What?" Chad said looking back over his shoulder.

"Should someone stay behind in case this guy doubles back on us?"

Chad turned and searched the darkness of the trees for the shadow man and caught a glimpse of its red eyes before it turned back into the darkness.

"Sure," Chad yelled back. "You and pussy boy stay behind." And then he continued into the woods.

Great, now I'm being called pussy boy, Grant thought as he waited out on the deserted highway.

Drew stayed in a low crouch and quickly scampered towards the highway. Within a minute he came to the guardrail about a hundred yards south of the group of men before stopping. Leaning against the metal barrier, he watched as their flashlight beams waved through the trees, causing elongated shadows to dance throughout as the men snaked their way into the woods. Two men with torches stood next to the guardrail watching their comrades as they penetrated into the darkness. "Come out, boy!" the last man yelled as he entered the dense tree line.

Stepping up onto the guardrail, Drew jumped down onto the pavement. It felt good to be on solid ground. At first, he welcomed not having his feet constantly getting tripped up in the underbrush, but he had just traded concealment for better footing and now found himself out in the open without a firing position.

Working his way across all three travel lanes towards the guardrail on the opposite side, which separated the highway from the medium, he hopped over the metal barrier and knelt down. Scanning the area, he checked to make sure he hadn't been seen and then rested the rifle on top of the rail. The two men with torches were off to his ten o'clock position. It took a few seconds until he was able to find a comfortable stance. The metal guardrail felt cold as he leaned up against it and took aim. It was easy to find the men as they were both bathed in light from the torches. One of them was sitting on the guardrail with his back to the woods while the other stood in the middle of the roadway pacing back and forth. Looking through the scope, he could see that both men were armed. Taking a deep breath, he sighted in on one the man sitting down. As Drew put his finger on the trigger, his target stood up and approached the other man in the roadway and stopped. Putting the crosshairs on his head, Drew squeezed the trigger.

BOOM! The silence of the night was shattered as the unfortunate man who was standing there holding a torch in the middle of the road had the right side of his head blown off. His body crumpled, and the torch fell from his hand, landing next to him. Blood from the wound spread towards the torch and began sizzling as it pooled against the flaming end. The other man instantly started running for the opposite side of the road. Drew sprung to his feet taking aim, tracking him. When the man reached the guardrail, he lifted up the torch, illuminating the whole area, as he tried to hop over the guardrail. Just as his feet left the ground Drew pulled the trigger. The bullet found its mark, sending the man somersaulting over the barrier and the torch went sailing from his hands, landing in a patch of dried leaves.

The air inside the sleeping bag became stifling as Steve waited, hearing the crunch of leaves as the men drew closer. He wondered when Drew was going to do something. Had something happened to him? A piece of him questioned if Drew had run off but quickly let that thought slip away as he had more faith in his friend than that. Then it came. That loud, distinct sound of Drew's rifle. He prepared for Cass to wake up screaming which she did, but her screams were muffled by Steve's ready hand.

"It's okay," he whispered, his breath hot in her ear. "They found us. Drew's trying to stop them."

Cass could tell that something was covering her head and panic started to set in. She brought her hand up to her face to remove whatever was covering it. Steve felt her arm move and grabbed it as he didn't want her to disrupt their concealment.

"Don't move. Drew covered us with leaves so they won't find us."

She lowered her arm and hugged him tight.

"It's going to be okay," he said.

She laid their listening to the men and their angered voices and began to tremble with fear, as the events from the day before started to haunt her. Visions of her friends being executed brought tears to her eyes. Steve felt her shaking and gently kissed her forehead. Hoping Drew could stop them, he recited a prayer: "Angel of God, my guardian dear, to whom His love entrusts me here, ever this night be at my side, to light and guard, to rule and guide. Amen."

Suddenly the night was filled with the distinct sound of machine gun fire. One of the men who had entered the woods turned around and headed back when he heard the first shot. As he exited the tree line, he saw Drew's second muzzle flash. Holding the machine gun by his side like Rambo, he pulled the trigger, sending bullets whizzing everywhere.

Drew moved just in time as bullets riddled the guardrail where he had just been firing from and dropped to the ground. One of the bullets came in low under the guardrail, and suddenly he felt an intense, searing hot pain in his left foot.

"God fucking dammit!" Drew said through clenched teeth.

He needed to get out of there before he was turned into Swiss cheese. The firing suddenly stopped as the machine gun toting man needed to reload. Drew lifted his head up high enough to see the man was having trouble reloading.

Drew took a deep breath, popped up, took aim and squeezed the trigger. His enemy staggered backwards and fell. The machine gun landed with a loud 'CLUNK'.

Drew dropped back to the ground just as other members of the group exited the tree line and began shooting.

Well this didn't go as planned, Drew thought as bullets continued to slam all around him. *I'm so fucked.* He was outnumbered and pinned down. *Please God, if you do exist, get me out of this.*

Suddenly Drew smelled something burning and within seconds found himself engulfed in thick, hot black smoke. Turning, he saw the median was on fire. The torch had set the pile of leaves ablaze, which quickly spread to the dry underbrush and its surroundings.

The smoke provided the concealment needed to make an escape. Barely able to see, Drew stood up and almost fell over from the excruciating pain as he put weight on his left foot. Using the guardrail to stable himself, he quickly began limping down the side of the roadway and tried taking several deep breaths to help push through the pain, but the smoke burned his throat, which caused him to choke and his eyes to water. He swore with each step as he fought through the agony. Behind him the fire intensified, and he could feel the heat on the back of his neck. Branches snapped and popped as the sap inside reached boiling temperature. The tops of trees seemed to explode, dropping flaming branches to the ground below, spreading the already rapidly growing inferno. The wind wafted hot embers everywhere and smaller fires began to pop up wherever they landed.

Drew stopped to wipe his eyes and reached back to grab the pint of booze from his back pocket. He took a swig and put it back. It was enough to do the trick, providing him with the boost he needed to keep going.

"Did you get him?" Chad shouted as he exited the woods.

"Over there!" one of the men hollered as he pointed down the road. Just then, thick smoke blew across the highway and they lost sight of him.

Chad turned and looked at the dark shadow man. Its eyes matched the intensity of the surrounding fire. Chad could sense it was staring at him, displeased that the man they came to kill had gotten away.

"Get after him!" Chad screamed.

Two men took off running down the road towards the last spot they had seen the man who had gunned down their comrades.

When he was certain the men had left his immediate vicinity, Steve poked his head out slowly and peeked around. The cold air felt refreshing on his face, but he was astonished to see a raging fire burning on the other side of the highway. It illuminated the whole area and he could see a few bodies laying out on the pavement. He dared not venture out for fear of being captured, executed, or accidentally shot by Drew. Scanning the highway further, his eyes focused on a strange dark silhouette moving along the highway.

"What do you see?" asked Cass.

"I'm not sure."

"You're not sure?"

"The woods on the other side of the highway are on fire," he finally answered after a slight hesitation. He decided it was best not to mention the ominous figure as the poor girl had enough fright in one day.

"What?"

Cass shimmied her way out of the sleeping bag, rolled onto her stomach and put her head on her hands. She was amazed by the size of the fire.

The minutes seemed to stand still as they both just stared into the vast openness of the woods, watching the flames grow, consuming the darkness. Off in the distance, they could hear the woods being devoured by the inferno. Hisses and pops filled the night air along with the smoke. Thankfully, there was a three-lane highway between them and the fire, and the wind was to their backs.

Grant came to just as the flames began to ignite his pants. "Whoa!" he shouted as he frantically patted his ankle and calf and used the barrier to help him get up on his feet. His head was spinning as he tried to get over the barrier, and he stumbled and fell over, landing hard on the pavement and scraping up his elbows and knees. Laying in the middle of the road, he began crawling towards the other side, trying to escape the heat that radiated onto the highway. He crawled past Tony, who had been shot just before he was hit. Luckily the bullet had slammed into his metal canteen on his hip, but the force of the impact had knocked him off balance just as he stepped onto the guardrail, and he'd gone careening over the other side, having landed on his head, which had rendered him unconscious.

The two men who raced down the highway after Drew stopped when their flashlights shined on fresh drops of blood painting the ground and leaving a trail that led into the tree line. "We're coming for you, asshole!" one of them shouted.

Drew glanced over his shoulder and saw them running across the three-lane highway towards him. Knowing they would catch up to him soon, he hobbled as fast as he could go. Blood had filled his boot and gushed with every step. His heart pounded, and he was drenched with sweat. A small cramp started to form on his right side, which took his breath away. Rubbing the cramp, he pressed on. He hadn't factored in running when he made his bold plan to attack the group of men, only that he needed to find a firing position, and fast.

Clutching onto the guardrail for support, he made his way through the darkness. Winching with every step, he wondered how bad his foot really was, knowing the booze and adrenaline were masking most of the pain. He glanced back over his shoulder to see how close the men were when suddenly the ground gave way.

Oh fuck! he thought as his right hand clenched tightly onto the guardrail, causing him to land hard on his back with the rifle striking the metal rail with a loud clang.

The two men quickened their pace and hopped over the guardrail, running hard toward the sound.

A wave of pain shot up Drew's left leg as he applied all his weight to his injured foot to prevent himself from sliding down. Clenching his teeth tightly, he let out a groan as his foot dug into the grass and dirt, which collected in the boot and wound. Taking a few deep breaths, he was able to sit up on his butt, and slowly started working his way down the embankment. Shooting his hands out into the darkness, he searched for something to hold onto.

After a few seconds, his hand touched something smooth and hard, the concrete abutment.

Placing his back against it, he slowly started making his way down. Looking up, the raging fire illuminated the roadway above. He prayed the two men giving chase were still running, as they would be unable to see the embankment, nor have time to react to the sudden drop and come plummeting down. Thankfully, he himself was only hobbling when he had reached it.

Drew took the shotgun off his shoulder and took aim at the top of the embankment.

Time seemed to be standing still as he waited, while his throbbing foot only added to the anticipation. *Had they seen the drop?* he wondered. *Did they stop, or had they possibly turned back around?* He contemplated yelling or going back up when suddenly a silhouette appeared, then quickly disappeared. Within seconds the man's body came tumbling down the embankment and he heard the distinct sound of a bone snapping, followed by the man's agonizing scream. Drew followed the sound with the shotgun, pulling the trigger as the man rolled past. The man's screaming became death curdling as the shotgun shell tore into his hip. Then the second man came tumbling past before Drew could pump the shotgun and take aim. The tumbling man landed hard on the first guy who was lying on the hard asphalt of the street below.

Drew pumped the shotgun and pivoted out from the wall on his left foot, sending fresh pain up his leg. Down below, the first man was screaming at the second to get off of him, but it was too dark to make out their entwined bodies.

He waited, listening to the men when he had a

sudden idea. The shotgun had five remaining shells, and he was willing to waste one in an attempt to locate both men. Readying his left hand to pump the shotgun as soon as he fired, he prepared to sacrifice the first round to illuminate the area below. Taking a deep breath, he squeezed the trigger, sending a chunk of hot lead to the bottom of the embankment, where pieces of asphalt peppered the first man's face and head. The muzzle flash was enough to give both men's position away, acting like a photo, burning the image into his mind. Moving the barrel of the shotgun slightly to the right, where he saw the second man standing, and pumping it as he moved, he pulled the trigger again. The second man was standing up, facing him with a look of terror on his face when he fired. The shell found his target, hitting him just beneath his chin, and damn near severing his head. With the second muzzle flash, Drew saw the first man still lying on the pavement below. He pumped and fired a third time. The man let out a blood curdling scream as the chunk of lead hit him directly in his left side, turning his insides to mush and causing him to bleed out in seconds.

Drew counted to sixty quietly to himself. Hearing nothing from the embankment below he figured both men were dead.

Slowly, he started making his way back up the embankment, grabbing onto the side of the wall, until he reached the guardrail at the top. Holding on tight, he flung his injured leg over the railing, and as he sat down, the glass pint bottle in his back pocket clinked against the metal surface. Pulling out the pint, he sat sipping the bottle while watching the fire in the middle of the medium, which was now three times its original size and growing. The pain in his foot was constant and he tried looking at it, but he couldn't see through the blood and dirt stained boot, and he dared not remove it in the event he couldn't get it back on. It was bad, but not serious. He was still in the fight.

Once the bottle was depleted, he decided it was best to get his bearings, reload and get going, as there were still three more men out there. He momentarily thought of Steve and Cass and prayed they were alright. *Hopefully they stayed put.*

Making his way down the road, he searched the area for the last of the men, turning his rifle whichever way he looked.

Steve watched as two men exited the woods beyond the fire and met up with a third near the bodies lying in the road.

"I think he was killed by the fire," one man said.

Steve's heart began to race at the thought of losing his friend, but kept his head about him, grabbing handfuls of leaves to cover up their spot that had become exposed. Cass's eyes began to well up with tears.

"What are we going to do?" Cass asked through her sobs.

"I don't know."

Cass hugged him tight and buried her face into his chest to muffle her cries. Steve wiped his tears and embraced her back.

Please Lord, don't let Drew die, Steve silently prayed.

The dark silhouette exited next to the fire, and

its eyes glowed like molten lava. It stared at Chad who could feel its outrage towards him for failing it once again. He was trying to think of something to say when one of the other men began to point and shout down the road.

Kill him, Chad heard from the sinister shadow, and without hesitating, he turned to his men. "Get him!" he barked.

All three men took off down the road.

Drew was stunned as he watched the men run towards him. *These guys just want me to kill them*, he thought as he brought the rifle up to his shoulder, aimed and fired. He shot the first man in the stomach, and the man dropped clutching at his abdomen and screaming in agony. The other two pressed on. Drew shifted his weight as he aimed. Pain coursed through his foot and up his leg as he pulled the trigger. He missed.

The men charging towards him began to fire and bullets zipped past him.

He took aim again and squeezed the trigger but nothing happened. As the shell casing from the last shot ejected, it became stuck in the ejection port, called a stovepipe, preventing the next round from loading into the chamber. Drew quickly reached up and tried removing the jam but in doing so it allowed his enemy to close in.

"Fuck!" he shouted as he dropped the rifle and unslung the shotgun. One of the attackers was almost on top of him as he pumped the weapon and dropped to one knee to try and make himself smaller and harder to shoot. The man came barreling at Drew and was just feet away when he fired. The round caught the man mid-chest, blasting him off his feet.

He was pumping the shotgun when suddenly a bullet found its mark and caught him in the left arm, spinning and dropping him. He started to crawl away, but the guardrail and a cluster of trees blocked his egress.

Chad ran up to him and aimed the gun at his head. The man had a fierce look in his eye, revealing to Drew the evil inside him.

Out of nowhere, the dark, ominous, shadowy figure appeared. Drew saw its red lava colored eyes, which squinted as if it was smiling.

The figure egged the man on.

Kill him, now! Chad heard as if a whisper carried on the wind. Drew heard it too.

The man leaned down putting the barrel of his gun inches from Drew's face.

"Thank you. You just killed all of the men, so now I won't have to. Now I can go back and take their wives as I planned, but without any of the mess."

"Fuck you! You sick fuck," Drew snarled as he stared into the barrel of the gun.

"Fucking is what I'm going to do to all of the women back at the retreat, and thanks to you, now I can" the man said as he leaned in closer. "Just like I fucked your little friends before shooting them."

Drew could feel the anger swell within him, but he was trapped and out of options.

Kill him now! Drew heard again and knew it came from the shadow figure.

"Fuck you too!" Drew yelled. He then snorted, producing a loogie and spat it at the thing.

Now! Drew heard and watched as that thing took a step closer to the man holding the gun to his head.

Chad thumbed the hammer back and began laughing as he said, "Say goodbye motherfucker!"

Drew closed his eyes. *I'm so sorry, Annabelle.*

The sound of the gun went off multiple times. Drew expected to feel no pain when passing into the afterlife. What he didn't expect was to feel nothing and continue breathing when the silence followed. He opened his eyes, and to his astonishment, his enemy fell forward onto the ground just beside him, flailing about as he grasped at his fleeting life. Bullet wounds were scattered about his back. Drew turned his head forward, and to his astonishment, saw another man standing before him, holding a torch in one hand and aiming a pistol at Chad's now still corpse with the other.

The shadowy thing let out a loud hiss and lunged at Drew's apparent savior, who had just gunned down its puppet. The man took a step back and tripped over a branch which sent him crashing down. The shadowy figure was about to strike when he shot the torch out in front of him. The red glowing eyes slammed into the burning flames, and suddenly it disappeared into a cloud of smoke.

Silence followed again as the two men lay on their backs, both breathing heavily and too stunned to speak.

When Drew's state of shock began to pass, he recognized the man as one from the group, but as he assessed that he was no longer a threat, he slowly got to his feet, hobbled over, and extended his hand to help the man up.

At first the man remained still, unable to

process what he had just seen. But soon his terrified expression in his eyes softened, and he accepted Drew's hand.

"What the hell was that?" the man wheezed, still shaking from the ordeal.

"I don't know," Drew replied.

"It was like a fucking demon or something."

Drew nodded. "Never thought things like that existed. But I've seen it once before, shortly after the sickness hit. Maybe that thing's what caused it, if it really is a demon."

"Holy shit! I think so," the man responded.

Drew gripped his left arm to apply pressure to the wound. "Name's Drew."

"Grant," the man said simply.

"Grant," Drew repeated. "There were six college kids travelling with me, and that fucker over there, along with two others in your group killed five of them, raping the girls before they did. Look me in the eyes, Grant, and tell me you weren't one of them."

"The fuck?" Grant gasped with astonishment as his eyes suddenly watered with remorse. "No way! I wasn't part of that! In fact, I had no idea!"

Drew peered into Grant's eyes. He'd questioned hundreds of people he had to help as an EMT, bluntly asking teens if they had taken any narcotics, asking women if their bruises had come from their husbands. Over the years, he became quite skilled at recognizing certain gestures, expressions, or changes in voice tone that suggested a person was lying. He could tell that Grant was telling the truth. "Okay. Mind telling me how you got mixed up in all this then?"

Grant wiped his eyes. "A bunch of us had come down here for a couples' retreat over at a nearby resort when the sickness hit. Some left, but a good number of us decided to stay put and hole up, figuring it was best to wait until it passed, or they found a cure. Somehow, Chad, that fucker over there, eventually took charge, claiming he had a military background and specialized in survival skills. I never liked him; he was aggressive and bossy. But everyone was afraid because of the crisis..."

"And it's during a crisis like this that people will quickly and blindly follow anyone who assumes command so easily," Drew commented.

"Yeah," Grant acknowledged. "I can see that now. And then he befriended several others that were willing to enforce his rules, saying that those rules were necessary for our survival. Next thing you know, he and his new buddies almost have absolute power. It was like fucking *Animal Farm.*"

"Never read it," Drew admitted.

"Anyway, this morning a large group of them went out hunting. Then later on, only Chad and two others came back, all up in arms, telling us that they were attacked by a lunatic who killed some in the group. Chad was very passionate, explaining to the rest of us men that it was up to us to hunt you down, that we owed it to the guys who lost their lives this morning. And that if we didn't do something about you, that you would come and kill us in the middle of the night."

"Well, I didn't attack those men," Drew explained. "Not until they beat my friend half to death and took those kids' lives."

"I'm sorry," Grant managed to get out through

a choked-up voice. "I didn't know that's what really happened. But knowing Chad and his friends, I believe it."

"And instead of letting him kill 'the lunatic,' you shot him in the back," Drew said with curiosity.

"Yeah. Well, hearing him say how he was gonna fuck my wife after I was gone was more than enough reason to do that."

"That *was* some crazy shit."

Grant looked around as if making sure they were alone. "I think that demon thing had something to do with it too," he whispered, almost afraid that just mentioning it would conjure it back into existence. "Like it gave him the idea to kill all of us men and take our wives. Or maybe I've just seen too many movies."

"A month ago, I would've said that you have," Drew whispered back. "But after what we both saw and heard, I think you're right. The only thing I don't get is why did it–"

Drew heard something rustling in the trees and turned to see Steve and Cass standing there. He smiled with relief at the sight of them, but he decided not to finish his sentence.

The sun was just coming up as Drew sat on the guardrail and Cass removed his boot. She had searched his bag and found the first aid kit. Inside was a pair of steel scissors which she used to cut the laces and the side of the boot. There was a chunk missing from it and the side was covered in blood. She cut the sock off and tossed it to the ground. Drew chuckled at the sight of the blood covered sock as it reminded him of the 2004 World Championship Boston Red Sox pitcher Curt Schilling, and his infamous bloody sock.

Cass dug through his bag again looking for the bottle of hydrogen peroxide, but instead pulled out a pint of booze.

"I'll take that," Drew said as he grabbed the bottle from her.

Steve just shook his head in disbelief.

"What, Steve?" Drew asked with that tone of his.

"It's not even eight in the morning yet."

"So."

"I thought you weren't going to drink anymore."

"Are you fucking kidding me? I just got shot... twice, while trying to save your ass, and now you're questioning me as I'm trying to relieve some of the pain." He took a long swig from the bottle and looked over at Grant, who just shrugged his shoulders.

"Well?" Drew asked, still looking at Grant.

"What?" Grant said.

"Don't you think I'm entitled to a drink?" He chugged the rest of the bottle and tossed it over his shoulder.

Grant looked over his shoulder at the now smoldering medium of the highway and the bodies of the men he was with yesterday that lay dead in the roadway, and then looked back at Drew. "Yeah, you deserve a drink after that. I could use a drink too. You got anymore?"

"There might be some left in that bag," Drew said pointing.

"You guys are unbelievable," Steve said as he picked up his bag and walked away.

Grant watched Steve walk away and made sure he was out of earshot. "What's his problem?"

"Me," Drew replied.

"It's complicated," Cass said looking up as she finished cleaning Drew's foot. "Now let me look at that arm."

Grant wasn't sure what to think of this misfit band, but he liked them. He liked them better than the group of men he was with, that was for sure.

The wound to Drew's arm was just a scratch. Thankfully, the bullet only grazed him. It could've used a couple stitches, but they didn't have any, so Cass just cleaned and wrapped it up. He figured if he kept it clean and dry it would heal on its own, but it would leave a nasty scar.

He sat with his foot elevated, letting it air out. After carefully inspecting the wound, he determined the bullet must've just torn off some flesh and didn't appear to have hit any ligament or bones, as he could still bend his foot. It just hurt like a bastard.

Drew looked over at the man who had saved him. "Thank you for saving my life last night, Grant."

"I'm just thankful I was able to stop that mad man. I knew he was messed up in the head, but I didn't know he was that bad."

"Yeah, he was one sick fuck."

"Indeed."

"Hey, can you grab that bag and see if there's any more booze in it? My foot is throbbing."

"Sure," Grant said as he walked over to the bag and picked it up. Plunging his hand into it, he expected to find a bottle of booze and not a bag full of bottles. He pulled out a liter of Southern Comfort and handed it to Drew.

"Thanks again," Drew said as he unscrewed the

cap and took a long pull, then gestured the bottle to Grant.

"Sure," Grant said as he accepted the offer and took a small swig. It burned going down. After taking another swig, he handed it back to Drew.

Drew wiped the top and took another long pull, burped and took another swig.

Cass sat on the cold pavement pulling leaves from her hair and asked, "So what now?"

"We head for home. Care to join us, Grant?"

"I need to get back to my wife and get the hell out of here. Hopefully our families are still alive."

"We can accompany you to find her," Drew said.

"Sure," Grant replied feeling safer travelling with others.

A short time later Steve returned, and they packed up and set off on their long journey home.

The ominous figure watched from beyond the trees. It seethed with anger that it had been unable to kill that man named Drew.

Chapter 51

The dark shadowy figure found Brian Phillips wandering the deserted streets of London. The time of the sickness had passed and now it was time to release him from his reign of terror. It waited in the shadows for him to pass. When he did, it stretched out its arm and uncurled its long black finger.

"You have done well my friend. Now go be with our creator," said the dark shadowy figure, which sounded like a whisper on the wind. It touched his head as he passed by, and Brian's heart stopped beating. His lifeless body fell in a darkened alley behind a nearby pub.

A light filled the alley, so bright the dark shadowy figure had to turn away from the intensity.

"My God!" Brian said as the radiant warm light enveloped him.

When the light dissipated, the dark shadowy figure turned back around and Brian Phillip's body was gone.

The ominous figure was now taking form. It moved from one location to the next with ease, no longer appearing in the sunlight like a shadow on the ground, but was taking on a human shape. Still lingering in corners, it walked down the streets and through the boroughs of New York City. Its size seemed to swell as it passed the mounds of bodies littered everywhere.

The modern city now resembled medieval times and the sickness had killed off twice as many people as its predecessor The Black Death. Bodies wrapped in sheets lined the streets. At first, trucks came and picked up the dead, bringing them to large fields to be burned. Soon, however, the trucks stopped coming. But many corpses remained. The city was soon filled with the most horrific smell and was infested with bugs consuming the cadavers.

People tried to flee the city, and at first the authorities blocked off roads preventing them from leaving. But soon the police departments started to dwindle and the remaining officers abandoned their posts to be with their families.

A slight gust of wind swept through the city streets, preceding the dark figure's presence. Sheets fluttered in the breeze, unmasking the horror beneath. Rotten corpses oozed blood and yellowish-green puss that ran down the gutters like rain water, pooling like puddles and flowing down storm drains.

It could feel its strength growing. Every death brought it closer to its physical form, in which it would be impossible to stop. This time it would not fail. This time it would make the oceans turn red with blood. The world would be His.

It turned left off of Madison Ave onto 49th street and approached the news mecca of the world. The time had come for War.

E.M. Kelly here, I have slayed my own dragons, and I'd love to hear your stories of how you slayed yours. So please feel free to drop me an email at: authoremkelly@gmail.com

If you or a loved one have a problem with drugs or alcohol, there is no shame in asking for help. Addiction is a tough and lonely road, but it doesn't have to be.

SAMHSA - Substance Abuse and Mental Health Services **1-800-662-4357**

To find an Alcoholics Anonymous near you please check: **aa.org**

Coming Soon!

Demons
&
War

Book II

Slaying Dragons: A Journey Through Hell

The Journey continues!

ABOUT THE AUTHOR

E.M. Kelly lives in Massachusetts with his wife and their daughter.